Becca's eyes widened. The gorgeous cowboy from the bar? What was he doing here?

His mouth curled in a slow, satisfied smile.

"Marc, you run along and take your shower," she instructed.

Her son, who was fairly well behaved for a second-grade boy, picked that moment to exhibit his rare rebellious streak. "Hi, I'm Marc."

The cowboy smiled as he came closer, his long-legged stride graceful and annoyingly mesmerizing to watch. "I'm Sawyer."

"Mr. Sawyer, do you like pizza?" Marc said.

"As a matter of fact, I do." Sawyer grinned.

"Then you should—"

"Marc! Scoot." Becca tried to cut him off.

"—have dinner with us," her son invited.

Becca bit back a groan; Sawyer's eyes glittered with knowing humor as he met her gaze. He was amused by her discomfort, which did nothing to raise her opinion of him, but he had the decency to wait until her son was inside to laugh outright.

"Well," he said as the front door slammed, "at least one of you likes me."

Lone Star Connection

New York Times **Bestselling Author**

Tanya Michaels

&

Cathy Gillen Thacker

Previously published as *The Cowboy Upstairs* and *His Baby Bargain*

Recycling programs for this product may not exist in your area.

ISBN-13: 978-1-335-50630-6

Lone Star Connection

The Cowboy Upstairs
First published in 2017. This edition published in 2020.

His Baby Bargain
First published in 2019. This edition published in 2020.

This edition published by arrangement with Harlequin Books S.A.

For questions and comments about the quality of this book, please contact us at CustomerService@Harlequin.com.

Harlequin Enterprises ULC
22 Adelaide St. West, 40th Floor
Toronto, Ontario M5H 4E3, Canada
www.Harlequin.com

Printed in U.S.A.

CONTENTS

Tanya Michaels, a bestselling author and eight-time RITA® Award finalist, has written more than forty books full of love and laughter. Tanya is a popular event speaker, an unrepentant Netflix addict and a mother of two. She lives outside Atlanta with two teenagers who inherited her quirky sense of humor and a spoiled bichon frise who has no idea that she's a dog.

Books by Tanya Michaels

Harlequin Western Romance

Cupid's Bow, Texas

Falling for the Sheriff
Falling for the Rancher
The Christmas Triplets
The Cowboy Upstairs
The Cowboy's Texas Twins

Harlequin American Romance

Hill Country Heroes

Claimed by a Cowboy
Tamed by a Texan
Rescued by a Ranger

The Colorado Cades

Her Secret, His Baby
Second Chance Christmas
Her Cowboy Hero

Visit the Author Profile page
at Harlequin.com for more titles.

THE COWBOY UPSTAIRS

Tanya Michaels

For H. I love you.

Chapter 1

"Sorry—I was trying to listen, but I got distracted by the hot cowboy in tight jeans." Even as Hadley made the apology, her gaze remained fixed across the dining room of the barbecue restaurant. The two women on either side of her craned their heads to look.

Across the table from the oglers, Becca Johnston sighed in exasperation. "Ladies, this is Cupid's Bow. Good-looking cowboys in Wranglers are a common occurrence. What's uncommon is a female mayor. So, could we focus?" If Becca won the election—no, *when* she won—she would be only the third woman in the town's hundred-year history to be mayor.

Sierra Bailey, seated next to Becca, smiled in encouragement, not at all distracted by the prospect of a hot cowboy—probably because she went home to her own cowboy every night. Locals had been placing bets on when her devoted rancher would officially pop the question. "You're going to make a wonderful mayor."

"Thank you." Becca truly appreciated the other woman's support and all the hours she'd spent volunteering on the campaign, in addition to her full-time job as a physical therapist. "You're forgiven for your poster idea." Sierra had suggested the slogan Vote for Our Favorite Control Freak!

"If it helps," Sierra said, "I meant it as a compliment. As Jarrett will tell you, I tend toward the bossy side myself."

In Becca's opinion, there was nothing freakish about wanting a life that was calm and controlled. Growing up in a house with six kids, she'd craved order. Now she planned to give that gift to her friends and neighbors.

Hadley refocused on the conversation, a glint in her dark eyes; the town librarian wasn't as blatantly outspoken as Sierra or Becca, but God help you if you defaced a book or interrupted patrons trying to read and study in peace. "In men, they call it leadership skills, but women get called 'bossy.' I say good for you—both of you—for not being afraid to take charge."

It isn't like anyone ever gave me a choice. Unwanted responsibility had been thrust on Becca as a kid. And again two years ago when her real estate agent husband fled town after a shady investment, leaving her a suddenly single mom struggling to pay the bills. Some money from a late uncle had helped her survive while she brainstormed new revenue streams, but survival wasn't enough. She wanted to triumph.

While Hadley had, thankfully, regained her concentration, Irene and Anita were still staring after the unseen cowboy.

"Who do you think he is?" Anita asked with a sigh. "Besides my future husband."

"Wait—none of you recognize him?" Becca swiveled in her chair, craning her head for a better look. She needed to know as many constituents as possible; if he was new to town, she should introduce herself. Then again, if a "hot cowboy" had just moved to Cupid's Bow, wouldn't she have heard the gossip by now? The local grapevine prided itself on speed and thoroughness.

She blinked at her first glimpse of the man. *Wow.* Hadley hadn't exaggerated his appeal. Unlike her friends, Becca wasn't usually drawn to rugged men. Her ideal type was more polished and urbane, like her ex-husband.

The man in the weathered straw cowboy hat stood facing local rancher Brody Davenport as they waited for a table; she could see only the stranger's profile, but it was impressive. Beneath the brim of his hat, a few curls of rich brown hair fell toward his eyes. His striking cheekbones were flawless and not even the unshaven stubble of an auburn-tinged beard lessened the effect of his strong jaw. And then there were his wide shoulders, corded forearms and, as promised, the breathtaking way he filled out his je—

Oh, *hell.* Suddenly Becca found her gaze locked with a pair of amused eyes. She couldn't tell their color from here, but the cocky merriment as he caught her staring was unmistakable. Heat flooded her cheeks, and she whipped her head back around. But the movement made her feel cowardly. Looking in his direction wasn't a crime, and she wasn't one to be intimidated by a man. Ignoring the prickle of embarrassment, she glanced back toward him and offered a casual, unimpressed smile.

He smirked.

Arrogant cowboy. She didn't want *him*; she'd just wanted his vote.

Despite being hungry and eager to try the barbecue Brody claimed was the best in Texas, Sawyer McCall was irrationally annoyed when the hostess showed them to a booth around the corner. Following her meant he couldn't get a better look at the group of women on the other side of the restaurant—specifically, the woman with pale red-gold hair who'd been scoping him out with such frank appreciation before she'd studiously tried to pretend otherwise.

Too late, sweetheart. She couldn't erase the spark of awareness they'd shared.

Once seated at the booth, he and Brody ordered a couple sweet teas. While Sawyer studied the laminated menu, his friend began once again praising the restaurant.

"Back when I was doing the rodeo circuit, The Smoky Pig is what I missed most about Cupid's Bow." Brody smiled, looking happier than Sawyer had ever seen him. "Of course, that was before Jazz came back to town, or she would have been what I missed most." Last month, Brody had married a former high school classmate, Jasmine Tucker, who'd left Texas after graduation and returned to her hometown only a couple years ago. Brody had fallen hard.

Sawyer still couldn't believe the bronc rider he used to go out drinking with was someone's husband now. "I can't wait to meet her." He grinned slyly. "Especially if she's as gorgeous as you say she is." According to her proud new husband, Jasmine had been a model in New York City.

"No flirting with my wife, McCall." Brody shot him a mock glare before his tone returned to normal. "You know the only reason you weren't invited to the wedding is because it was so small and so far away, right?" Brody had admitted that he'd suggested the Caribbean ceremony because he'd wanted to prove he could be worldly, too—that marrying him didn't mean being "stuck" in Cupid's Bow.

"You sure the real reason you didn't invite me was because you were afraid she'd take one look at me and decide *I* was the better-looking cowboy?" Sawyer smirked, but then said, "Nah, I understand. I think it's great you two put a couple stamps in your passports. I've always had wanderlust myself." Granted, most of Sawyer's travels had been regional—Texas, New Mexico, Colorado, Wyoming.

"On-the-Move McCall. When was the last time you were home?"

Sawyer shrugged, as if the answer didn't matter. "My life's a thrilling blur of cattle drives and training horses, pretty cowgirls and small-town motels."

At the mention of motels, Brody frowned. "Are you sure you don't want to stay with us until after the trail ride? You'd be more than welcome."

Cupid's Bow was about to have its centennial celebration, a week of Western-themed festivities culminating in a three-day trail ride that would recreate the journey of the town's founders; on the strength of Brody's recommendation, Sawyer had been hired as one of the ride leaders. Getting here a week early allowed him plenty of time to catch up with his friend, a chance to compete in a rodeo in the next county and the opportunity to finish a series of articles he'd been writing for a Texas travel magazine. *Plus, you had nowhere else to be.* He hadn't been back to the family spread since his older brother had made it clear Sawyer was no more than a glorified ranch hand.

"I appreciate the offer of letting me bunk with you." Originally, that had been Sawyer's plan…or as close as he came to "planning" in advance. But he'd realized today just how smitten Brody was and how awkward the role of third wheel would be. "You and Jazz are newlyweds, though. You don't need me underfoot. I'll check into a hotel after lunch." It would be an added expense, but he'd had a good year between prize money and breeding rights for the bull he'd invested in. His only splurge was a new truck.

"Sure, there are a couple of hotels close by. Or you could—never mind."

Sawyer raised an eyebrow, his curiosity piqued. "What?"

"Well, Becca Johnston has a room to rent. Since you'll be staying for a couple of weeks, that might be more comfortable than a hotel, but she's—"

"You boys decided what you want to eat?" A blonde waitress with a polka-dot manicure and thick drawl set their drinks in front of them. "Sorry I took so long. Lunch rush."

Both men ordered their entrées, but as the waitress turned to go, Brody stopped her with a question. "Hey, Leanne, how would you describe Becca Johnston?"

"Terrifyingly efficient," she said over her shoulder.

"That pretty much nails it," Brody agreed. As the waitress walked away, he told Sawyer, "If you rented a room from Becca, your lodgings would be spotless, the meals would be tasty and she could answer any question you ever had about Cupid's Bow. But you don't want to cross her. Last man who did that is still missing."

Sawyer froze with his glass halfway to his mouth, sweet tea sloshing, but then decided his friend was messing with him. "You made up that last part."

"Exaggerated, maybe. But it's true no one knows where her ex-husband is—including Becca. Long story short, she's still pretty ticked. And she would hate you."

"What's wrong with me?" Sawyer demanded. "I've been told I have a winning personality."

"Becca likes structure and setting rules. While you… are a pain in the ass."

"But a charming one."

Brody snorted. "Not as charming as you think. Is that our food?" He perked up at the sight of Leanne carrying a tray in their direction.

"Do you have her phone number or address?"

"Leanne's?" Brody asked, sounding perplexed.

"Becca's."

"I'm telling you, it's a bad idea. Although, I suppose that's why you're pursuing it."

"What's that supposed to mean?"

Brody gave him a knowing glance. "Never met anyone who hates being told what to do more than you."

"It's not like I'm being stubborn for the sheer hell of it," Sawyer defended himself. "A private room is bound to offer more peace and quiet than a hotel filled with tourists in town for the centennial celebration."

"I'll give you directions to Becca's place, but it's your funeral if you track in mud or pick an argument with her."

"Pretty sure I can handle myself."

"Maybe. If not…can I have your truck?"

Chapter 2

Marc Johnston watched the soccer ball, a whirl of white and black as it came at him, and wished it would roll far away. Off the field. Into the street. His mama would never let him chase it into the street. No ball, no soccer practice. He could go home to play in his room! It was too hot outside.

But that was a dumb wish. If the ball rolled into the street, his mama would chase it down and bring it back to him. She'd told him a zillion times, "I'm always here for you." Not like his daddy, who'd gone away. Mama was never far.

Right now, she was coaching from the side of the field. "Kick the ball, Marc! You can do it!"

He swung his leg. It wasn't really a kick, not a good one. He brushed the side of the ball, which kept moving, and lost his balance as it rolled under his foot. He wobbled, then fell on his back, the sting just enough to make him suck in a breath. *Ow.*

Mama jogged toward him, her face crinkly with worry. She helped him up, brushing grass and dirt off his uniform. "You okay, champ?"

"I guess."

She patted him on the shoulder. "Maybe you should take a break and drink some water."

He'd rather have soda from the machine by the bleachers, but knew better than to ask. Mama handed him a water bottle, then turned to give instructions to Jodie Prescott, who was taller than Marc even though his birthday was before hers. He didn't like Jodie—she called him Shorty—but he was glad she was keeping Mama busy so he could go sit in the shade. There was another boy there, not in Marc's grade, playing on a Nintendo 3DS.

"Are you here for soccer practice?" Marc asked.

The kid grunted. "Does it look like I'm playing soccer? My dad's coaching my sister's team over there." He flung an arm toward another field without looking up from the screen. "I'm waiting."

"You're lucky you have a DS." *And lucky you have a dad.* And, also, lucky he didn't have to play soccer. "Can I have a turn?"

"No. But you can watch me." He scooted a little closer so that Marc could see the screen.

It was the best soccer practice ever. Marc almost forgot how hot it was. He even almost forgot about his mama, who had to call his name twice when it was time to go home. On their way to the van, the way she watched him made him feel bad for not trying harder at soccer.

She brushed the back of his shirt again. "We'd better get this straight in the washer if I'm going to get the stain out."

"Sorry." His mother didn't like stains. Or running in the house. Or when he forgot to swallow his food before telling her interesting stories, like how Kenny Whittmeyer's pet snake got out of its cage. Marc had learned at dinner last night she also didn't like stories about Kenny Whittmeyer's pet snake.

"You don't have to apologize. You didn't do anything wrong—everyone falls down."

"Even you?" It was hard to imagine Mama falling. She never messed up.

"On occasion." She hit the key button that made the doors unlock. He got in the backseat, wishing he was big enough to sit in the front. It felt lonely back here.

Although she started the engine, she didn't drive anywhere. She looked at him in the mirror. "Marc, are you enjoying soccer?"

If he told her the truth, would he still have to play? *Probably.* She was the coach. They couldn't just quit the team. "Soccer's okay."

"You know you can talk to me, right?"

"Yes, Mama."

She sighed. She made that sound a lot. Marc didn't remember her doing it so much when his dad lived with them, but those memories were blurry, like when he tried to see underwater at the community pool.

"Mama? A girl in my class has parents with a divorce."

"Parents who are divorced."

"She says she lives with her dad in the summer. Is it summer soon?"

"Next month, after the election."

"Will I live with Daddy then?"

"No, I'm afraid not, champ." Her eyes were shiny in the mirror, like she might cry, and Marc wished he hadn't asked. "But I'll do my best to make sure you and I have a great summer. Okay?"

"Okay." He looked out his window. "Is Mr. Zeke coming back?" For months, the bald, smiling man had been around their house, making what Mama called ren-o-vations. Mr. Zeke had shown Marc cool drills and saws.

"Not anytime soon. The attic's finished now, so he's moved on to his next job. But now that the attic apartment is ready to rent, maybe we'll have guests."

That would be nice. It would be even better if whoever came to stay with them was as cool as Mr. Zeke.

Becca had mixed feelings about her son's silence on the drive home. On the one hand, she'd had a very long day and appreciated the few minutes of peace. But she was worried; quiet reflection was not the seven-year-old's natural state. Was he still in pain from his fall? *More likely he's still in pain from his father's defection.* The questions about when he would see his dad, followed by whether or not the general contractor would be back, made it pretty clear that he missed having a man to look up to in his life.

Her throat burned. Nothing mattered more to her than her son, but she couldn't be everything to him. The town's upcoming centennial celebration was taking up her time for the next couple weeks. But maybe after that, she could invite Zeke, a widower in his late fifties, over for dinner—a home-cooked thank-you for a job well done.

By the time they rolled into the driveway, the stillness in the minivan was becoming oppressive. This called for emergency measures. "How about I order pizza for dinner while you take your shower?"

The excited whoop from the backseat made her smile. She'd barely pulled the keys from the ignition before her son flew out of the vehicle and up the three wide porch steps. There, he sat dutifully to remove his cleats. She took a minute to stare at the house, gleaming white in the Texas sunshine, and remembered the day she and Colin had moved in. It was a beautiful two-story home, complete with a porch swing, surrounding rosebushes and gorgeous maple trees in the yard. It had all symbolized how far she'd come from an overcrowded double-wide trailer on a gravel lot. To her, this house had been the castle at the end of the fairy tale.

It still can be. She clenched her fists at her sides, summoning determination. Okay, yes, Colin had turned out to be more fraudulent frog than prince. But she didn't need him for a happy ending. She would become mayor and raise a wonderful son.

"Mama, I can't get this knot out."

Joining Marc at the top of the steps, she knelt down over his shoe. Her promise of pizza must have really improved his mood, because by the time she'd unlaced both cleats, he was happily chatting away. She didn't even register the sound of the vehicle at the bottom of the driveway until the door closed.

"Excuse me," a deep masculine voice called, "are you by any chance Becca J—"

As she turned, the man stopped dead, recognition

striking them both. The cowboy from the bar? What was he doing here? Stalking her?

"You," he breathed. His mouth curled in a slow, satisfied smile. "You're the woman who was checking m—"

"Marc, you run along and take your shower," she instructed. She was about to throw this man off her property. It was probably better that her son didn't witness it...or overhear any of the man's lewd commentary on what she may have been "checking." Unbelievable. She'd ogled a stranger *once* since her divorce, and he'd followed her home. What were the odds?

"Uh, Mama? The door's locked."

Right. She knew that. She fiddled with the key, but the dead bolt got only part of her attention. The sense that she could feel the man's gaze on her was distracting. "There you go, champ." She swung the main door wide open, expecting her son to reach for the handle on the inner screen door.

Instead, he hesitated, waving at the approaching cowboy. "Hi, I'm Marc."

The cowboy smiled, his long-legged stride graceful and annoyingly mesmerizing to watch. "I'm Sawyer."

Marc's eyes widened as he caught sight of the man's gold belt buckle, etched with a cowboy on the back of a bucking horse; Becca read the word *champion* before realizing that she was staring in the direction of the man's groin, and averted her eyes. "Did you win a rodeo?" her son asked.

"Quite a few."

"That is so cool! Maybe I'll ride in a rodeo someday," Marc said, surprising Becca. He'd never expressed any interest in that. "I take riding lessons from Ms. Meredith. She's nice, but I like Ms. Kate better. She's my piano teacher. She gives me cookies."

Hearing him list his teachers out loud, Becca mentally kicked herself. She'd inadvertently surrounded him with women. Why hadn't she checked to see if Jarrett Ross was taking on any more riding students over at his ranch? In Becca's defense, Marc's soccer coach was supposed to have been a man. But when he'd broken his leg the first week of the season, she'd stepped up to fill the void.

Sawyer winked down at her son. "Keep at that piano practice. The ladies love musicians."

Yeah, that's what her seven-year-old needed—advice on picking up women. From the cocky way Sawyer carried himself, she just bet he had plenty of experience in that area. "Ladies also love hygiene," she said wryly. "Now about your shower…"

Marc opened the screen door. "Back in a minute!"

"Take your time and do the job right," Becca cautioned. "There's no rush."

"But I'm *hungry*. If I hurry, I get pizza faster. Mr. Sawyer, do you like pizza?"

"As a matter of fact, I love it."

"Then you should—"

"Marc! Scoot."

"—have dinner with us," her son invited.

Becca bit back a groan; Sawyer's eyes glittered with humor as he met her gaze. He was amused by her discomfort, which did nothing to raise her opinion of him.

"Well," he said as Marc disappeared inside, "at least one of you likes me."

Now that he was on the step just below her, she could see his eyes were green, flecked with gold, and she hated herself for noticing. "If you'll excuse me for a moment," she said tightly, "I need to call in an order for pizza." That would give her an opportunity to regain her composure.

He smirked. Didn't the man have any other expressions? "Want to know what toppings I like?"

She shot him a look that should have vaporized him on the spot, leaving nothing but his memory and scorch marks on the sidewalk.

"I'll just wait here then," he said, moving past her to make himself comfortable on the porch swing. He even took his hat off and ran a hand through his brown hair. In the sunlight, a few threads shone a deep coppery red, much darker than her own strawberry blond.

His hair was thick, wavy, and she wondered errantly if it was soft to the touch. *Rebecca Ruth Baker Johnston, pull yourself together.* Just because she hadn't had sex in the two years since Colin skipped town was no reason to become unhinged in hormonal desperation. She marched into the house, locking the door behind her. No matter how good-looking he was, Sawyer was a stranger; she was a single woman with a child to protect. She called the pizza place, but she was so preoccupied that there was no telling what she ordered. For all she knew, instead of a large pepperoni pie with extra olives, dinner tonight might be a piece of garlic bread and six liters of soda.

Well, that's what she got for stalling. Her philosophy had always been to tackle problems efficiently, then put them behind her. Time to figure out why this cowboy was here and send him on his way. She returned to the porch, her tone brisk as she asked, "So is Sawyer your first name or last?"

"First. Sawyer McCall." He extended a hand. "Pleasure to meet you. Officially."

Her fingers brushed over his in something too brief to qualify as a handshake before she pulled away. "Becca Johnston. What are you doing here?" *Besides bonding with my son and trying to mooch free pizza.*

"Brody Davenport sent me. I don't know if you happened to notice while you were undressing me with your eyes—"

She exhaled in an outraged squeak.

"—but he's who I was having lunch with. Brody and I are old friends. He contacted me a few months ago about coming to town to help with the centennial trail ride and to finally meet Jasmine. I need a place to stay."

That place sure as hell wouldn't be under *her* roof. "There are two motels in the Cupid's Bow area," she said. "I can draw you maps to both of them."

He bobbed his head. "Yeah, Brody said you were pretty much an expert on this town—which would be useful to me, since I'm writing a travel piece. Brody also said that if I stayed here, the room would be spotlessly clean and the food would be excellent."

She bit the inside of her lip. When she'd had the bright idea to rent out her attic, she'd been thinking more in terms of single women who might feel vulnerable staying alone at a hotel, or who would appreciate bubble baths in the spacious claw-foot tub. Maybe she could even rent the room as a long-term apartment to a woman like herself, divorced and needing to regroup. She certainly hadn't considered giving the key to a smug, sexy stranger. "I think I would prefer female tenants," she said. "At least until I get a guard dog."

He raised an eyebrow. "You don't strike me as a dog person."

She wasn't; training and grooming seemed like a lot of work when she was already stretched thin with limited hours in the day. But she resented being pigeonholed. "You don't know anything about me, Mr. McCall."

"No, but from what Brody said..." He cleared his throat, looking sheepish.

Ah. So there'd been more to the rancher's characterization of her than the promise of a clean house and good food. All Sierra's teasing about being a control freak echoed in Becca's head.

"Do you currently have any female tenants scheduled?" Sawyer asked.

"Well, not yet."

"I can pay up front. Cash. And I can give you a list of references, including Brody and his aunt Marie, to assure you I'm not some whack-job."

She'd known Marie Davenport, a now-retired 911 operator, for years. And there was no denying Becca could use the money; her salary running the community center and her stipend as a town-council member were barely a full-time income. That's why she'd decided to invest in renovating her attic to an apartment in the first place, so she could rent it to a paying customer. *Yes, but...him?*

Becca had spent her life mastering the art of structure. During the happier moments of her marriage, she'd relaxed, grown complacent, and she'd paid for it with scandal and divorce. Now, she was more determined than ever to keep her life smooth and orderly. Sawyer McCall might be smooth, with his glib manner and roguish smile, but instinct screamed that life would be anything but orderly with this cowboy living upstairs.

"Mr. McCall, I really don't think—"

The screen door banged open and a mini tornado gusted across the porch in the form of her son, his green dinosaur pajamas plastered to the wet chest and limbs he hadn't bothered to dry. "You're still here! Are you staying for pizza? Mama, can I show him my space cowboys and robot horses?"

Becca studied her son's eager face and tried to recall the last time she'd seen him look so purely happy. "Mr. McCall and I aren't finished talking yet, champ. Why don't you go set the table for three?" She wasn't convinced she would rent the room to Sawyer, but a slice of pizza was a small price to pay for her son's beaming smile.

Marc disappeared back inside as quickly as he'd come.

She took a deep breath. "The attic apartment has its own back stair entrance and a private bathroom. No kitchen, although there's a small refrigerator up there for beverages and snacks. Whoever I rent the room to is welcome to join Marc and me for meals—but in exchange, I was hoping to find someone with a bit of child-care experience. Occasional babysitting in trade for my cooking." She'd only just now had that brainstorm, realizing how much it would mean to Marc to be around a man, but it sounded plausible. And if Sawyer said no, it would help justify turning him away.

He shrugged. "Sounds reasonable. I'm no child-care expert, but I've worked with kids at equestrian camps and on family trail rides."

She sighed, regretting what she was about to say

before it even left her mouth. "Then, assuming your references check out, you've got a deal, Mr. McCall."

His grin, boldly triumphant and male, sent tiny shivers up her arms. "When do I get to see my room?"

Chapter 3

Sawyer braved his landlady's glare, her blue eyes like the center of a flame. Fiery was a good description for her—hot, but projecting the aura that a man should stay back for his own safety. At the restaurant earlier, he'd seen her sitting down. She was a lot taller than he'd expected, trim and shapely in her polo shirt and shorts. When he first drove up, her kid had been wearing a numbered practice jersey; Becca wore a whistle on the cord around her neck. Team coach, maybe? She seemed like the kind of person who wanted to be in charge.

And not at all like a woman who changed her mind easily. Despite his claims at lunch that he was charming and likable, Sawyer was almost surprised she'd agreed to rent him the room. Her expression when she'd first seen him in the driveway had suggested she was more likely to back over him than take him in as a guest.

"Come on," she said irritably. "We might have enough time before the pizza comes for you to see the room." She opened the door, but stood there, barring his entrance as she studied his boots. "You can leave those on the porch."

Her tone rankled. He wasn't her damn kid. "Yes, ma'am. I promise to wash my hands before eating, too."

She gave him another narrow-eyed glare. *Probably deserved that one.* Instead of halfheartedly apologizing for his sarcasm, he gave her a winning smile. She pressed a finger to her forehead as if physically pained.

Maybe he should stay at a hotel, after all. Brody was right about him—Sawyer had a habit of provoking bossy people. Wouldn't sharing a house with a woman who already disliked him needlessly complicate life?

Nah. In only a matter of minutes, he'd convinced her to change her mind about renting to him. In a matter of weeks, he could win her over entirely. Sawyer liked a challenge. Besides, in the unlikely event that he failed, it was just a few weeks out of his life. After that, he'd be putting Cupid's Bow behind him.

He placed the boots neatly by the front door. "After you."

Brody hadn't exaggerated when he predicted the place would be spotless. The hardwood floors gleamed; the creamy walls looked freshly painted. There were no toys scattered about or fingerprint smudges. If he hadn't seen Marc with his own eyes, Sawyer never would have believed a little boy lived here.

The narrow hallway opened up into a living room and Sawyer winced. "Is my room this…pink?" The low-backed sofa and two armchairs were all the same shade, coordinating with a striped circular rug that took up most of the floor.

"Mauve," she corrected, studying the furniture with him. "With cranberry accents."

Cranberry? An Aggies football fan, he would have called the dark throw pillows and decorative candles "maroon." At least then it would be showing team support for Texas A&M.

Her tone was defensive. "I think it looks nice, but to answer your question, no, this isn't the color scheme I used in the attic." She suddenly brightened. "Still, I completely understand if the accommodations here aren't to your liking. I can still give you directions to either of those hotels."

He should probably be insulted that she was so eager to get rid of him. "I'm sure the room will be just fine. Even if the bed's lumpy, with mismatched sheets, it'll be better than all the times I've slept on the ground during a trail ride or stayed in a crappy motel room." He'd been to rodeos in luxury Vegas settings and tourist-destination stockyards, but those weren't the norm.

"Mr. McCall, I do not make up beds with mismatched sheets."

He couldn't help grinning at her affronted tone; the woman took her linens seriously. "I've always cared more about what happens between the sheets than about whether they match."

She sucked in a breath, but the doorbell rang, saving him from a potentially blistering retort. Redirecting her anger, she glared toward the front of the house. "That better not be the pizza already!"

Was she that set on having events unfold according to

her timeline? "Most people are happy when they don't have to wait long for delivery."

"There are three regular drivers," she said, as she dug through her purse. "But Keesha only works weekends. Which leaves D. B. Janak, who I happen to know has the flu, because I ran into his girlfriend at the store, and Callum Breelan, who is proving to be just as bad as his disreputable uncles." Money in hand, she strode toward the door, rattling off the rest of her explanation over her shoulder. "Only seventeen and he already has one speeding ticket and two warnings—Deputy Thomas went easy on him. I don't need lead-foot Callum using my dinner as an excuse to mow down pedestrians and small animals."

Sawyer blinked at the unexpected blast of information. She'd been talking too fast about people he'd never met for him to process all of it. The upshot seemed to be Becca knew *a lot* about her neighbors. And had strong opinions.

While she stood at the door haranguing the delivery boy about his driving habits, Sawyer found his way down the hall to a huge kitchen, the kind that was big enough to include a full-size dining room table and china cabinet. Marc stood on his tiptoes at a marble-topped island, trying to pour lemonade into a red plastic superhero cup. Sawyer lunged forward, taking the pitcher from the boy's hands just as it started to wobble.

"Here, better let me get that for you. I'm guessin' your mama doesn't like spills."

The boy shook his head, eyes wide. They were the same color as Becca's. "She hates messes. And snakes, even though they're cool."

"Not all of them," Sawyer said. He'd had a few

close encounters with rattlesnakes and copperheads he'd rather not think about. He eyed the pitcher on the counter, noting the slices of fresh lemon bobbing inside it; obviously, Becca did not serve lemonade that came from powder. "Where can I find a glass?"

Marc directed him to a cabinet next to the stainless steel refrigerator—not that it was easy to see the silver steel beneath the clutter. The kitchen was pristine—no dirty dishes in the sink, no mail sitting on the counter—but the fridge was practically wallpapered in Marc's schoolwork, crayon drawings and photos. As he looked closer, Sawyer realized there were also a number of newspaper clippings that all seemed to be about Cupid's Bow events. One mentioned a Watermelon Festival, while another—

"Can I help you find something in particular?" Becca asked from behind him, her voice icy.

Busted. He straightened, making light of his snooping. "Guess I was just curious about the family I'll be staying with, trying to reassure myself that you and Marc here aren't—" he'd been about to say ax murderers, but murder jokes weren't appropriate in front of the little boy "—aliens from outer space." That made the kid giggle, and Sawyer winked at him. "Or dangerous robots. Or spies for the CIA!"

"That's ridiculous," Becca said, exasperated. "Our CIA handler is the one who gave us all that fake documentation to support our covers in the first place."

Sawyer rocked back on his heels. So she did have a sense of humor? Good to know. The next few weeks were looking up already. He grinned at her, but she turned away to set the pizza on the table, almost as if she were hiding her smile.

"Marc was kind enough to show me where the glasses are," he said, pulling one from the cabinet. "The lemonade looks delicious. Want me to pour you some, too?"

She cocked her head, seeming confused by the question.

"Becca?"

"Sorry, I'm not used to someone else serving me in my own kitchen. Lemonade would be lovely, thank you."

Sawyer remembered Brody mentioning an ex-husband who'd bailed on her and the boy. How long had she been alone, that something as simple as someone else pouring her a drink was jarring?

"Wait, Marc, slow down!" Becca batted her son's hand away from the open box as Sawyer joined them at the table. "The pizza's still pretty hot."

"Guess what, Mama? I've decided not to get a pet snake when I grow up."

"Oh, good." She dropped her arm around his shoulders in a brief hug. "I was going to talk you out of it, anyway, but this saves me the trouble."

The oval table was big enough to seat eight. Marc and Becca sat next to each other, toward the center, and Sawyer went around to the other side, taking the chair opposite Marc.

"It's so cool Mr. Sawyer could have dinner with us!" Marc grinned so broadly that Sawyer noticed for the first time that the kid was missing one of his bottom teeth.

Becca hesitated. "Actually, he might be staying a few days. Or longer."

"In the new upstairs room?" Marc shot out of his seat with a whoop of excitement.

"Marc Paul Johnston, what kind of table manners are those?"

"Sorry." He slid back into his chair, his tone sheepish. But he was still smiling.

Sawyer locked his gaze on his plate, not wanting to make eye contact with the kid. If he returned Marc's grin, Becca might think he was encouraging the boy's rambunctious behavior. Besides, it was discomfiting to be the source of so much joy. He'd signed autographs for kids at rodeos and assisted tourists with children, but he'd never had prolonged exposure to one. *You'll be an uncle soon.* Would he be close to his future niece or nephew? Doubtful. He sure as hell wasn't close to his brother.

Charlie hadn't even been the one to share the news that he and his wife were expecting; Sawyer's mom had told him the last time he talked to her on the phone. The next day, Charlie had sent a terse email and Sawyer had replied with dutiful congratulations. That had been a couple weeks ago, and he could still hear his mother's chiding tone in his head.

"Gwen's due at the end of October. Surely you'll want to arrange your schedule so that you can be here?"

He'd told her he really couldn't say what his schedule would be in the fall, but that he'd be in touch. Then he'd quickly found an excuse to get off the phone. The truth was, even if he could make it, what would be the point? His sister-in-law was a nice lady, but her own family lived close to the ranch, so she had plenty of support. And as for Charlie… Ever since his older brother had returned to the ranch from college, the two of them could barely be in the same room without an argument erupting. Their father always sided with Charlie. Their mother just wanted everyone to get along. In her mind, that meant Sawyer—the outnumbered younger son—should cave.

"Something wrong with your pizza?" Becca asked tentatively.

Sawyer realized he was scowling. "Uh…you were right about it being hot. I burned the roof of my mouth," he lied.

"Kenny Whittmeyer's dad burned his hand when he took Kenny and me camping," Marc volunteered. "We were roasting marshmallows and he said a whole *bunch* of bad words. I—"

A trumpet sound came from beneath the table, and Becca shifted in her seat, pulling a cell phone from the pocket of her shorts. She glanced at her son. "You know I'm only checking this because of the race, right?"

He nodded, informing Sawyer, "Mama has a no-phone rule at the table. But we make ex-sections 'cause of the race."

"Exceptions," Becca corrected absently, reading a text. She frowned, but put the phone away rather than responding. "Who wants the last slice of pizza?"

Sawyer shook his head, letting the growing boy snag it, and reached for his glass. "What's this race you mentioned? Are you a runner?" He could easily imagine her in a marathon. She seemed disciplined enough, and judging from her toned figure, she did something to keep in shape.

"Not literally. I'm running for mayor."

Sawyer choked on his lemonade.

"You find that funny, Mr. McCall?"

Hell, yes. Weren't politicians supposed to kiss babies and suck up to people? Becca was far too imperious for that. She hadn't even been able to pay for a pizza without lecturing the hapless delivery boy.

She misinterpreted the smile he was fighting. "I'll have you know that women are *every bit* as capable as—"

"Whoa. No argument here. I've known plenty of badass women."

"So what's the big joke?" She challenged, those eyes sparking again.

He doubted there was any answer that wouldn't get him in trouble. Might as well go with the truth. "The idea of you courting votes is a *little* funny, don't you think? You seem like someone who speaks her mind, whether the opinion is popular or not."

"And that's bad? Community leaders should be honest and straightforward."

"In theory, sure." Feeling Marc's gaze on him reminded Sawyer that there was a seven-year-old listening to his cynicism. "But don't listen to me. I'm just an outsider. What do I know about the people of Cupid's Bow?"

Becca stood, gathering up the empty plates. "About that—you being an outsider? Would you mind finishing your lemonade on the porch and enjoying the evening breeze while I call Brody Davenport? I need to start checking your references."

"No problem." He scraped his chair back. "Checking up on me is the responsible thing to do."

She gave him a smile that was part apology, part

amusement. "Well, I'd hate to accidentally rent the room to a dangerous alien robot."

"That would be awesome!" Marc said.

"Which," she told him affectionately, "is why *I'm* the one who makes the decisions around here."

Sawyer understood not letting a second grader run the household, but alien robots aside, he was pretty sure Becca preferred to be the one making decisions no matter who was involved. *Just like Charlie.* But a hell of a lot prettier.

After Becca finished her phone call, she tucked in Marc, who was supposed to read for thirty minutes, then go to sleep. From the excitement on his small freckled face, she suspected he wouldn't be falling asleep anytime soon. She wasn't sure yet how she felt about her new tenant, but she had to admit he'd been great with her son.

She should go thank him. And let him know the room was officially his.

She stepped onto the front porch, where the heat was sticky in comparison to the air-conditioned house but not intolerable. Intolerable came in August. Sawyer glanced up from the swing with that too-appealing grin that could've belonged to a movie star; the spectacularly vivid sunset behind him added a cinematic effect. The only thing missing was a musical score. Becca told herself she was unaffected and had always liked books more than films, anyway.

"Did Brody vouch for me?" he asked.

"He said I should kick you to the curb—that you're a pain in the ass who likes to get his own way."

Sawyer shrugged. "Well, who *doesn't* like to get his way?"

Hard to argue that. Brody had also said Sawyer was dependable, loyal and never drank to excess or let himself get goaded into bar fights, like a few of their former rodeo friends.

"Let me show you the room. Pay me cash for tonight, and you can decide in the morning how long you're staying, after you've had a chance to judge the accommodations for yourself." She almost said something about making sure the bed was comfortable, but stopped herself, recalling his comment about sheets earlier. She did not need to hear any jokes about what took place in his bed.

He unfolded himself from the swing, and she took a moment to appreciate the novelty of being with someone taller than she was. Only a handful of men here in Cupid's Bow were. In elementary school, she'd hated being the tallest in her class—probably the tallest in the whole school. But she'd decided her height was an advantage at home. Towering over her siblings helped her secure their obedience.

She'd foolishly taken it as a good sign that she and her ex-husband had been the same height; she'd joked to a friend that there was no better way to start a life together than seeing eye to eye. *Nice symbolism, lousy results.* Pushing aside memories of her failed marriage, she opened the door.

After Sawyer's reaction to her "pink" furniture, she was hyperaware of her feminine decorating touches as she led him to the back of the house. The hallway was lined with pictures of her and Marc in scallop-edged and filigree frames. A curved glass vase of yellow roses sat on the kitchen counter. The delicately patterned stair runner that went up to the second floor looked like lace from a distance.

Although Sawyer would never see it, her own bedroom was a frilly, silky haven complete with scented candles and ornamental pillows too small to have any practical purpose. Becca prided herself on being sensible and getting things done; she wielded coupons with genius, killed bugs and occasional rodents and could single-handedly fix a lot of the plumbing problems that came with home ownership. But after growing up in a grungy trailer with three brothers—and later, two sisters who wore their brothers' hand-me-downs—she couldn't resist surrounding herself with soft, girlie indulgences.

The staircase felt uncharacteristically cramped with Sawyer on the steps behind her, as if he was closer than decency permitted. She suddenly wished she was wearing a loose T-shirt that hung down past her butt instead of a tucked-in polo shirt. *Don't be ridiculous. There's nothing wrong with your butt, and you don't care about his opinion of it, anyway.* Although…turnabout being fair play, it would make them even if he noticed her body. She'd certainly ogled his earlier today.

"The master bedroom, guest room and Marc's room are all on this floor," she said, as they reached the landing. "The attic is one more flight up."

The extra trip involved a narrow spiral staircase with an iron railing.

A quarter of the way up, Sawyer huffed out an exaggerated breath. "Good thing I'm in shape. But just in case, do you know CPR?"

Of course she did. She'd taken half a dozen first-aid

and emergency preparedness classes when she'd been pregnant. But she said nothing, refusing to encourage any jokes about her mouth on Sawyer's—which didn't stop the forbidden image from flashing through her mind. The man might be cocky and unapologetically brash, but he'd demonstrated moments of thoughtfulness this evening, too. The right combination of confidence and attentiveness could make for a devastating kiss. Her toes curled inside her sneakers.

Get a grip, Rebecca.

She had no business thinking about kissing her tenant. Or anyone else, until the centennial celebration was over. She was the chairwoman of the centennial committee, and a flawless series of public events would help her win this election. *Stick to the plan.*

While she was at it, she needed to stick to an impersonal, informative tour—more letting him know where the clean towels were, less imagining where his hands would be if he were kissing her. "Coming up from the outside will be a lot easier than this. The house was built into a little bit of a hill, so the staircase is short. Not to mention, using the private entrance will be less disruptive to me and Marc if you keep late hours."

Would he be staying out late? He was a good-looking single man in a town with two bars and a popular dance hall. Opportunities abounded. Her stomach clenched. What if he wasn't alone when he came back to his room at night?

She bit the inside of her lip, conflicted. She didn't really have the right to insist he be celibate while he was in Cupid's Bow...but she *was* responsible for the impressionable child sleeping one floor below.

The attic door wasn't a standard size; they both

needed to duck slightly to go through it. Inside the room, the ceiling was comprised of crazy, irregular angles, but nothing that Sawyer would bang his head on.

"Cozy," he said, looking around. "I meant that in a good way, promise."

To their left was a queen-size bed covered in a quilt she'd won in an auction at the Cupid's Bow Watermelon Festival; to the right was a small sitting area with two antique chairs, a bookshelf and a modest-sized, flat-screen TV. He would also have his own microwave and mini fridge. The windows were tiny, reminiscent of the portholes on a ship. When she'd had Zeke install the back door, she'd also asked him to include sidelights for a little more sunshine.

"See? No pink," she told him. The general decorating theme up here was "furniture I didn't need anywhere else in the house" but she'd tried to tie everything together with navy and cream. "Bathroom's around the corner. Everything you need should be in the linen closet, but let me know if I overlooked anything."

He poked his head through the doorway and laughed. "I haven't seen a tub like that since Granny's house."

"And where did Granny live? Brody talked about how long he'd known you, but didn't mention where you're from."

"Most of my family is west of here, toward the Hill Country. We have a… My father and brother run a spread in Kerr County."

"Are you close to them?"

He rocked back on his heels, thumbs in his belt loops. "Let's just say, I thought it would be better to strike out on my own."

"I can relate to that," she said softly, more to herself

than him. Her earliest memories were of her trucker father kissing her goodbye and telling her to take care of "Mama and the baby" while he was gone. Her younger brother Everett hadn't even been a year old when their mother got pregnant with the twins. That had been a complicated pregnancy, with a lot of doctor-mandated bed rest, and Odette Baker had never really been the same afterward. By the time Becca was ten and the first of her sisters was born, she was actively fantasizing about the day she could move away.

"You're not from Cupid's Bow?" Sawyer asked. "With you running for mayor and talking like you know everybody in town, I figured you were born here."

"Nope. I grew up a little over an hour away." Cupid's Bow was separated from her hometown by eighty minutes...and a world of experience. Back home, all she'd ever wanted was to escape. From the minute Colin had brought her to Cupid's Bow, all she'd wanted was to belong. She *loved* it here. She loved the people and the open spaces. She loved that she could see an unending blue horizon unimpeded by skyscrapers, and brilliant stars not strangled by city lights or air pollution. "Cupid's Bow is the perfect size for me. The population's under four thousand, so it has small-town charm, but it's not so small that the only businesses are eponymous."

He raised an eyebrow. "E-pony-what-now?"

"Self-named. In the town I grew up in, there was one restaurant—Ed's Diner. Never mind that it sucked. And the only place to get your hair cut was Shirl's. Owned and operated by—"

"Let me guess—Shirl?"

She nodded. "There's healthy market competition

here in Cupid's Bow, but we haven't been overrun by generic franchises. It's the perfect balance."

"And you want to become mayor so you can maintain that balance?"

"Well, that...and I like telling people what to do."

He laughed. "I feel sorry for the poor slob running against you."

"That would be the incumbent," she said, her mood darkening as she remembered Sierra's text from earlier. Last election, Mayor Lamar Truitt had run unopposed. Displeased that Becca had the nerve to challenge him, he was constantly looking for chances at passive-aggressive sabotage. "Which reminds me, I have some phone calls to make. I should let you settle in." She reached in her pocket for the key to the attic entrance, but hesitated. "I'll have breakfast on the table at 6:00 a.m. I know that's early, but I have to get Marc to school."

"Actually, I'll already be gone by then. Brody and I plan to get in some sunrise fishing before heading to look at livestock. He's thinking about expanding his herd."

She wasn't so much interested in his plans tomorrow as she was in making a necessary point. "While you're here, Mr. McCall—"

"Sawyer." He gave her a chiding smile. "I insist."

"While you're here, it's best if you come down to breakfast alone."

His smile faded to a perplexed expression. "I just told you, I won't be here for breakfast."

"I don't mean tomorrow, I mean in general. It would be better if you don't bring any...guests to breakfast."

Comprehension lit those gold-green eyes. After a

moment, he smiled. "I see. Rest assured, I will only show up at the breakfast table as a party of one."

Relieved to have that settled, she wished him a good night and turned toward the door.

She was on the staircase when he called from behind her, "No need to bring guests down for food, anyway. I can just keep the fridge stocked and serve breakfast in bed."

Chapter 4

It was still dark outside when Brody called to say he was turning onto Becca's street, but, judging by the enthusiastic dawn chorus of birds outside Sawyer's room, sunrise was coming. He went down the flight of stairs behind the house and had just reached the bottom when a pair of headlights shone across the driveway. He swung open the passenger door of Brody's pickup, greeted by the welcome smell of coffee.

"You survived the night," Brody observed.

Sawyer climbed into the cab. "Sorry to disappoint you—I know you want my truck if Becca decides to spike my food with hemlock. Give her time. I don't generally drive people to homicidal rages until they've known me at least twelve hours. I hear you were completely unhelpful as a character reference, by the way."

"You wanted me to lie to her? Cupid's Bow is my

home." Brody sipped from a travel mug, handing a second one to Sawyer. "After you get on her nerves and she runs you out of town—or buries you in the city park—*I* still have to face her."

"Don't want to run afoul of the new mayor, huh?"

"It'll be interesting to see who wins the election. Truitt's sort of...blandly competent. Not someone who inspires devotion, but his cronies have a fair amount of combined influence in town. Becca could be great, if anyone bothers to vote for her. She's outspoken—"

"Gee, I hadn't noticed."

"—and may have stepped on a few toes during her time on the town council. Half the town is afraid of her, and Jazz and I haven't decided if that's going to work for or against her. Maybe people will be too scared *not* to vote for her."

Sawyer chuckled. "Well, she doesn't scare me." Rather, she intrigued him, her steel-spined demeanor a seeming contradiction to the house she'd decorated with soft, frilly things. And she amused him, with her unexpected playful side, as well as impressing him with how much she clearly loved her kid. Sawyer had a lot of respect for mothers; the only person in his family he tried to maintain a relationship with was his mom.

"Wait a minute." Brody peered at him in the dim light of the glowing dashboard. "You like her, don't you? I thought the two of you would drive each other crazy."

Because she was admittedly bossy and he had a habit of provoking people—especially when it brought fire to a pair of unforgettable blue eyes? "Like I said, give it time."

* * *

"...and you just *know* the bastard did this on purpose," Sierra concluded, pacing the length of Becca's living room as she ranted.

Seated on the sofa with her legs tucked beneath her, Hadley Lanier nodded, her dark ponytail swishing. Her summary of the situation was the same as Sierra's, but with significantly less cursing. "This is another lame attempt to sabotage you."

Originally, Becca had invited the two women over for a girls' night, since Marc was spending his Friday evening at dinner and a movie with the Whittmeyers. But plans for lighthearted conversation over sangria had become an impromptu strategy session now that Mayor Truitt had abruptly cut the budget for the upcoming centennial celebration.

"Emergency reallocation of funds, my ass," Sierra said, snagging her wineglass as she passed by the coffee table on her next lap. "Everyone associates you with the celebration, which means you could lose the election if people are disappointed enough with the festivities. He's manufacturing obstacles just to make you look bad."

"Let him try," Becca said calmly. The idiot had been trying to steer public opinion about her ever since January, when the paperwork had come in with enough signatures to officially qualify her as a candidate. At the Valentine's Day celebration—which she'd chaired—he'd been careful to praise the job she'd done, while vocally "worrying" that the town's needs were cutting into her family time with Marc. In an April interview with the *Cupid's Bow Clarion*, Mayor Truitt expressed his gratitude for the support of his wife and grown children, subtly undermining Becca by saying he couldn't imagine how difficult the job would be for a single parent.

In response, Becca had reminded everyone that Sheriff Cole Trent, the best sheriff in three generations, did his job successfully while raising two daughters alone. Of course, his circumstances had recently changed, now that he'd met and married Kate Sullivan, but Becca's point had been made.

"You're taking this remarkably well," Hadley said, her tone admiring. "I was so mad that on the drive over here, I was imagining far-fetched schemes to have Truitt disgraced. One of them involved costumes and code words and his ending up in a South American prison."

Becca shook her head at the younger woman. She'd wanted the librarian on her campaign because Hadley was bright and creative, but sometimes her imagination went to weird places. "We don't need elaborate schemes—"

"Code names could be fun," Sierra said.

"—when we have talent and skill," Becca finished. "Truitt is shortsighted. He can create unnecessary obstacles, but I'll look twice as good to voters when I overcome all of them."

Sierra tapped her index finger against her chin. "Only if the general populace knows about the behind-the-scenes obstacles. If *you* talk about problems that crop up, you risk sounding whiny. But the rest of us can strategically spread the word. Manuel and I make all kinds of small talk with our patients while trying to distract them from the pain of their workouts. And Kate's grandmother Joan can casually mention your committee progress at her quilting club and weekly senior-center poker games."

Becca nodded, although she temporarily lost her train of thought when she heard a vehicle engine outside.

Hadley cocked her head, her expression shrewd. "Everything okay? That's the third time tonight you've tensed when a car passed by."

"It is?" *Damn.* Becca had impressed her friends by being unfazed by Mayor Truitt's shenanigans, yet she was as high-strung as a horse during a thunderstorm when it came to the idea of her new tenant returning.

True to his word, Sawyer had been gone when she got up this morning. She had no idea when to expect him back—or if she'd even encounter him, given his private access to the attic. The big problem was that she hadn't informed the other two women of his presence. Earlier, she'd almost told them that she'd rented the room, but realized they'd ask to whom. She'd balked at admitting it was Hadley's "hot cowboy in the tight jeans."

Better get it over with it. This was Cupid's Bow. She was lucky they hadn't heard about Sawyer already.

Sierra laughed. "She's probably just listening for Marc to come home and you've found some way to turn it into a mystery."

"Actually, I was listening for my new tenant." Becca stood, giving the explanation casually as she carried their empty snack tray toward the kitchen. "I finally rented out that attic apartment. I told him he was welcome to use my kitchen for dinner, but I'm not sure when—or if—he'll be in tonight."

Both women were right on her heels as she refilled the platter with cheese, crackers and grapes.

"He?" Sierra asked. "Somehow I always imagined you with a female roommate."

Me and you both, sister. "Maybe I'll rent to a woman next. He won't be here long." Just a few weeks...although if she stayed this antsy the entire time, it was going to feel like a lot more.

"Who is he?" Hadley asked.

"A friend of Brody Davenport's. He's going to help with the centennial trail ride, and in the meantime he's writing some travel articles about—"

"Whoa!" Hadley's dark eyes were huge. "You don't mean the guy who was with Brody yesterday at The Smoky Pig?"

"Um, yeah." Becca cleared her throat. "That's him. Sawyer."

"I can't believe your luck!" Hadley said.

Frowning, Sierra leaned on the kitchen counter. "I'm not sure if this is good luck."

"Are you kidding me?" Hadley demanded. "She's got the hottest cowboy since *your* man living under her roof."

Sierra smiled faintly at the reference to her boyfriend, Jarrett, but her tone remained wary. "You guys know I love my adopted hometown." She'd moved to Cupid's Bow from Dallas almost a year ago. "But people here can be a little...old-fashioned in their thinking. The worst of them question whether a woman can do the job of mayor—which, hell, yes—and even the well-meaning worry about her juggling the demands with being a single mom. How is it going to look that said single mom is shacking up with—"

"Hey!" Becca objected.

Sierra waved her hand in an impatient gesture. "I'm

not implying a damn thing. But you know how gossip flows in this town."

Faster than champagne at an open-bar wedding.

"Well, then you should introduce him to me," Hadley suggested with a cheeky grin. "If he and I are dating, it removes you from any speculation."

Sierra snorted. "Way to take one for the team."

"Okay, I'm not subtle," Hadley admitted, "but we don't all have gorgeous ranchers in our lives."

Sierra grinned. "Jarrett *is* gorgeous. And sweet. And more sensitive than he wants anyone to know." Her expression glowed. Witnesses would be able to tell from twenty paces that she was in love.

Had Becca looked like that in the early years of her marriage? When she was the happiest she'd ever been and fully expected that happiness to last the rest of her life? She drained her glass, trying not to feel bitter as she listened to Sierra joke about Jarrett's latest attempts to get her to try camping.

"He knows I'm not outdoorsy," Sierra was saying, "but the idea of cuddling in a sleeping bag with him does have merit."

"Aren't you going on the centennial trail ride?" Hadley asked.

"Nope. I'm all for celebrating the town's big anniversary, but I'm not a native. I'll celebrate from indoors with cake. And air-conditioning." She checked her watch. "Speaking of Jarrett… I told him I might be home early enough for us to watch a movie."

"A movie, huh?" Hadley smirked. "Is that what the kids are calling it these days?"

"Smart-ass." Sierra lightly shoved the other woman's

shoulder. "How would I know what the kids are calling it? I'm older than you are."

As the only woman over thirty in the room, Becca rolled her eyes. "Neither of you are allowed to use the word *old*."

"You're not much older than we are, but you're definitely wiser," Sierra said. "One of many reasons why you'll make a great mayor. Do you want to work on revamping the celebration budget? I can text Jarrett that I'll be late."

"Thanks, but no. You go home to your rancher, and let me crunch the numbers." The funny thing about Truitt trying to rattle her with a reduced budget was that *nothing* he threw at her could be as big a shock as her husband leaving and Becca suddenly finding herself the head of a single-income family. Before that were the years she'd tried to cobble together a grocery budget for a large family out of spare change from the sofa cushions and her brother's lawn-mowing money. Making do with less was her entire wheelhouse. "I'll call you guys this week after I've done some math."

Hadley grimaced. "Not to be an English-major cliché, but count me out. Slogans and speeches, I've got your back. Math? You're on your own, madam mayor."

As Sierra, who had a head for numbers, heckled the brunette about passing up an opportunity to improve her skills, they gathered up their purses and put on their previously discarded shoes. Then they said good-night, leaving Becca in the suddenly still house. She stayed so busy with Marc and her community activities that the peace and quiet was almost startling.

And then the phone rang.

My fault for not appreciating the silence while I had

it. She picked up the cordless phone from the kitchen counter. "Hello."

"Rebecca?"

Becca flinched. "Mother?" Had something happened to one of her brothers or sisters? It was difficult to imagine anything short of an emergency prompting Odette to call. Becca could count on her fingers the number of times they'd spoken since she left home. Her dad's funeral, her sister's wedding…the wheedling phone calls when Odette realized her late brother-in-law had left Becca all his money. When Becca had been pregnant with Marc, she'd reached out to her mother, but Odette had refused to take her calls, still holding a bitter grudge because her oldest child had eloped. "What's wrong?"

Her mother sniffed. "Does something have to be *wrong* for me to miss my firstborn?"

Concern for her siblings dissipated, suspicion filling the vacancy. Her mother had alternately relied on her and resented her over the years, but they'd never been close. "The last time you 'missed' me, it was because you'd run through the bulk of Daddy's life insurance settlement and wanted money."

"Rebecca Ruth, I did not raise you to be disrespectful. And taking care of children is not cheap."

What children? Everett drove 18-wheelers now, earning a living the same way their father had, Courtney was married in Oklahoma and Becca's twin brothers, Sean and Shane, ran their own auto body repair and paint shop. Only eighteen-year-old Molly still lived at home. There were moments Becca suffered pangs of guilt for not maintaining a relationship with her little sister, but the age gap between them didn't leave them with much in common.

Is that the real reason you haven't made more of an effort? Or are you just selfishly reveling in your freedom? Becca had given so much of herself to her siblings for so long that her relationship with her family had felt parasitic by the time she left home. Was it selfish to distance herself from them, or simply an act of self-preservation?

Even these few moments on the phone with her mother were draining her. She sagged into a kitchen chair. "You're not much older than we are," Sierra had said. But sometimes Becca felt ancient. Being forced into a caretaker role at four years old aged a woman before her time.

"I've had a long day," Becca said. "How about we get straight to the reason you called?" She spared a glance at the digital clock above the stainless steel stove. Would she have enough time to squeeze in a bubble bath before the Whittmeyers brought Marc home? But then her mind strayed to Sawyer and when he might return. The idea of being naked except for a layer of scented bubbles with the cowboy in the house made her feel oddly vulnerable. *That's ridiculous. Are you planning not to bathe or change clothes while he's staying here?* Still…

"It's about your sister," Odette said with an aggrieved sigh. "Molly's been out of high school since January, and all she's managed to do is get fired from three jobs and date two inappropriate men. The one who just dumped her is almost forty! Bet she'll go running back to him if he calls. She did last time."

Becca's stomach clenched, regret burning like an ulcer. Molly had always had good grades, nearly as good as Beccca's had been, and she'd earned enough credits to graduate a semester early. *Maybe if we'd kept in better touch, I could have helped her develop some ambition for college.* Or for anything. Knowing Odette, Becca guessed she'd been leaning on her youngest as live-in help, so why would she foster Molly's desire to leave?

It sounded as if mother and teen weren't getting along. On the one hand, discord between them might finally motivate Molly to seek greener pastures. But Becca wanted to see her sister in community college or IT courses or dental hygienist school—*something* productive—not shacked up with a man twice her age because she didn't have the income to live on her own.

"She's impossible," Odette complained. "I don't know what the hell I'm supposed to do with her."

Parent her. But there was no point in saying that. For all that Odette had given birth to six of them, she'd never been overly invested in raising children. In fact, Becca was almost surprised her mother even cared enough to seek guidance over Molly's behavior. "Have you talked to Courtney to get her input?" Becca's second-youngest sibling knew Molly a lot better than she did.

"The situation is beyond 'input.'"

"But… I thought you were calling to ask my advice?"

"Typical. You're hoping to mumble a few parenting tips, then wash your hands of us. Is that it?"

The seething accusation in her mother's voice might have wounded Becca if she hadn't built up an immunity over the years. Odette had used the same tone when she'd labeled Becca a spoiled ingrate for going away to college when her family needed her. She'd used it when she asserted that Becca had eloped out of spite—never mind that it had been a financial decision—and again when Becca had refused to turn over her inheritance from her uncle. Odette had called her a heartless miser who'd let her family starve rather than share her windfall.

"I don't need advice," her mother said now. "I need you to look after your sister."

"No." The rush of anger was dizzying, and Becca grasped the edge of the table as her blood pressure soared. "I'm not your unpaid babysitter anymore. I'm a grown woman with my own child and a mayoral campaign who—"

"I bet you have all those Cupid's Bow voters conned into believing you value family."

Becca had too much self-control to hang up on anyone...but just barely. "If *you* value family, talk to your daughter. Molly's young. There's time for her to get her life on track before she makes an irreparable mistake."

"You be sure to tell her that when she gets there."

"When she gets here?" Becca echoed, praying she'd heard wrong.

"I was calling as a courtesy. She's probably on a bus by now. Hateful girl told me to go to hell, declared she was moving in with you, and stormed out. The two of you should get along great." And with that, her mother disconnected.

Becca sat frozen, barely registering the unpleasant buzz of the dial tone. Was Molly *really* coming here, or had she given Becca's name as a decoy because she didn't want their mother to know where to find her? Considering how long it had been since the two sisters had spoken, it seemed more likely that Molly would crash with a friend or one of those "inappropriate men" Odette had mentioned.

The sound of a vehicle in the driveway finally

spurred Becca into motion. She put the phone back on its charger cradle and went to look out the window, expecting to see Sawyer. Despite her conflicted feelings about the man, at the moment she'd welcome a distraction. But it was the Whittmeyers.

She walked out barefoot to meet them. "I wasn't expecting you for another hour at least," she told her son as he hopped out of the minivan.

Lyndsay Whittmeyer rolled down her window, her Texas-sized blond curls filling the frame. "The movie was sold out, so we drove to Turtle for a round of minigolf and then brought him back."

"It's probably just as well," Becca said. "Now he can get plenty of rest before his game in the morning." They were scheduled to play at nine, which meant arriving at the soccer fields by eight thirty.

"Kick the other team's butts," Kenny called from inside the vehicle.

Marc laughed even as he cast a cautious look at Becca to make sure she didn't object to *butts. Not tonight, kiddo.* Between Mayor Truitt's pettiness and having to talk to her mother, Becca found her mental vocabulary was a bit more colorful than usual.

She was making sure her son had remembered to thank the Whittmeyers for taking him along when a taxi pulled up behind them, blocking their exit from the driveway. For years, there hadn't been any cab service in Cupid's Bow, but Arnie Richmond had decided he could make good money driving inebriated patrons home from the local bars on the weekends. Had Sawyer and Brody gone out drinking?

But it wasn't the tall cowboy who climbed out of the backseat. A curvy redhead emerged, barely topping five foot three in her boots. She glanced around nervously as Arnie popped open the truck, but then she locked gazes with Becca and smiled.

Becca blinked. “Molly?” The young woman might not have gotten much taller since they’d last seen each other, but she’d definitely grown up. The interior light from the cab showed that the tips of her sister’s layered bob were streaked magenta and electric blue. And she filled out her black halter top in a very adult way.

Molly took a gigantic camo duffel bag from Arnie, handing him a crumpled wad of bills in exchange, then turned back to Becca. “Hiya, sis. Long time no see.”

Chapter 5

Becca felt dazed, moving on autopilot as she waved goodbye to the Whittmeyers and ushered her sister up the porch steps. She managed an absent "You remember your aunt Molly?" to Marc, even though she doubted he would. It seemed only yesterday that Becca had been applying bandages to Molly's scraped up, preschool knees. Now her sister was a woman in painted-on jeans and high-heeled boots.

"You look...good," Becca said diplomatically. Beneath the foyer chandelier, her sister's heavy-handed makeup looked a little garish, but the teenager was still beautiful. Besides, Becca had too much guilt over their estranged relationship to open with criticism.

"Mama always said I look like you. The redhead part, maybe." Molly's laugh was self-conscious. "Definitely not the height." She dug inside her purse and pulled out a green pack of bubble gum. "Want one?" she offered Marc, as she unwrapped a piece for herself.

He nodded eagerly.

"You okay with sour apple?" she asked. "I've also got grape, watermelon and fruit pun—"

"I'm sure sour apple will be fine," Becca said. "Marc, why don't you put on your pajamas and watch a DVD in my room? I need a few minutes to catch up with Aunt Molly."

"'Kay, Mama. Thanks for the gum."

"Sure thing, kid." As he took off toward the staircase, Molly smiled after him. "He's cute. I always wanted a little brother. Thought it might be fun not to be the baby of the family."

Being the oldest was no picnic, either. "You're definitely not a baby anymore. You're a grown woman who gets to make adult choices. Like leaving home, apparently."

Molly's face flushed. "About that..."

"Odette only called fifteen minutes ago. The bus must have made good time."

"I decided to save the money I would've spent on the ticket and bummed a ride from a couple of guys headed in this general vicinity. We parted ways at a bar just outside town."

"*Please* tell me these were guys you knew." Becca had an appalling mental image of her sister hitchhiking on the freeway.

"Uh, it was more like a friend-of-a-friend thing," she said evasively. "But since I'm not twenty-one, I couldn't go into the bar for dinner. You got anything to eat?"

"Come on, I'll fix you a sandwich."

Molly followed slowly, studying her surroundings.

"This place sure looks different than back home." There was an edge to her voice. Jealousy? Disapproval? Had she subscribed to Odette's claims that Becca should be doing more to financially assist her family? "Is there a guest room?"

What was Molly's backup plan in case there wasn't—sleeping on the sofa? "Yes."

Her sister looked away, blowing a green bubble that popped loudly. "I know you and I don't talk much, but I can't afford to get all the way to Oklahoma to stay with Courtney. Can I stay here?"

The inevitable question. Becca didn't want to think about where Molly would end up if she said no. "You can stay. But there are a few house rules and conditions."

Molly's gaze hardened. "I don't need you telling me what to do."

"You just showed up in the middle of the night on my doorstep, courtesy of a few 'friends of friends' who only got you close enough to call a cab, so maybe you should keep an open mind about sisterly advice. What do you have to lose?" Instead of waiting for an answer, she went to the refrigerator. Molly might be more amenable to guidance with food in her stomach. "I can do a bacon, lettuce and tomato sandwich or grilled cheese." She eyed a small container of leftover chili. "Or nachos."

"Grilled cheese. Courtney used to make me that with tomato soup."

And I used to make it for Courtney. It had been one of Becca's go-to dinners because the local supermarket often had canned soup as a buy one, get one free special. These days, there was soup in the house only when Marc got a cold and she cooked homemade chicken noodle. "I could heat you up a cup of chili with your sandwich."

"Just the sandwich is fine."

Silence stretched out while Becca buttered slices of bread. "You want to tell me about your fight with Odette?" she prodded.

"It wasn't my fault! You must know how unbearable she is. Everyone says you couldn't wait to get out of there."

"I got out of there with a plan—and a college scholarship. Maybe you need a plan, too." Or at least opportunities. Becca knew of a few places that were hiring in Cupid's Bow; none of them were particularly glamorous, but they didn't require specialized skills, either. If Molly was only able to find part-time work, maybe she could also do some volunteering. Becca pondered options as she flipped the sandwich in the small frying pan. Volunteering in the community would allow Molly to make contacts, while keeping her out of trouble.

"Dwayne and I had a plan. He plays guitar and I sing. We were gonna save up bus fare and an apartment deposit, go to Nashville and get famous. But then he got back together with his ex-wife. Maybe they'll break up again."

Becca wasn't sure which to address first, the statistically unlikely odds of "getting famous" or the inadvisability of fickle lovers. "First piece of sisterly advice? Don't make your plan dependent on a guy."

"What happened to your man? Mama cackled some about your getting taken down a peg, but never said why you divorced."

Becca sucked in a breath. Odette had *laughed* over it?

Given some of the things her mother had said directly to her, that shouldn't come as such a hurtful surprise. Turning off the stove, she reminded herself of the positives in her life. "The divorce represents my past. What's important is my future, raising Marc and winning this mayoral race. What do you see in *your* future?"

"Dunno. Guess I'll figure it out as I go along."

"Something smells good down here."

Sawyer! Preoccupied by the arrival of her sister, Becca had stopped listening for his return. She whirled around to find him hatless, his hair a shaggy yet somehow appealing tangle, with his chambray shirt unbuttoned over a white T.

He flashed an apologetic smile. "Didn't meant to interrupt, just wanted to grab a quick bite."

"And who might you be?" Molly asked, her eyes wide with interest. "I didn't know Becca was involved with anyone."

Becca shook her head emphatically. "Our only involvement is the rent he pays me for the apartment upstairs."

"Oh." With that breathy proclamation, Molly rose from her chair and sidled closer to him. Her attraction to Sawyer was even less subtle than Hadley's ogling yesterday.

Becca's stomach tightened as she wondered uncomfortably if the attraction would be mutual. The heavy makeup Molly wore obscured her age—assuming Sawyer was even looking at her face and not the cleavage revealed by the clingy halter top.

"Sawyer McCall, ma'am. Pleasure to meet you."

As he shook Molly's hand, Becca slapped the plated

grilled cheese on the table. "Sawyer, this is my sister... my *teenage* sister."

Molly glared. "I'll be nineteen in a month. That makes me practically twenty."

No, that makes you practically nineteen. Sawyer could date whomever he wanted—assuming she was a legal adult and didn't show up at breakfast—but Becca refused to sit idly by and watch her sister pursue another doomed liaison.

"Molly Baker." Her voice was a purr as she smiled up at him. "I'm staying here, too, so we're neighbors. Guess we'll be seeing a lot of each other."

He stepped back, softening the retreat with a smile. "You know what? After a hot day in the pasture, it was just bad manners for me to come down without showering first. Apologies, ladies. I'm going to get cleaned up."

Becca was half-afraid her sister would offer to wash his back for him, but he left the room without giving her the chance.

The minute his boots hit the stairs, Molly's smile disappeared. "You went out of your way to make me sound like a little kid!"

"I made you sound like exactly what you are. Besides, didn't we talk about how you need goals that don't include a man?"

"I'm not divorced and cynical, like you." Molly dropped back into her chair. "*I* believe in true love."

And you expect to find it with a drifter rodeo cowboy at least a decade older than you? "I'm not saying love doesn't exist. I just believe in making smart choices."

"You think I'm stupid?"

"Of course not. You did great in school. I think you can do anything you set your mind to. You just need a plan." A logical approach to life, without taking rides from strangers and throwing herself at men she'd met seconds ago.

"How would you know what I need? You barely know me."

"Well, I guess it's about time we fix that. Tonight we can—"

"My day was very draining," Molly said, her expression mutinous. "I'm going to turn in early."

"No problem." Actually, that gave Becca longer to strategize. "Tomorrow, after Marc's soccer game, we'll talk."

When her mother had called earlier, Becca had been furious that Odette was once again dumping the job of parenting on her. But, truthfully, Becca regretted not being a better sister to her youngest sibling. Starting tomorrow, she would make up for it. Becca was goal-oriented, and now she had a new goal to add to the running list: help Molly turn her life around.

When you were trying to set a good example for a child—not to mention demonstrate your moral fiber to a townful of voters—you rarely indulged in vices. Becca didn't smoke, rarely swore in front of others, kept her alcohol consumption to a minimum and hadn't had sex in years. But everyone had at least one weakness. She had never been able to resist the tart temptation of key lime pie.

The one downstairs in the refrigerator was currently calling to her.

It was after midnight, a terrible time for extra calories. The smart decision would be to go back to sleep. But her sleep hadn't been restful, anyway. She'd bounced through a chaotic tangle of dreams that were half make-believe and half memory. Having Molly here had not only dredged up Becca's childhood, it reminded her how much she'd adored her father. He'd been on the road constantly, trying to provide for his family, but the days when he'd come home had been like Christmas and birthdays and the Super Bowl rolled into one, cause for Texas-sized celebration.

Even Odette, who spent hours in bed with nausea when she was expecting and fatigued headaches between pregnancies, had got excited about his return, emerging from her room with bright eyes and a warm smile that gave Becca temporary hope her mother would change. But when he left, the brightness faded. And after he'd died? The only light she'd ever glimpsed in her mother was permanently extinguished. Odette was a bitter woman with a martyr complex, always complaining about how her children didn't appreciate her.

Am I *turning bitter?*

Only a few hours ago, Molly had characterized her as a cynic whose worldview was tainted by divorce. Logically, Becca knew better than to let that upset her. Yet she was bothered enough to reach for the stained-glass lamp on her nightstand. Screw all this tossing and turning—life would look better after a slice of key lime.

Rather than turn on the hall light and risk disturbing Marc or Molly, Becca used the thin beam of her cell phone flashlight to guide her way downstairs. She frowned when she noted light coming from the kitchen; the fixture above the counter was on a timer and should have turned off an hour ago. Apparently, her groggy mind was too jumbled to draw the obvious conclusion—someone was in there.

It wasn't until she entered the room and met Sawyer's gaze that she belatedly made the connection. *Too late to go upstairs and pull on a robe.* There was nothing scandalous about her pajamas, but she felt a little silly in front of him—barefoot in a pink T-shirt and shorts set that was covered in pandas. He sat at the kitchen table in a thin white T-shirt and pair of faded jeans, polishing off a sandwich and a glass of milk.

"Did I wake you?" His apologetic expression gave way to a slow smile as he studied her. "Cute pj's."

She held her head high, attempting dignity as she marched to the refrigerator. "They were a birthday present from Marc. And no, you didn't wake me. I wanted a glass of water." Which sounded more mature than she'd come down to stuff her face with pie in the middle of the night. Then again, this was her damn house, and who cared what he thought of her sleepwear or her eating habits? "And pie. I *really* want pie."

"I was hungry, too. I never did get dinner earlier. Figured it would be best to let you and your sister catch up without an audience, then nodded off while checking the baseball scores. Woke up with my stomach growling. You don't mind my raiding the pantry, do you?"

"Not at all. Just, if you finish something, write it on the grocery list so I can get more." She tapped the magnetized notepad on the fridge. "And don't *ever* finish the last slice of key lime pie. I'd have to kill you in your sleep."

"Nah. You wouldn't stoop to a sneak attack. If you decided to take a man out, he'd see you coming."

"Thanks. I think." When she opened the fridge door, she saw that there was over half a pie left in the fluted dish, and turned toward him. "You want some of this?"

He arched an eyebrow, his gaze wicked. "Just to clarify what you're offering, sweetheart—"

"Oh, grow up." She should be cold from the refrigerator, not tingling with warmth over his juvenile single entendre. Slamming the door shut, she retorted, "You know perfectly well what I was—and was *not*—offering."

"Sorry," he said, with an unrepentant grin. "Did Brody warn you I have a bad habit of teasing? I made one playful comment to Jazz today at lunch, and for a second I thought he was going to come across the table. He should know better than anyone that I didn't mean anything by it."

"And *you* should know better than to flirt with other men's wives." But her tone wasn't sharp. Habitual flirt or not, Sawyer had been polite but restrained with her sister, and Becca was grateful. She carried her plate of pie to the table. "Thank you for not encouraging Molly."

"Hit on your little sister under your roof? Oh, hell, no. I'm much too afraid of you for that." He leaned back in his chair. "Besides, she's not my type."

"You don't like redheads?" Why had she asked that? Sawyer's taste in women was irrelevant, and God forbid he think she was fishing for compliments. It was not a Sensible Becca question. It was a midnight, key lime, to-hell-with-the-consequences question.

"I have nothing against redheads. I like women of all shapes, sizes, skin tones and hair colors. But getting involved with a girl that young?" He pretended to shudder, then flashed a wolfish smile. "I like experienced women."

She just bet he did. "I'm going to pretend you mean life experience."

"How do you know I didn't? There's something very appealing about a woman who's had time to figure out who she is, who knows her own mind." He held Becca's gaze, and heat prickled over her skin like a full-body blush—one she hoped was invisible.

Looking away, she reminded herself that she was not foolish enough to take his words as a personal compliment. He was a chronic charmer whose flirting, by his own admission, meant nothing. Yet the thought of a man who could appreciate a strong-minded woman was heady. Since the divorce, her few attempts at dating had shown that too many guys were looking for a female who would defer to the big strong man in her life. The guy who'd come the closest to appreciating Becca had been Will Trent, who'd taken her to dinner last December, and praised Becca's blunt, forthright nature. But she'd spent the evening exercising said bluntness and telling Will that if he had any sense, he'd win back the local florist who loved him. *And I was right.* Will and Megan had been together ever since.

Sawyer crossed the kitchen and returned with his own slice of pie. "Not that it's any of my business, but you didn't mention your sister was coming. Surprise visit?"

"Surprise doesn't begin to cover it. Molly and I haven't spoken much in the last few years."

"Is she your only sibling?"

"Hardly. There are six of us."

He gave a low whistle. "You said you could relate to my putting distance between me and my family, but that's *a lot* of family."

Hence the distance. "I love my brothers and sisters.

I just didn't want to be bogged down by them." She sighed. "Is that selfish?"

"You're probably asking the wrong guy. I do what I want and go where I want and barely remember to call my mom on Mother's Day. But given how much you care about Marc and this whole town? Selfish is the last thing I'd call you."

Until he said it, she hadn't realized how much she needed to hear the reassurance. "I'm glad I rented you the attic." She grinned at him. "Despite my original misgivings, you're not completely terrible."

"Thanks. I think."

Marc sat on the kitchen floor, trying to pull up the bright blue socks; they were tight, because of the built-in shin guards. This was taking too long. His cereal was going to get soggy. He hated soggy cereal. One time, at Kenny Whittmeyer's house, Mrs. W let them have *cookies* for breakfast. She'd said cookies probably weren't any less healthy than doughnuts. Marc loved his mom, but no way would she ever serve cookies for breakfast.

"Morning." Mr. Sawyer walked into the kitchen, pausing on his way to the coffeepot to ask, "Whatcha doing down there?"

"I have to put on these socks."

"You sure those are socks?" Mr. Sawyer filled a coffee mug and took a sip without stirring in all the extra stuff Mama used. "They look long enough to be pants."

"They're special. For soccer." Suddenly, Marc had an idea so excellent that he forgot all about soggy cereal and how he couldn't kick the ball too good. "Do you wanna come to my game? You can cheer for my team, the Unicorns."

"The Unicorns?" Mr. Sawyer didn't say anything mean, but Marc could tell from his expression that he thought the team name was kind of dumb. "Was that your mother's idea?"

"No. Everyone on the team had to suggest an animal, and then we voted. I said T. rex, but Jodie Prescott wanted *unicorn.* I guess unicorns are okay. They're just like horses 'cept with sharp horns they can use to stab their enemies."

"I don't know much about soccer, but I think stabbing the other team is a foul."

Marc grinned, climbing up from the floor to sit at the table with his new friend.

"Afraid I can't make the game this morning," Mr. Sawyer said. "I promised to help Brody on his ranch before the day gets too hot. Do you have another game soon?"

"Oh, yeah. Tuesday." Marc had almost forgotten that he had to play a makeup game for one that got rained out. "Horse riding Sunday, piano on Monday, soccer on Tuesday." Every Wednesday, they had dinner and choir rehearsal at the church.

"Sounds like you have a pretty full week."

"Yep. On Thursday, we have soccer again. Practice, not a game." Marc dipped his spoon in the cereal. Maybe it would rain on Thursday. Practice could get canceled. *Mama would just reschedule it.*

Mr. Sawyer frowned at him. "You don't sound very enthusiastic. Do you like soccer?"

Marc glanced at the door to the garage; Mama had gone out to the extra refrigerator to get bottled water for the team. She would be back any second. "It's fine, I guess."

"Want to try that once more with feeling?"

"What?"

"Never mind." He followed Marc's gaze toward the door. "Do you not want your mom to know how you feel?"

"I..." Marc didn't want to complain about Mama. At school, there had been an assembly where the principal talked about bullying. She gave them a list of mean things they should never do, including talk "behind someone's back." Was that what he and Mr. Sawyer were doing? Marc got out of his chair and carried his bowl to the sink.

"Sorry, buddy. Didn't mean to upset you."

"I'm not upset." Marc smiled over his shoulder, the same kind of smile he gave adults when they talked about his daddy and Marc didn't want anyone to know he was sad. He didn't want to be called a crybaby; getting called Shorty was bad enough. Even though Kenny Whittmeyer was Marc's best friend, sometimes Marc got mad at him for stupid reasons—like being taller, even though Kenny couldn't help it. And not having *any* lessons after school. Kenny used to take a karate class, but Mrs. W made him stop when he kept karate chopping stuff at the house, including his big brother, Coop.

A snake, no lessons and cookies for breakfast. That was the life.

From behind him, Mr. Sawyer said, "Tell you what, I will definitely come to your game on Tuesday."

"You will?"

"Just let me know what time, and I'm there. Go, Unicorns!" He waved his hands in the air.

Marc laughed. This had been the best week since his birthday. First, Mr. Sawyer showed up. Then Aunt

Molly, with her cool hair and bubble gum. If exciting surprises kept happening, soon *Kenny* might be jealous of *him*.

By the time Sawyer returned midmorning, the rain was coming down in horizontal sheets. Cupid's Bow might be well east of the infamous Texas Tornado Alley, but the town was subject to major storms that rolled in off the coast. He'd been at Brody's for only a couple hours before both men realized ranch work would be impossible today. Sawyer had decided to return to his room and work on an article, leaving the newlyweds free to enjoy their rainy afternoon.

He parked in the driveway and sprinted for the front porch, rather than go all the way around the house to his private entrance. Becca had given him keys that would work for either door. He was removing his boots beneath the wooden roof when her van pulled up alongside his truck. The driver's door opened, and a navy blue umbrella blossomed like some mutant nylon flower.

She hustled Marc beneath the umbrella, concentrating her efforts on shielding her son rather than herself. The brief distance from the van to the porch left her as soaking wet as Sawyer was. He'd been considering taking off his damp shirt and leaving it on the porch swing to dry. Not an option for Becca, whose sodden polo shirt was clinging to the lacy bra beneath. Trying not to leer, Sawyer lowered his gaze…but then stole a peek from beneath his lashes.

Damn, her curves were sexy. He'd struggled against noticing last night, when she'd been braless beneath the thin material of her pajamas, but it was impossible to miss with her clothes plastered to her lush body. Turning away, he wrung out the hem of his shirt and tried to think appropriately G-rated thoughts. She had her kid with her, for crying out loud.

He cleared his throat. "Some weather, huh? Did your game get canceled?"

"No, we had time to finish before the rain started," Marc muttered.

"We won," Becca said cheerfully. "Six to four."

"Because of Jodie Prescott," Marc said. "She made most all of our goals."

"Yep, Jodie's quite a talent," Becca agreed.

Mother and son didn't seem to be having the same conversation. Becca was radiating pleased pride; Marc sounded as if he'd be happy to never see a soccer field—or Jodie Prescott—ever again. Surely Becca had noticed that her son wasn't interested in being the next David Beckham? *None of my business.* Maybe Becca had overruled his objections because the exercise and fresh air were healthy. Marc might not like broccoli, either, but there wasn't anything Sawyer could do besides shrug sympathetically. And make himself scarce from the dinner table on broccoli nights.

Becca knelt down to untie her son's shoes and help him out of his shin guards. "You change into dry clothes as fast as you can, and I'll see if we have the ingredients for hot chocolate. Not a typical drink for May, but this isn't exactly 'typical' weather." She rose, reaching for the door. "Actually, this storm is an excellent opportunity."

Sawyer stared skeptically at the rain. "For what?" Turning the streets into canals and attracting tourists with gondola rides?

"Well, you and Brody can't get any ranch work done in *this*."

"Definitely not. Which is why I came back to—"

"And on the day I rented the attic to you, we agreed that occasional babysitting would cover your meals here."

"True. But—"

"And my sister is in desperate need of a job. The sooner she starts applying, the sooner she'll find one."

"You want to go running around town now? I hope you have a boat in the garage."

"Her willingness to seek employment in this weather will make a good impression. It demonstrates tenacity and a strong work ethic."

Molly's "willingness"? Somehow he didn't think the young woman was going to get a choice in the matter—much like Becca wasn't giving him any. Then again, he did agree to periodic babysitting. "Sure. I can watch Marc for a few hours."

"I was hoping you'd see things my way. He's not a picky eater, so lunch can be whatever's simplest to make. He's allowed one soda, as long as it's not caffeinated. Thank you, Sawyer." Becca beamed at him, her smile so approving that for a split second he felt like a hero. He would have agreed to almost anything she asked. Thankfully, instead of making more requests, she turned and went inside.

When he'd moved in, he'd told himself he could charm his disapproving landlady into liking him. But he had underestimated *her* charm. If Becca ever realized the true power in her smiles, he might end up wrapped around her manicured little finger.

Nah, no reason to panic. He hated being told what to do. That hadn't changed. It was just damned difficult to say no to a beautiful woman in a wet shirt.

Chapter 6

The storm had not let up in the hour since Becca had loaded her scowling sister into the minivan, both of them in raincoats. If anything, the wind had increased and the thunder was growing louder. Sawyer stared out the window, trying to ignore just how uncomfortable he was with the idea of her out driving. *Since when are you a worrier?* He used to have casual conversations on the sidelines of rodeo arenas while his friends risked life and limb on the backs of fifteen-hundred-pound bulls. Becca had done just fine taking care of herself before he came along, and she didn't need his concern.

Another thunderclap rattled the house, and he turned toward the sofa, where Marc was supposedly reading a book. It had been ten minutes since he'd last turned a page. They could both use something productive to do.

"Want to help me look for candles and flashlights?" Sawyer asked. "In case the electricity goes out."

The kid frowned, his tone perplexed. "Even if the lights go out, we don't need candles. It's *daytime*."

True. Becca had said she'd be back by four, or would call if Molly had a strong lead and needed more time to interview. "You're right. Guess I'm just..." *Worried? Preoccupied by your mother? Hoping that raincoat keeps her dry so no SOBs are leering at her in wet clothes?* "Bored. Want to play a video game or something?"

"We don't have a console. Kenny Whittmeyer has an Xbox. Even Jodie has a PlayStation."

"Maybe you can ask for one for Christmas?" Sawyer suggested sympathetically.

Marc flopped back on the couch. "That's what Mama said, too. Do you know how far away Christmas is?"

I'll be an uncle by then. It was a surreal thought. He and Charlie used to torment each other with stupid pranks. Hard to believe that the obnoxious kid who once stuck a frog in Sawyer's boot was going to be someone's father.

Thinking about those pranks, Sawyer felt a pang of nostalgia. As much as he and Charlie had plagued each other, they'd both adhered to the unspoken rule of no tattling. They'd relied on creative revenge rather than running to their parents—and woe to anyone outside the family who messed with either of them. They were a united front against perceived enemies. *We were partners.* Equal in worth, if not age. That had changed when Charlie went to college and became the first McCall to finish his degree.

"What about a board game?" Sawyer asked. "Or cards?"

"Do you know how to play checkers?"

"It's been a while, but yeah. Want to play at the kitchen table and finish off the key lime pie?"

Marc's eyes went wide. "That's a bad idea. Key lime is Mama's favorite."

"Don't worry, buddy, I was only kidding. But I could rustle up a snack if you're hungry."

He shook his head. "Can we play out on the porch? I want to see the rain."

"The thunder doesn't scare you?" Sawyer was impressed; that was some significant weather out there.

"It used to. But Mama and I watch the lightning from the porch swing sometimes."

"Sounds good to me."

As Marc scampered off to get the checkers board, Sawyer found himself imagining what it would be like to share that swing with Becca, her soft curves cuddled against him as the two of them marveled at the pyrotechnics of a Texas storm. *Except it wouldn't be the two of us.* Becca was a package deal—and even if Sawyer's life were stable enough that he felt comfortable dating a single mom, it was difficult to believe Becca would voluntarily snuggle up to him.

Difficult, but not impossible.

Sure, she was more subtle than her sister, but that didn't mean she was indifferent. There'd been those admiring glances across the barbecue restaurant, and since then, her teasing last night and the intimate way she'd smiled at him when he'd agreed to babysit. In general, he avoided complications and bossy people. But for the chance to find out if the attraction went both ways...? *It's not like you can avoid her, anyway. You live together.* More or less.

"Found it!" Marc called. He returned, holding a battered cardboard box with masking tape around the corners.

Sawyer pushed aside indecent thoughts about Marc's mom and opened the door for the kid. "You do realize that even with the roof, we're going to get a little wet? The rain will blow onto the porch." The sound of the howling wind reverberated all around them. Wait—that noise was more than the wind.

Marc cocked his head. "Do you hear that, Mr. Sawyer?"

"Yeah." The intermittent sound wasn't exactly a howl; it was a high-pitched whine coming from somewhere in the yard below. Blinking rain out of his eyes, Sawyer leaned over the railing and saw a black-and-gold tail, stubby hind legs and a wiggling butt that suggested frantic movements from the unseen front half of the body. A small dog, probably no more than a puppy, had tried to get under the porch and appeared to be stuck in the latticework.

"That's a *dog*!" Marc was breathless with excitement, his words running together. "We have to save it."

Sawyer was already on his way down the steps. If the dog kept up its panicked struggling, it would either break the lattice or injure itself, or both. "You stay put," he told Marc, "and I'll—"

But the boy scrambled past him, jostling Sawyer, missing the bottom step and nearly landing on his face on the sidewalk before making a wobbly recovery. Sawyer's heart was in his throat as he envisioned having to tell Becca that her baby's nose was broken, yet Marc seemed unfazed by his near tumble on the concrete.

"Do you think he's okay, Mr. Sawyer? What kind of dog is it? Where did he come from? Does he have a collar?"

The kid's rapid-fire delivery gave Sawyer a better understanding of Becca's no-caffeine rule. It was easy to see what Marc would be like after downing an energy drink.

"I won't be able to tell if he has a collar on until I free him," Sawyer said, keeping his voice low so that he didn't spook the animal further. "And I won't be able to help him until you move out of my way."

Marc scrambled to the side in such haste that his shoes slid in the mud and he toppled over. He grinned sheepishly. "Oops."

Reassured that the boy was unhurt, Sawyer focused on the squirming dog. "This would be easier if you'd hold still a second," he muttered, wrapping his hands around the animal to steady him. The dog yowled in protest, but was free a moment later.

It was a German shepherd puppy, little more than a black-and-gold fur ball, with big clunky feet that hinted at his eventual size. Correction, Sawyer noted, lifting the puppy by the scruff of its neck, *her* eventual size. "It's a girl."

"She's so cute!"

"Maybe when she's dry," Sawyer said. "Right now, she's a wet, dirty mess. And frankly, so are you. We should get you inside and cleaned up before your mom gets home."

"What about the puppy? We can't leave her out

in this storm!" A well-timed thunderclap punctuated Marc's words.

Sawyer stood, carrying the puppy up the stairs. No way could he bring it into Becca's house, but he and Marc should at least finish their conversation out of the rain. The kid was going to catch a cold at this rate. "Maybe I can rig up some kind of pen for her out here."

"We can't leave her out here *alone*. She'll be scared."

"She can't run loose through your house, either." Although, technically, the puppy didn't seem interested in running. Worn-out from trying to escape the clutches of the evil lattice, she was now nestled into Sawyer's body heat, her breathing a soft, growly snore.

"She can stay in *your* apartment," Marc suggested, a gleam in his eye. The hint of rebellion made him look like a completely different kid than the miserable boy Sawyer had chatted with that morning, the one who'd struggled into shin guards for a soccer game he didn't want to play.

For a moment, Sawyer considered the idea. The only things of value he had with him were his laptop and his guitar, both easily placed out of the puppy's reach. "Your mom wouldn't like it."

Marc's face fell. "No, I guess not. She doesn't like video games. Or sodas. Or sn—"

"Or snakes. I remember."

Becca liked order and rules and sending her son to a structured activity for every day of the week. Sawyer thought again of the pranks from his youth, the scrapes he and Charlie got into that had been so much fun they'd almost always been worth the consequences. He and his brother might not see eye to eye as adults, but they'd shared a hell of a childhood. Marc lived in a spotless house with pink furniture and no siblings. In the years to come, what would his treasured memories of mischief be?

"We're *only* taking the puppy upstairs to get her out of this storm," Sawyer stated, finally relenting. "And you have to bring me a towel to dry her off first. If the rain stops before your mom returns, we can ask a few of your neighbors if they're missing a dog. Her owner probably lives close by."

"What if she doesn't have an owner?"

Sawyer suddenly found himself grinning at a memory of his first day here. Becca had said she wanted a guard dog. *Careful what you wish for, sweetheart.*

"Well, that was a *very* productive afternoon," Becca chirped, injecting as much positivity into her tone as humanly possible. Her optimism might rub off on Molly.

Eventually.

For now, Molly was sighing heavily in the passenger's seat. "Yeah, I'm sure we set some record for the most food-service forms filled out in a storm." Under Becca's supervision, she'd completed six applications, starting with one for the concessions booth at Cupid's Bow Cinema and ending at the local deli, where they'd picked up food for dinner. "Gee, do I want to serve overpriced popcorn for a living or glop mayo on people's sandwiches? Hard to pick between two dream careers."

If they'd been at home, where Becca's attention wasn't divided between conversation and the dwindling visibility as evening approached, she would have pointed out that the Reyes family, who owned the deli, were some of the town's most well liked citizens or that Molly would be *lucky* to get a call from the movie theater manager after smacking her gum through their entire conversation and answering his questions with sullen curtness. But now was not the time to provoke an argument.

"At least the movie theater job offers later hours," Becca commented. When Molly had opened one eye long enough to refuse an invitation to the soccer game that morning, she'd mumbled that she was more of a "night person." Becca turned her windshield wipers to their highest speed, keeping her observations conciliatory. "Whatever job you end up with now doesn't have to be a long-term career. Look at it as a stepping stone." And perhaps the necessary motivation to come up with a better plan. "If you don't want to live with me or Odette forever, you need a steady income."

"Or I could just get married."

Rainy conditions or not, Becca couldn't help jerking her gaze off the road long enough to glare at her sister. "What an appalling thing to say."

"Plenty of wives don't have jobs. Mom never did."

"But that's no reason to get married! And for the record, being a mom or dad *is* a full-time job. More than a job, actually." Such a simplistic term couldn't begin to sum up the difficulties and joys of parenting. Odette had tried to delegate away the difficulty; by doing so, how many of the joys had she cheated herself out of?

"Let me get this straight. Finding a husband was okay for you, but would be 'appalling' for me?"

"Molly, I hope you do fall in love and get married. Someday. Years from now." *And I hope it turns out a hell of a lot better than my marriage did.* "But I met Colin while I was in college. If I'd never dated him or anyone else, I still would have left the university with a degree and a plan for the future. It was my scholarship, not my marriage, that allowed me to—"

"Escape the rest of us?" There was genuine pain in her soft question.

"Molly…"

"Whatever. I get it. Must have sucked, taking care of a bunch of bratty brothers and sisters." She stared out the window. "I can barely take care of myself, right?"

As Becca turned into the driveway, she felt a twinge of cowardly relief that getting out of the vehicle would provide a convenient end to the conversation. Normally, she wasn't one for avoidance. But in this case? She didn't know what to say. Molly had her faults, but resentment toward the big sister who'd abandoned her wasn't unwarranted.

Becca couldn't resolve that, not in the next ninety seconds, but she hated for their afternoon to end on such a sour note. "You were really good with those kids at the library. I know Hadley will appreciate you volunteering a few hours a week."

Since they'd been next door to the library, Becca had dropped by to introduce her sister. In her midtwenties, Hadley might be a good role model, while being closer to Molly's age. And if Molly was sticking around Cupid's Bow for a while, she should meet people—people who weren't inappropriate men.

When the conversation had turned to the election, Molly had wandered off and helped a little girl find a book. After that, Hadley had wrangled Molly's agreement to come read stories a couple times a week.

In a perfect world, Hadley could hire Molly for a paying job, but the town library had suffered some budget cuts. If—*when*—Becca was elected, maybe she could find a way to redistribute funds. Not for her friend or her sister, but because she thought access to books was a much better priority than some of Mayor Truitt's showy pet projects.

"Thanks," Molly said. "Hadley seemed okay."

"Would you be interested in a job working with kids?" Becca asked. "There's a day care center and a preschool at the church. They aren't open on Saturdays, and I'm not sure if either is actively hiring, but we—"

"I'm hungry and I want to put my wet feet into the warmest socks I can find." Molly yanked her door open. "Maybe give the career-counselor bit a rest?" Without waiting for a response, she stomped toward the house.

That could have gone better.

Could've gone worse, too. Rather than focus on negatives, Becca decided to count today as a victory; less than twenty-four hours after arriving in town, Molly had multiple job leads and had met a potential new friend. It was a decent start.

Gathering up the bags from the deli, she followed after her sister. In the living room, Marc was lying on the floor with a deck of cards. She was surprised to find him showered and in his pajamas before dinner. After setting the food on the kitchen counter, she returned, leaning down to kiss the top of Marc's head, breathing in the apple scent of his children's shampoo and marveling at how fast her little boy was growing. "Hey, champ. What are you up to?"

"Trying to build a house out of cards. Mr. Sawyer showed me earlier, but I'm not very good."

"Not yet, but that's why we practice, right? Where is Mr. Sawyer?"

"Why?" Marc's gaze jerked to her face, then slid

away. "Do you need him? He went upstairs when we heard you and Aunt Molly outside. We probably shouldn't bother him. He might need some alone time. Mrs. Whittmeyer is always sending Kenny and his brother and his dad camping so she can have 'alone time.'"

Becca laughed. "Yes, well, the Whittmeyer boys can be a handful. Did you give Mr. Sawyer any trouble?"

"I was real good. I read my book and took a shower."

"So I noticed. It's a little early for pj's. Tired after soccer this morning?"

"No. But my clothes were dirty. F-from playing checkers with Mr. Sawyer!"

She had to remind him to bathe after horseback-riding lessons and soccer practices, but he found the condition of his clothes unacceptable after a checkers match? "I didn't realize checkers was such a rough-and-tumble sport."

"So there's a full-contact version?" Molly leaned against the doorjamb, standing on one foot as she peeled off a damp sock. "I'll have to ask Sawyer to teach me."

Becca shot a quelling glance at her sister. *You, behave.* Her cell phone rang and she saw that Kate Trent was calling, probably about the festival, which kicked off a week from tomorrow. She left the room to take the call.

Kate didn't bother with a hello. "Parade emergency!" Her voice was tremulous, unlike the calm, patient tone she used when teaching Marc's piano lessons. "The roof of Jed Harker's decrepit barn collapsed."

"Oh, God, is he okay?"

"No one was in it. But he was storing three floats for us."

Becca knew that the local fire department had offered Jed money in the past for the barn, wanting to burn it down as a training exercise. It was not exactly a shock that the building had fallen apart. She was just glad no one had been hurt. "I'll go through the festival phone tree and put together a list of people who can help repair floats—"

"At least one of them is beyond saving. Completely destroyed!"

"People who can help build floats," Becca amended, "and I'll get back to you tomorrow night. Don't panic. We still have a week before the festival."

"Right. Of course you're right. I don't know why I got so emotional about a few parade floats."

Becca grinned, glad her friend couldn't see her knowing expression. She had a pretty good idea why Kate had been so emotional lately—and why, green faced, the sheriff's wife had suddenly bolted from the campaign meeting Thursday, claiming that the barbecue hadn't agreed with her. Did Kate not yet realize she was pregnant again, or were she and Cole waiting until the second trimester to share the news?

"The floats are under control," Becca promised. "You've done a great job coordinating the parade."

"Thank you," Kate said, finally sounding like herself. "Your notes from last year were so organized that it's been easy. Except for this slight building-caving-in hiccup."

"I'll call around and look for new places to store the floats. Structurally sound edifices only, I swear. Meanwhile, why don't you relax and get that handsome husband of yours to rub your feet or something?" Hanging up the phone, Becca realized that it felt like a different lifetime since she'd romantically pursued Cole Trent—not that romance had been her motivation exactly. After the divorce, trying to date him had seemed sensible, another case of being goal-oriented. He was a good father, a good person and good-looking. With her being on the town council and him being the sheriff, they would have been the Cupid's Bow version of a power couple. It could have canceled out her feelings of failure.

But as soon as Kate had entered the picture, Becca had been able to admit Cole wasn't the right man for her. *My own husband wasn't the right man for me, either.* Was there a right man for her? As she'd told Molly, a strong, independent woman didn't need a man. Oh, but there were times she wanted one.

Focus. She had a sister to rehabilitate, a festival to run and an election to win. *But first, dinner.* Since the deli had done most of the work, all that was left was some mixing and reheating. As she pressed buttons on the microwave, she thought she heard a strange sound over the beeps and the ongoing white noise of the rain. It had been sharp and high-pitched. Some kind of animal, maybe?

She tilted her head, waiting to see if it came again. But other than the muffled sound of Sawyer's footsteps two stories above, there was nothing. Obviously just something outside. Or maybe the cowboy was watching the Discovery Channel and had the volume up too loud.

Dismissing her curiosity, she did a mental run through of centennial events. The official kickoff was Sunday morning. She, as festival chairperson, would give a brief welcome address in the downtown gazebo, followed by a speech from Mayor Truitt. She would attempt to not publicly roll her eyes while he was talking. Then came the parade.

Sunday night was her big triumph, the sold-out concert that was drawing in tourists from neighboring regions. She'd called in a favor and booked a young woman originally from Cupid's Bow who'd won a reality TV singing contest a few years ago; thinking of the girl's resulting celebrity made Becca feel guilty that she'd been so quick to dismiss Molly's hope of musical fame. But—

There! It was that same sound as earlier. And it definitely hadn't come from outside.

Marc came around the corner in a hurry. "Hey, Mama—"

"No running in the house," she reminded him. "Did you hear that noise?"

"Wh-what noise? I didn't hear a noise. That's not why I came in here! I'm hungry. That's why I came to the kitchen. Is it time for dinner?"

"Pretty much." Her son was acting squirrelly. "Want to set the table while I go tell Sawyer we've got food ready?"

"No!"

"Marc Paul, what on earth is going on?"

"N-nothing. But remember about his alone time?"

"Did he specifically say he needed to be left alone?" She wanted to know what Sawyer was up to and exactly how he'd spent the hours he was supposed to be watching her son.

"No." Marc hung his head, not meeting her gaze. "But...what if he's taking a nap?"

"I heard lots of movement up there. Don't worry, he

isn't asleep." Before her son could suggest any other obstacles, she marched up the first flight of steps.

Above her, she heard the door to the attic apartment open and close. Sawyer met her halfway down the spiral staircase, moving so quickly it was on the tip of her tongue to tell *him* not to run in the house; they almost collided in the narrow space.

"Hi." His smile was casual, as if there was nothing odd about him barreling down the steps like a one-man stampede. "How'd it go with your sister?"

"Not bad." She'd need to move in order for him to come down the rest of the way, yet she stood where she was, peering past him, unable to shake the feeling that he was hiding something. "How did it go here?"

"Great."

"Are you sure? Because Marc is—"

A sharp bark interrupted her, followed by a long, plaintive howl.

Sawyer scrubbed a hand over his face. "I can explain."

Chapter 7

From the way Becca's eyes narrowed to accusing slits and the delicate flare of her nostrils, Sawyer half expected her to shove him down the stairs. He had the height and weight advantage, but fury could provide an adrenaline boost. *This is what I get for ignoring Brody's warnings. Hope he takes good care of my truck.*

But when Becca struck out with one hand, it was only to nudge him to the side as she tried to squeeze past. It didn't work. They ended up wedged in the stairwell together. Under the circumstances, he probably shouldn't be enjoying it so much, but her angry breathing exaggerated the rise and fall of her breasts under her shirt and she smelled so good…

"You smuggled a dog into my house?"

"I temporarily sheltered a puppy in need."

She angled her hips to slip free. The wiggle was

pleasant to watch, as was the view as she stomped up the remaining stairs. "What if it chews up my attic while you're eating dinner with us? Did you even think about that? And how dare you encourage my son to be dishonest! What kind of example is that setting for Marc and Molly?"

It was your son's idea. But no self-respecting man blamed a seven-year-old. "You do realize Molly is technically an adult and not an impressionable child who needs to be protected?"

Apparently, that was the wrong thing to say, because Becca blasted him with a fulminating glare over her shoulder as she opened the attic door.

After lining the floor with copies of the *Cupid's Bow Clarion* from the recycling bin and removing everything he could from her reach, Sawyer had put the puppy in the small bathroom with a bowl of water. Now she was pawing frantically at the bathroom door, whining at their approach. The moment Becca turned the doorknob, the shepherd launched herself forward, running in circles as she yipped.

Shaking her head, Becca scooped up the dog. "I should've expected you."

"You recognize her?" That made sense. As he'd told Marc, the puppy probably belonged to a neighbor.

"No." Trying to shush the dog, Becca sat in the nearby chair. "But they say trouble arrives in threes. First you. Then Molly. This just makes sense."

Had she just compared Sawyer to some kind of dark omen? "Hey! I thought you decided you like me."

"Doesn't mean you aren't trouble."

Smart woman. "On a scale of one to I'm evicted, how ticked off are you about the dog?"

"I don't mind that you brought her in out of the storm. What kind of monster do you think I am? But letting Marc think it's okay to lie—especially when you both so clearly suck at it—was pretty crappy of you."

He should be regretting that, not watching her fingers stroke the dog's coat, noting that Becca was naturally affectionate and wondering what it would take to coax some of that physical affection his way. "So, uh, you really haven't seen her before?"

"Nope. And I don't know of anyone in the neighborhood who owns a German shepherd. I can ask around and put up signs, but if no one claims her..." She scratched behind the puppy's ear. "What am I supposed to do with you, trouble?"

"You can't call her that. You'll give her a complex."

"Yeah." She studied the dog, sprawled on her back with her paws in the air and tongue lolling out to the side. "I can see she's distraught." After a moment, Becca cast a sidelong glance in Sawyer's direction. "Will it give you a complex if I call *you* trouble?"

"Nah, I'm tough. Unless you're attracted to vulnerable, sensitive men. In which case..." Pressing a palm to his heart, he did his best to look wounded.

She chuckled, but there was an endearingly self-conscious undertone to her laugh. "I don't—"

"Hey!" Molly's voice reached them before she actually made it to the top of the stairs and poked her head in the room. "You two are taking a long time up here. Marc was worried. He sent me to make sure you hadn't 'kicked out Mr. Sawyer.'" She blew a purple bubble as she surveyed the situation. After it popped, she said, "Cute dog. Are y'all coming downstairs or what?"

Becca nodded. "We'll be there in a minute. And you

can assure Marc that I'm not tossing Mr. Sawyer out into the street." She shot him a warning glance. "Not tonight, anyway."

Sawyer was not surprised that dinner conversation revolved around the puppy. Rather than leave the dog upstairs, unhappily alone, Becca had fashioned a makeshift crate out of a large laundry basket lined with old towels. After wolfing down a few bites of the chicken Becca pureed in the food processor, the puppy curled up and slept in a corner of the kitchen.

"What if we can't find her owner?" Marc asked eagerly.

Feeling delayed guilt about how he'd handled the situation, Sawyer tried to intervene before the kid started pressuring Becca to keep the dog. "I'll bet Cupid's Bow has an animal shelter of some kind. Maybe she could stay there until someone adopts her into a good home."

Becca clapped a hand to her forehead. "Oh, that'll go over *great*. Truitt can paint me as a heartless woman who dumped a puppy at the pound. How can I convince voters I can take care of our town if I can't take care of a single dog?"

Sawyer hadn't quite thought of it that way. "We might still find out where she belongs. And if not… maybe she can help you in the election. There's a long tradition of political pets. Hell, wasn't there some book about a dog in the White House?"

"Mr. Sawyer," Marc said in a loud whisper, "we don't say *h-e-l-l*."

"Right. Sorry." Trying to coax a smile from Becca, he added, "Who knows? Maybe adopting Trouble could be your first step on the path to global domination. Today, Cupid's Bow. Tomorrow, the world."

Molly giggled, but Becca just rolled her eyes. "All I need is Cupid's Bow, thanks. That's the difference between me and Truitt. He bases too many decisions on what might advance him to 'bigger things.' I'm not trying to launch a political career, I just want to do right by this town."

It was apparently something she felt strongly about because twenty minutes later, when Molly and Marc had taken the puppy outside and Sawyer was handing Becca containers of leftovers to put in the fridge, she was still discussing her plans. Plans she insisted were for the good of the citizenry, not for her own selfish benefit.

"Take the community center, for example." Shoving the small box of potato salad onto the shelf with enough force that it toppled over, she launched into a detailed accounting of the town budget. She lamented about services she felt Truitt was willing to overlook in favor of new, splashy efforts that got him more press—and possibly more votes. "By his logic, why even have the children's library, right? Kids can't vote. And his attitude toward the senior center—I mean, most of those men and women have lived in Cupid's Bow for decades. They *made* this town! For him to..."

Sawyer gamely tried to listen, but it was easy to get lost, staring at her expressive mouth, appreciating the fire in her eyes, watching her body bounce and sway as she gestured for emphasis.

She stopped abruptly, blowing out a breath. "I ranted for too long, didn't I? See, this is why I need Hadley to help me prep for speeches. So no one thinks I'm boring."

"You aren't boring. You're...passionate." His tone was more intimate than he'd intended. Consciously, he'd only meant to signal encouragement. But subconsciously, he had been mentally replaying the image of her in that wet shirt all afternoon...

Blinking, she leaned against the refrigerator door, uncharacteristically speechless. When she found her voice, it was soft, questioning. "Look, if this is my imagination running amok, tell me to get over myself, and I won't bring it up again. But upstairs, joking about me being attracted to you, and just now... Are you flirting with me?"

Busted. He grinned sheepishly. "Not very well, if you have to ask. Want to give me pointers?"

Her mouth quirked in an attempted answering grin, but she smoothed it away with a shake of her head. "I'd be flattered, if you hadn't already admitted that you flirt with every woman—teenagers notwithstanding. Regardless, it isn't a good idea. Things could get... complicated between us. You live here."

"Which means I'm conveniently located."

"Sawyer! Be serious. I have a very full plate—and a kid—and you'll be gone from Cupid's Bow in, what, two weeks? Two and a half? So never mind what kind of man I find attractive. Or how..." her gaze slid away "...passionate I am."

"So this is a bad time to ask you out?" At her glare, he raised his palms in front of him. "Kidding! I was kidding." But only because he already knew the answer would be no. Whatever else could be said about her, Becca was beautiful and smart and kept him on his toes. There were far worse ways to spend two and a half weeks than in her company. "I'm going to retreat upstairs and quit hassling you. Want me to take the puppy back up with me?"

"Are you going to keep her? Take her with you when you leave Cupid's Bow?"

"Hadn't planned to." He liked dogs, but he was on the move a lot. The cab of his truck didn't seem like the best environment for a puppy.

"That's what I thought. She can sleep in my room. Tomorrow, I'll try to find where she came from, and if that doesn't pan out, I guess I'm now the proud owner of a German shepherd."

He winced. His impulsive decision this afternoon may have landed her a pet for the next decade. Sawyer was unaccustomed to thinking long-term. The closest he'd come was investing in prize-winning livestock, because he'd known he wouldn't be able to ride forever. And even then, someone had approached him with the opportunity. "I guess it's good you're a dog person."

"I never said that. I…implied it, but I was fibbing." She sighed heavily. "Marc's wanted a pet for a long time, though, and Trouble's young, so she can be trained without my having to overcome years of bad habits. I'll work everything out."

"Undoubtedly." The people of Cupid's Bow would be fools not to vote for her. As far as he could tell, she calmly and logically overcame every problem thrown her way—from divorce to unemployed siblings to surprise canines. "I hope it's not too flirty to pay you one last compliment? You're about the most capable woman I've ever met, Becca Johnston."

That earned him a real smile, a wide curve of generous lips he deeply regretted not being able to kiss. "Even if it was flirting, maybe I'll overlook it. Just this once."

* * *

Sunday was proving to be a mixed bag. Becca's attempts to determine where Trouble had come from were futile—with each passing hour, it became clearer that she was now a dog owner. *Yippee.* But in the win column, the manager of the Cineplex called during lunch to offer Molly a job. Becca hoped her sister showed more gratitude in person than she did while on the phone.

Molly was scowling as she rejoined everyone at the table. "I'll have to wear a uniform."

So? Was she afraid the vest with the movie theater logo on it would be less flattering than the men's shirt she currently wore with ripped shorts? Becca shoved a forkful of salad in her mouth to keep from commenting. She darted a glance in Sawyer's direction, recalling how he'd laughed when he discovered she was running for mayor. *See? I can be tactful.* Sort of.

"He said to be there by three," Molly added, "so he can show me the ropes before it gets busy tonight. Can I borrow your mom-mobile?"

Becca hesitated. Lend her only vehicle to the young woman who'd been impatient for Becca to speed up during yesterday's storm, even though road conditions were dangerous?

"I'm a good driver. Shane and Sean taught me a ton about cars." Molly had been the twins' receptionist at their auto body shop for six weeks before it became apparent that three Bakers under one roof made for a tense working environment. As far as Becca could tell, that had been the start of her sister's downward career spiral.

"It's not a question of your driving skills," Becca said. At least, it wasn't a question of *only* that.

"I could take her," Sawyer volunteered. "I was thinking about running into town, anyway. Brody says there's a tack-and-supply shop downtown. The zipper on my gear bag broke, and I need more rosin before the rodeo." He'd told Becca not to expect him for any meals on Wednesday because he was making an overnight trip to Refugio to ride in an exhibition rodeo.

Seated next to him, Molly laid a hand on his sleeve, looking far more enthusiastic about his offer than she had about being gainfully employed. "That would be *so* nice of you."

"Or we could all go together!" The words erupted out of Becca before she'd even had a chance to consider them. "I have to get puppy supplies. That's why I was reluctant to give you my car, Molly. Because I have errands to run. Why take more vehicles than we need, right?" Forcing a smile, she met her sister's irritated gaze, refusing to back down. Becca's interference was for the greater good—she would serve as a buffer between her sister and the disinterested Sawyer, keep Molly from making a fool of herself and pick up dog supplies. Which she really did need.

Her suggestion was motivated by sound reasoning. *Not* a moment of irrational jealousy at the idea of Molly alone with Sawyer and the pretty young woman undoubtedly throwing herself at him again.

"Sounds like a plan." Sawyer rose from his chair, carrying both his empty bowl and Marc's to the sink.

Her son looked absolutely thrilled. Becca wasn't sure what excited him the most, the increasing likelihood that he would get to keep Trouble or a shopping trip with his new hero.

"If we're all going to be out of the house," she told Marc, "Trouble will have to stay in the bathroom. Your job is to play with her between now and then and wear her out, so she'll take a long nap and won't feel lonely when we leave. Deal?"

"Deal!" He was already sprinting to liberate the puppy from her temporary pen.

Molly stood, too, her expression sullen and her salad unfinished.

As her sister turned to go, Becca eyed the dishes left on the table. Granted, it would take her only a moment to clean them up, but Molly needed to take responsibility for herself. "Molly, I think you forgot to rinse out your bowl." Her tone was the same polite but firm one she used when certain members of the town council refused to see sense.

Molly slowed, but didn't immediately stop. Was she going to ignore Becca and go upstairs, anyway? At the last minute, she pivoted, clearing her place and stomping to the sink, muttering under her breath the entire time.

Becca fought down her own rising temper; an argument now would just make their ride even more awkward. If such a thing was possible. A hyper kid excited about his new pet, a ticked-off teenager and a too-appealing cowboy Becca had told herself just yesterday she needed to keep a distance from—*oh, yeah, best trip into town ever.*

Awkward silences, Becca decided, were a problem only if you didn't fill them. She used town trivia like handyman Zeke's putty, spackling over tense moments with such skill they were barely discernible.

As she steered the van into the theater parking lot, she shared the building's history, how it had been owned decades ago by a local family who showed only G-rated films on the single screen. When the couple who owned it got divorced, the husband got the theater while the wife got their ranch and their truck. In bizarre retribution, the husband had showed only R-rated movies for a year. The town council at the time halfheartedly tried to stop him…which would have been more successful if 80 percent of the councilmen hadn't been paying customers. Eventually the single-screen theater was bought by new management and expanded into neighboring space when the drugstore moved to a different location.

"Now the theater can show three movies at a time," Becca said. It had been a big deal in Cupid's Bow when that happened. "Who knows? Maybe one day we'll go as high as five."

Sawyer grinned from the passenger seat. Marc was too engrossed in a comic book to respond and Molly had barely said a word since they'd left the house. Becca didn't appreciate the way her sister slammed the door when she exited the vehicle, but at least after she got out, the mood lightened.

Becca drove toward the downtown, continuing to highlight points of interest, from the huge gazebo in the center of town to the limited but tasty restaurant selections to the new old courthouse.

Sawyer's brow furrowed. "I'm sorry, the 'new' old courthouse?"

"The original one was built right after the town officially incorporated, in 1917. But it burned down in the eighties and they replaced it with a pink, glass-paneled monstrosity that was supposed to 'modernize' Cupid's Bow. It was damaged in the storm fallout after a hurricane a few years ago. There have been repairs since then, but the county finally decided to rebuild, honoring the area's heritage with a structure that closely mirrors the first one. So it's like the old courthouse all over again, but new."

"Huh." Sawyer sounded bemused. "Cupid's Bow is… To be honest, I'm not sure how to describe it."

"Weird," Marc chirped from the backseat. "But good weird."

Sawyer grinned over his shoulder. "There are worse things to be than 'good weird.' Thanks for the impromptu tour," he told Becca. "It's nice to get a little history before I help with the centennial ride."

"There's a lot to love here." Did she sound like a manic travel brochure? She couldn't help it. Even when she wasn't trying to fend off tense silences, she gushed about Cupid's Bow. She'd never been as attached to any place as much as she was to her adopted home. Not the blink-and-you'll-miss-it town where she'd been born or even the city where she'd gone to college. "You should check out the park when you have some free time—it's gorgeous as long as the river isn't overflowing. One of my goals if I'm elected is to have the town explore methods of flood control. Too often the park is a bog. And you have to see the old railway station before you leave town."

"Mr. Sawyer gets to see the soccer fields, too," Marc said. "At my game on Tuesday."

Becca winced at her lack of foresight. If she'd realized Marc planned to invite his new friend, she could have explained that Sawyer had his own schedule while he was in the area. As good-natured as the man was, she doubted he wanted to spend an evening watching seven-year-olds chase a ball with varying degrees of skill and team spirit. "That's a nice idea, champ, and I'm sure Mr. Sawyer appreciates the invitation, but I don't think—"

"It's okay," Sawyer said. "I promised I'd be there, and I keep my promises."

"Oh." She cut her eyes toward him, trying unsuccessfully to read his expression in too brief a time. "I hadn't realized you two already discussed it."

"That isn't a problem, is it? If I go with you?"

Yes. The more time he spent with Marc, the more the kid grew to idolize him. And the more time *she* spent with the cowboy, the harder it was to remember why she shouldn't flirt and smile and soak up his compliments.

But she'd always applauded peopled who lived up to their promises, even more so since Colin had flaked out on his marriage vows and his implied promise of raising his son. So she sounded almost sincere when she replied, "On the contrary, I'm thrilled you'll be joining us."

Sawyer waited for Marc to return his attention to reading, then lowered his voice. "This is what your 'thrilled' face looks like?" he teased softly. "Not what I would have pictured."

"I am happy you're coming with us." Happy-ish, anyway. "It just caught me by surprise."

"Me, too. I don't spend a lot of time at kids' soccer matches. But nothing's been quite what I expected since I got here."

"I know that feeling." Her life had been turned upside down for the last few days. Sawyer wasn't the only reason for the turmoil, but he was definitely at the center of it. "My life's gotten weird lately."

He grinned. "Good weird, or bad?"

"Too soon to tell." The puppy, unhappy about her confinement, had howled for part of the night, so Becca was sleep deprived, as well as frustrated by her sister's attitude. Plus, she was anxious over an upcoming debate and knew that bringing a good-looking stranger to Marc's soccer game was bound to cause whispered speculation.

Still, with sunshine streaming through the windows, her son humming cheerfully in the backseat and Sawyer smiling at her, life felt pretty damn good at the moment.

Chapter 8

Becca didn't work at the community center on the weekends—not officially, anyway—and Monday was usually hectic. She spent it making sure rooms that had been rented out for Saturday and Sunday events had been restored to the proper condition, following up on inquiries, firming up the schedule for the coming week. This particular Monday morning was no exception, yet amid the controlled chaos, inspiration struck…with a little help from Sammy Pasek.

She was sitting at her desk in the administrative office just off the lobby when her phone rang. It was Sammy, calling between classes to ask if he could come in an hour early today in order to leave an hour sooner, to take his sister to the orthodontist. Eighteen-year-old Sammy was in a special honors program where he finished his school day early and used afternoons for volunteer service. He'd be leaving for college in August, and Becca had written him a hell of a recommendation letter.

Once she assured Sammy that the schedule change was no problem and disconnected the call, her thoughts turned to Molly. Her sister could benefit from exposure to resolute role models like Sammy. Then there was Vicki Ross, only a year or two older than Molly, who came in every Monday and Wednesday to use the weight room. Vicki's sophomore year of college had been postponed due to serious injuries she'd suffered in a car accident; she'd done physical therapy with Sierra for months. But now Vicki was healed, rebuilding her strength and planning a girls' trip with her mom to Lake Tahoe to celebrate her progress over the past year.

Becca had no point of reference for mother-daughter bonding; if she had to fly to the West Coast with Odette, she'd probably parachute out of the plane somewhere over the Grand Canyon. But that didn't mean she couldn't attempt some strategic *sisterly* bonding.

She reached for the phone, optimism welling. Granted, Molly had been annoyed yesterday when Becca hijacked her ride to work with Sawyer, but how long could the younger woman hold a grudge? A free lunch and a chance to meet some people her own age might cheer her up.

The phone rang unanswered until voice mail kicked in, so Becca hung up and tried again after updating some new rental agreements.

Finally, on her third attempt, she got an answer.

"Hello."

At least Becca assumed the greeting was "hello." The word was distorted by a huge yawn.

"Did I wake you?" Becca frowned at the clock in the corner of her laptop. It was almost eleven.

"Well, I did work last night," Molly said defensively.

"I know. I drove into town to pick you up, remember?" Becca had wanted to hear about Molly's first day, but her sister had rested her head against the window and feigned sleep until they got home. But today was a fresh chance. Better get to the reason for her call before Molly withdrew again. "I was thinking, how about I come get you and we have lunch in town together? There's an incredible barbecue place. Then you can come to the community center with me."

"Why?"

Becca hadn't expected such an incredulous response. Marc happily hung out here whenever she put in a few hours on the weekend; there were basketball courts, ping-pong tables and even a small reading nook, suggested by Hadley. "To see where I work, to introduce yourself to more of the community." She almost added "to meet a boy your own age" but was afraid it would sound judgmental. Besides, she wasn't certain whether Sammy Pasek was currently seeing anyone. "Come on, it's just a few hours," she cajoled, "and you get free food out of it."

"Fine." But the surly agreement wasn't quite as promising as Becca had hoped.

Molly's mood had not improved an hour later, when she trudged out of the house wearing enough eyeliner for all the Dallas Cowboy cheerleaders combined and a skimpy tank top, her expression daring Becca to say something.

Not walking into that trap. Her sister was about as subtle as Truitt's past attempts to publicly bait her. Besides, Molly's skin-baring fashion choices weren't *that* over-the-top for late May in Texas. People didn't take on this heat in sweater sets and slacks.

"We didn't have a chance to talk about it last night, but how was work?" Becca asked encouragingly.

"People wanted to see movies, I sold them tickets. People wanted popcorn, I filled buckets. Riveting, huh?"

Becca sighed, not objecting when her sister reached for the radio dial and filled the minivan with country music.

Luckily, not even Molly's sour mood was a match for the food at The Smoky Pig. She dug into her brisket and fries with gusto, not pausing to say much, but clearly enjoying her meal. Meanwhile, a succession of folks came over to discuss the festival with Becca. The crushed parade floats had been the first in a series of minor setbacks, but she wasn't worried. Problems were only opportunities to find solutions.

Cousins Kim and Tasha Jordan, who worked for the county EMT service and fire marshal respectively, stopped to discuss crowd control for the concert Sunday. When their order number was called at the counter, Becca bade them goodbye and turned back to see Molly looking impressed for the first time.

"You really talked Kylie Jo Wayne into doing a concert for you?" Molly asked around a bite of coleslaw.

"Well, I pleaded my case to her parents, who still live out by Whippoorwill Creek, and they eventually put us in touch. Kylie's from Cupid's Bow. She was glad to do something to give back to the community that supported her when she was on that reality show." Becca hoped she sounded modest enough, without downplaying the achievement so much that Molly lost interest. This was the first time she'd been engaged all day.

"I love her music," Molly gushed. "Do you think... do you think there's any chance you might be able to introduce me to her while she's here?"

"I honestly don't know. Her schedule will be pretty tight, and she travels with security and a manager and her band. But I promise if there's an opportunity, I will seize it."

Molly surprised her with a grin. "I believe you. You're not exactly shy."

Becca laughed. "No, I guess I'm not." Good thing. Monday night, she had a debate in town hall against the mayor, one of her last chances to officially make her case. It was on the tip of her tongue to ask Molly if she might want to come along. Would she be interested in seeing her big sister in action, or bored by the small-town politics? Before Becca had decided how to frame the question, they were interrupted by Gayle Trent, stopping by to volunteer her son Jace, in case more help was needed with float repairs.

After Gayle bustled off into the crowd, Becca realized how late it was getting. "Shoot! I'm supposed to be back in the office in ten minutes."

"Yeah, but aren't you the boss or something? No one's going to yell at you if you're late getting back."

"Maybe not, but what kind of example would I be setting for all the employees who work for me? Besides, I take pride in my work ethic. The point is to do a job well—not just well enough to avoid getting yelled at."

Molly rolled her eyes, but reached for the purse hanging on the back of her chair. "Guess we'd better head out then."

Dial it back a notch, Becca advised herself as she counted out bills for the waitress's tip. She didn't mean to sound self-righteous every time she opened her mouth, but she was trying hard to make up for lost years, time when she could have been steering Molly in the right direction. Lunch had been a start. Her sister had actually smiled at her. Hopefully, a couple hours at the community center would further the cause.

They ran into Sammy in the parking lot, and when Molly met the handsome varsity swimmer, her face lit up like the town fireworks over the Watermelon Festival. Becca tried not to grin, afraid she'd look smug about how well her plan was working. She sent the two teenagers off to the filing room with a stack of folders, and was surprised when Molly stalked back into the administrative office half an hour later, scowling. Sammy walked past not long after to help some kids retrieve a basketball that was stuck, darting a crestfallen glance in Molly's direction. She pointedly ignored him.

Should Becca broach the subject once she finished the phone call she was on?

Before she had the chance, though, Vicki Ross came into the center. When the blonde stopped to fill out the sign-in sheet for the weight room, Becca introduced her to Molly.

Vicki grinned at the magenta and blue streaks that framed Molly's face. "I like your hair. My family would probably lose their collective minds if I did something like that."

Doubtful. In Becca's opinion, the Ross family was so happy to have Vicki healthy and whole again, they wouldn't blink if she shaved her entire head and tattooed her face.

But Molly was nodding, her expression empathetic. “Family members can be super judgy.” She cut her gaze toward Becca.

Trying to help someone find their footing wasn’t the same as judging them. Mentally rolling her eyes, Becca returned to her desk. The girls talked for a few more minutes, then Vicki asked if Molly wanted to be her spotter in the weight room.

When Sammy poked his head into the office to update Becca on an equipment delivery, he looked disappointed not to find Molly with her. He leaned against the door frame, not meeting Becca’s gaze. “Did, uh, your sister say anything about me?”

“Like what? Did something happen?” Becca’s protective instincts rose. She wouldn’t have thought Sammy was the type to make a move on a girl he’d just met, but if he—

“I don’t know,” he said miserably. “We were talking about the pool and how she hasn’t been yet.” Cupid’s Bow had a very nice aquatic complex, funded years ago by a donation from an oil tycoon. “And I mentioned my swim scholarship. I didn’t mean to brag, but I, uh, wanted to, you know, impress her. Maybe it sounded too obnoxious? She suddenly stormed out. I’m real sorry if I made her mad.”

From what Becca knew, she would have expected her sister to be flattered that Sammy wanted to impress her. “I’ll mention that you apologized, but honestly, I wouldn’t worry too much about this. She may have been in a bad mood because of something completely unrelated to you. Now, can you go check all the thermostats? I want to make sure the air-conditioning units are working properly after those repairs last week.”

"Yes, ma'am."

Today was the start of a brand-new class in wood carving. Becca was in the lobby giving directions to a group of retired gentlemen who'd looked lost, when Vicki Ross strolled toward the exit, whistling cheerfully.

"Vicki, hold up!" Becca darted around a brochure stand to catch up with the young woman before she left the building. She lowered her voice. "Can I ask… Did Molly seem okay to you? I think she was upset earlier, and I just wanted to see if her day had improved."

Tilting her head to the side, Vicki considered the question. "I wouldn't say she was upset. She has a really sharp sense of humor—sarcastic, but funny. We're going out on Thursday, because that's the next night she has off. She did get sort of quiet. Perked right up when Jace Trent came into the weight room, though. She's still there talking to him." Vicki pushed open the door, her smile impish as she turned to go. "Can't say I blame her."

Becca gritted her teeth. Although the sheriff's younger brother was closer to Molly's age than, say, Sawyer, Becca thought Jace was too old for a not-quite-nineteen-year-old.

Still, Becca had known the upstanding Trent family for years and trusted everyone in it. Jace might smile at Molly's flirting, but nothing untoward was going to happen in the heavily windowed rec-center weight room, where any number of citizens could see in. Ignoring the overprotective instinct to drag her sister out of there bodily, Becca returned to her office, her earlier triumphant mood deflated.

It wasn't a complete wash. Molly and Vicki had made plans. That counted toward establishing friendships. Of course, Vicki would be headed to Tahoe in June and back to university in August, but Molly would be more settled in by then.

Becca pushed aside thoughts of her sister long enough to answer some emails, adjust a few numbers in the summer budget and sit through a meeting with representatives from a group looking for a place to hold a haunted house in the fall. Their plans sounded too disturbing—and potentially dangerous—to host at the community center, but she agreed to a second meeting if they wanted to rethink their approach.

It was almost time to leave so Becca could pick up Marc from his after-school art program and get him to his Monday evening piano lesson. Molly was still nowhere to be seen. Jace Trent had left over an hour ago, poking his head into Becca's office to get an update on parade floats. She'd politely thanked him for his willingness to help, biting back any snarled reminders that Molly was just a kid.

Becca checked in the weight room for her sister, without luck. It would be handy to text her, but unlike many other teenagers, Molly didn't have a cell phone. She'd mentioned her ex-boyfriend giving her one, but the plan had lapsed since they broke up. Luckily, the rec center was only three stories. Becca started on the bottom floor and worked her way up, frowning when she discovered her sister in the doorway of the basketball court, smiling up at a shirtless Larry Breelan. The Breelan brothers had a reputation for trouble; the oldest, Daryl, had been arrested for fighting, public drunkenness and a number of pranks gone awry. His unapologetic "boys will be boys" attitude was particularly ludicrous now that he was approaching forty.

She cleared her throat, inserting herself between Molly and the leering Larry. "I've been looking all over the building for you," she told her sister.

"Well, you found me. Larry here was just telling me about the time he and his brothers—"

"You can tell me all about it on the way to pick up Marc. We need to go." She shot a dark look at Larry. "Now."

Molly folded her arms across her chest. "And if I'm not ready to leave? Maybe I can find my own ri—"

"You have to get ready for work tonight. Remember? Come on, I don't want Marc to think I forgot about him."

That got Molly moving. Something flashed in her expression, and Becca wondered if Odette had ever neglected to come get her once Molly's older siblings had left home. Sean and Shane had stayed in the same town, but as young bachelors enjoying their first apartment and being legally old enough to buy beer, they probably hadn't spent a lot of time in the school carpool line.

Becca gave a sigh of relief when her sister willingly followed her down the corridor. Almost as if to counteract it, Molly turned to give Larry one last wave. "Come by the Cineplex sometime."

And bring a date, Becca wanted to add. *Someone age-appropriate.*

Life would be simpler if Becca could just tell people what to do and they would listen. But politics and family matters required at least a little finesse. If she couldn't deal with her sister tactfully, how could she hope to win the election? Becca tamped down the urge to snap *what the hell were you thinking?* as they crossed the parking lot.

Instead, she silently counted to one hundred, then smiled at Molly while buckling her seat belt. "So did you have a nice afternoon? Not too boring, I hope."

"It was okay."

"When Vicki left the center, she mentioned the two of you might go out this week. That should be fun."

"Uh-huh."

"And Sammy—"

"Mr. Honor-Student-Captain-of-the-Swim-Team?" Molly rolled her eyes. "Did you ask him to come to the center so he could inspire your screwup sister with his rousing college pep talk?"

"Of course not! He works here. He comes in every day. And I didn't say a word to him about you beforehand. What you're calling a pep talk was just his misguided attempt to impress you."

"Right. Well, I'm sure he'll have the chance to impress plenty of girls on campus next fall."

"Look, Molly, I'm sorry if Sammy upset y—"

"I'm not upset with Sammy. *He* isn't the one who made sure I spent my afternoon with people who all have big plans and places to go. College. Lake Tahoe. Meanwhile, I'm stuck here like some loser."

Stuck? Becca's blood-pressure skyrocketed. Molly was completely ungrateful that Becca had given her a place to live and helped her find a job. *I should put her butt on a bus right back to Odette.* Sure, Becca could do that. But would she be able to live with herself afterward?

"Cupid's Bow is a wonderful place," she said firmly. "But if you don't want to be here, explore other options."

"Like school?" Molly sneered. "Did you know that Jace Trent dropped out of college?"

"Yes." His parents had been disappointed when he'd moved back to Cupid's Bow and taken up bartending, along with several other odd jobs.

"He's been in school a lot more recently than you, and he says it's not all it's cracked up to be."

"So rather than keep an open mind about your future, you've decided to limit your options based on casual conversation with a guy you just met?" Becca was going to wring Jace's neck. *After* he finished rebuilding those floats.

Molly glared, but didn't respond. Probably just as well—they'd reached the elementary school.

Marc climbed in the car, telling them all about his day before he even had his door closed. Becca studied his freckled face in the rearview mirror, the sight of him filling her with love. She adored her son, and he would grow up knowing that.

Molly's own childhood situation had been different than Marc's. The encouragement she received was likely erratic, coming from siblings when they had time for her or Odette if she was in a rare good mood. Maybe Molly didn't dream bigger because she had trouble believing in herself. With time and patience, Becca could help her overcome that. So what if today hadn't gone perfectly? Bringing Molly to work had been a mere plan A.

And if plan A failed, there were plenty other letters in the alphabet.

"Mama! My lucky cereal isn't here!"

"Lucky cereal?" Sawyer paused in the hallway just outside the kitchen; he'd been on his way to retrieve the boots he'd left on the front porch. It was almost time to leave for Marc's soccer game.

Currently, Marc was standing in front of the open pantry, scowling fiercely. "I always have a bowl before my games. The cereal circles look like little soccer balls." He lowered his voice to a confidential tone. "And they're *chocolate*."

Ah. Sawyer guessed the kid was more invested in the splurge of almost-junk-food than he was in the athletic superstition. "Your mom took Trouble out back. Want me to look on the high shelves? Maybe the cereal just got moved."

"Hurry," Marc urged. "Or we'll run outta time."

Sawyer did his best, shuffling pantry ingredients that were so organized they were damn near shelved in alphabetical order, but there was no chocolate-flavored cereal to be found. "Sorry, buddy, I—"

"What are you guys doing?" Becca asked, as she and the puppy came in through the door from the garage. There was an undercurrent in her tone, the faint apprehension of a woman who didn't appreciate others rearranging her stuff.

"My cereal's missing," Marc explained. "Mr. Sawyer was helping me find it."

"Trying to, anyway. I'm afraid I came up short." The kid looked so crestfallen that Sawyer offered, "What if I buy you a chocolate shake after the game? We could go to the diner for supper."

Becca frowned. "Oh, I don't know about that. I—"

"Brody said the diner has awesome key lime pie." In the middle of helping his friend put out hay yesterday, Sawyer had surprised himself by asking where to find the best key lime pie in town. Sawyer's personal favorite was pecan. The request had forced him to admit that he wanted to know where to take Becca in case she ever rescinded her no-flirting policy and went out with him. It had been a random, far-fetched impulse—and yet he was glad he'd prepared. Because now her blue eyes sparkled in anticipation.

"They *do* serve good pie there," she admitted. "And it would be nice not to cook after such a long day..."

Marc let out a whoop of joy.

Becca raised an eyebrow. "I haven't technically said yes."

"But you will, right, Mama? Pretty please!"

"I suppose if you promise to show a little of that energy out on the soccer field, I can agree to the diner afterward. I have to put Trouble in her crate. Can you scoot upstairs and tell Aunt Molly we're ready to go? We need to drop her off on our way to the game."

As the boy raced out of the room, Sawyer knelt down to scratch behind the puppy's ear. "I can take care of Trouble if you need a minute to fix the pantry."

She tried hard to fake confusion, her eyes wide and her tone nonchalant. "I don't know what you mean."

"I moved some things around. I don't think all your salad dressings are in order by height anymore."

"Very funny. I'm not *that* bad." But she was already reorganizing boxes according to whatever System of Becca she used. "I'm just very busy between work and parenting and the election. It saves me time if I know where everything is. Like the cereal. It should be right here."

"I didn't touch it, I swear." He latched the metal door to Trouble's kennel. "I get in enough trouble for turning off lights when I leave a room." Go figure. He'd been brought up to believe that not wasting electricity was responsible behavior.

"Only when you turn off the ones I—"

"I'm ready," Molly announced, shrugging into her uniform vest as she entered the kitchen. "We leaving or what?"

Nodding, Becca closed the pantry door. "By any chance, did you eat Marc's cereal?"

Molly froze, her gaze turning guilty, then defensive. "I didn't see his name on the box."

"You're welcome to anything you want in the kitchen. But please, if you use something up, write it on the refrigerator list like we've talked about."

"Sorry," Molly mumbled. "I guess college-educated people never forget to do crap like that."

The sarcasm was a holdover from the day before. When Sawyer had returned from Brody's yesterday evening, the two sisters had been "discussing" regional colleges. The discussion consisted of Becca cheerfully lecturing while Molly popped bubble gum.

There was nothing cheerful in Becca's demeanor now. She balled her fists at her hips. "Are you determined to be negative about everything? My pointing out your potential was a *compliment*. Going to college—"

"A college degree isn't everything." Oh, hell. *Why did I say that?* The last thing Sawyer wanted was to get involved in the sisters' argument.

Both women swung their gazes in his direction, their matching expressions of surprise highlighting the family resemblance. Molly's shock faded to a smirk when she realized she had an ally.

Meanwhile, Becca eyed him like he was something unpleasant on the bottom of her shoe. "No," she said tightly, "of course it's not *everything*. But school is a decent starting place for a girl with academic promise and no plan."

He wouldn't know about that. Although his grades had been all right, no one had ever told him he had "academic promise." He functioned better in wide-open spaces than in classrooms. "I didn't mean—"

"You don't have to apologize to her!" Molly interjected. "People are entitled to their opinions. Even non-Becca-approved opinions. She thinks she can go through life bossing people around."

Becca's eyes narrowed dangerously. "I was *trying* to *help*. But, no, you—"

"Uh…ladies?" Though it went against his sense of self-preservation to interrupt a second time, Sawyer deemed it necessary. "Maybe this conversation should be tabled until later, so no one's late for work. Or soccer."

At the reminder of soccer, Becca whirled toward her son, paling. "Are you okay?" she asked Marc.

He looked more fascinated by the raised voices than emotionally scarred. "Fine."

"I didn't mean to lose my temper with Aunt Molly," Becca said, her tone contrite. "Sometimes adults just disagree."

Marc nodded. "I know. Mrs. W disagrees with Mr. W all the time. Kenny says his dad brings home flowers and then his parents take a nap and everything's okay."

Sawyer choked back a laugh at the mention of make-up naps.

Becca looked unsure how to respond. "Yes, well. Glad they, uh, have a system that works for them. Now, if everyone's ready, we should get going." She grabbed her car keys off the hook on the wall and strode toward the front door.

Sawyer got there first, opening the door for her. She sailed past without looking in his direction, and he wondered how badly he'd screwed up by opening his big mouth back there. He'd be happy to buy her flowers to make up for interfering, but he was pretty sure she'd never agree to a conciliatory "nap." No matter how nicely he asked.

"I'll get those for you."

Another time, Becca might have appreciated the unsolicited offer of assistance. Now, it just made her want to slam her trunk shut—not that she could, because the automatic hydraulics kicked in, lowering the trunk with measured speed, but still. Even though it was an immature impulse, more in line with the behavior of a sulky eighteen-year-old than a pillar of the community, she didn't care. Sometimes, a woman wanted to slam something.

Or kick a very good-looking cowboy in his denim-clad shin.

Before she could tell Sawyer that she was capable of carrying the cooler and the collapsible soccer chairs she brought to every game, he was already reaching for them, taking them from her with an earnest expression.

Nice try, but it's going to take more than green-gold eyes and strong arms to win my forgiveness. No matter how great those arms looked in the short sleeves of his dark T-shirt. Who did the man think he was, butting into her conversation with Molly and undermining Becca's point? He was a guest in her home, not a family therapist. When he'd interrupted her, Becca had been so blindsided she hadn't known how to react. Too bad she didn't have that moment to do over again, she thought, as she nodded hello to team parents and the volunteer referees. Because she had a few choice words for the man.

It was unusual for her to remain this irritated—Mayor Truitt had been publicly disagreeing with her for months, and her normal response was faintly amused exasperation. So why was she so upset that Sawyer had voiced an opposing opinion? Anger was heating her blood even more than the May sun, and she impatiently pulled a rubber band from her purse, looping her hair into a ponytail. Fanning herself with her clipboard, she called the names of the kids who would play the first quarter and resolved to ignore Sawyer entirely.

But it was impossible not to notice a man on the sidelines enthusiastically yelling "Go, Unicorns!"

On some level, Becca may have been hoping that if she didn't interact much with him, then other parents wouldn't start asking questions about his association with her—a frankly ridiculous wish. Every female gaze had been drawn in Sawyer's direction from the second he put down the cooler, some admiring, but most of them quizzical. As the second quarter started, it became clear Sawyer was specifically cheering for her son. He clapped for the team in general, but Marc was the only kid whose name he knew. The quizzical glances shifted from Sawyer to Becca. As she swapped out a couple players, she struggled to ignore the unspoken questions shimmering around her like heat waves.

But what she *couldn't* ignore was the giddy expression on her son's face. Marc had never looked this happy playing soccer. Ever. And she knew she had Sawyer to thank for that.

Just moments before the halftime whistle, Marc kicked in a goal. Pride crashed through Becca, and she barely checked the urge to rush over and hug her kid. He might not appreciate that in front of all these people, and, as coach, she should treat her players equally. So she clapped him on the shoulder and said "Good job" just as she would have congratulated Doug or Jodie. But inside, she was turning cartwheels. *I knew you could do it, champ.*

When the players cleared the field for their halftime break, Sawyer helped distribute water and orange slices from the cooler. Behind her, Becca heard Mrs. Prescott asking him, "Are you Marc's uncle?"

"No, ma'am. I'm just renting an apartment from the Johnstons until after the centennial celebration."

"Oh." Cecily White, the single mother of twins, sighed audibly. "It's a shame you can't stay longer. You seem to be bringing our team good luck."

"I appreciate that," Sawyer said, "but I suspect the team is doing well thanks to its stellar coach."

Becca's cheeks tingled with warmth. *Charmer.* Did he know she could hear him? Did he really think she was doing a "stellar" job, or was this another attempt to get back in her good graces?

A moment later, Cecily elbowed Becca in the ribs, whispering, "I can't believe you've been hiding him up in your attic!"

Hiding implied keeping secrets—a less than ideal reputation for a political candidate. "He's a tenant," Becca said coolly, "not a hostage. Free to come and go as he pleases."

Cecily hadn't heard a word. She was too busy ogling Sawyer as he high-fived the smallest player on the team. "You are a lucky, lucky woman."

Becca almost laughed at that. While she certainly had her share of blessings—namely her son and the friends she'd made in this town—*lucky* did not describe how she'd been feeling lately.

"I was so sad for you when Colin left," Cecily continued, "but if I'd known *he* was going to come riding into your life..."

Yeah, well. Pretty soon, he'd be riding right back out of it. "Cecily, if you don't mind, I want to talk to the kids about their passing strategy before we start again." She also needed to remind them that the teams switched goals after halftime. Many was the game when Dylan Ellis got so excited to find himself in control of the ball that he kicked to whichever net was closest and scored a point for the other team.

She gathered the kids around her, but while she was waiting for the last stragglers to join the semicircle, Amy Prescott sidled up to her.

"Kudos on your new cowboy friend," Amy said. "I don't know where you find the time—or the energy—with everything else you've got going on, but—"

"Amy. Sawyer is renting a room from me. Period. It doesn't take much extra time or effort to deposit his rent check."

Amy winked broadly. "Hey, no judgment here. You're my hero."

Becca ground her molars, turning her attention to the antsy seven-year-olds, who were turning out to be far less frustrating than their parents.

To Sawyer's credit, his behavior throughout the entire game was impeccable. He was friendly but not flirty with the moms, overlooking their obvious titters and speculation. He cheered heartily for the Unicorns but politely clapped when the other team did well, underscoring all Becca's lectures about sportsmanship. And not once did he crowd her or monopolize her time, instead hanging back and letting her coach.

Yet she could feel his gaze on her so often, like the prickly warning of sunburn. She'd slathered both herself and Marc with UV protection; too bad they didn't make a Sawyer-block that would keep her from getting emotionally burned. She'd had time for her anger to cool, and now realized that while she'd been annoyed that he jumped into her conversation with Molly and contradicted the point Becca was trying to make, what she'd really been feeling was hurt. Betrayed, even. It was an overreaction that underscored how important Sawyer's opinion was becoming—how important *he* was becoming—to her.

She could tell anyone who would listen that he was nothing more than a tenant, but if that were true, he wouldn't have the power to hurt her feelings. From the first time she'd laid eyes on him, there had been attraction. Now there were stirrings of emotion that wouldn't do either of them any good in the long run. *And I always think long-term.* Becca had goals and plans and a track record of success…except when it came to men.

After two and a half years together, her high school sweetheart had accused her of caring more about her potential scholarships than she did about him; their relationship dissolved when she told him he was absolutely right. In college, she'd met her husband-to-be, and he had seemed like her fairy-tale prince, everything she'd ever dreamed of in the man she would someday marry. Then she'd come with him to Cupid's Bow and got her happily-ever-after. Sort of.

The truth was, even though she was a mother past thirty, she didn't have a lot of experience with men. She could count on her fingers the number of guys she'd dated. She wasn't used to flirting or casual relationships, and now that she was divorced, she sure as hell wasn't looking for Fairytale Prince: The Sequel. So she was unsure how to handle Sawyer. Could she go on a few dates with someone and enjoy the pleasure of his company, knowing that there was no future in it, or would it feel like a counterproductive waste of her limited time?

Next to her, Amy Prescott shouted, startling Becca from her thoughts. Jodie had scored. *My team got a point and I was too distracted by a man to even notice.* Some coach she was.

Becca belatedly cheered on her star player, working hard to stay focused on the game for the last few plays. But once the final whistle blew and Sawyer helped her gather gear, she felt uncharacteristically shy, self-conscious in a way she hadn't experienced since her dramatic growth spurt in elementary school.

"Thanks," she mumbled as he handed her the clipboard. "Not just for helping me carry stuff or pass out snacks, but for being here. It meant a lot to Marc." The Fighting Frogs had defeated the Unicorns 7–5, but from the way her son was beaming, no one would ever guess his team had lost. Marc had scored two goals, a season record for him, and both times he'd turned immediately to Sawyer to exchange a thumbs-up. Now Marc was jogging toward them with a rare swagger.

She ruffled her son's hair. "You more than earned that milk shake. There may even be onion rings in your future. Great job, champ."

"Thanks, Mama. What did you think, Mr. Sawyer? Was that great? What was your favorite part? I liked scoring goals, but also that time when the other team thought I would pass to Jodie but actually I kicked it to Doug, and they didn't even see him coming! And when Dylan wiped out, making that totally awesome kick—it's okay, he said he's not hurt—and…" Marc kept up a mile-a-minute sports commentary as the three of them walked to the minivan.

Listening to his high-energy recap made Becca realize how much her own energy was flagging. After a full day's work, the argument with her sister and the game, she was beat. Although she'd never say a word to dampen Marc's enthusiasm for their trip to the diner, what she really wanted was to go home to a hot shower, silky-soft pajamas and a good book. Sighing, she hit the remote that unlocked the van doors. *I'd be willing to forgo key lime pie for the chance to kick off my shoes and take off this bra.*

"You okay?" Sawyer asked.

"Of course. It's just been a long day."

"Want me to drive?" he asked. "I've been tooling around town enough that I can find my way to Main Street from here."

Her instinctive reaction was to refuse; she believed in projecting an image of strength. But, honestly, being able to close her eyes in the passenger seat for a few minutes sounded like heaven. "Here." She gave him the keys, her hand brushing his.

His warm, callused fingers against hers sent a pulse

of awareness through her, but the brief physical contact wasn't nearly as intimate as his reaction. He went still at her touch, his only movement a shuddery breath as his eyes locked with hers. She might not have abundant experience with the opposite sex, but there was no mistaking the desire she saw in his gaze. It made her feel wanted and feminine. And powerful.

Her earlier fatigue evaporated as if it had never been. Once again, key lime pie sounded like a splendid idea—or at least like a safe substitute for what she was really craving.

Seated next to her on the padded vinyl bench, Marc was buzzing with so much excitement that the salt and pepper shakers on the table were living up to their name.

And I ordered this kid a chocolate milk shake? Becca was having serious second thoughts about filling him up with sugar. On the plus side, after the crash, maybe he'd go to bed early. Yeah, there was some A-plus parenting.

While Becca perused the salad choices, Marc leaned across the table. "Do you know what you want, Mr. Sawyer?"

Sawyer's eyes were on Becca, his menu unopened in front of him. "Yes."

Heat flooded her cheeks, and she glanced away, trying not to project her own lust onto the cowboy. She noticed the Ruiz family at a corner table; she was fairly certain their little boy had been in Marc's class last year. "Hey, Marc, isn't that one of your friends?"

Marc spun around, climbing up on his knees for a better look. "Uh-huh. That's Alejandro. He sits at the same art table as me on Fridays. He's a real good draw-er."

"Do you want to go say hi?" she asked. "We have

plenty of time." His milk shake would be out soon, but they hadn't ordered their food yet. It would be at least another ten minutes before dinner was served.

"Okay." He scrambled down and darted into the path of an oncoming waitress. Luckily, she had the reflexes of a superhero and didn't spill any of the drinks she carried.

"Walking feet!" Becca called after her son. Then she turned to Sawyer with a wry smile. "Is it wrong that I desperately want him to become better friends with someone who doesn't own a snake?" She fiddled with the straw in her sweet tea. "No, in all seriousness, I'm incredibly grateful he's got a best friend who's helped him get through some tough transitions. But I worry that because of my schedule he's spending too much time with the Whittmeyers."

Sawyer cocked his head, his expression puzzled. "Whittmeyer… Whittmeyer… Gee, the name doesn't ring a bell."

That made her laugh. "If I had a dollar for every time I heard a story that started with 'Kenny Whittmeyer,' I'd be the richest woman in Texas." She glanced fondly at her son. From his exuberant body language, she guessed he was reenacting the soccer game for his friend, especially the parts where Marc scored goals. "I know I told you this already, but thank you for coming to the game."

"I had fun," Sawyer said, sounding vaguely surprised. "And now there's something I should have told you already. I'm sorry about what happened at the house, with your sister. No one asked for my input, and I should have kept my trap shut. College is…a sore spot for me."

"Because you didn't go?" she asked carefully. Though she hadn't admitted it to him, she'd looked up some of his articles online. His intelligent, evocative writing had impressed her. He was descriptive enough to bring to life sights and sounds and tastes of places she'd never been, witty enough that she'd laughed aloud at her computer screen. And when referencing a historic massacre that was an uglier part of the state's history, and how people could learn from it, his words had been poignant enough to make her blink away tears. He was definitely as smart as any of the college friends who'd graduated alongside her.

"I didn't mind not going," he said. "I was being honest when I told Molly that I don't think a college degree is the be-all and end-all. People take different paths in life. But when my brother came home from college…"

Had Sawyer resented his brother's education? Had he felt somehow inferior? It was impossible to imagine the cocky cowboy ever feeling not good enough. "What did—"

The waitress returned to the table with Marc's milk shake and an apology for taking so long. "I've got a party of twelve over there, including two dairy allergies and a gluten allergy." She nodded to the other side of the room, where tables had been pushed together to accommodate half a dozen kids in soccer jerseys and their parents. The Unicorns were only one of the teams who'd recently finished a game. "Checking with the chef on substitutions and ingredients got hectic."

Becca assured her that the wait was no problem. Truthfully, she'd been so caught up in wanting to learn more about Sawyer's past that she'd forgotten about food entirely. But her son certainly hadn't. As if he'd been keeping one eye on the table for the arrival of his milk shake, he materialized immediately, wriggling back into the booth with a huge smile and a request to take Trouble for a walk in the park sometime with Alejandro's dog, Scottie.

Guiltily, Becca realized that she was a little disappointed that Marc had returned so soon, curtailing her grown-up conversation with Sawyer. *It would be nice to have dinner alone with him.* The thought triggered an unsettling realization. Although she'd told Sawyer he shouldn't flirt with her, shouldn't ask her out, if he did…she would say yes.

She took a deep breath, not sure whether to hope he honored her request or to hope he was stubborn enough to ask anyway.

Chapter 9

"This is *not* me giving in to your 5:00 a.m. howls," Becca told the puppy sternly. "Because that would be reinforcing negative behavior. This is just me taking you outside to further your house-training, since we're both awake, anyway."

Trouble didn't seem to care what the reasoning was. She bolted forward with her customary enthusiasm the minute Becca unlatched the kennel. Since Becca had sleepily stumbled into the master bathroom, where the dog was, it seemed inconsiderate not to also give the shepherd the chance to go potty. She carried the puppy downstairs, where the leash hung on a newly installed hook, and as she did so, the most delicious aroma in the world washed over her. *Coffee.*

Maybe that had been what woke her, not the puppy's intermittent whimpering. *Truth time, Rebecca—did you come down here to walk the puppy or to say goodbye to Sawyer before he hits the road?* Well, it wasn't as if the two were mutually exclusive.

Refugio was only a couple hours from here; she was stunned that someone would voluntarily make a trip this early. But Sawyer said he was stopping at a ranch along the way to have breakfast and check on some business investments. It sounded as if he had friends in the area that he wanted to visit, too. Like Brody, here in Cupid's Bow. Thinking of Kate and Sierra and Hadley, Becca wondered what it would be like if her friends were scattered throughout the state. She couldn't decide if Sawyer was blessedly popular, with so many people in his life, or lonely. Maybe those conditions weren't mutually exclusive, either.

As she padded into the kitchen, she wondered… Did Sawyer also have lovers all over the state, women he called when he was in town who would be happy to see him?

Her tone was sharper than she'd intended when she greeted him with, "You turned on the wrong light. Again." She had one programmed; it helped give the house the appearance of being occupied when she was away and insured that she didn't come downstairs to total darkness on early mornings. When he used the switch manually, he disrupted the timer.

"Good morning to you, too."

"Sorry. The puppy's been interrupting my sleep." She had no qualms about blaming her mood on the squirming bundle of fur in her arms. At the shepherd's insistent wiggling, she set Trouble down, freeing her to run to Sawyer with floppy-pawed adoration. Trouble's feet were comically big for her body, but she didn't let awkwardness stop her from throwing herself atop Sawyer's boots for a tummy rub. The dog obviously loved him—and why not? He had rescued her from a storm and given her a home. Yet after a moment's affection, she loyally returned to Becca.

He grinned. "She knows who the alpha of the pack is."

Now if only the rest *of the pack would recognize my authority.* As she took the puppy into the backyard, Becca thought irritably about Sawyer disrupting her light settings, and Molly finishing the oranges in the produce drawer and the milk *and* the last of Marc's cereal without writing any of it down on the grocery memo pad. Did no one respect Becca's carefully ordered world, the effort she put into keeping life's chaos at bay? *Don't panic.* It was only some lightbulbs and supermarket items. That didn't mean she was losing control. Yet.

She went back inside, hoping caffeine would improve her outlook. Sawyer leaned against the kitchen counter, watching her pour a cup of coffee.

He slid her the sugar canister. "Not going back to sleep?"

"No point. I have to be up in less than an hour to get Marc ready for school, anyway." All year, her son fought getting out of bed. It was ironic that only in the final two weeks of school, excited by the promise of summer, did he wake alert and cooperative. "Besides, I have a grudging respect for this time of day. I don't like it, exactly, but I appreciate the peace of it." They were speaking in hushed tones, careful not to wake the rest of the household. Outside was hushed, too. At

5:00 a.m., the world was just waking up and the chaos hadn't kicked in.

She stirred her coffee. "What about you? Natural morning person?"

"Not inherently, no. But after so many years of my dad waking me for early morning chores, the habit sank in. It helps when I wake up to a pretty lady, but as long as there's coffee, I can cope."

She ignored the pretty-lady crack; she doubted a woman with tangled hair and light-timer issues qualified. They finished their coffee in companionable silence.

Rinsing his mug out at the sink, he gave her a crooked smile. "Will you miss me while I'm gone?"

She rolled her eyes. "If you want me to miss you, you have to stay away for more than one day."

"Can't. Your cooking's got me too spoiled."

Another eye roll. Conversations with Sawyer were like ocular calisthenics. "I get it—you're an irredeemable charmer who can't help laying it on thick. But, come on. Respect my intelligence, would you? In the week you've been here, we've had pizza, deli takeout, diner food and hamburgers *you* grilled." In fact, now that she recounted the list aloud, she felt vaguely embarrassed. She actually was a fair cook, but she'd been so busy lately…

"You're right, commenting on the food was an inferior use of my charm. I can do better." He cleared his throat, his expression faux solemn. "Rodeos are dangerous work, ma'am. I'd be much obliged if you'd send me off with a kiss for good luck."

For one ludicrous second, she imagined actually

doing it, going up on her toes and pressing her lips to his just to see his shocked expression. It would be priceless. *And that would be your* only *motivation?* Well, no. There was also the rediscovery of what it would be like to kiss a man—to kiss this man, in particular. *Bad idea, Becca.* Yet her heart sped up, and anticipation fizzed through her. Gripping her coffee mug, she stood rooted to the spot. Her common sense was strong enough to overcome anticipation. For now.

Sawyer grinned, and the reckless moment passed with him none the wiser. "Okay, that line was terrible, too. I can't do my best work at this hour."

"You're not supposed to be flirting with me, anyway, remember?"

"Of course." His expression was all innocence. "That was only hypothetical flirting. It didn't count. And I still get to be *friendly*...that's just good manners."

How long would her self-discipline hold? She grabbed his truck keys from the counter and held them out. "You should go. Now, before morning traffic picks up. Be a damn shame if you got stuck in Cupid's Bow rush hour." All nine cars and two school buses of it.

He laughed, taking his keys and tipping his hat in farewell. Beyond the kitchen, too far in the shadows of the hallway for her to see his face, he paused for just a second. "Now that I think about it, maybe it isn't the food here I like so much. Maybe it's just seeing you across the table."

"You were incredible!"

Any man would appreciate hearing that from a pretty woman, and Sawyer smiled at the willowy brunette in her halter top and skintight jeans. But most of his attention was on the chute, where one of his best friends was about to ride. Lewis had been injured last winter, and this was his first official event back in the saddle.

"Thanks, darlin'," Sawyer said absently. He'd sound ungracious if he disputed her compliment, but today hadn't been one of his better performances. *Because you weren't focused enough.*

He'd been distracted and out of sorts. His morning had started off so well, teasing Becca in the cozy confines of her kitchen. Good coffee, better company. But when he'd reached the ranch where his friend and business partner, Kaleb, lived, he'd felt a pang of… Not quite bitterness, but perhaps an envy that men like Brody and Kaleb had a place where they belonged.

How long had it been since Sawyer felt that? Maybe it was why he'd been so angry at Charlie—not just for coming back from college with a condescending disrespect for the work Sawyer had done in his absence, but for making Sawyer feel like the ranch wasn't equally his, like he belonged less.

Although Sawyer still enjoyed traveling, discovering quirky new places and regional customs to write about, the word *home* was starting to hold an allure he hadn't experienced since he'd driven away from his family ranch with a muttered good riddance.

Only distantly registering that his brunette fan had faded back into the crowd, he cheered for Lewis, eager to replace the ugly memory of his friend's accident. *You're lucky* you *didn't have an accident today.* Bronc riding was not something that should be half-assed. What had happened to the thrill of the ride?

Sawyer used to love the crowds and the noise; always happiest outdoors, he hadn't minded the gritty heat. Even the sensation of his teeth rattling in his skull had made him feel alive, sending jolts of adrenaline through him. He knew cowboys who participated in rodeos well into their sixties, albeit on the senior circuit, but when Sawyer thought about the decades to come, this wasn't what he wanted for his future. At least, it wasn't *all* he wanted.

But the packed stand of a Texas rodeo was no place for introspection. Someone jostled his shoulder, and he turned to find Gabe Delgado, champion roper, standing there.

"Been a long time." Gabe winced in mock sympathy. "Sorry to see you've gotten even uglier since I saw you last."

"You haven't—but then it's hard to go down when you were already at rock bottom."

Gabe cackled at that. "Did Lewis talk to you about tonight? A bunch of us are going to The Catfish Shack. Knock back a few cervezas, charm some pretty senoritas… You in?"

"Absolutely." For the beer, anyway. Sawyer's interest in flirting with attractive women was as halfhearted as his lamentable ride. *Not true.* He recalled the way Becca had looked this morning, when she'd grinned at him and sassed that he needed to get out of her house before rush hour. As tired and dusty as he was, he knew that if *she* were at the restaurant tonight, where scheduled bands performed everything from zydeco music to Czech polkas, his interest would be boundless. He'd want to take her out on the dance floor...and back to his hotel room.

With the festival kicking off this weekend, there would be numerous events where he could indulge his first wish; maybe she would agree to dance with him. As for his second wish? *Ha.* Yet it felt as if the magnetic pull between them had been steadily growing. Was there a chance Becca had changed her mind?

Sawyer grinned, already looking forward to seeing her tomorrow. The thrill of rodeo riding might be starting to fade, but there were plenty of other challenges that could keep his life exciting.

Good to be back home. The uncensored thought jolted Sawyer worse than the potholes that had threatened his tire rims and shocks just outside the county line. He turned off the truck, staring through the windshield at Becca's place. This was no more "home" than any of the circuit hotels he'd stayed in or bunkhouses he'd shared with other ranch hands when he picked up seasonal work. And yet it felt more welcoming than the tiny apartment he rented as his base of operations, probably because he was never there long enough to settle in or decorate beyond the essentials—a bed and a TV.

Never mind the "home" part, he told himself as he rounded the house to the back stairs and his private entrance. *It's just nice to be back where there's a generous-sized tub.* He'd awakened this morning with some predictably sore muscles and a few new bruises. Some mineral salt and a soak in that claw-foot tub sounded like heaven. After the nonstop activity of the rodeo yesterday and last night's rollicking good time at the noisy club, he was looking forward to the peace and quiet, too. He doubted anyone would be home midmorning on a Thursday. Marc should be in school, Becca was probably at work and Molly… No telling, but he was sure Becca had her somewhere—applying for a receptionist job, volunteering at the local food bank, taking an aptitude test.

He didn't doubt that Becca's intentions were good, but did she realize that her manic efforts could backfire? Molly might resent being pressed into service 24/7 and rebel. What if she got herself fired from the theater or tanked a community college application just to give herself a break?

None of my business, though. He'd interfered once and regretted it. From here on out, the Baker sisters would have to work out their own differences of opinion.

Still…seeing their sibling relationship with the clarity of an outsider's perspective was making him think more about his own brother. They'd been so close once; part of him missed that. Maybe he'd give Charlie a call some night soon. He still hadn't congratulated him in person about the baby—not that over the phone was in person, exactly, but it was better than a text.

As expected, the house was empty.

But not entirely quiet. He'd just removed his shirt and pulled the mineral salt from the cabinet under the bathroom sink when he heard Trouble barking furiously. Obviously, she'd heard him moving around upstairs. She'd probably been in her crate for hours; taking her outside before he indulged in his bath was the humane thing to do.

He had to pass through Becca's room to reach the master bath where the kennel was, and being in her private sanctuary felt odd. The room was so intensely *female*…from faint lingering perfume in the air to the pale pink curtains and the jewelry box on her dresser. Her bed almost made him laugh; it was made with military precision. Although he'd never do it, his fingers itched to scoot one of the decorative throw pillows a millimeter to the side, as an experiment to see whether Becca would notice. *Of course she would. Then she'd rightfully toss you out into the street for touching her personal things.*

No more fixating on her bed. Or the idea of her in it. Or the pleasant fantasy of sharing it with her. He groaned. At this rate, he should skip the muscle-healing bath and take a cold shower instead.

From the bathroom came a yip of impatience, and he gave himself an inner shake. Right. Dog, bath, move on with his day. As he unlatched the kennel, Trouble tripped over her own feet, scrabbling to reach him and lick his face.

"Could we turn the adoration down to, like, a nine?" he asked, holding her at arm's length. "I like you, but no doggy kisses."

Growing up, he'd talked to the pintos and Arabian horses in the barn, so he didn't feel self-conscious about his one-sided conversation with Trouble. At least, he didn't until he heard Becca advise from the bedroom beyond, "Maybe you should start with holding paws and work your way up to kisses."

A dozen reactions hit at once—from being embarrassed to hoping she wasn't angry at his intrusion to being plain old happy to hear her voice—and he lost his grip on the puppy. Trouble bounded over to meet her mistress. Sawyer rose slowly, following at a more dignified speed. "Hope I wasn't overstepping in here," he called. "I just got in and thought Trouble could use..." He caught sight of her for the first time and her expression robbed him of words. She was gaping at him with raw appreciation that made his pulse quicken. He didn't know what he'd been about to say; he only knew that if she kept looking at him like that, his jeans were going to get seriously uncomfortable.

She swallowed. "You, ah... Your shirt."

He'd forgotten he was only half-dressed; it hadn't seemed important when he'd had the house to himself. "Sorry?" He couldn't commit to the word. While he hoped he hadn't offended her, he couldn't regret the way her gaze greedily traveled over him. "I thought you were at work."

She nodded, her voice huskier than usual. "I was. The school called—Marc forgot his lunch, so I was going to grab it and drop it off. But I figured I should let Trouble out while I was here..."

"Great minds think alike," he teased, stopping in front of her. But neither of them was actually moving to let the dog outside. Instead, they stood still, only inches apart, and Sawyer wondered if kissing her would be the smartest or dumbest thing he'd ever done. Damn, he wanted it, to feel her mouth beneath his, but she'd warned him off and he wasn't going to push without a clear signal from her that she wanted it, too. So he balled his hands into fists to keep from reaching for her, and willed her to do something crazy—like pull him down on that perfectly made bed and have her wicked way with him.

When Trouble barked, breaking the moment and stealing Becca's attention, he felt a flare of irrational resentment toward the dog. *I snagged you a home, and this is how you repay me? Thanks a lot, mutt.*

Becca scooped up the puppy. "I better get her outside before there are consequences."

"Probably a wise choice." To his own ears, his voice sounded thick with disappointment. Did she notice? It was difficult to tell, since she was speed-walking in the opposite direction.

Sawyer followed her to the kitchen, where she was hooking the leash to Trouble's collar. "I'll take her out. You have to get back to work and swing by the school, so..."

"And you have writing to do?" she asked, as he opened the door.

Right. Travel articles about the great state of Texas and places where the cowboy way of life still persisted. He'd only ever written nonfiction, yet he suddenly felt inspired to try his hand at erotic short stories.

"They're good," Becca said sincerely.

Blinking, he whirled around to face her. She enjoyed erotic short stories?

"Your pieces, I mean."

"Oh." Reason belatedly caught up to his brain. But then he felt confused again. "You've read them?"

Her smile bordered on shy. "A few. They made me realize that even though I've lived in Texas all my life, there are a lot of places I've never visited, landmarks I'd love to see. New experiences I'd like to try."

Be glad to help with that, sweetheart. "I'm glad they had an effect on you. That's gratifying to hear."

Marc's lunch box in hand, she followed him outside, choosing to go around the house to her minivan instead of through the front door. "Then I'm glad I told you. I was…a little embarrassed to admit it."

"Embarrassed you read a couple of nonfiction articles written in the specific hopes people would read them? Why?"

"Embarrassed to be looking you up on the computer when I was supposed to be working. Or after I crawled into bed at night. It was a surreal experience, reading the words of a man who happened to be sleeping one floor above me."

She'd been in bed thinking about him. Without the tail of a shirt to help camouflage his growing erection, he turned away, letting Trouble explore some bushes in the opposite direction.

After a moment, Becca said, "I'd better scoot. Have a good afternoon."

"You, too." He tried to sound casual and not like a man choking on his own lust. "I'll see you tonight." And no doubt be thinking of her in all the hours in between.

Becca stirred the peppered white gravy that had once won a Cupid's Bow cook-off; it was funny to think about how hard she'd worked to impress the judges when she first moved here and realize that next week *she* would be one of the judges. Also, now that she thought about it, it might be a little funny that they even had a gravy cook-off. Did other places do that? Maybe it was a small-town Texas thing; the quality of one's chicken-fried steak was determined largely by the gravy that went over it.

And tonight she was making her from-scratch chicken-fried steak, gravy and mashed potatoes. Normally, she coached soccer practice Thursday evenings, but since they were under a storm warning and the kids had just played two nights ago, she'd exercised her coach's prerogative and canceled. For the first time since Sawyer had moved in, she was demonstrating her real cooking skills. Hopefully, it would impress him—because she was psyching herself up to ask him out.

She could no longer deny what she wanted. Those few moments when he'd been shirtless in her bedroom today? Hotter than the last few times she'd actually been in bed with her ex-husband.

Only a few days ago, she'd told Molly that she was someone who seized opportunity. And, with soccer practice out of the way, tonight was a unique opportunity. Molly and Vicki had headed into town for an evening at the local dance hall, and once Marc went to take his shower, Becca and Sawyer would have a few minutes of privacy. She could ask him to the concert Sunday. Or they could make reservations for the nice restaurant over in Turtle. Even the idea of opening some wine and watching the storm after Marc went to bed sounded like a promising date. Since Vicki would be bringing Molly home after their girls' night, Becca had nowhere she had to be.

Last night, when Sawyer had been away, she'd spent a lot of time thinking about him, thinking about how he'd be gone for real soon. And she'd come to realize that if they didn't have at least one date before he left, she'd regret it. It had been a lonely two years since her divorce, and she might be in for quite a few more. Meanwhile, fate had delivered to her doorstep a funny, articulate, dead-sexy cowboy whose abs could have been sculpted from marble. Who was she to ignore that gift?

The fact that he was so good with her kid was also heart melting. He was outside with Marc now, helping him pick flowers to press for science class.

When the door banged shut and the two of them came in, Trouble on their heels, Becca admonished her son to wash his hands extra carefully before dinner.

"Good idea," Sawyer said. "I'm going to my room to wash up, too." He was back a few minutes later in a fresh T-shirt, holding his hands out toward Becca. "I used soap and everything," he teased. His playful expression faded as he inhaled deeply. "Lord, it smells good in here. Amazing, actually."

"Let's hope the food tastes that way, too," she said lightly. She wasn't worried. Well, not about the dinner, anyway. Thinking ahead to later gave her butterflies. *Get a grip. You are not afraid to make the first move.*

But maybe the butterflies weren't a sign of fear. Maybe the fluttering was just giddy expectation. Now that she'd stopped trying to fight her attraction to him, it was stronger than ever. Each glance in his direction left her a little breathless, quivery with awareness and suppressed need. She wouldn't have been surprised if she dropped a plate while trying to set the table.

Marc returned, and once he'd presented his hands for inspection, they all sat down to eat. After his first bite of food, Sawyer gave a low moan, his expression one of rapture.

"You can cook like *this*, yet you still order pizzas?" he demanded.

She grinned, pleased by the compliment. "Well, this is pretty time-consuming. If it weren't for practice being rained out..." She cast a guilty look at the sunshine streaming through the kitchen window. The weather front that had originally been forecast for this evening had veered south of them. "Anyway, I love to do it when I get the rare opportunity, but life doesn't always cooperate. So eat up. Tomorrow we're probably back to hot dogs or frozen lasagna."

Marc scrunched his nose. "Why would anyone eat lasagna that's frozen? Blecch."

"No, I'd cook it in the oven first."

"Then it wouldn't be frozen," he pointed out with exaggerated patience. "You're weird, Mama."

Sawyer winked at her from across the table. "But good weird."

Most days, Becca would give just about anything to slow down time—so that she could have more hours to spend with her son, more hours to research the feasibility of plans for the town, more hours to exercise and work off all that key lime pie. Yet tonight was moving so slowly that she wanted to scream in frustration. Dinner had been wonderful; if the way to a man's heart was really through his stomach, Sawyer would be proposing any minute now.

But as soon as they were done eating, while Becca struggled to find a reason to send Marc up to shower an hour early, her son tugged Sawyer into the other room so they could finish watching an eighties' sci-fi movie they'd started before Sawyer had gone on his overnight trip. Marc had been waiting days to see the end. So while the guys laughed through a movie with terrible special effects and no discernible plot line, she cleaned the kitchen. Thoroughly. She had a lot of excess energy tonight, and while scrubbing counters and appliances wasn't her first choice for burning through it, chicken-fried steak *was* a messy meal to prepare. Might as well put her vigor to good use.

When she heard the music of the end credits, excitement tingled through her. There was a definite spring in her step as she moved to the doorway of the living room. "Marc, honey, why don't you head up and take your shower now? Or…"

Inspiration struck. "Would you rather take a bath? You still have that art kit Ms. Hadley gave you for your birthday." It included colored bubbles and special crayons that could be used on the tile and generally made a mess—which Marc loved but she did not. Tonight, she would be willing for him to linger a bit longer in the tub while he colored and played. *I am a very selfish mom.*

He grinned eagerly. "Cool! Can I get my toy boats and my water gun, too?"

She was going to be mopping up puddles from the floor afterward. "Sure."

Sawyer chuckled as he rose from the sofa. "I think I've been doing baths wrong. I had one earlier today, but it lacked art supplies and a fleet of ships."

Becca smiled over her son's head and almost joked that now she knew what to get Sawyer as a parting gift, but the idea of saying goodbye to him made something inside her clench. Instead she told Sawyer, "I'm going to run upstairs and help Marc start his bath." If she didn't supervise the pouring of bubbles, the entire second floor would be suds city. "But after that, I, uh, I was hoping you and I could talk."

His eyebrows rose. "Did I forget to write something on the grocery pad?"

"It's nothing like that."

"Well, you have my interest piqued. How about I take Trouble for a quick walk, you take care of Marc and we'll meet back here in about ten minutes?"

Her heart raced. "Deal."

Chapter 10

Don't jump to conclusions, don't jump to conclusions. It had been Sawyer's mantra all the way up the street. Just because Becca wanted some time alone with him didn't guarantee that she wanted to further explore the chemistry that had sizzled between them earlier today. Still, with that impressive homemade dinner and the way she'd smiled when they agreed to meet back in a few minutes, it was difficult not to get his hopes up.

"Hello, Sawyer!" Elderly Mrs. Spiegel was playing chess with her husband on the front porch, and they both waved in his direction. Earlier in the week, Sawyer had helped Mrs. Spiegel get her car started after her battery died. He'd heard from Brody—who'd heard from his aunt Marie—that Mrs. Spiegel was telling everyone in town that Sawyer was a hero.

He waved back at the Spiegels, trying to look like

a respectable citizen and not a pervert who wanted to get naked with his landlady at the soonest opportunity. *You may have misread the signals.* But just in case, he quickened his steps, urging Trouble back to the house. When he took the leash into the kitchen to hang on its appropriate hook, he found Becca pouring two glasses of wine.

She peered up at him from beneath her lashes. "I hope you like red."

Truthfully, he was more of a beer guy, but with any luck, this was a special occasion. "Red is perfect."

"I have a confession to make," she said. "You remember when I told you that you'd have to be gone for more than a night for me to miss you?"

He nodded.

"I lied. Turns out I did miss you last night. Does that sound ridiculous?"

"Not even a little." Should he admit that the whole time he was out with his buddies, surrounded by pretty women, he couldn't get her off his mind? "I—"

The phone rang, and Becca swore. He almost laughed; her uncharacteristic cursing perfectly matched how he felt about the interruption.

Leaning over to glance at the caller ID, she frowned. "It's the deputy. Probably just festival red tape, but I'd better take it."

"I'm not going anywhere." Now that he was sure they were both feeling the same way, he was suddenly calmer, more centered. He didn't have to wonder *what if* anymore; he could afford to be patient for the space of a phone call.

She gave his hand a brief, grateful squeeze, then

picked up the cordless receiver. "Hello?" A second later, she paled.

"What is it?" Sawyer blurted. He hadn't meant to interrupt, but worry for her eclipsed courtesy.

She barely seemed to hear him, anyway. Wearing a dazed, shell-shocked expression that was very un-Becca, she nodded into the phone. "I… Yes, thank you. I'll be right there."

As soon as she hung up, he stepped closer, folding her in a loose hug. Despite the erotic thoughts he'd had about her, he didn't have any ulterior motives for holding her now; he was simply driven by the need to comfort. "Everything okay?" *Dumb ass. Police officers don't call at night for no reason.*

"Fine." She expelled a shaky breath. "Except for my underage sister being loudly drunk and kicked out of the dance hall."

He winced. Molly certainly wasn't the first teenager in the world to have a couple drinks—Sawyer was relieved the news hadn't been worse—but this must be a blow to Becca. She'd been working hard to shape her sister into a model citizen; he wouldn't be surprised if Becca saw this as a failure on her part.

She moved her glass of wine away, suddenly eyeing the alcohol as if it was corrosive acid. "I need to go get her."

"Want me to come with you?" The offer was automatic. As much as he hated family drama, it turned out that he hated seeing her upset even more. He desperately wanted to make this better for her.

A half-formed smile ghosted across her lips. "That's sweet, but no. Can you stay with Marc while I run out?"

"Of course. And Becca?" He gave her his most solemn expression. "I promise not to adopt any more pets while you're gone."

She laughed then, a peal of pure amusement, and in that moment, he felt every bit the hero Mrs. Spiegel said he was.

When Becca rolled into the gravel parking lot, she spotted her sister immediately. It was difficult to miss Molly, who was gesticulating wildly next to a police car parked in the corner. Becca squinted, studying the scene in the dim orange glow of sporadic light poles. Molly looked furious even though she was at fault, not at all grateful that Deputy Thomas had called her sister instead of hauling her to the station.

On the rare occasions Becca had overimbibed, she tended to become chatty, giggly or weepy. *The lesser-known dwarves.* It occurred to her for the first time since the deputy's call that Molly might be an angry drunk. While Becca couldn't bring herself to believe her sister would turn violent or ever hurt Marc, she had no trouble imagining Molly dropping f-bombs from one end of the house to the other.

Turning off the car, Becca hurriedly scrolled through her contact list. A moment later, Lyndsay Whittmeyer answered with a chirpy hello.

"Hi, Lyndsay. It's Becca. I hate to ask this on such short notice, especially on a school night, but is there any way Marc could sleep over? I'm having a bit of a… situation." This was Cupid's Bow. Lyndsay would hear all about Molly's public intoxication by tomorrow, but Becca didn't have time to get into it now.

"Of course. Coop's baseball game went into extra

innings, and we're on our way back from Turtle, but we'll swing by and get Marc just as soon as we can."

"Thanks! You're a lifesaver." Becca disconnected with a mental promise to make a batch of her friend's favorite pecan bars in the very near future. She opened her door. *Time to get this over with.*

She briskly crossed the lot. "Deputy Thomas—"

"Great." Molly stumbled, propping herself up on the hood of the deputy's car. "My big shister comes bargin' in."

"I'm not 'barging' anywhere. I'm your ride."

The deputy stepped between them, his expression sympathetic and his voice soft. "I got a cup of coffee in her, ma'am. Not sure it's done much good yet. She's… in a state."

"I'll make sure she doesn't end up in this state again," Becca vowed. "Come on, Molly. We're going home."

"Your home," the girl slurred. "Your rules. It's ridicu…it's rid…it's *stupid*!"

Becca took her by the arm, trying to keep her steady. Molly pitched to the left, and they almost went over.

Gritting her teeth, Becca recovered her balance. "How did you even buy drinks? Fake ID?" Most of the bartenders could spot them, especially Jace Trent, who'd been coached by his brother, the sheriff. Plus Molly was supposed to have been with Vicki. Everyone around here knew Vicki Ross wasn't yet legal drinking age.

"Didn't buy 'em. My friend did."

"Let me guess—a male friend. One older than you."

"*Larry* likes me." She managed to make it an accusation.

I like you. Not so much right at the moment, but there was potential for the two of them to be friends. Or was there? Maybe Becca had been fooling herself about her ability to be a good influence, about their being able to find common ground. She leaned over to make sure Molly's seat belt was buckled properly.

"You don't have it in the slot," she said.

"Can't do anything right for you!" Molly cried, swatting away Becca's attempts to help. "Mama never cared if I finished the last of the cereal! Or smiled at a guy."

Odette didn't care—there was breaking news. And Larry Breelan hadn't been feeding an eighteen-year-old drinks because he'd been hoping for a smile. First thing tomorrow, Becca was calling the sheriff and asking him to kindly go tase the offending Breelan.

"Well, I do care," Becca said. "I care about you not making self-destructive choices. And I care about your future. And I care about how this is going to look to the people in my community." She'd been trying so hard to help Molly make friends, wanting her to know that same sense of belonging Becca felt here in Cupid's Bow.

"You care about the *election*!" Molly smacked her hand on the dashboard. "You're afraid someone might not vote for you because your sister got a little tipsy!"

"You passed *tipsy* four or five exits ago. What happened to Vicki? Did she see you get thrown out? I don't want her worried."

"She went home—said her legs were starting to bother her. I told her I had another ride."

"Larry Breelan?" Forget going through the sheriff; Becca would tase the opportunistic lech herself. "Do you have any idea how—"

"Vicki talked about you all night. How you were there for her when she was in a wheelchair last summer, how you're always there for this town. When the hell are you there for me?"

Since the minute you showed up at my door needing a place to live, you ingrate. Becca had been introducing her to people, giving her rides to and from work, encouraging her to want more for herself. But making those points now would be wasted breath. Her sister was too irrational.

Within seconds, Molly went into a full-on rant about the injustice of life, including how her ex had taken her for granted and how it wasn't fair both of her sisters had met their perfect men. She must be using an alternate definition of perfection, one that included shady real estate deals and divorce.

Needing to be free of the escalating verbal abuse, Becca pulled into the driveway at a crooked angle. Then she dutifully came around the side of the car to help, but Molly shoved at her arm.

Becca took a deep breath, fighting the urge to say something she couldn't take back. *Oh, go ahead. She probably won't remember it in the morning, anyway.*

Molly spilled from the car, unsteady but managing not to face-plant on the driveway.

"Need a hand?" Sawyer's voice came from the porch, and Becca glanced his way, torn between gratitude that he was there and humiliation that he was witnessing this.

"Not you, too!" Molly wailed. "Bad enough I'm *her* pity project." She stomped up to the front porch, removing her shoes as she went. One landed sideways on a step. *Cinderella goes on a bender.*

Becca hurried after her, pausing to ask Sawyer, "Where's Marc? Did he—"

"I got him out of the tub and suggested he read in bed, told him you were giving Aunt Molly a ride."

"Could you help him pack a bag with his toothbrush and clothes for tomorrow? He gets to have a rare school-night sleepover. The Whittmeyers are on their way." Recalling how she'd joked about Marc spending too much time at their house made her feel guilty; she was damn lucky to be friends with a family who always had her back.

"On it." Sawyer held the door open for her, then headed up the stairs.

Becca found her sister in the kitchen, trying to pour orange juice and spilling it all over the counter. Molly gave her a look of pure malevolence. "You're outta OJ. Better write it on the damn list."

Retaliation burned on the tip of Becca's tongue, the urge to snap. *And you wonder why Odette didn't want you under her roof and your boyfriend didn't love you? Because you're awful.* "We'll discuss this tomorrow. When you're sober. For now, you need to go sleep this off." *Before I stick your ass on a bus to Oklahoma.*

No. She would not dump this on Courtney the way Odette had always dumped her parenting responsibilities on Becca.

She was a little surprised when Molly actually headed toward the stairs instead of doing something to spite her. Still, she didn't fully trust her sister to get into bed without causing further destruction, so she followed along.

Her presence seemed to enrage Molly. "Go away!"

"It's *my* house."

"Mama?" Marc appeared at the top the staircase, freshly bathed and wearing monster truck pj's. His voice was tremulous, the note in it one she normally heard only after a nightmare or during tornado watches.

Her maternal instincts superseded the rage she was feeling, and she softened her tone. "It's okay, baby. Just go wait with Mr. Sawyer." But this *wasn't* okay, and the fact that her little boy was witnessing any of it made the rage bubble hotter.

"Yeah, be a good little boy, Marc, and do what Mommy says," Molly sneered. She grabbed the newel post at the bottom of the steps, pivoting back toward Becca. "You. You think *I'm* seven, too, but I'm not. And you aren't my mommy. You barely want to be my sister!" She wobbled on the second step.

Becca jerked forward to help. "Be careful."

"*Stop telling me what to do!* I'm. Not. A. Kid."

"Then grow the hell up!" Becca realized she was shaking. She couldn't remember the last time she'd lost her temper.

Molly glared at her, angry tears shimmering in her eyes, and whirled around to resume her climb. She made it three more steps before misjudging one, losing her balance and grappling unsuccessfully for the banister.

Marc gasped as his aunt tumbled to the hardwood floor below, narrowly missing Becca, who'd flattened herself against the wall. Molly shrieked, either in fear or pain, but the scream quickly gave way to sobbing. Becca realized her own cheeks were wet.

Kneeling beside her sister, she gingerly poked and prodded to make sure nothing was broken. "Can you wiggle your fingers? Do you think you can stand?"

Suddenly Sawyer was there, strong and steady, first helping Molly to her feet, then picking her up and carrying her upstairs.

As Becca watched the cowboy she was crazy about disappear into her sister's bedroom, she had to bite back hysterical laughter over how wrong the night had gone.

The night air was cool, and the relative peace of the neighborhood was a relief after the yelling and tears inside. Sawyer darted a sideways glance at Marc, who wasn't saying much as they waiting on the porch for his friend's family.

"You okay, buddy?"

Marc seemed startled by the question. "I'm not the one who fell."

"Your aunt will be okay. Your mom's taking care of her now." From the noises Molly had started making before he'd backed out of the room, Becca was probably holding Molly's hair back while the girl heaved. Having been in Molly's position himself a time or two, he wasn't without sympathy. Still, he figured a hellacious hangover might make the teenager think twice before reaching for a drink again.

"They're both really mad," Marc said.

"Yeah, but not at you. Brothers and sisters fight sometimes."

"Kenny and Coop call each other names. But Coop is nice. He helps us with math sometimes and got us to the next level of Ultimate Fortress Strike." The little boy stared into the distance. "I don't have a brother. I don't even have a daddy. He went away."

"I'm sorry, kid." *Your dad sounds like a jackass.* "But you've got your mom. And she's special. Having her in your corner is like having three or four parents."

"I only need two." Marc sighed. "Mr. Sawyer?"

"Yeah, buddy?"

"Are you gonna leave, too?"

The lump in Sawyer's throat made it difficult to answer. He hadn't expected so much sadness in Marc's eyes, eyes that were a lot like his mom's. Sawyer hated to let the kid down, but he cared about him far too much to lie. "Yes. You and your mom have been great—everyone in Cupid's Bow has been—but this is your home, not mine."

The boy's lower lip trembled, but he nodded. "Where's your home?"

I don't know. Luckily, the Whittmeyers pulled into the driveway before Sawyer was forced to explain that.

How could he summarize his life in a way that made sense to a seven-year-old when Sawyer himself was starting to have questions he couldn't answer?

Mrs. Whittmeyer kept knocking on the door to Kenny and Coop's room to check on the boys. That's what she claimed, anyway. "You boys okay? You boys need anything?" But they all knew she was really checking on Marc, peering down at him in a way that made him wish he could shrink into the beanbag chair the same way turtles hid in their shells.

He started to tell her he was fine, just so she'd stop looking at him like that, but Kenny interrupted. "Marc's sad. Brownies would cheer him up."

She was quiet for a moment. "All right—I'll whip up a batch, but after that, you guys have to go to bed. School tomorrow."

Once she was gone, Kenny grinned from the other beanbag. "Video games and brownies on a school night! This is the best."

"Uh-huh." Marc tried to smile.

Coop glanced over from the homework he was doing at his desk. "Wait. Are you *actually* sad?"

Marc shrugged. Tonight had been a little scary. He didn't like seeing Mama mad or seeing Aunt Molly fall, but Sawyer promised his aunt would be okay. What made Marc's tummy hurt was the rest of the conversation he'd had with Sawyer. *I don't want brownies.* He just wanted the cowboy to stay.

"I think Mama likes Mr. Sawyer." She was different with him here. Still Mama, with her rules and her election stress, but Sawyer made her laugh. She said yes to more stuff, like milk shakes and bath crayons. And Trouble! *I have a dog.* Before Sawyer came, Marc had asked if he could have a pet about a million times. She always said no.

"Does the idea of her dating bother you?" Coop asked. "Some of the kids at my middle school have divorced parents, and it can be a difficult transition—"

"Shut up!" Kenny tossed a pillow at his brother. "I hate when you try to talk like a grown-up."

"It's called *maturity*, butt face."

"I wouldn't mind if she dates Mr. Sawyer," Marc said. "But how can she if he's leaving town? He doesn't want to stay in Cupid's Bow."

"That's dumb," Kenny said. "Cupid's Bow is great."

Coop put his chin on his hand. "He just needs a reason to stay."

Marc had learned in social studies that there was a president and a vice president; even the school had a principal and a vice principal. Was there such a thing as a vice mayor? Maybe Sawyer could work for Mama after she won.

Coop rolled back his chair—it was the cool kind with

wheels on it, the same as the one Marc sat in when he was at his mom's office. "You said she likes Sawyer. Does *he* like *her*?"

Marc shrugged. "How do you tell? He doesn't take her flowers or kiss her or anything."

Kenny always made throw-up sounds when his parents kissed, but Marc didn't mind if his mama wanted to kiss Mr. Sawyer. Daddy was never coming back, but sometimes Marc still wanted a family. A family like Kenny and Coop had, with two parents who fought sometimes but who also made each other laugh and snuggled together.

"Does he wear a lot of stinky body spray?" Kenny pinched his nose. "That's what Coop does when he likes a girl."

"Hey, Angie Heller said I smelled great when I took her to the Spring Fling dance. That gives me an idea," Coop said excitedly. "Last Halloween, a bunch of us watched a slasher movie. Angie got so scared she buried her face in my shoulder. I think that's when she started liking me. Does your mom ever watch horror movies?"

"Never."

"I got it!" Kenny snapped his fingers, which used to make Marc jealous, because he couldn't do it right. But Kenny couldn't whistle, so they were even. "You can borrow Slither. Your mom's afraid of snakes. If we let Slither loose in your house, Sawyer can capture him and your mom will be so happy she might kiss him or something."

Maybe—but Marc would be grounded for a *long* time. Like, until he was older than Coop. Or even Aunt Molly. "I don't think that will work. Besides, I have a dog now." He sat a little taller in his beanbag. "A real good dog. If Trouble saw a snake in the house, she'd probably kill it to protect us." Dogs could do a lot more than snakes could.

"I think grown-ups have to go on dates to see if they like each other," Coop said.

"That's dumb." Kenny had a long list of things that were dumb. "Why would you even go if you didn't like a person? Hi, I hate you, wanna have a date?"

Coop ignored his brother. "If Sawyer takes her to dinner or asks her to dance, you'll know he likes her."

And then he might stay. Marc grinned for the first time since Mrs. Whittmeyer had picked him up.

Life had been interesting lately, which was nice, but if Sawyer stayed with Mama, life just might be perfect.

Becca stood at the bottom of the spiral staircase. She and Sawyer still had an important conversation to finish. Besides, she wanted to thank him again for his help. Only lingering embarrassment stalled her. The Baker girls had not been at their best tonight.

You're not a Baker anymore.

Oh, but she was. She was beginning to realize she always would be. That her recent quest to have voters see her in a positive light had actually begun years ago, when an awkwardly tall, poor girl had yearned for the respect of her classmates and teachers. Was her need to distance herself from that past why she'd kept her married name after Colin had bailed on their marriage? Even as a jilted wife who'd been publicly humiliated, Becca Johnston had been a step up from Rebecca Baker. "Mayor Johnston" would be still further from those humble beginnings, but winning the election wouldn't change who her family was.

And fidgeting pointlessly at the bottom of the steps wouldn't change what Sawyer had witnessed tonight. Lifting her chin, she started climbing the stairs.

The soft, bluesy strains of a guitar drifted from his room; she assumed he was listening to the radio or an iPod. It wasn't until she stood outside his door, which was cracked open a few inches, that she realized *he* was playing. He sat on the bed in a white undershirt and jeans, an acoustic guitar across his lap. Apparently the calluses on his long, capable fingers weren't just from ranch work.

The notes trailed off as he glanced up, meeting her gaze.

"Sorry to interrupt," she said, wishing he hadn't stopped. Watching him had been mesmerizing, especially the expression on his face, somewhere between bliss and concentration. It was easy to imagine him with the same rapt focus when he was touching a woman, bringing her pleasure as unerringly as he'd brought those soulful chords to life.

"No apology necessary," he said. "I left the door open so I could hear you if you needed me. Is she doing better?"

"She's passed out cold." Arguably an improvement over vomit-rama, which had been so gross Becca had gone for a hot shower after she had her sister changed into clean clothes. Now she stood in Sawyer's room in a silky pajama set, her damp hair drying in ringlets over her shoulder. Given their early morning kitchen encounters, this was far from the first time he'd seen her in pj's. But being alone in his bedroom with him felt a lot different than leaning against the counter as they both waited for the coffeemaker to finish.

The attic itself seemed cozier than usual in the muted light of matched lamps, with the house quiet below. It was at once peaceful and charged with an electric tension that built with each step she took toward him. Ignoring the two chairs she passed, she sat next to him on the bed. The mattress creaked a soft whisper of greeting and Sawyer welcomed her with that too-appealing tilted smile. She had the impulse to trace her thumb over his lips.

Instead, she nodded toward the guitar. "I didn't know you played." There was a lot she didn't know about him. And yet she felt so close to him, able to confide in him as if he were a friend, repeatedly trusting him with her son.

He regarded the pale wooden guitar as if seeing it for the first time. "This was my brother Charlie's. He asked for it for Christmas his freshman year of high school, took lessons for a few months. But then he got hyperfocused on school and keeping his GPA scholarship-worthy. The guitar ended up in the hall closet, and I stumbled across it when I was bored one rainy afternoon. Taught myself with the help of the workbook he'd left in the case and some online videos."

"Your parents must have been glad the investment wasn't wasted." She was speaking as someone who was financially responsible for things like piano lessons, but immediately wished she'd said something warmer, like, "your parents must be proud of your talent."

He made a noncommittal noise, dropping his gaze as he strummed the strings. "Got any requests?"

"Not really. Just no songs about booze tonight." Dread slithered through her as she thought about how many people had been at the dance hall and how many more would hear about it tomorrow. "I know it's self-centered to take this personally, to worry about how Molly might make *me* look, but with Truitt scrambling for reasons to skewer me…" She forced a tight smile, trying not to borrow trouble. "But every family has its troublemakers, right?"

"My family sure did. You're looking at him."

"Were you really that bad?" She tried to imagine him as a hell-raising young man. There was always a hint of wickedness in Sawyer's smile, but he was also someone who helped with second-grade homework and assisted little old ladies with car trouble.

"I guess 'bad' depends on your perspective. As a kid, I was a prankster. It probably started because I wanted to be just like Charlie. We had practical joke battles right up until April Fool's Day of his sophomore year in college. Harder to organize pranks long-distance, but we were creative."

The affection in his tone made her feel wistful. She and her own siblings hadn't shared that kind of bond—which shouldn't depress her, because she didn't even like pranks. People could get hurt. Yet it was obvious he and his brother had been close.

"Then Charlie buckled down, got serious and made the dean's list. I was proud of him—we all were. Until he graduated with a bachelor's degree in pompous arrogance. With honors. I'd always thought, as my dad got older, that Charlie and I would run the ranch together. But it was…challenging after he came home. I decided to strike out on my own. I worked ranches, accumulated rodeo wins. There were wild nights that I cannot, as a gentleman, discuss."

Becca didn't want a gentleman tonight. She wanted

to relive the gripping passion she'd felt this morning when she'd thought he might kiss her; she wanted to blot out the last few hours, put aside her tangled relationship with her family and explore how good she and Sawyer could be together.

"I never had the chance to be a troublemaker," she said. "I was busy taking care of my younger brothers and sisters, my son, this town. Don't get me wrong, I'm no martyr—I love Marc and I love Cupid's Bow. But trying to be good for everyone gets exhausting." She trailed her fingers over his collarbone.

He inhaled sharply, but otherwise didn't react.

She closed the distance between them, her pulse erratic and her voice low. "Don't I deserve the chance to be bad?"

Chapter 11

Knowing how direct Becca was, Sawyer shouldn't have been so surprised when she pressed her lips to his. Yet for just a moment, he couldn't believe this was happening.

Need sparked through him as he breathed in the scent of her skin, registered the warmth of her soft curves through his clothes. *Yes.* Yes, this was really happening. He cupped the nape of her neck, angling her head to deepen the kiss. Gently at first, so he didn't rush her.

But then she threaded her fingers through his hair, tugged him closer and knocked his world sideways.

Damn, the woman could kiss. His heart pounded faster with each beat, and desire pounded through him even harder. She sucked at his lower lip, and he went almost light-headed with desire. Had he pushed her down on the mattress or had she pulled him across her? When had they gone horizontal?

He groaned, trying to pull back from her addictive mouth long enough to assess the situation. "This is moving fast."

"And fast is bad?" she asked coyly.

I don't know. Selfish desire warred with concern for her.

Her smile faltered, and she propped herself up on her elbows. "Do you not want…"

"Are you kidding me, woman? I'm hard-pressed to think of anything I've ever wanted more." He glanced pointedly at his lap. "*Very* hard-pressed. But you've had an emotional night. I don't want to take advantage."

She sat up, her fingers skimming beneath the hem of his thin shirt. "Okay, now I want you even more. I appreciate the concern—and it has been an emotional night—but I wasn't upset when I wanted you to kiss me this morning. Or when I wanted to touch you in the kitchen, before we were interrupted. You've thought about it, too, right?"

He leaned forward to kiss a path from the curve of her neck to her cleavage. "Sweetheart, I've barely been able to think of anything else since the first time I saw you."

She gave a murmur of approval at his words, arching her back when he palmed one breast through her top. "I want this," she said breathlessly. Her body gave him the same message, her nipples hard against the satiny material of her pajamas, her hips subtly rocking against his, beckoning him closer.

Eager to accommodate, he unbuttoned the sleep shirt, baring her generous breasts. He rubbed his thumb across one peak, feeling both reverent and possessive. When he bent down to replace his thumb with his tongue, she made a sharp, sexy sound, so he did it again.

He wanted to give her everything, wanted to make her shake with desire. “Tell me what you want.”

“You.” She shuddered as he licked and suckled her. “Wait, there is one other thing…”

“Name it.”

Her voice was pure seduction. “Can I be on top?”

With a grin, he rolled over. “You do like to be in charge, don’t you?”

She straddled him. “Don’t worry, cowboy. I’ll make sure you like it, too.”

Becca woke disoriented to predawn birdsong outside the window, stiffening when realization hit her. *I’m naked! I’m naked in Sawyer’s bed!*

Well, technically, she owned the bed. And the house. Which would make leaving easy—she only had to go down one flight of stairs—but could make everything else awkward. There would definitely be no avoiding each other. Not that she *wanted* to avoid him, necessarily. She didn’t regret any of the three times they’d had sex throughout the night, each one better than the last. But being in the same house didn’t give her time or space to process what had happened.

“I know you aren’t a morning person,” Sawyer murmured, without raising his face from the pillow next to her, “So I’m trying not to take your panic as an insult.”

“Panic? Who’s panicking?”

“I’ve been to petrified forests where the wood isn’t as rigid as you are right now. Do you want to talk about it?”

She expelled a breath, vastly reassured. He was just

as wonderful now as he had been last night. "Not really. But it means a lot that you offered. I don't want you to think I have regrets. It's just been a long time since I woke up next to a man. And I've never woken up next to any man except for Marc's father."

Sawyer sat up, his expression perplexed. "You mean since the divorce."

"I mean since ever." She'd slept only with her ex-husband. In high school, she'd never even been tempted. Growing up with a mother who was habitually pregnant had left Becca convinced that the reward wouldn't be worth the risk. "Colin and I married young. And before that, I was too worried about the possibility of accidental pregnancy. You may have noticed I was very adamant about the condoms."

He chuckled. "That's not the part of last night that stands out in my memory."

"It was all pretty memorable." She sighed. "In a perfect world, I could stay and we could do it again, but I have work. Plus, I should check on Molly. And call the Whittmeyers to make sure Marc is all right."

"I'll bet he's hanging in there—you're raising a great kid. Will I see you tonight?"

"Unless I miraculously turn invisible. I live here, remember?"

He smirked. "Ha-ha. I meant—"

"I knew what you meant," she said softly. Would there be any repeat of this, of them together? "Marc will be back home tonight, and my current relationship with my sister is...volatile, to say the least. I'd like to set good examples for both of them."

"So no cuddling on the couch, making out in the stairwell or throwing you down on the kitchen table?"

Her face heated. "That was a joke, right? I mean, it's not something you've actually thought about while we're sitting there having coffee?"

"No comment."

Damn. Now *she* would be thinking about that the next time they were in the kitchen together. "I have to be discreet. As for when I might find myself up here again… Can we play it by ear?"

"Of course." He pulled her close, kissing her shoulder. "You know where to find me."

Before Becca left for work, she hadn't been able to get any response from the motionless lump that was her sister. So she'd left water, aspirin and a note saying she'd check back later on the nightstand. She returned on her lunch break, after the most productive morning she'd had in months; either sex left her energized or she was working *really* hard in order to avoid thinking about last night. She wasn't ashamed of anything they'd done, but she was in the habit of thinking long-term. With Sawyer, that thought process was null.

Luckily, she had plenty of other things to concentrate on—like a full-time job, a town-wide celebration, a debate in three days and a pain-in-the-ass sister.

When she pulled up in front of the house, Sawyer's truck was gone. He'd mentioned exploring a fort today for a piece he was writing that included a lot of the area's history. She was both relieved she and her sister wouldn't have an audience within earshot of their conversation, and paradoxically disappointed not to see him.

After letting Trouble out, she went to Molly's room with a bowl of soup; she'd stopped to buy a couple cans on the way home.

"Knock, knock," she said, not shouting, but making no effort to keep her voice down, either. If Molly had a killer headache, that was her own fault.

Molly mumbled something unintelligible.

Becca put the soup on the nightstand. "I don't mean to be a hard-ass about this, but I need you to wake up. There are some things we have to discuss before Marc comes home this afternoon."

"Oh, God." Molly shoved a tangle of hair out her face. "Marc. I was awful to him."

"You were awful to everyone," Becca said matter-of-factly. "But you can't ever do that again in front of my son. If you do, you're out."

Molly nodded silently, her eyes glittering with tears. After a moment, she reached for the tissues on the nightstand, sniffling. "You love him so much. Do you think...do you think our mother ever loved us?"

The question caught Becca off guard. "Yes." In the beginning, maybe, when they were snuggly babies and not unruly toddlers or kids with increasingly complicated lives. Odette liked cradling newborns, but in the years that followed, she was crap at parenting. When Becca was young, it had never occurred to her to question why her mother kept having babies. They'd lived in a rural town surrounded by family-owned farms, with a predominantly Catholic population. Large families were not uncommon. Looking back, though, Becca wondered if their mother had been trying to recapture that early love she'd felt for her children.

I'll probably never know. While Becca had made her peace with that, it was clear Molly was still tormented by her upbringing, by questions of whether she'd been wanted. There was one certainty Becca could give her sister. "Daddy loved us…so much. He *adored* you. There were complications when the twins were born, and I don't think he ever expected to be a father again after that. Then you came. I remember how excited he was when they brought you home from the hospital. I wish you could've known him longer."

"Me, too. I only have a few memories, but they're all good. I feel like my happiest childhood moments were with him."

"Do you think… Is that maybe why you're drawn to older men?" Becca asked gently. Maybe once Molly identified the underlying cause of her actions, it would be easier to change her behavior.

But Molly recoiled, her face tight with anger. "That is *gross*! And you don't know what you're talking about. Who died and made you a licensed therapist?"

"I'm sorry. I—"

"Out." Molly grabbed the plastic wastebasket Becca had left next to the bed, brandishing it in front of her like a weapon. "I'm gonna be sick again. So unless you want to stay and watch…"

Hell, no. After last night, she never wanted to hear the sound of retching again. Yet it seemed important that Molly know she wasn't alone. "If you need me, I'll stay."

Her sister looked startled by the offer, but then waved her hand in a shooing motion. "No. You should go."

With a nod, Becca turned toward the door, touched when Molly added quietly, "But thank you."

Because Molly called in sick to work Friday, everyone was home that night. The mood was odd—not tense, in Becca's opinion, but unnaturally subdued.

Marc was quiet through dinner; Lyndsay had admitted on the phone that she'd probably let the boys stay up too late. Molly had insisted on joining them at the table, as if it was some kind of penance, dining on weak tea and crackers without saying much. Sawyer was…

Actually, Becca had no idea what Sawyer was doing or thinking, because she'd barely allowed herself to look at him all evening. She was paranoid her smiles or glances would reveal too much, that anyone who saw them together would somehow know they'd been intimate. Ridiculous, yet she couldn't quite shake the irrational fear.

It wasn't until after dinner, when Molly retreated to her room and Marc took the puppy out, that Becca felt comfortable enough to address Sawyer directly. Even then, she kept her gaze on the dinner dishes she was scrubbing furiously, rather than make eye contact.

"I'm not trying to ignore you," she apologized.

"I know." His tone was amused, affectionate.

Still, she felt bad for giving him what a less understanding man might deem the cold shoulder. "This is all so new to me and I'm having trouble acting natural, but it doesn't mean you've done anything wrong or—"

"I know, Becca." He gently squeezed the nape of her neck, and she almost jumped.

She glanced back, meaning to smile at him, but frowned instead. "You're taking this awfully well." Because he'd had so many affairs he could be sophisticated and blasé about having seen her naked?

"I'm not taking it nearly as well as you think. I wanted to kiss you all through dinner, wanted to call you a least a dozen times today, and of course, there's that kitchen table right there…"

She followed his gaze, her pulse quickening as she recalled his words this morning. She couldn't remember ever having had fantasies about doing it on the table, but she was pretty sure there were some in her future.

"But," he continued, "you indicated this morning that you needed a little time to adjust. The last time I backed off and let you come to me, it worked out *very* well." He gave her a lazy grin that didn't mask the predatory gleam in his eyes. "Gives a man hope."

She smiled back, but knew that hope of his wouldn't be paid off tonight. She was spending the evening with Marc and planned to stay close by if he needed her—no sneaking up to the attic. "You may have a little bit of a wait."

His gaze darted back and forth, and once he'd ensured there were no witnesses, he ducked in for a lightning-quick kiss, over before it began, but still enough to make her tremble. "You're worth it."

When Marc came back inside, Sawyer made small talk with him for a few minutes and then excused himself, gracefully giving Becca the space she needed. *He's damn near perfect.* Except for the pesky leaving-in-a week part. She decided not to think about it.

"Mama, when are we going to hear the TV lady sing?" Marc asked.

"You mean the concert? Day after tomorrow. Are you looking forward to it?"

Marc nodded, but he seemed more dismissive than excited. "Is Mr. Sawyer coming with us?"

"Yep." She'd given him one of her VIP tickets.

"Maybe since there's music, you should dance with him."

She frowned at the uncharacteristic suggestion, trying to remember if she'd ever heard him mention dancing before. Where was this coming from? "I suppose it's a possibility." Maybe if she danced with a couple different people, so it didn't look as if she was singling him out…

Did Sawyer like to dance? He was a rodeo champion, so he obviously liked physical recreation. And after last night, she could attest that he had a keen sense of rhythm.

"Did you and Daddy ever used to dance?"

This line of questioning was getting weirder; Marc rarely ever mentioned his dad. "We did at our wedding. Would you like to look at the photo album sometime?"

While she personally didn't want to dwell on her romance with Colin, she didn't want to erase Marc's sense of having a father…even if Colin had been more a figurehead than a hands-on parent. He'd showed up to play proud dad at T-ball games and church choir concerts, had always smiled brightly in their family Christmas photo, but when it came to the nitty-gritty of their daily lives? Becca had run everything, from selecting the pediatrician to deciding Marc's bedtime and extracurricular activities. In retrospect, she was ashamed that she had never pushed Colin to take a bigger role. Because she'd liked being in charge, it hadn't bothered her. Colin worked long hours to support their family, and she'd thought the two of them were simply playing to their strengths. If she'd encouraged him to spend more time bonding with his child, would he have stayed for Marc's sake?

Shaking off the past, she smiled brightly at her son. *I'll just have to love him enough for both of us.* "Why the sudden interest in dancing? Want me to teach you how it's done?"

He backed away, looking vaguely horrified. "No, I just thought *you* might like to dance. With Mr. Sawyer."

Wait, was this her seven-year-old trying to play matchmaker? "I'll ask him about it," she said neutrally. If the concert were in a neighboring county where she didn't know anyone, she'd like nothing better than to spend the evening in Sawyer's arms.

But here in Cupid's Bow? She'd been insisting to others that he was a tenant and nothing more; if she snuggled up to him publicly, she'd get some serious side eye. Well, except maybe from Amy Prescott, who'd probably just want to high-five her.

"Honey, you know that Mr. Sawyer isn't my…boyfriend, right?" *No, definitely not a boyfriend, just my secret lover.* Guilt suffused her. Was she a terrible mom for sleeping with a man she'd known only a week?

Marc didn't answer. "I'm going to get the checkerboard. You said you'd play after dinner," he reminded her.

She nodded, glad they weren't playing anything more mentally taxing. Her thoughts had been jumbled all day, and now she had new worries. She was glad her son thought so highly of Sawyer, but she didn't want to give him false hopes. He'd already been abandoned by his father; if Sawyer broke his heart, the kid might end up needing therapy.

Thinking of her conversation earlier with Molly, about their childhood and whether or not their mom had loved them, Becca sighed inwardly. *Frankly, we could all benefit from a little counseling.* Maybe they could get a group discount.

* * *

"Hate to say I told you so," Brody said with faux sympathy, "but I don't think your landlady likes you. At all."

"Is that so?" Sawyer tipped back his straw cowboy hat and pulled a handkerchief from his back pocket to wipe the sweat off his face. This morning's sun, though warm, had been bearable; the afternoon temperatures weren't playing so nicely. Oh, this would be nice enough weather for fishing on the shaded bank of a river or napping in a hammock—preferably with Becca cuddled against him—but the last few hours of assembling booths and makeshift stages for the festival had been grueling manual labor.

Brody put down the toolbox he'd carried over from the other side of town square. "Well, she's bossing all of us around—it's Becca way—but she *really* seems to have it in for you."

Sawyer grinned inwardly, thinking of how flustered she'd been that morning when they'd had their customary encounter by the coffeepot. She'd started to admit that she'd had a dream about him last night, but had abruptly cut herself off, cheeks reddening. *She likes me just fine.* In fact, he'd love to tell his friend about what had happened—not because he wanted to brag about going to bed with her, but simply because she hovered in his thoughts constantly. Being unable to share any of those thoughts was stifling.

Before the two of them had left the house that morning, Becca had reiterated that it was important everyone see them as platonic, for Marc's sake. Recalling how vulnerable the kid had seemed when he'd asked if

Sawyer was going away, Sawyer had readily agreed to play it cool in public.

Becca, however, was overcompensating. She was an all-or-nothing woman, and acting casual was clearly not in her repertoire. First there'd been her refusal to so much as glance at him at dinner. Now she was going out of her way not to show him any favoritism, even though he was the only nonlocal who'd volunteered to help set up the festival. Last night he'd been amused by her terrible show of feigned indifference. Today, he was…oddly aroused. Turned out there were times he could appreciate a bossy woman, especially when he vividly recalled her climbing atop him two nights ago.

Besides, her determination to keep him busy made him feel like part of the inner circle. The longest break he'd had all day was the last thirty seconds, which was akin to how she ran Molly's and Marc's lives. She meant well, trying to keep Molly out of trouble and wanting Marc to be well-rounded with his music lessons and sports and junior civic duties. It was hard to fault her intentions, even if Sawyer didn't particularly agree with her methods. In her own manic, she-should-probably-cut-back-on-caffeine kind of way, keeping people active was how she showed she cared.

Now, if only the rest of the town realized that.

While Brody's heckling about her was more of a running joke than a real accusation, some of the other volunteers were grumbling about how hard Becca was working them.

An hour later, waiting for his turn to fill a cup of water from the cooler, Sawyer tried to defend her. "She has a fun side," he protested.

A bald, burly man in a Cupid's Bow Fire Department

T-shirt raised his eyebrows. "Who are you, again? And how do you know Becca?"

"Sawyer McCall." He shook the man's hand. "I've been renting a room from her for the past week."

"Ah. Maybe she's more relaxed at home," the man said skeptically, "but my cousin worked at the community center last summer, said Becca is a total perfectionist."

"That would be a good quality in a mayor," Sawyer said. "You know she'd never do a half-assed job."

"But a big part of the job is being able to work with others. If she alienates everyone, how will she get anything done? Assuming she can even win the election."

"It'll be close." Manuel Diaz, who'd introduced himself to Sawyer that morning, reached for the paper cups stacked next to the ice water. "But she has my vote. Sierra's been telling all of us at the hospital what a great job Becca will do. It may come down to the small business owners—they're the backbone of the town's economy, and Truitt's been wooing them with grand promises. I hope they keep in mind on voting day how few of those promises he kept this term."

The bald man grinned. "Damn, Manny, didn't realize you were so interested in local politics. Maybe you should be on the town council."

Manuel chuckled. "Sierra and my girlfriend both say that, too."

After that, conversation turned to local gossip and Sawyer walked away with a polite nod, sipping his water and thinking over everything he'd heard. He wouldn't be in Cupid's Bow much longer, but maybe he could do some good while he was here.

Sawyer sat behind the steering wheel, watching

through the windshield as Becca finished talking to an elderly lady in a Houston Astros shirt, and a short bearded man. Even though Sawyer was tired and ready for a shower, he didn't mind the wait—not when he had this view of sunlight shining on Becca's red-gold hair or the sway of her body as she gestured. But then she turned toward the truck, and he dropped his gaze so that he wasn't caught staring.

"Sorry I took so long," she said as she climbed in.

"No worries. You did warn me, after all."

When he'd suggested riding into town together, she'd originally declined, pointing out that, as festival chair, she might have to stay longer. Wanting time alone with her—even if it was just the fifteen-minute ride back to the house—he'd told her he'd wait if necessary. He'd eventually cajoled her into agreeing, teasingly reminding her that one vehicle was better for the environment than two, and she had voters to impress.

Speaking of which... What was the best way to tell her about the brainstorm he'd had earlier?

Her head fell back against the seat. All day, she'd projected an image of being in charge, reassuring people who came to her with problems, and "motivating" would-be slackers to get the job done right. Now she sighed, her expression showing hints of vulnerability. "I'm exhausted."

Oh, boy. That might make tonight a less-than-ideal time for the houseguests he was about to spring on her. But it was still early evening. "Think you have time for a nap before dinner?"

She stifled a yawn. "If I lay down now, it would be too hard to get back up."

"I worry about you running yourself ragged." It was

almost enough to make him feel guilty about that third time they'd had sex Thursday night, and how little sleep she'd gotten. *Almost.*

"Things are just crazy right now, with the centennial and the mayoral campaign," she said. "I'll catch up on my rest after the election."

He snorted. "After the election, you'll be too busy running the town."

"Then I'll delegate someone on my staff to take naps for me." She reached over to squeeze his hand, and he wanted to stop the truck and kiss her. "You really think I'm going to win?"

She would if he had anything to say about it. "You know how you've said I should feel free to use the common areas?" She'd told him to make himself at home in the living room and kitchen, so long as he cleaned up after himself and respected her policy about grocery inventory.

She frowned at the non sequitur. "Sure."

"And you meant it, right?"

"Yes." But she said it warily.

"Great—because I invited a few people over tonight."

"Tonight?" Her voice was shrill, one might even say edged with panic. She took a deep breath. "How many is 'a few'?"

"Four or five. Enough for a rousing game of poker at the kitchen table."

She pinched the bridge of her nose. "And it had to be tonight? The festival kicks off tomorrow, and I'm trying to prepare for the debate on Monday."

And he wanted to help. If tonight went well, maybe there'd be a few more friendly faces in the audience at that debate. "I promise my motives aren't selfish—they're political."

She laughed. "Cynics would say those usually go hand in hand."

"You know Manuel Diaz, right?" At her nod, he added, "He thinks some of the local business owners could be very important in this election. But you have a certain…reputation in town. For being…"

"Controlling? Bossy? This is Sierra's posters all over again," she muttered.

"Whose what?"

"My friend Sierra. She works with Manny in physical therapy at the hospital. You wouldn't believe what she wanted to put on the campaign posters."

"Becca Johnston for Global Domination?"

She rolled her eyes. "Vote for Our Favorite Control Freak. As I told her, there's nothing freakish about being organized."

"You are not a freak of any kind. You're smart. And determined. And funny. And bighearted." He could name a dozen more things he loved about her—but it wasn't his good opinion she needed. "But it's possible some people in town haven't had a glimpse behind the public image yet, at the real you. So I invited Manny, who's already on your side, and a few men in town he thinks are influential."

"Just men, huh? I'll have you know, women can be excellent poker players. In college, I won enough one semester to pay for all my textbooks."

"For the record, I also asked two women, but neither of them could make it on such short notice. Thank God you play, because this will work a lot better if you join us."

"Why would anyone decide to vote for me just because I play a couple hands of poker with him?" She clenched her jaw. "If you think for a second I'm going to let someone win—"

"Nah, I would never ask that of you." And he wouldn't respect her half as much if she stooped to that kind of manipulation. "Be yourself. Just don't gloat too much if you kick our asses."

"I make no promises."

Chapter 12

Manny rose from his chair, looking toward the dealer. "Count me out this round—I have an early morning." He flashed a teasing smile. "Plus, I've lost all the money I can afford to for one night."

Becca checked her watch. "I actually have to leave to pick up Molly in about fifteen minutes, anyway."

As people stood around the table, Sawyer allowed himself a self-congratulatory smile. Tonight had turned out even better than he'd expected. Not financially—he was down nineteen bucks—but for Becca. He watched her now, as she joked with the editor of the local newspaper, the *Cupid's Bow Clarion.* She looked relaxed and happy…and thirty dollars richer. Conversation had centered around the festival and some good-natured trash talking.

As a scowling Roger Sands approached Becca, however, Sawyer realized that the town councilman was getting less good-natured by the moment. "A Johnston taking my money," the balding man growled. "Just like old times."

Becca stiffened. So did everyone else, eyes on her as the men in the room waited to see how she responded. Manny took a step closer to Becca, as if preparing to intervene on her behalf.

But she wasn't one to shrink from confrontation. "I'm sorry you lost some money in Colin's last property investment deal," she told Sands, her voice so quiet Sawyer could barely make out the words. "But Marc and I lost more than anyone. Our family—my marriage—fell apart."

Sands lowered his gaze, shamefaced, barely mumbling a goodbye before hustling toward the front door. It banged shut behind him. Once they heard his car start, it was as if everyone else exhaled in relief.

Manny squeezed her shoulder, and Sawyer was surprised by the irrational flash of jealousy that went through him. "This has been fun," the physical therapist said. "It'd be *more* fun if we don't invite Sands next time."

Everyone trickled out with polite farewells, thanking Becca for her hospitality. None of them knew it had been involuntary. Then the house was quiet, with Marc already in bed and Molly still at work.

Becca sighed. "We've never really talked about my ex."

"Do you want to?" Sawyer could be a good listener, if that was what she needed, but she didn't owe him any explanations about her past.

"No. Maybe." She reached for the now-empty bowl

of queso on the table and carried it to the sink. "Colin was always ambitious—it was one of the reasons I was attracted to him. But I think that ambition got corrupted somewhere along the line. He convinced people in our community to invest in a resort on the coast, and the whole deal fell apart. When he left, I thought he was embarrassed, that he'd been duped. Took me a while to realize it had been a scam and that he was probably fleeing criminal charges. No one ever found enough evidence to convict him, but thank God I kept my own financial accounts, separate from him and his company. Even now, when I think about it, I feel so stu—"

"Hey." Sawyer pulled her into a hug. "*You* didn't do anything wrong."

"Except fall in love with a fraud."

If Sawyer had felt a prick of jealousy over Manny's casual contact, it was nothing compared to the wave that swamped him hearing her say she loved another man. *Of course she loved him—he was her damn husband.* Maybe what bothered him wasn't the statement of the obvious so much as the realization that he would never hear her say she loved *him*.

His stomach clenched, knotted in a riot of conflicting emotions. He'd barely even considered the prospect of a steady girlfriend before; he had little experience with commitment. He couldn't really want a single mom—and prospective mayor—to fall in love with him. That was commitment squared.

Becca pulled away, her voice soft. "Do you think I'm running for mayor because deep down I want to prove I still have the town's respect? I tell myself I have noble goals, but what if this is just a way to distance myself from what Colin did?"

"You love Cupid's Bow. No one who's talked to you for more than five minutes could ever doubt that. And, okay, maybe you also have some personal motivation, but so what? As long as you do the best job you can for the community, does it really matter what prompted you to run?" Her ex had ruined enough for her and Marc without also making her second-guess her campaign. *Bastard.* "Too bad you don't know where he is—I'd be willing to rearrange his face."

Becca gave him a sunny smile. "You'd have to get in line behind me."

"Little known fact—concerts are actually supposed to be fun."

The rollicking chorus of Kylie Jo's latest hit made it practically impossible to hear conversation. But Sawyer had murmured his teasing reprimand right at Becca's ear, close enough for his breath to feather over her skin, and she shivered at the sensation. It was so tempting to lean back and let her body melt into his.

Instead, she stood straight, hoping their nearness only made them look like two people crowded together in front of the stage, not like two people who'd seen each other naked.

"I am having fun," she said. More or less. The songs were upbeat and she did her best to clap along with everyone else, while also mentally reviewing for tomorrow night's debate, keeping an eye on Marc, who was a few yards away with Kenny Whittmeyer, and trying to find Molly in the surrounding crowd. She'd said she was going to get a soda; Becca wanted to make damn sure her sister didn't get distracted by a beer vendor or a Breelan.

Sawyer placed his hand on the nape of her neck, pressing with his thumb and rotating it in a slow circle that made her moan.

"That feels incredible," she said, her body sagging against his despite her resolve.

"You're tense. What are you doing later tonight?" he whispered, his voice coaxing. "I could give you an excellent full body massage. You need to relax."

Reluctantly, she took a step away from him. "What I need is to work on my to-do list. Tomorrow is—"

"Delegate," he suggested. "Make sure you leave a little time for you. By which I mean *us*."

Her breath caught. It was such a seductive idea—that she and Sawyer were a united "them." But there were only a few days until the trail ride, where they would be surrounded by others. Becca would never risk sneaking into his tent, and after the trail ride, he was leaving. *I can count on one hand the number of nights we have left together.* The realization ached in her chest.

She swallowed hard, changing the subject. "Do you see Molly anywhere?"

His sigh sounded exasperated.

"What?" Craning her head, she turned to look at him. "What's wrong?"

"Nothing." A moment later, he gave her a halfhearted smile. "But it's a slap to the ego that I'm trying to put the moves on you and you're more interested in what your sister is doing. She's eighteen. She can find her own way to the concession stand and back."

"You think I'm overprotective."

"I… It's really none of my business." He glanced toward the stage, where the band was finishing up the song Kylie Jo had won the TV competition with. "And this probably isn't the place to discuss it, anyway."

Though Becca nodded, she continued to think about what he'd said. Yes, technically Molly was an adult. But hadn't he seen how much trouble she'd gotten herself into less than a week ago? Becca had cause to worry.

"Hey, Mrs. Johnston!"

As the opening guitar notes of a ballad played, she glanced down to find Kenny and Marc. "Hey, guys—having a good time?"

Her son nodded. "But we're hungry. Can I have a waffle cone?"

"Is Mrs. W. going to stand in line with you? I don't want you wandering in this crowd without an adult."

"Coop said he'd take us," Kenny chimed in.

"Then I guess—"

"Mama!" Marc tugged on the lace-edged sleeve of her peasant blouse. "This song is so slow even *you* could dance to it."

Ouch. If Sawyer wanted to experience a real slap to the ego, he should try parenting. Kids were hell on the old self-esteem.

Marc had redirected his focus to the cowboy. "Do you like dancing, Mr. Sawyer?"

He smiled. "I guess there's only one way to find out. Becca?"

"Oh, but I don't…" She couldn't bring herself to say no—not when she so badly wanted to be in his arms. So she gave her son a ten-dollar bill for ice cream and, as the boys scampered away, laced her fingers with Sawyer's.

He pulled her close, and need sizzled through her. Aside from a few stolen kisses at the house, he hadn't really touched her in days. She missed him. How much worse was it going to be after he was gone? They swayed to the music. She should be enjoying herself, loving the way his body brushed hers, but she couldn't relax into the moment. Her mind was racing.

"I know the city is paying you to help with the trail ride," she said, "and that you win money from the rodeos, but have you ever thought about…something else?" Would he be bored, planting roots in a small town like this one?

"Like what?"

"I don't know." She thought about how moved she'd been reading one of his articles. "Maybe writing a book someday?"

He laughed. "There are days when I curse my way through trying to finish a two-page piece. Not sure a whole manuscript would be for me. That's a hell of a commitment."

Right. "Stupid idea," she muttered. "Forget I said anything."

He tipped her chin up with his finger, studying her face. "What's troubling you, sweetheart?"

Lots of things. But at least she knew how to fix one of them. "Sexual frustration." She went up on her toes so that she could whisper in his ear, "I will definitely be coming upstairs to visit you tonight."

His grip on her tightened, making her smile despite her brief moment of melancholy. "Hot damn. How soon can we get out of here?"

Becca couldn't remember ever sleeping through her alarm before, but that's exactly what she did on Monday morning. After several wonderful hours spent in Sawyer's room the night before, she'd staggered drowsily to her own bed and crashed into blissful sleep. But when she woke up forty minutes late and caught a glimpse of the time, any remaining bliss wore off in a hurry.

She was frantic as she scurried around the kitchen while Marc got dressed, shoving coffee filters into his lunch box instead of back into the cabinet where they belonged.

Sawyer shot her a guilty glance from the end of the counter, where he was waiting for caffeine and trying to stifle his yawns. He'd also slept later than usual today, but he wasn't the one who had to get a kid to school, a dog to the vet and a newspaper reporter to the senior center. As part of the centennial week, the paper was interviewing the oldest living citizen in Cupid's Bow, but on her bad days, Miss June confused easily, and Becca wanted to be there to help make sure the interview went smoothly. She wished she could assign that chore to Sawyer—maybe he might be interested in working for a paper someday. It could be a nice steady job that allowed him to settle in one place. But Miss June got flustered around strangers.

Maybe he'd be willing to help with something else; delegating had been his idea, after all. "I hate to ask this of you, but—"

"Sweetheart, after last night, you could ask for one of my kidneys. Or my truck." He cocked his head to the side, considering. "Okay, maybe not the truck. Seriously, just tell me what you need."

"Can you take Trouble to the vet for me this morning?" she asked, as Marc's footsteps thumped down the staircase. He was moving fast, well aware from her half-dozen reminders that they were running late. She bit her lip. “And maybe take Marc to his piano lesson this afternoon? I’ve got the debate tonight and—”

“Done.”

“Thank you.” If Marc hadn’t been barreling into the room, she would have kissed Sawyer to show her gratitude. “I wish I could...”

“I know.” He gave her a lopsided smile. “Me, too.”

Becca didn’t need a town poll or a recap in the local paper to gauge how she did in the debate; she had Olive Truitt in the front row. The more fiercely the tiny woman glared at her, the better Becca knew she was doing.

When Becca had first declared her intention to run, the mayor’s wife had been all sweetness and light to her—saying that it was great to have a woman in the race, claiming that she admired Becca’s gumption. But as it became clear that Becca had a real chance—thus jeopardizing Olive’s standing as First Lady of Cupid’s Bow—the woman’s demeanor had changed. She and her two friends, Helen and Sissy, gossiped about Becca whenever they thought they could get away with it, not getting caught in outright lies, but certainly distorting the truth beyond recognition. Sierra had privately nicknamed Helen and Sissy “Hateful and Spiteful.”

Sierra was also in the front row and her discreet thumbs-up signs throughout also let Becca know that she was doing well.

When Becca had arrived at the town hall two hours ago, Olive had cornered her by the water cooler. “I understand you hosted a poker game at your house. Very hospitable.” Then she’d paused, a calculating gleam in her silver-gray eyes. “Although...one wonders if gambling is setting a good example for your son. Wouldn't want him to grow up with the same reckless disregard for money as his father."

Becca had been too furious to respond; the only words that had leaped to mind would make her look crass or volatile, and she refused to hand Olive that ammunition. So she'd clenched her jaw and saved her replies for the debate itself. Now, listening to Mayor Truitt give his closing remarks before she took her turn, she supposed she was lucky *he* hadn't brought up the Johnston history with money, trying to smear her by association to Colin. She figured the only reason he hadn't was because he and Colin had done a number of business deals together, deals that Truitt had made substantial money on. The good mayor probably didn't want to remind voters of his own association with the shady real estate broker.

The debate had barely concluded when Becca's phone buzzed with a text—from Sierra. YOU WERE AWESOME! Apparently her friend thought it would be undignified to tackle hug Becca and squeal her congratulations where other people could overhear, but the string of emojis that popped up on Becca's phone made Sierra's feelings clear.

Becca spent a few minutes shaking hands and thanking supporters, but the debate had been the draining conclusion to an already long day. She couldn't wait to get home. On the drive to her house, she felt a twinge of regret that Sawyer hadn't been there tonight. He'd volunteered to stay with Marc, and it wasn't as if he had any stake in local politics, anyway. Still, she could just imagine the expression on his face if he'd been there, the pride shining in his hazel eyes. The unspoken but unmistakable *way to go, sweetheart.*

Becca had wonderful friends—and greatly appreciated their support—but encouragement from Sawyer lifted her in a way that was different than when Sierra or Hadley verbally high-fived her. He liked to tease her about global domination, but sometimes the way he smiled at her did make her feel empowered enough to take over the world. *Becca Johnston, benevolent tyrant.*

She pulled into her driveway with a faint smile, ready for pajamas and pie and a stolen kiss or two.

The porch light wasn't on—despite the timer that was supposed to ensure she never had to climb the steps in the dark—and her eye was automatically drawn to the only light shining from the house, the bathroom window in the attic. Sawyer hadn't bothered to lower the blinds, and she could see just enough to know that he was shirtless and kneeling, partially out of view. Curious to find out what he was doing, she went inside. The downstairs was completely quiet; up above, she heard a shriek of laughter from Marc and the answering rumble of Sawyer's low voice. A high-pitched bark followed.

By the time Becca got to the top of the spiral staircase, she could also hear splashing sounds. The door to the attic apartment stood wide open and she went in to find Sawyer and her son giving Trouble a bath. From what Becca could tell, there was as much water on the floor as in the tub and the two guys were almost as wet as the puppy. Laughter burbled up inside her, and Sawyer whipped his head around, his expression guilty.

"You're home already!" He didn't sound particularly happy about that. "How'd it go?"

Hearing Becca's voice, Trouble lunged suddenly, trying to make a break from the tub. Water surged over the side as Sawyer tried to calm the puppy.

He glanced from the puddles on the tile back to Becca. "I, uh… You know I'll clean all this up, right?"

"Clean does seem to be the goal here," she said, biting back another laugh when the dog gave a full body shake, spraying Sawyer and Marc with droplets.

"Trouble rolled on somethin' dead," Marc announced, with a little boy's fascination for the gross. "She smelled worse than a skunk. Now she'll smell like shampoo."

"A definite improvement," Becca agreed. "You, however, are going to smell like wet dog. You'd better scoot down for a quick shower before bed."

His face fell. "Aww. But we aren't done!"

"I'll finish up," Sawyer said. "You listen to your mama. Okay?"

Marc nodded. "Yes, sir. Good night."

"Night, buddy." Sawyer gave her son a smile full of so much affection that tears pricked her eyes.

Years ago, Becca had thought she was on the path to a fairy-tale ending and had instead stumbled into divorce and scandal. She'd told herself that she was too wise now to make the same mistake again. But the sexiest man she knew was giving her dog a bath and looking at her kid with love. It created the illusion of family. Of happily-ever-after.

She followed her son downstairs, trying to keep her tears in check. There was no ever-after with a man like Sawyer. He'd walked away from his own family and didn't seem interested in putting down roots anywhere.

As a grown-up, she didn't think the most fantastical thing about fairy tales were the enchanted slippers or magic wands; it was that the charming princes were so ready and willing to commit. In real life, they all too often had one foot out the door.

Becca's big festival challenge Wednesday afternoon was relocating three dozen fourth graders. They'd been scheduled to sing after the community theater performed a historic reenactment, but Becca deemed the ancient risers the kids stood on unsafe. The elementary school music teacher had twice requested that the collapsible stage be replaced, because the supports were starting to give way. So far, she'd been denied due to budgetary reasons, but after hearing how the metal creaked as the kids filed into place, Becca was already planning a fund-raiser to get new risers.

Meanwhile, she moved a cooking demonstration out of the gazebo to give the kids a place to perform, then headed off to find ice water and a portable fan for Marianne Schubert, who was having hot flashes in the arts and crafts tent. Once that was accomplished, she joined Lyndsay Whittmeyer and the boys, who were watching a glassblowing demonstration. Sawyer would be swinging by to pick up Marc and take him to his riding lesson.

"Hey." Lyndsay greeted her with a smile. "Got everything running to perfection?"

"Perfection? No. But I like to think I've brought order to the chaos."

"Your specialty. Honestly, you should give a seminar at the community center sometime on staying organized. I don't know how you do it...but you'll certainly be a darn good mayor."

"Fingers crossed."

"Sorry I couldn't make the debate the other night.

I was feeling under the weather, afraid I was coming down with something. Whatever it was, I'm glad it passed quickly."

"Staying home was the right call," Becca assured her. "You wouldn't want to risk getting everyone sick."

"I know. But I would've liked to watch you wipe the floor with Truitt—Sierra said it was awesome. Besides, there was something I wanted to ask you about. In person."

Becca raised an eyebrow. "Well, we're talking face-to-face now."

Casting a quick glance toward the boys, Lyndsay sidled a few feet away, then a few more. Once they'd put some distance between them and the kids, she asked, "So...you and the cowboy?"

Becca stalled. "What do you mean?"

"Is there something going on between the two of you? You looked pretty cuddly at the concert." She hesitated before adding, "You looked *happy.* And maybe it's none of my business, but you should know, I overheard the boys talking about it and—"

"The boys?" Her blood ran cold. Had Marc been talking about her and Sawyer as a couple? *Can you blame him? Sawyer's spent more quality time with him in the past two weeks than his father has in the past five years.* This was exactly the kind of disappointment she'd wanted to avoid for her son. "They don't think we're involved, do they?"

"I'm not sure. They clammed up when they noticed me. I just heard something about you and Sawyer and dancing. But, really, would it be such a bad thing to be involved with someone like him? You must have at least thought about it."

The urge to confide in her friend was overwhelming. Each day that brought them closer to goodbye threatened to crack Becca's calm, organized facade, leaving her in near-constant emotional turmoil. But as she debated whether to trust Lyndsay with her secret, she noticed Sissy Woytek in her peripheral vision. Best friend to the mayor's wife, Sissy was trying to look as though she wasn't shamelessly eavesdropping. Becca knew better than to care about what others thought of her personal life, yet she couldn't help feeling defensive, not just as a mayoral candidate but as a single mom. She didn't want others judging her affair and she sure as hell didn't want local gossip affecting Marc.

Instead of giving Lyndsay a straight answer—or worse, lying—she replied with a question of her own, one that wouldn't fuel any rumors from Sissy. "Does Sawyer really seem like the kind of guy I'd let myself fall for?"

Her friend was quiet for a long moment. "I guess not. He's certainly not anything like Colin. But you… Oh!" Her face flushed, and she raised her hand in a quick wave. "Hey, Sawyer."

Becca turned to find him behind her, gorgeous in the afternoon sunlight. "Everything go okay with the horses?" While some of the people going on the trail ride had horses of their own, some tourists would be on borrowed mounts provided by Brody and other local ranchers. Sawyer had gone with his friend to double-check the temperament and health of the animals before embarking on the three-day trip.

He nodded. "We're in good shape for the ride. Marc ready to go to his lesson?"

She signaled to her son, who trotted over with a

broad smile. Becca hugged him. "Have fun riding. I'll see you back home for dinner."

She watched the two of them walk up the hill together, Sawyer laughing at something the boy said while Marc gazed up with blatant hero worship. No, Sawyer was nothing like the slick, urbane, all-style-and-no-substance Colin. That was the problem. If he'd been more like her ex, she would have done a much better job of protecting her heart.

Does Sawyer really seem like the kind of guy I'd let myself fall for? The question echoed in Sawyer's head over and over until he found himself gnashing his teeth. Luckily, Marc and his instructor were on the other side of the ring, so the kid didn't notice Sawyer's mood. The boy had been excited for Sawyer to see him on horseback, so whenever Marc looked over, he did his best to look happy and encouraging.

But he hadn't felt very happy in the last forty-eight hours. He and Becca had shared an amazing night Sunday after the concert with no one the wiser about her midnight trip to visit a secret cowboy lover. It was beginning to chafe that she didn't want anyone to know about him. It felt…sordid.

Despite the incredibly intimate connection he'd felt with her Sunday night, he'd barely seen her Monday until she'd come home during Trouble's bath. Maybe it was just her busy schedule with the festival, but he had the damnedest sense that she'd been avoiding him since then. What had he done wrong?

Maybe the problem has nothing do with a what, a snide inner voice whispered, *but a who*. As in who he was—a rodeo cowboy with no college degree. Was she ashamed of him because he wasn't some businessman in a suit? Sawyer had left home feeling as if he wasn't good enough for his own family, so it didn't seem like a stretch that perhaps the future mayor of Cupid's Bow didn't think he was good enough for her, either.

She'd been dropping bizarre hints lately about career options. Write a book? Because that was a more prestigious, potentially more lucrative, job than bronc riding and ranch work? She'd said herself she'd been attracted to her ex because he was ambitious. *And how did that work out for you, sweetheart?*

It added to his cranky mood that Becca had been giving him little assignments, from asking him to drive Mrs. Spiegel to the mechanic's to putting him in charge of Marc's lesson today. Granted, Sawyer had told her he wanted to help, but the adorable novelty of her bossing him around was wearing off. His naturally rebellious nature was rising to the fore. Listening to her chide Molly bought back too many memories of Charlie lecturing him, and if Sawyer had to hear one more word about those lights on timers… What the hell was wrong with just turning lights on and off as needed? But no, Becca Johnston had to have things *her* way.

Yet beneath his increasing frustration was the suspicion that he might be overreacting. It was possible that his surliness had nothing to do with light timers and being cajoled into giving her son a ride. Maybe what really chapped Sawyer's ass was the knowledge that she was about to move on to a new important position, while he would be moving on with his life in an opposite direction. Would he see her again? *Hell, she barely lets you see her now*—at least, not in any way she was willing to admit in front of voters. It stung more than it should, and he was torn between wanting to get out of Cupid's Bow and away from the ache she caused, and wanting to stay as close to her for as long as he could.

By the time the guys returned from Marc's lesson, Becca had a spitting headache. She'd been arguing with Molly, who wanted to borrow the car to go hear a band in Turtle tomorrow. "Do you really think you've proved yourself responsible enough for that?" Becca had challenged, knowing her sister would be surrounded by men and booze in the club.

Molly had acted as if she had slapped her. Just as Becca was setting the table, her sister retreated to her room and refused to come out for dinner.

Although Sawyer didn't resort to stomping and slamming doors, his mood seemed almost as dark as Molly's. He didn't say much as he sat down.

"She's being impossible," Becca said, needing someone on her side.

He gave her a chiding glance over the top of the ice tea glass in his hand. "Maybe from her perspective, it seems like you're being impossible."

"Me? I'm the one doing her a favor!"

"And do you ever let her forget that? I know she's made mistakes, but that's how people learn. You can't be naive enough to think she's the first teenager to get dr—" Thankfully, he stopped himself, with a quick glance in Marc's direction. "People screw up. But constantly pointing it out can do more harm than good. Do you want to drive her away?"

"Is Aunt Molly going away?" Marc asked, sounding distraught.

Becca glared at Sawyer. "No, she's sticking around."

Unlike the cowboy. He had a lot of nerve, telling her how to manage her family when he didn't even speak to his own. She changed the subject for her son's sake. "How was your riding lesson?"

"Great." Marc's face brightened as he told her all about the horse and how much better he was getting and how he might be ready to try a canter or gallop.

She gave him a fond smile. "You're really enjoying it, aren't you?"

"A lot more than soccer," Sawyer muttered.

Both Becca and her son whipped their heads in his direction. Marc looked stricken. "Mr. Sawyer!"

"It's okay," Sawyer encouraged. "She should know."

"But..." His lip quivered.

Becca was livid. This was the second time in one meal Sawyer had offered his unsolicited opinion, and now he'd made her son uncomfortable. She glanced at Marc's mostly empty plate. "Would you like to be excused?"

He didn't have to be asked twice. Nodding, he scampered away from the table. Becca pressed her lips tightly together, trying not to explode while he was still in earshot.

Sawyer stood. "I think I'll go, too. I don't really have much of an appetite."

"Wait!" They needed to talk about this.

But the look he gave her made her suddenly question the wisdom of having the discussion now.

"Word of advice?" he said in a low voice. "When they elect you mayor, try not to order everyone around. They might stage a coup."

"You sound as melodramatic as Molly. Asking people to pitch in and giving people suggestions is not the same as 'ordering everyone around.' But while we're on the subject of ill-advised behavior? What was that about Marc and his soccer games?"

"He doesn't like it."

"I realize that."

Sawyer gave her a look of disgust. "But you make him play, anyway?"

She tried to silently count to ten to keep from shouting. "I don't 'make' him play. He wanted to sign up originally because Kenny Whittmeyer thought it would be cool, but didn't follow through. I've asked Marc point-blank if he likes playing. I'm trying to encourage him to be honest with me—if he could bring himself to say he wanted to quit, I'd pull him out. It's important to learn to stand up for yourself. Meanwhile, it's good exercise for him and he's getting better every week. Who knows? By next year, he might actually enjoy it." Sawyer wouldn't be here next year; he wouldn't even be here next month.

Angry that he'd become so enmeshed with their lives when he wasn't sticking around, she lashed out. "But none of this is *your* business. You're not his father. You're not even my boyfriend. You are—"

"Just a tenant. Got it." His expression was so cold that the temperature in the kitchen dropped ten degrees.

She hadn't meant to belittle him. She'd only been trying to establish boundaries, struggling after the fact to keep herself safely isolated. "Sawyer..."

"Nah, you're one hundred percent right, sweetheart." His bared his teeth in a sardonic smile. "As always."

When Sawyer came downstairs in the morning after a brutally sleepless night, he found Becca at the table, bleary-eyed and cradling her head in her hands. Guilt twisted inside him; he hadn't meant to hurt her. But then, he hadn't been making the wisest decisions lately. He'd known from the start that an affair with a single mom would be complicated, much less a high-maintenance single mom who pushed all his buttons. Yet he'd ignored his own common sense.

"Sawyer." Her voice was raw, as if she had a cold. Or as if she'd been crying. "Glad I caught you before you headed out for the day."

"Actually..." He shifted his weight. "I'm headed out, period. I'm going to stay with Brody and Jazz tonight and leave with him for the trail ride tomorrow."

"What? I—"

"Truck's all loaded up," he said, trying to stick to his decision. If he remained here, there were only two likely outcomes—more fighting, which he didn't want. Or making up. Kissing each other, touching, growing closer...all of which would make their inevitable parting even worse. "I only came down here to leave this." He held up an envelope with his final rent payment and a note wishing her well.

"You were going to leave without saying goodbye?" She swallowed hard. "I guess taking off is what you do, though, huh?"

He stiffened at the accusation. "It wouldn't be permanent. I'll see you on the trail ride."

"Maybe not. I...have a lot to do before the election."

Liar. She was going to cancel because of him. The worst part was, he didn't know whether to be disappointed or relieved about not having to see her. Maybe it was best to get this whole thing over with. She obviously thought so if she was skipping the ride.

He tipped his hat toward her, his voice tight with emotion when he said, "Take care of yourself, Becca. And give Marc a hug for me."

"He's going to miss you."

I'll miss you both. But he wouldn't miss the way he'd felt the last few days—as if he was a dirty secret to be kept from voters. As if he was, yet again, not quite good enough. So he kept his words to himself and left, wincing when Trouble barked, as if she was calling him back. *Sorry, puppy.* It was time to go.

Chapter 13

"You okay, sis?"

Becca glanced up from the book she hadn't been reading; she wasn't even sure what it was. "I've been better." The election was this week and she should be obsessing over her chances, trying to sway any last-minute undecided voters, but the days had been a hazy blur since Sawyer left. She knew her son was sad to see him go, but Marc's heartbreak was mitigated by school finally being out for the summer.

"I'm all ready for work," Molly said gently. "Still willing to drive me?"

Becca tossed the book on the coffee table, rising from the couch to get her keys. "Actually, why don't you take the car? I don't have anywhere I need to be today." She was taking a much-needed rest in the aftermath of what everyone was calling a very successful festival.

"Oh, wow, you're worse off than I thought." She hesitated. "You miss him, right?"

Becca blinked. Maybe her discreet affair hadn't been as discreet as she thought. "What do you mean?"

"He was gorgeous and great with Marc and even cooked sometimes. Plus, I saw how he looked at you. How could you *not* miss him?"

Excellent question—and one Becca was struggling to find the answer to. "Letting you use the car has nothing to do with any supposed feelings for Sawyer. I'm offering it because you're a smart adult working hard." In addition to the movie theater job, Molly was working minimal hours in the library, earning a stipend Hadley had managed to scrape together. "I've been thinking about it, and I need to treat you more like an adult. Maybe the reason I couldn't before was because I hated to admit we lost all those years. I was a crappy big sister to you."

"No you weren't!" Molly enveloped her in a tight hug. "You are the best."

"We'll see if you still feel that way in a minute," Becca said. "You should have adult responsibilities. I was thinking you could move into the attic apartment, come and go as you please—and that you should pay rent." Sawyer had accused her of constantly reminding Molly that this was a favor, that she was an imposition. Well, now that would change. "We can discuss the specifics tonight, but what do you think?"

Molly's eyes glittered. "I think I'm lucky to have you, and I won't let you down. I promise I'll drive exactly at the speed limit and come home right after my shift. Now, can I give you a piece of life advice?"

Becca raised her eyebrows, surprised, but trying to

keep an open mind. "I suppose that's fair, after all the suggestions I've made."

"Go get your cowboy."

Loss burned in her chest, and Becca tried in vain not to picture his face. That teasing smile, those hazel eyes. "He's not mine. I don't even know where he is." *But Brody Davenport might.* "All I need to make me happy are my family and winning this election."

Her chances had never seemed better. Recent informal polling after the festival put her way ahead of Truitt. She should be feeling confident and eager. Not hollow.

Molly eyed her with a combination of skepticism and pity. "You're sure that's all you need?"

"Well...and key lime pie." And time. She'd healed from her divorce over time. Wouldn't this be the same? In a few weeks, she'd be so busy running this town, she'd barely remember Sawyer McCall.

"I hope I'm not interrupting, but can I talk to you for a minute, Madam Mayor?"

Becca turned from the owner of the bowling alley, who'd been telling her how glad local business owners were that she'd won, to see Sierra Bailey, especially gorgeous in a strappy green cocktail dress. Plenty of wedding receptions had been held in the community center "ballroom," but tonight it had been elegantly decorated for Becca's victory party. She was thrilled, but feeling slightly overwhelmed by all the congratulations and people who wanted to shake her hand. It would be relaxing to just talk to a friend for a few moments.

She flashed Sierra a grateful smile. "You're allowed the occasional interruption—I couldn't have done this without you! If you'll excuse me for a moment?" she asked the bowling-alley manager.

"Absolutely. Guest of honor needs to circulate." He held up his glass. "I need a refill, anyway." With a polite nod to Sierra, he ambled toward the cash bar.

"I've been dying for a chance to get you alone all night!" Sierra said. "Short of stalking you on your way to use the ladies' room, this seemed like my best opportunity."

"It has been hectic. Good hectic, obviously. Who could possibly complain about such an outpouring of felicitations?" Odd, though, that she had talked to dozens of people tonight and still felt so lonely. "What can I do for you?"

Sierra bit her lip. "Okay, I hope this isn't an incredibly insensitive faux pas—I know tonight's a big night for you—but I have something I need to tell you."

"Out with it then." Of all Becca's friends, Sierra was the one who most bluntly spoke her mind. Now that she had her attention, what could be slowing her down? Unless she was afraid of ruining Becca's jubilant mood? "Is it bad news? Did Truitt demand a recount or something?"

"Nothing like that! Just the opposite. I have great news." She leaned close so that Becca could hear her whisper over the chatter of partygoers. "I'm engaged."

Becca barely managed to contain an undignified whoop of glee. "Seriously? Oh, honey, that's fantastic!" She squashed her friend in a hug that no doubt wrinkled both their dresses. "When did this happen?"

"This morning. He proposed on a napkin."

"He what?" Becca raised an eyebrow, about to be disappointed in Jarrett. He'd lived his whole life in Cupid's Bow and knew all the most romantic places. What was this nonsense about a napkin?

Sierra, however, was beaming, no trace of disappointment in her glowing expression. "It's this thing he does…leaves me romantic notes next to my morning coffee, written on napkins. This morning's said 'Will you marry me?' Then when I said yes, we ditched the coffee in favor of celebratory mimosas, and he carried me back to our bedroom and—" Her cheeks went rosy. "Well, it was all much more romantic than it probably sounds."

"Actually, it *does* sound romantic." The idea of waking up to someone who adored you each morning? Someone who showed his affection by making coffee and jotting love notes? A twinge went through Becca as she thought of the times she and Sawyer had shared in her kitchen, those predawn moments when it had been just the two of them, him teasing her over the rim of his coffee mug and making her grin even though smiling at 6:00 a.m. seemed vaguely unnatural.

Enough with the melancholy. Tonight is a celebration! Not just for her, but for one of her closest friends. "So is there a ring yet?" she asked, looking down at Sierra's hand.

"Yes, but I didn't wear it tonight. We didn't want to upstage you with a public announcement—only family knows—but I had to tell you! I'm hoping you'll be my maid of honor." Sierra grinned. "If you're not *too* busy running Cupid's Bow."

"Oh, I will be such a good maid of honor," Becca vowed, touched that Sierra had asked her. "I'm very detail oriented. And I have pull. Anything you two want for the ceremony, it's done."

"See? This is why you're my favorite control freak! But honestly—" she sighed, peering through the crowd until her gaze landed on her handsome rancher "—the main thing I want for the ceremony is just to walk down the aisle to that guy right there."

As if he sensed her gaze, Jarrett glanced up from the conversation he was having with Sierra's coworker Manuel. When his eyes locked with his fiancée's, his expression became so intimately tender that Becca almost felt like a voyeur standing there. The two of them were going to be so happy together—a fairy-tale ending she could believe in.

No, what they had was better than a fairy tale. It was a partnership.

That's what I want. And yet she was used to running her own household, unaccustomed to thinking of anyone as an equal partner. She knew from her divorce that it was a risk, depending on someone and suddenly waking up one day to find they were no longer there. But for happiness like Sierra and Jarrett shared, wasn't it worth the attempt?

Sawyer smiled at his family, touched to be here sharing Sunday dinner with them for the first time in years. When he'd come home five days ago, things had been awkward at first, tentative. It had probably helped smooth the way when Sawyer declined his brother's offer to formally become part owner in the ranch.

"I appreciate it," Sawyer had said sincerely. "But this isn't where I want to be permanently. I'm still weighing options."

"Oh, thank God." Charlie had looked relieved. "Because the offer was genuine, but I still have some control-freak tendencies."

Sawyer had clapped him on the back, his smile bittersweet. "Some of my favorite people do."

Since that conversation, tensions in the house had eased considerably. And now his mother was standing, her eyes glistening with emotion, honoring him with a toast. "To Sawyer. All I've wanted was for you to make peace with your brother and father, return to the bosom of your family. And my prayers have been answered!" Smiling, she pressed a hand to her heart. "Now, are you going to leave of your own volition, or do I have to kick you out?"

He blinked. "Pardon?"

"Honey, we love having you on the ranch, and you're always welcome," she said. "But, um, isn't there somewhere else you'd rather be?"

"She means with Becca," Charlie added, "in case you're too much of a chucklehead to suss that out for yourself."

"Wh-what?"

"Oh, come on." Charlie rolled his eyes. "You've been to how many places since we saw you last, won how many rodeos? But have you been telling us about any of them? No. We keep hearing stories about your landlady and a little town called Cupid's Bow."

Even taciturn Charles Sr. spoke up. "You're obviously in love with the girl, so she must be special. McCall men don't run from commitment." The loving glance he exchanged with his wife was mirrored at the other end of the table between Charlie and Gwen.

Sawyer should have felt uncomfortable, like a fifth wheel. Instead, what he experienced was a sharp mental clarity that had eluded him since he'd left Cupid's Bow with a bruised ego and a half-assed plan to make amends with his family. He *was* being a chucklehead. Did he want to stay here, seeing Becca only in the *Cupid's Bow Clarion* articles he looked up at 3:00 a.m. like some sort of internet stalker, or did he want to admit that he should have been more patient? More understanding about her reservations? She had a child to think about and a divorce behind her; she couldn't just throw herself headlong into a relationship with a guy she'd known less than a month. The only reason Sawyer had even wanted her to was because he'd fallen so hard for her.

He turned to his older brother. "You are absolutely right."

Charlie leaned back in his chair. "You want to run that by me again?"

Sawyer laughed. "No. Once-in-a-lifetime kind of thing."

"Still… Sawyer McCall willing to say I was right. I guess miracles do happen."

Good. Because he might need one to make things right with Becca.

Saying goodbye to his family hadn't been difficult, since Sawyer didn't plan to wait so long this time before seeing them again. Still, he appreciated the few minutes of privacy with Charlie out by his truck. He had a few things he needed to say to his brother.

But Charlie was staring past him, squinting at a minivan coming down the drive. "Now, who do you suppose that is?"

Sawyer's heart turned over in his chest, thudding in wild hope. "She's here."

"Becca?" Charlie grinned, then started loping toward the house. He called over his shoulder, "Try not to screw this up, man."

Sawyer took deep breaths, but the sight of her as she climbed out of the van shook his composure. God, he'd missed her. "B-Becca?" He couldn't believe he was seeing her in person.

Her smile was crooked, endearingly uncertain. "Surprised?"

"Stunned. What are you doing here? Not that I'm unhappy to see you," he hastily added.

"I needed to talk to you—about us. If there's still a chance we can be an 'us.' Sawyer, I'm so sorry about how I handled our relationship." Guilt shone in her eyes. "I want to be with you. I want everyone in Cupid's Bow to know, which probably doesn't mean as much to you now that the election's over—"

"Are you kidding me, woman?" He reached for her, tugging her into his arms. She wanted him. Enough to track him down and drive all the way here, down unpaved roads MapQuest didn't know existed, to tell him in person. "It means more than I can put into words. My life is flexible, ungrounded. I should have recognized that, with all your responsibilities, you have to be more cautious. I pushed too hard, and I'm sorry."

He crushed her in a fierce hug. Having spent the last couple miserable weeks without her, he never wanted to let her go again. He expelled a breath that was half groan, half chuckle. "Dammit, I was going to ride back into town and sweep you off your feet, but you beat me to it." That was his Becca; she knew her own mind and took action.

She met his eyes, her gaze searching. "You aren't really annoyed I'm here, are you?"

"Hell, no. I'm annoyed at myself for letting wounded pride come between us, but mostly I just feel grateful." He wanted to kiss her with all the pent-up need and longing he felt, but was intensely aware of the witnesses no doubt crowded together at his mother's kitchen window.

Instead, he rocked back on his heels and cupped Becca's face in his hands. "I love you."

"I love you, too."

Joy welled inside him—not just happiness, but a sense of contented, soul-deep belonging. "I was serious about being on my way to see you." He jerked his chin toward the bags that sat in his truck. "I'm willing to make Cupid's Bow my home...if you're okay with that."

"There's nothing I'd like more. I should warn you, though—the attic's taken. Molly just paid me rent for the whole month. Seems wrong to kick her out."

"I wouldn't expect to live with you." Not until everyone saw how serious they were and he could get Marc's blessing on proposing to his mama. "How would that look, the mayor of Cupid's Bow moving a boy toy in so soon after the election?"

She gave him a lopsided smile. "You assume I won?"

"I believed in you, yeah, but... I looked it up online just to make sure. Congratulations, Madam Mayor. I'm proud of you." To hell with the onlookers. He *had* to kiss her.

She eagerly met him halfway, rising up on her tiptoes and clutching at his shoulders. Their fervent kiss was a celebration, a reunion, a pledge. When he finally forced himself to pull away, they were both gasping for air.

"I desperately want to get you alone," he growled, "but my family will never forgive me if I don't introduce you first."

"I want to meet them, too." Yet she hesitated, her expression endearingly vulnerable. "They just got you back. Brody said you and your brother are getting along better than you have in a decade. Will they resent my taking you away from home?"

"Home is with you." Was it too soon to say something of that magnitude?

Apparently not. She beamed at him with so much love he felt invincible. He could win every rodeo in the world and not feel anything as sweet as the triumph of knowing he'd won her heart.

Lacing his fingers through hers, he led her toward the house. "I really do like Cupid's Bow, and I've put out some feelers for jobs in the area. But the important part is that we're together. I want to be where you are, want to help you with Marc—not that you need it," he said, backpedaling.

She squeezed his hand. "Sure I do. Everyone can use *some* help, and there's no one I'd rather turn to. I need your perspective and your ability to make me laugh when I least expect it. And the way you can block out the rest of the world with your kiss," she added huskily.

He stopped, trying to recall why they had to go inside instead of ducking into the barn and frantically undressing each other.

Her cheeks grew rosy under his stare, and she attempted a breezy tone. "Plus, there's the obvious—I need you to keep me too busy to accidentally attempt global domination."

"Oh, I have some ideas about how we could occupy

your time." He raised her hand to his lips, brushing a quick kiss across her knuckles. "But, sweetheart? If you ever want to take over the world, I'll be right there beside you, cheering you on." And feeling damn lucky that she'd altered *his* world, now and forever.

* * * * *

Cathy Gillen Thacker is married and a mother of three. She and her husband spent eighteen years in Texas and now reside in North Carolina. Her mysteries, romantic comedies and heartwarming family stories have made numerous appearances on bestseller lists, but her best reward, she says, is knowing one of her books made someone's day a little brighter. A popular Harlequin author for many years, she loves telling passionate stories with happy endings and thinks nothing beats a good romance and a hot cup of tea! You can visit Cathy's website, cathygillenthacker.com, for more information on her upcoming and previously published books, recipes and a list of her favorite things.

Books by Cathy Gillen Thacker

Harlequin Special Edition

Texas Legends: The McCabes

The Texas Cowboy's Quadruplets

Harlequin Western Romance

Texas Legends: The McCabes

The Texas Cowboy's Triplets
The Texas Cowboy's Baby Rescue

Texas Legacies: The Lockharts

A Texas Soldier's Family
A Texas Cowboy's Christmas
The Texas Valentine Twins
Wanted: Texas Daddy
A Texas Soldier's Christmas

Visit the Author Profile page
at Harlequin.com for more titles.

HIS BABY BARGAIN

Cathy Gillen Thacker

Chapter 1

"I told you. I'm not doing it."

Sara Anderson stared at the ex-soldier standing on the other side of the half-demolished pasture fence. Matt McCabe had come back from his tour in the Middle East eighteen months ago and, despite the efforts of family and friends to draw him out, had seemed to go deeper into his self-imposed solitude every day.

This kind of moody isolation wasn't good, even for a newly minted Laramie County rancher.

Hadn't she learned that the hard way?

Heaven knew she wasn't going to willingly allow another similar tragedy to happen again. And especially not to someone she'd once been close to, growing up. Not if she could possibly help it, anyway. And she was determined that she could.

Shivering a little in the cool March air, Sara stepped

around the heaps of old metal posts and rusting barbed wire strewn across the empty pasture. She plastered an engaging smile on her face while taking in his handsome profile and tall, muscular physique. With his square jaw and gorgeously chiseled features, Matt had always been mesmerizing. Even when, like now, he did not put much effort into his appearance. His clothes were old, clean and rumpled. Boots scuffed and coated with mud.

The dark brown hair peeking out from under the brim of his black Resistol was a little on the long side, curling across his brow and over his ears, down the nape of his neck. And though he had clearly showered that morning, he hadn't shaved in days. All of which, combined, gave him a hopelessly rugged, masculine look.

The kind that set her heart racing.

And shouldn't have.

Given the fact she had definitely not come here to flirt or see where the age-old attraction between them would lead. An attraction they hadn't ever dared to explore, even in their reckless high school days.

Sara drew a breath. Tried again. Picking up the conversation where they'd left off.

"And I told you—" with effort, she held his stormy gray-blue eyes "—I'm not giving up." She was determined to enlist his help…and save him along the way.

With a scoff, Matt swaggered away from her, his strides long and lazy. He bent to pick up the pieces of a wood fence post scattered across the field, then tossed them into the bed of his battered Silver Creek Ranch pickup truck. "Well, you should retreat," he advised over one broad, chambray-clad shoulder. His dark brow lifted in a warning that set her pulse racing all the more. "'Cause I'm not changing my mind."

Like heck he wasn't!

Sara put on her most persuasive smile and stalked through the knee-high grass and the Texas wildflowers getting ready to bloom. "Never say never," she warned cheerfully. Especially when she had set her mind to something this important.

Matt pushed back the brim of his hat with his index finger. Brazenly looked her up and down in a way that heated her flesh, head to toe. "And why is that?" he challenged softly.

Sara focused on the nonprofit organization and the ex-soldiers she was helping. Her actions every bit as deliberate as his, she moved closer still. "Because if you ever deign to meet him, you just might fall in love with Champ, the remaining black Lab puppy from the latest West Texas Warriors Association's litter." She certainly had. Not that she was signing up to train a service dog. Not when she would soon be going back to work as a large-animal veterinarian and had a six-month-old son to raise.

Matt folded his arms across his muscular chest and let out a sigh that reverberated through his entire six-foot-three-inch frame. "Good thing I'm not planning on visiting the puppy, then."

Time to play the guilt card, and appeal to the legendary McCabe chivalry. "You're seriously opposed to helping out other returning military veterans in need of a therapy dog?"

Irritation darkened his eyes and he pressed his sensual lips into a thin, hard line. "Of course not." He gestured offhandedly. "Just tell me where to send the check and..."

She held up a staying palm. "We've got money, Matt." At least for the needs of the current litters. "What we *need* are more hands-on trainers to help socialize the puppies."

His expression grew even more impatient. "Well, that's not me," he countered curtly. "Haven't you heard? I'm not exactly a dog person these days."

Actually, she had learned he'd become mysteriously averse to pets. Which was strange. When they'd grown up together, there hadn't been an animal who didn't automatically gravitate to the personable cowboy with the exquisitely gentle touch.

Deciding to call him out on this—and anything else that needed to be challenged—she scoffed, "Oh yeah. Since when?" What had happened to him in the time he'd been away from Laramie County? That had made him decide to clear a two thousand acre ranch, all on his own?

Their eyes met, held. For a moment, the years of near estrangement faded and she thought he might answer, but the opportunity passed, with nary a word.

Matt squinted right back at her. Shrugged. "I've got a question, too, darlin'." Deliberately, he stepped into her personal space. "When did *you* get so darned pesky?"

The endearment, coupled with the insult, worked just as Matt hoped.

Sara's slender shoulders stiffened and she drew herself up to her full five feet, nine inches. She glared at him resentfully. "I've always been extremely helpful and forthright!"

He grunted and reached for the metal cutters. Walking along the fence, he snipped through the lengths of rusting barbed wire. Irritated to find she was still fast on his heels.

"Is that what they're calling your do-gooding these days?" He slanted a glance at her, and noted the way the breeze was plastering the soft knit of her sweater against her delectable breasts. Ignoring the hardening of his body, he turned his gaze back to her face. "And here I was thinking you were just bossy and interfering."

She dug her boots into the hard ground beneath them and propped both her hands on her denim-clad hips. "I go where I'm needed, Matt."

The fact she, like so many others close to him, apparently saw him as a charity case rankled. Gathering up the wire, he walked back to toss it into the bed of his pickup truck alongside the stack of weathered metal posts. "I don't remember calling for a large-animal vet."

She continued shadowing him, getting close enough he could inhale the lilac of her perfume. "Then I guess it's your lucky day," she announced. "Me, showing up here—"

"Uninvited," he turned to point out.

She held her ground. "—and all."

This ornery woman had no idea who she was playing with. "Uh-huh." Matt moved closer, drinking in her fair skin and sun-blushed cheeks. Damn, she was pretty, standing there in the spring sunlight. Her cloud of golden-blond hair drifting across her shoulders and framing the delicate features of her face.

In an effort to further repel her, he let his gaze move lower, to the lithe build of her body. From her dainty feet and long sexy legs, to her slender waist and the lush fullness of her breasts, she was all woman.

Still enjoying the view immensely, he returned his focus to the elegance of her lips, cheeks and nose. The jade depths of her eyes. "Sure you're in the right place? Talking to the right ex-soldier?"

"Definitely." She trod even closer and tilted her chin up to his. "And believe it or not, I'm strong enough to handle you, cowboy."

"Sure about that?" Matt asked gruffly, wishing he hadn't noticed how feminine and perfect she was. All over.

"Yes," she repeated.

Funny. She hadn't seemed strong when she'd lost her husband a little over a year before. She'd seemed vulnerable. Achingly so.

To the point, every time he'd run into her, he'd been tempted to take her in his arms and hold her close. Not as the platonic friends they'd once been in their high school days. But as an ex-soldier comforting another ex-soldier's wife.

There were several problems with that. First, he'd already gone down that route before—and learned the hard way that any relationship based on rebound emotions was a huge mistake.

And second, she was so damn pretty and accomplished these days, he knew he'd never be able to leave it at that. Holding Sara close would make him want things he couldn't have and had no business wanting.

Because, thanks to the mistakes he'd made and the guilt he still harbored, having a wife or a family of his own was no longer in the cards for him.

Clearly misunderstanding the reason behind his long

pause, Sara pleated her brow. She looked at him more closely, then queried cautiously, "Really, Matt? You seriously *doubt* my inner strength?"

"No," he conceded honestly. "You're as feisty as they come."

"Feisty," she said, repeating the term distastefully. "Really."

He grinned, thrilled to be getting under her skin.

It was that friction that would help keep them apart.

Watching the color come into her high, sculpted cheeks, he removed his hat and let it fall idly against his thigh. "Don't like the term?"

Her pretty green eyes narrowing, she watched him run his fingers through his hair. "It's condescending!"

He settled his Resistol squarely back on his head. "Yeah?" he retorted sardonically. "In what way?" Because she was feisty and then some. Always had been.

Oblivious to how much he liked her spirit, Sara let out a lengthy sigh. "In the sense that *feisty* is an adjective usually attached to a female or small animal one would *not* expect to defend itself."

He rolled his eyes at her deliberately haughty tone. "Spoken like a veterinarian," he said. Then seeing a way to needle her further, added, "A *woman* veterinarian."

Now she was spitting mad. She planted her hands on her hips again. "You just keep digging yourself in deeper, don't you, cowboy?"

He shrugged in a way designed to rankle her even more. "Hey. If it annoys you, maybe you should leave." He went back to pull up some more aging fence posts.

"Not until you at least agree to come to my ranch and see the puppy."

He turned so suddenly she nearly slammed into him.

He inhaled another whiff of her lilac perfume. "Why me?" he asked as his gaze drifted over her fitted suede jacket and dark, figure-hugging jeans. "Instead of someone else a hell of a lot more amenable?"

Sara sighed and folded her arms beneath her breasts, her action plumping them up all the more. "Because we need more veterans actively involved in helping other returning military personnel," she stated softly, her breasts rising and falling with each agitated breath.

He rocked back on the heels of his worn leather work boots. "Isn't that the mission of the West Texas Warriors Association?" Of which, he knew, there were hundreds of members.

Her expression turned even more serious. "We need everyone, Matt."

He rejected her attempt to make him feel guilty for not wanting to dive back into the world of his nightmares. "I don't think so."

She glowered at him. "Why not?"

"I like my solitude."

She made a face and then, to his mounting frustration, tried again. "Listen to me, Matt," she beseeched, hands outstretched. Her gentle eyes filled with compassion. "I know how hard it was for Anthony to really reconnect after he came back to civilian life..."

So, the rumors about her late husband's unhappiness...and maybe hers, too...were true.

He scowled, not sure why the comparison bothered him so much. "I'm not your late husband, Sara."

She acknowledged that with a nod, then pushed on despite his gruff, unwelcoming tone. "Working with dogs can help alleviate PTSD-related depression and anxiety."

Now what is she trying to infer? "Do tell," he prodded.

She tilted her head to one side and offered a tantalizing smile. "Who knows?" Another shrug. "It might help right your temperamental attitude, too."

Not sure whether he wanted to haul her close and kiss her, or demand she leave *now*, he sent her a censuring look. "Thanks, but I've got my bad moods covered, Sara."

She huffed, her eyes narrowing all the more. "Spending all your time alone?"

"Making the Silver Creek Ranch a cash-generating enterprise," he corrected.

Sara seemed unimpressed. "By tearing down tons of trees and ripping down sections of old fence?"

He went back to snipping barbed wire. "First of all, the fence is so old it's a hazard. Second, Texas barbecue restaurants need either oak or mesquite. And I've got plenty of both."

Sara tapped one boot-clad foot impatiently. "And then what? When you clear-cut all this land?"

She sounded like his folks. Constantly complaining that whatever he was doing wasn't enough.

He yanked out a rusting metal post and added it to the pile on the ground. "I'm going to plow the weeds and sow some grass. Put up new pasture fence and lease out the land to my brother Cullen so he can run some of his cattle here."

Giving him room to work, she took a moment to consider that. Probably finally realizing he did indeed have a business plan.

"Not planning to buy any of your own?" she asked eventually.

He shook his head. The last thing he wanted was to

be responsible for another living thing—person or animal. "Did enough cattle herding growing up."

That, she did seem to understand. It didn't mean she let up. Her gorgeous honey-blond hair blowing in the spring breeze, she followed him down the fence line. "You know, you could do all this a lot faster if you hired some help. Or even enlisted some of your family members and friends."

Her unsolicited advice irked him. He turned and studied the guileless look in her eyes. "Don't want me to be alone, huh, darlin'?"

She pursed her lips in a worried frown. "I don't think it's healthy and neither does your family, Matt."

So now they were finally getting down to it, he thought wearily.

She stepped closer, once again invading his space.

Her soft, feminine voice took on a persuasive lilt. "Your mom came to see me. She thought maybe I could talk you into rejoining the community again."

Matt shook his head at Sara's naïveté. His mom hoped for a lot more than occasionally getting him off the Silver Creek spread. "She only did that because..."

Sara beamed, turning on the full wattage of her neighborly charm. "What?"

He edged closer. "She knows I'm attracted to you."

She laughed in disbelief, the ambivalent sound filling the air between them. Her lower lip took on a kissable pout. "You're just saying that to get me to leave."

He surveyed her indignant expression. Leaned in closer. "Is it working?"

The look in her eyes grew turbulent. "No."

He dropped his head. "Then how about this?" he taunted softly, taking her in his arms.

Rather than step away, she put her hand on the center of his chest, and gave him a small, purposeful shove.

That sent him exactly nowhere.

"No." She glared at him heatedly. "But nice try, cowboy."

He reluctantly let her go and stepped back, his own temper flaring. "Then maybe you should rethink this plan you and my mom cooked up. Because I'm not the guy who's going to treat you with kid gloves, darlin'." And he was pretty sure, at the end of the day, that was what Sara wanted.

Her eyes narrowed. "I don't want you to treat me with kid gloves."

He came back to her, took her in his arms again and lowered his lips, just above hers.

Damn, if she didn't make him feel ornery.

He smiled as she caught her breath. "Sure about that?" He rubbed the pad of his thumb across her lower lip.

Her brows furrowed as she began to see where this standoff between them was likely headed. "Yes," she said, stubborn as ever, trembling even as she held her ground.

Loving the delicate feel of her body so close to his, he asked, "Really sure?"

"Completely sure," she taunted right back. "In fact, cowboy," she went on to dare in spunky delight, "you could *kiss* me and—"

The gauntlet had been thrown down between them.

Matt never gave her a chance to blurt out the rest.

His mouth touched hers, laying claim to every sweet soft inch. Only, the indignant slap he expected—the one that would have heralded his immediate gentlemanly release of her, and her quick, fiery exit—never came.

Sara told herself to resist the sensual feel of his lips moving over hers. But her body refused to listen to the wary dictates of her heart. She had been numb inside for so long. Responsive only to the needs of her adorable infant son.

Now, suddenly, she was alive in a way she had never expected to be again. The yearning to be touched, held, appreciated for the woman she was came roaring back. Made her tingle all over. Opening her lips to his, she pressed closer to the unyielding hardness of his chest, and, lower still, felt his undeniable heat and building desire. With a low moan of surrender, she went up on tiptoe, wreathed her arms about his neck and tilted her head to give him deeper access. He uttered a low moan of approval. His tongue twined with hers. He brought her nearer still, delivering a kiss that scored her soul. Left her limp with longing and trembling with acquiescence. Her middle fluttering, she melted against him. And then all was lost, as she experienced the masculine force that was Matt. For the first time in her life, she was with a man who didn't hesitate to give her the complete physicality she craved and had always longed to explore. Excitement roaring through her, she reveled in the thrill of his commanding embrace. The hard, insistent pressure of his kiss, and the tantalizing sweep of his tongue; for the very first time in her life, she experienced the temptation to surrender herself completely. Forget her worries about the future. Live only in the moment she was in.

Had her life not already been so complicated—full of

the grief and guilt she still felt for not doing as much as she could have, or should have, when she'd still had the chance—and had she not intuited that Matt's own private world was much the same as hers and her husband's had once been, who knew what might have happened had their make-out session continued on this brisk and sunny spring day?

But they did both harbor secrets and heartache.

And combining the two would only risk further hurt. For her, for him, for her baby boy.

So she did what she should have done all along, and finally put her hand on the center of his chest and tore her lips from his.

Just that quickly, Matt let her go.

They stared at each other, breathing hard. To her surprise, he looked every bit as shaken as she felt.

Compelled to save them both and downplay this, however, she took another step back. Gave a hapless shrug, looked into his eyes and said, "Just so you know, cowboy, you're not the first man who's made a move on me since Anthony died."

He was the first one who'd made her feel something, though. Too much, actually. Way too much.

Emotion warred with the skepticism in his eyes. "Trying to make me feel competitive?"

No! Heck, no! Sara thought, chagrined. "I'm just saying," she returned as calmly as possible, "I wasn't interested then. And I'm not interested now."

The corners of his lips turned up as his gaze raked her luxuriantly, head to toe. "Your kisses just said otherwise, darlin'."

Once again, she shook her head. Embarrassed. Humiliated. And worst of all, still wildy turned on. Swallowing around the ache in her throat, she held his eyes deliberately and corrected him. "My kisses said I'm human, Matt." *Human and oh so lonely, deep down. So ready to get out of my own misery and help someone else in need. Like you, Matt. And how crazy is that?*

She waited a moment to let her words sink in. Then said, "As are we all."

It didn't mean she had to be a fool for a second time.

And especially not with the far too irresistible Matt McCabe.

Chapter 2

"Is this a good time?" Matt asked, from the porch of Sara's Blue Vista Ranch house the following Saturday afternoon.

For you, Matt McCabe, Sara thought, still reeling from the hot, audacious kisses he had delivered the last time they'd seen each other, *there will never be a good time. Not ever again.*

But not about to let him know how much he had affected her, or how often and passionately she'd thought of him over the last week, she merely looked him up and down.

The reality was, he was the last person she had expected to see standing on her doorstep, given how acrimoniously they had last parted.

But here he was, as mouthwateringly handsome as ever. Looking mighty fine in a blue button-down shirt that made the most of his brawny shoulders and rock-solid abs. New jeans that did equally appetizing things to his long, muscular legs and hips, and shiny brown boots. He'd shaved and showered, too, although his thick, wavy dark brown hair was just as unruly as she'd come to expect. His dark gray-blue eyes just as wryly challenging.

"Depends on why you're here," she replied tartly, wishing she were clad in something other than a peach tunic and white yoga pants stained with drool and baby formula. She looked down her nose at him, pausing to make sure he knew just how unwelcome he was. "If it's to pick up where we left off last week..."

His sensual lips lifted into a tantalizing smile. Excitement lit his eyes. "Kissing you?"

She flushed at the memory of his delicious body pressed against hers, his lips stirring up needs best forgotten. She was a widow, after all. Determined to never make the mistake of turning her heart over to a man again.

Never mind the strong, silent, stubborn type.

"Arguing."

He chuckled and ran a hand across his jaw. A wicked grin deepened the crinkles around his eyes. "Is that what we were doing?" he drawled, tilting his head.

So she wasn't the only one who'd been remembering! Huffing in aggravation, Sara folded her arms tightly in front of her. "Let's just say our discussion made me realize you and I will *never* be on the same page, McCabe." And she refused to chase after lost causes, so...

An infant wail went up from somewhere behind her. Sara tensed in distress and lifted a staying hand.

Saved by the baby.

"Hang on a minute." She rushed off to gather up her son and returned with the red-faced infant in her arms, ready to direct Matt on his way. Instead, she found him looking down at her little boy with surprising interest.

"This Charley?" Matt asked tenderly, taking in her son's sturdy little body, cherubic features and shock of fine blond hair. The long-lashed eyes that had started out blue and were now more dark green.

Surprised, Sara asked, "You know his name?"

Matt shrugged as he and Charley locked gazes and the infant momentarily stopped crying, then ever so slowly began to smile. "I know a lot of things," he murmured.

Charley reached for Matt, and when Matt offered his hand, the baby latched on tight to the tall cowboy's pinky.

In the same soothing tone that would have done a baby wrangler proud, Matt continued, "Including the fact you've told everyone to give up on ever getting me involved in the West Texas Warrior Association's therapy-puppy raising program."

Sara had indeed put out the word.

Figuring there was no reason to stand in the doorway while they talked, she ushered him in. He shut the door dutifully behind them. "And that bothers you because…?"

Sara perched on the edge of the living room sofa, a little embarrassed by the mess around them. She settled Charley on her lap, while Matt—who still had his hand linked in Charley's little fist—settled next to them.

Exhaling, the handsome cowboy looked deep into her eyes. "Since you talked to my mom, every member of my family has come out to the Silver Creek to see me."

Glad to see the indomitable Matt off-kilter for once, Sara grinned. "What's the matter, cowboy?" she teased, knowing there wasn't a finer group than Rachel and Frank McCabe and their offspring. "Don't like family?"

Appearing more besotted than ever of the tall rugged man with the deep, soothing voice, Charley reached up to hold on to Matt with both of his little hands.

Matt grinned down at her son, looking happier than Sara could recall in a long, long time.

Apparently realizing he hadn't answered her question, Matt let out a long exhalation of breath, then turned his attention back to her once again. "I love 'em," he said, before adding, "when they're minding their own business."

Sara regarded him pensively. She understood that. She had two college-professor parents and five older brothers who'd been in her business for years. Fortunately, all of them were now scattered across the country, busy living their own lives. And though she could have relocated next to any of them after Anthony died, she had chosen to stay on the small ranch where they had hoped to bring up Charley.

Part of that had been because she still considered the rural Texas county where she had grown up home, and hadn't wanted the stress of finding another job at another veterinary practice and another place to live.

The rest had to do with her not wanting to clue any of them in on the private misery she'd been unable to share with anyone. Least of all those who might have judged her for not being the kind of wife she should have been.

But her own heartache had nothing to do with Matt's problems now. She settled Charley a little more comfortably on her lap and drew a breath. "I get you have a problem, McCabe, but I don't see where I come in."

Charley finally let go of Matt's finger.

Matt got up and paced over to the fireplace, stood with his back to it, admitting gruffly, "The problem is they're not going to give up on what they want for me."

Sara saw where that would be a problem for a man who professed to only want to be left alone. She bit her lip, acutely aware that things were getting way too intimate between them again, way too fast. "What? Can't kiss them to make them go away?" she quipped.

He let out a belly laugh.

At the low masculine sound, so foreign in Sara's small cottage-style bungalow, Charley's brows knit together. He began to cry again, so heartrendingly this time it was all Sara could do to swallow the lump in her throat.

First she had failed as a wife. And now, this…

Matt frowned in alarm.

Sara's lack of sleep made her own eyes well, too. She stood and began to walk the floor with Charley, jostling him a little as she moved in the hopes that the slight, swaying motion would soothe him. It did not.

"What's wrong with him?" Matt asked.

That was the bitter irony. "I don't know." And as his mother, she certainly should have. She rocked him back and forth.

Matt strode closer, his handsome features etched with tenderness. He lifted his hand to Charley. This time, the baby howled all the louder and batted Matt's palm away.

"Then why is he so fussy?" Matt had to speak up to be heard over the wailing.

Sara arched a brow, irritated to have him constantly finding ways to make her feel off balance, not to mention seeming more inept than she already was. "If I knew that, do you really think he'd still be crying?" she demanded.

Ignoring her pique, Matt gently touched her son's cheek, as if checking for fever. Again, Charley batted his hand away.

Taking the cue, Matt backed off. "Is he sick?"

Glad to have someone to share her concern with, Sara shifted Charley to her other shoulder. She continued gently soothing him, as best she could. Looking over his blond head at Matt, she admitted, "I thought he might be since he's so cranky and doesn't want to eat, but he doesn't have any fever. He's not pulling at his ears the way he did when he had an ear infection, either."

"Is his throat red?" Matt asked, while Charley warmed to the audience and wailed even louder.

Was this what it would be like to have someone big and strong and male to share the parenting duties with? Telling herself she was really losing it, Sara pushed the ridiculous notion away. "I can't answer that, either. I haven't been able to get a good look." And in fact, she had been considering going into the emergency pediatric clinic in town, if this went on much longer.

Matt pointed out, "His mouth is open now."

Figuring as long as she had help she might as well use it, she retrieved the flashlight she kept on the kitchen counter. Then turned back to Matt. "You want to hold him?"

For the first time, Matt hesitated.

"Listen, cowboy, either be part of the solution or leave. Because I don't need any more problems today."

From the pen in the corner of the living room, Champ, the nine-week-old black Labrador puppy Sara had been trying to get Matt to help socialize, lifted his head and began to jump up against the three-foot wooden sides of the whelping pen, in rhythm to Charley's wails.

Matt turned in the direction of the noise. He locked eyes on the puppy.

And in that instant, Sara knew.

Matt wasn't a dog person.

Not in the slightest.

Not anymore.

Matt swore silently to himself as he clamped down on the memories he worked so hard to quash.

When he'd set out for Sara's ranch, he'd figured he would see her baby. He'd even been sort of looking forward to it. Why, he couldn't exactly say.

He hadn't figured she'd have one of the pups from the litter there. But she did and as the puppy continued whimpering with excitement and trying to climb over the sides, it was all he could do not to break out into an ice-cold sweat.

Over a harmless little black Lab pup, of all things.

"Matt?" Sara's hand was on his arm. Her tone as gentle as it was inquiring.

"Sorry," he rasped, turning his back to the rambunctious retriever. "I'll hold Charley while you try and get a look at your son's throat."

Ignoring the stuff of his nightmares, Matt held out his arms. Sara shifted her son over. Oblivious to Matt's private grief come to life, Charley wailed even louder.

Whatever questions she had—and she seemed to have plenty—could wait.

On task once again, Sara cupped her son's chin in her hand and shined the flashlight in that direction. While the puppy gave up trying to escape, opting instead to pick up a squeaky toy and then roll happily around with it in the pen, Charley twisted his head to the side, buried his head in Matt's chest and firmly clamped his lips shut.

Sara seemed even more nonplussed.

"Why don't you hold him? I'll look," Matt said.

Nodding in frustration, Sara set the flashlight down and took Charley back in her arms. The moment she had him, he glared at her, as if he blamed *her* for whatever was bothering him, and began to howl again, even more vociferously.

Matt hunched so he was at eye level with Charley—and trained the light low, so it only hit the lower half of her son's face. He surveyed the back of his throat. "Looks fine," Matt said in surprise. The way Charley was carrying on, he'd expected to find it beet red. "A healthy normal pink."

"No spots? Even on the roof of his mouth? Red or white?"

Matt looked again, as Charley began to cry in earnest once again. "Not a one."

"Oh, Charley, honey, what's wrong?" Sara said, swaying her little boy back and forth.

Noting the puppy was now drinking water, and vastly relieved his own unexpected memories were now subsiding, Matt whipped out his phone. "How old is Charley?"

Sara shifted her son onto her shoulder and walked

over to the puppy pen. She reached down to give Champ another toy to occupy him. Turning back to face Matt, said, "He turned six months old ten days ago."

Figuring the sooner he was able to get out of there, the better, he punched in a number.

Sara came closer, a still-whimpering Charley cradled in her arms. As she attempted to see what he was doing, her shoulder bumped up against the center of his chest. "Who are you calling?"

"Cullen's wife, Bridgett."

His brother's wife was a neonatal nurse at Laramie Community Hospital, and a mother to a one-year-old boy, with another child on the way. Luckily, she answered right away. "Hey," he said. "I'm at Sara Anderson's ranch, and we've got a little problem..."

While Matt described what was going on, Sara carried Charley into the kitchen and got a bottle of apple juice out of the fridge. She offered it to the baby. Still sniffling, he took it in his chubby little hands, put it in his mouth and started to sip, then let out another wail and pushed it away.

Matt came back. He hated to pry, but Bridgett needed to know if she was to help. "Are you still nursing?"

As he spoke, his eyes slid to her breasts. Although it was a natural reaction on his part, Sara flushed self-consciously.

"I switched him to formula when I had the flu last month."

Averting his glance, Matt relayed that, too.

By the time he'd turned back to her, Sara had composed herself once again. "Bridgett said to check his gums to see if they are red or swollen or if there is any sign of a tooth pushing through. She said sometimes they can teethe for a few days or weeks before the tooth actually shows."

Sara ventured a look, but Charley pressed his lips shut again. With maternal resolve, she eased the tip of her index fingertip along the seam of his lips, trying to gently persuade him to open up. Eventually he did. Just enough so she could get her finger between his gums.

With a scowl, Charley clamped down tight.

"Ouch!" Sara winced in surprise.

"Feel a tooth?"

"No." She shifted Charley a little higher in her arms, so they were face-to-face. Now that he'd bitten her, he was beginning to look a little more content. Satisfied he'd gotten his point across, maybe? Matt wondered.

"But," she mused as she pulled his lower lip down, "his gum does look a tiny bit swollen here on the bottom. Right here in the middle."

Matt relayed the information then said, "Bridgett wants to talk to you." He set his cell phone aside while he eased Charley from her arms. "I can't believe I didn't even think of that," Sara told his sister-in-law.

He walked the little boy back and forth, while the two women talked. Eventually, Sara hung up. She walked into the kitchen and took a children's medical kit from the cupboard. "Bridgett said their son Robby's first tooth caught them by surprise, too."

"I remember."

"She said to try numbing medicine."

"Hear that, little guy? Your mommy is going to fix you right up."

Charley lounged against his broad chest. Tears still gleaming damply on his cheeks, he gazed up at Matt adoringly. Sara turned back to Matt as she worked the protective seal off the numbing cream. "You're good with little ones," she remarked.

He shrugged, aware that was a talent he came by naturally. "You know the McCabes. Lots of little ones around. Seems like someone is always putting a baby in my arms."

Sara regarded him skeptically. "You could say no," she pointed out wryly.

Lately, he usually did. Trying not to wonder why he hadn't in this particular case, Matt shrugged again and turned his attention to sparring with his old friend. "Actually, darlin'," he drawled, "I believe I do refuse things every now and again." He lifted his brow, reminding. "Like your repeated requests to recruit me for the therapy-puppy training program?"

She came close enough to rub a little medicine on Charley's gum. Her son wrinkled his nose, too surprised to protest. As the moment drew out, Charley's jaw relaxed and his little shoulders slumped in relief.

So his mouth had been hurting, Matt thought. Poor little fella.

Without warning, Charley held out his arms to his mommy. Reluctantly, Matt transferred the little boy, surprised to find how bereft he felt when he was no longer holding him.

Wordlessly, he watched Sara cuddle her baby boy. They were the picture of bliss. Enough to make him want, just for one ill-advised second, a wife and child of his own to love and care for…

Sara tossed him a wry glance. "Speaking of the WTWA therapy-puppy raising program…if you gave yourself half a chance, I bet you would be really good with our puppies, too."

Just like that, his genial mood faded. "No," he said firmly. "I won't."

Once again, Matt noted, he had disappointed Sara. Deeply.

Seeing the puppy circling in the pen, Sara handed Charley back to Matt and rushed to pick up the sleek little black Lab. She carried him outside to the grass next to her ranch house.

"Then why are you here, if not to volunteer to train a puppy as I asked?"

Matt positioned Charley so he could see outward, and then held him against his chest, one of his forearms acting as the seat for the baby's diaper-clad bottom, the other serving as a safety harness across his tiny chest.

He shrugged. "I wanted to give money. You said you needed more volunteers, especially military. I want to *fund* an effort to recruit and train more puppy handlers."

He expected her to immediately jump at his offer. She didn't.

"For someone who has been adamantly opposed to becoming involved in any way with the therapy and service dog program, this is quite the turnaround," Sara stated, looking him up and down with the same savvy she'd exhibited in years past. "What's the catch?"

Of course she would figure out he had an ulterior motive. Matt proposed, "You let my family know that I've become 'involved' so they'll stop haranguing me."

Sara sent a glance heavenward. "I'm not sure they'll consider writing a check *involved*, cowboy." She mimicked his deadpan tone. "But you do have a good idea.

Especially if we were to combine the recruiting efforts with the first annual WTWA service-dog reunion picnic we're hosting in a few weeks."

Aware that sounded like more than he could handle, without triggering a whole new slew of nightmares, Matt lifted his hand. "Listen, I'll help out with anything that needs to be done organizationally…"

Her eyes glittering with disappointed, Sara seemed to guess where this was going. "But you still don't want to help in the hands-on socialization of Champ."

"No." Aware the pup had finished peeing and was hopping around his feet, begging to be picked up, Matt steadfastly ignored him. "Not my thing."

Sara picked up a ball and threw it, then watched Champ bound off to retrieve it. "What's happened to you? I don't remember you having an aversion to animals growing up."

The truth was he hadn't.

"Did you get bit or attacked by a dog or something?"

Once again she knew him too well. Despite the time that had elapsed since they'd been friends.

"No."

She peered at him in concern. "Lose one you cared about so deeply that you can't bear to be around another?"

Comforted by the feel of Charley snuggled up against him, Matt pushed away the unwanted emotions welling up inside of him. "I told you. I don't have the patience to train a puppy."

"Really?" she echoed skeptically. "Because you seem to have a lot of patience with my son." Her gaze drifted over him and Charley before she tossed the ball again.

He turned his attention to the close fit of her white

yoga pants over her spectacular legs, and felt his body harden. "It's different."

She continued to study him as Champ raced off.

His gaze drifted up to her peach knit tunic top. The fit was looser, but it still did a nice job of showing off her luscious breasts and trim midriff. He liked the half-moon necklace and matching earrings she wore, too.

In fact, liked everything about her. Maybe too much.

"Something's going on with you," she persisted.

He cut her off brusquely. Not about to go down that path. "I don't have PTSD, if that's what you're inferring."

She regarded him with steely intent. "Sure about that? I heard your last tour was pure hell. That's why you quit the army when your commitment was up."

He shrugged. "I came back. I'm alive."

Another telling lift of her delicate brow.

"Maybe the question, then, is," she countered softly, "who didn't?"

Again, right on point.

Silence fell.

Wondering if it would always be like this between them—her challenging, him resisting—he said nothing more.

The puppy came over, panting. Sara gathered him in her arms. "Time to eat, buddy."

Matt followed her inside. Figuring it was his turn to question her on her choices, he said, "I'm surprised you took on a puppy when you already have your hands full with Charley."

She filled a food bowl and set it back inside the whelping pen, next to the water bowl and the puppy. "I didn't plan to, but Alyssa Barnes, the soldier who was going to raise Champ and help with his training, had a setback." She straightened and went to the sink to wash her hands, then came back to him and took Charley in her arms.

"She's going to be in the hospital another week, and then a rehab facility here in Laramie for about twenty-one days after that," she explained. "But she still wants to do it, and I'm not about to take that away from her, when this is all she's been looking forward to. And since you wouldn't even consider helping me, cowboy, even on a short-term basis, I volunteered myself."

Guilt flooded Matt. Along with the surprising need to have her understand where he was coming from. He trod closer, appreciating the sight of Charley nestled contentedly against her breasts. Noting how sweet they looked, he spread his hands wide. "Look, it's not that I'm selfish or heartless." He drew a deep breath and confessed what he had yet to admit to anyone else. "I just don't want to be around dogs, okay?" Even one as technically cute and lively as little Champ.

She settled Charley in his high chair, persistent as ever. "And again I have to ask… Why is that, Matt? What's changed?"

Annoyed, he watched her snap a bib around Charley's neck. Wishing he didn't want to haul her against him and kiss her again. Never more so than when they sparred.

Working to keep his emotional distance, he let his glance sift over her in a way he knew annoyed her, then challenged, "Why do you care?"

Especially after she'd already told everyone she was giving up on him. And walking away…

A fact that had somehow irked him.

"I don't know." She plucked a banana from the bunch. Looked over at him and sighed. "Maybe it's because I feel disrespected by you."

Disrespected! "In what sense?" He'd come here to extend the olive branch. Not drive her away with bad behavior the way he had a week ago. And yet here they were, bringing out the worst in each other…again…

Setting the peeled banana on a plate, she frowned and said, "In the sense that people tend to not tell me sad or upsetting stories since Anthony died." She raked a hand through her hair, pushing it off her face. "It's as if they're afraid that I'm so fragile, if they say or do the wrong thing, they'll push me over the edge."

He lounged against the counter, opposite Charley. He empathized with her. "I'm familiar with the walking-on-eggshells part."

She wheeled her son's high chair closer to the breakfast table, sat down and began to mash the fruit with a fork. "Then you can also understand my frustration at having apparently been tasked with getting your help and yet simultaneously been cut out of the loop. Because there is clearly something more going on here than what I'd been told."

He could see she felt blindsided, when all she'd been trying to do was help. The wounded vet, Alyssa Barnes. Him. Champ. And in that sense, he did owe her. So…he drew up a chair on the other side of Charley, sat down and said, "You want to know what happened?"

She nodded, expression tense.

Matt gulped. "I saw a dog get blown up right in front of me." *And worse...* "His death was my fault."

Chapter 3

Sara stared at Matt, hardly able to comprehend what he had just said. "And your family knows you were a part of such a terrible tragedy?" she asked, aghast. Or more horrifying still, that he felt *personally* responsible?

His expression closed and inscrutable, Matt watched her begin to feed her son. "I'm not really sure what they know."

Sara spooned up a bit of mashed banana from Charley's chin. "But you haven't told them," she ascertained quietly.

As he exhaled, his broad shoulders tensed, then relaxed. "It would freak my mom and dad out to know how close I came to dying. So no, I didn't give them any specifics other than what was reported in the news. That our base was hit by suicide bombers in the middle of the night. And there were no injuries or fatalities among our soldiers."

Thank heaven for that, she thought. Resisting the urge to jump up and hug him fiercely *only* because she thought such a move would be rejected, she asked, "Was it a bomb-sniffing dog who saved you?"

"No," Matt said hoarsely. "Mutt was one of a half dozen strays we picked up over there and took in."

Sara caught the note of raw emotion in his voice. She slanted Matt another empathetic glance, then rose and got two bottles of water from the fridge. "The army lets you do that?"

He tilted his head. "It depends on the commanding officer and the situation." Matt relaxed when Charley turned and grinned at him. He stuck out his hand, and Charley latched on to his palm, banging it up and down on the tray. "Our CO thought having dogs around was good for morale. Reminded us of home. Gave us something other than the war to think about."

Sara could see that. Relieved that he was finally confiding in her, she walked back to join Matt and her son at the breakfast table.

"So he let us keep them and train them, but no one person was allowed to adopt any one dog. The deal was the pets belonged to the unit, and we had to rotate their care," Matt related. "Anyone who was interested could sign up, and on the day and night you were assigned, you fed and walked a dog, and got to sleep with that particular dog next to your bunk."

Sara knew full well the healing power of animals. "Sounds nice." Their fingers brushed when she handed him his water.

For the briefest of seconds, Matt leaned into her touch. "It was."

Still tingling from the casual contact, Sara uncapped

her water, took a sip, then resumed feeding Charley. She needed to hear the rest of the story, as much as Matt needed to tell it. "So what happened to make you feel responsible for Mutt's death?"

Matt gently extricated his palm from Charley's fingers. He looked away a heartrending moment, then took a long drink. "You really want to hear this?" he finally asked.

Her heart went out to him, and again, it was all she could do not to stand up and hug him. "I really do," she answered softly. It was the only way she'd begin to understand him and what he'd been through. The only way he'd begin to heal, too.

Wearily, Matt scrubbed a hand down his face. He seemed reluctant, but began to relate: "I had Mutt that night. He woke up around two in the morning, and he was nosing my hand, signaling he needed to go out."

Made sense.

"It seemed urgent, and I thought it was a routine potty break, so I stumbled out of bed and opened the door to our barracks. Then all hell broke loose."

Sara's heart lurched as she pictured the scene.

Matt shook his head, unable to completely camouflage his grief. "Mutt picked up the scent of whatever he'd heard and bolted away from me at top speed, barking his head off. Woke everyone and all the other dogs up."

Sara could imagine that, too.

Matt jerked in a shuddering breath. "Turned out we had a dozen suicide bombers in the compound, ready to kill us all." His voice caught at the unbearable pain of that memory. "Mutt attacked the closest one, and the guy blew himself up. And Mutt along with him."

Briefly, he couldn't go on. His eyes glistened. "Just like that, they were both dead. And a minute or so later, thanks to the swift action of our soldiers," he said hoarsely, "so were all the other enemy combatants."

This time she couldn't resist. Sara reached over to touch his arm, her fingers curving around the hard, thick muscles. "Oh, Matt..." she said, aware it was all she could do not to burst into tears herself.

Her attempt to comfort him, even a little, failed.

His forearm remained stiff, resisting. He shook his head, a faraway look in his eyes. In abject misery, he confessed, "The hell of it is, if I had just been a little more alert, or wary... If I would have had my gun, I would have taken out the bomber before Mutt got to him. But I didn't." He swallowed hard.

Aware her initial instincts not to touch Matt had been on point, Sara dropped her hand and went back to feeding a now sleepy-looking Charley the last of his mashed fruit. At least Matt was talking; she held on to that.

"What about the other dogs?" she asked softly, wanting him to get the rest of the story out, to have that much-needed catharsis. "You said there were no troop injuries..."

His glance still averted, Matt released a breath. "There were some injuries. Shrapnel. None of the other dogs were killed." Hands knotting, he shook his head. "But it could have very easily gone another way," he admitted rawly.

With multiple fatalities of soldiers and canines, Sara thought.

Matt drained the rest of his water. "That incident made me realize my time to be effective was gone." Regret tautening his masculine features, he slanted her a look. "I'd already notified the Army I would be resigning my commission and heading back to the USA when my tour was up. And so, that's what I did."

Sara offered Charley a sippy cup of milk.

"And your family…?" Did the McCabes know even part of what he'd just told her?

Apparently not, from his reaction.

Matt's brows lowered like thunderclouds over his gray-blue eyes. "They know I don't talk about what happened over there."

"Except you just did."

He frowned. "Only because I want you to know. So you'll stop asking me if I can be hands-on with Champ or any other puppy, because I just can't. I don't want that kind of responsibility." His grimace deepened. "Not ever again."

Talk about a textbook case of PTSD. Sighing, she got a washcloth and cleaned Charley's face and hands. Removed his bib.

Matt came closer. His mood shifting, now that his heart-wrenching confession had been made, he gazed gently down at Charley, who was now slamming both his palms happily on the high chair tray. "So I'll gladly write a check. But as for the rest," he gritted out, "there is just no way, Sara."

Sara understood guilt, unwanted memories and unbearable pain. More than he would ever know.

Matt exhaled. Then moved so she had no choice but to look into his eyes. "And I would appreciate it," he said, as their gazes locked, held, "if you didn't talk to anyone else about what I've just told you."

Even if it would help him eventually? Sara wondered, conflicted. Still, she knew a confidence deserved to be kept. So she did what she knew in her heart was right for their friendship, which miraculously seemed to be resuming.

"Okay," she said, letting out a long breath, and lounging against the counter, too. "I won't tell anyone what you went through over there. But if you do want to talk to someone…someday…"

He moved away again, his manner as gruff as his low voice. "No. All I want to do is put it behind me."

Easier said than done, she thought.

But she understood.

Sometimes the only way to get past pain that immense was to stop reliving it and move on. Survive and advance. Hour by hour…day by day.

He removed a checkbook and pen from his shirt pocket.

"So, what do you think it will take to fund a drive for volunteer puppy raisers? Will a thousand dollars be okay to start?" He squinted at the hesitation he saw on her face. "What?"

Noticing Charley was beginning to look very sleepy, she lifted him out of his high chair, walked into the living room and sat down in the rocker glider. She brushed her lips across the top of his head, then positioned him so his chest was cuddled against hers, his head nestled in the crook of her shoulder.

Aware Matt was watching her closely, appearing to feel the same tenderness for her son that she did, she returned. "New ideas, and the money to fund them, are always appreciated."

He followed and settled on the ottoman opposite her. Knees spread, hands clasped in front of him. "But?" he asked quietly.

She smiled ruefully, as Charley sighed and closed his eyes. "I'll be blunt. I don't think this is going to solve your problem with your family."

Matt frowned. "Why not?"

Since Charley was drowsy enough to put down, she rose and carried him over to the Pack 'n Play in the corner of the breakfast nook. When she'd settled him, she turned back to Matt and said, "Because I know your sister, Lulu, and your mother, and they're going to see *any* extroverted action by you, no matter how small, as a much-needed breakdown of the walls you've put up around you since you came back from the Middle East. And they are going to want to *expand* on that."

Matt frowned. "So their nagging will increase, not decrease. Is that it?"

"Pretty much." She went into the kitchen to put on a pot of coffee.

Arms folded in front of him, Matt lounged against the counter again. "So what do you suggest?"

She shrugged, wishing he didn't fit into her household quite so easily. "It's your family."

He watched her measure coffee into the paper filter. With a wry half smile, he pointed out, "You come from a large family, too, darlin'."

As always, the endearment melted her heart and made her way too aware of him. Physically, and in other ways, too. She poured water into the reservoir.

"Yes, but mine are spread out all over the country now. So their ability to badger me in person is limited mostly to phone calls and texts. They generally don't just show up on my doorstep. Well," she amended hastily at his skeptical expression, "my parents have come to see us a few times, and hinted that I should start looking for a job close to the university where they live and teach in Colorado Springs. But for now at least they've accepted that I want to raise Charley in the community where Anthony and I grew up."

His glance drifted over her. "Think you will ever change your mind?"

Good question, one she was still wrestling with. "I don't know. Maybe. But I like my job at Healing Meadow Veterinary Hospital. They've been really good about extending my maternity leave past the terms I initially thought I wanted."

Although it had been rough, going through the last six months of her pregnancy alone, after her husband's death. She'd had the support of her work colleagues and other single moms that she knew. Plus, her parents had come to Texas for Charley's birth, and helped her for a few weeks after that, but since then, she had been mostly on her own, with help from friends whenever she needed and or wanted it. Of course, it wasn't the same as going through a pregnancy with a loving husband at her side, sharing every moment of Charley's growth and development with his daddy. Having Matt around today had shown her that. Made her long for an intact nuclear family, and the kind of hope-filled future a situation like that would bring.

Luckily, Matt had no way of knowing how emotional she was feeling, deep down inside.

Still, his attention deepened in a way that warmed her from the inside out. In deference to her sleeping son, he moved slightly closer and kept his voice low. "What terms did you want from your employer?"

She swallowed and tried not to flush. She may have had an unrequited crush on Matt once—when they were teens—but they were destined to be nothing more than friends now.

"Six months."

Turning away, she forced herself to ignore the intense yearning for closeness, and the flutter of desire that swept through her. "But now that Charley is six months old, I can see I'm not quite ready to go back full-time."

Ignoring the masculine warmth and strength emanating from his tall body, she busied herself wiping down the high chair. "So I'm going to stay on leave another three months, and then ease into work by taking emergency calls every other weekend, and seeing patients one day a week."

Matt observed, "And you're taking on Champ, too."

Who, Sara noted, was curled up in a ball in his indoor puppy pen, fast asleep.

"For just a month or so." She hoped, anyway. "But yeah, I really am going to have to find someone to help me with that."

She got out the cream and sugar and set them on the island, along with a plate of oatmeal-cranberry-pecan cookies.

Matt watched her fill two mugs. "What about Charley?"

Their fingers touched as she handed him his mug. Aware she was tingling more now than she had been before, Sara furrowed her brow. "What do you mean?"

"You said you were going to need help to work with Champ and watch your son simultaneously."

Sara stirred in cream and sugar. "Right."

Matt drank his black. "Would you consider letting me assist you with your son?"

Sara paused. Was this guilt talking—or something

else? She looked him up and down. "Let me get this straight. You... Mr. Lonesome...want to be Charley's baby wrangler?"

Matt's broad shoulders lifted in an affable shrug. "Why not? He likes hanging out with me. I like hanging out with him." He paused. "Don't trust me?"

Sara blushed. Yet another obstacle to her going back to work. "Actually," she admitted with chagrin, "I don't really trust anyone except for Bess Monroe, and your sister, Lulu, with Charley—if Bess is around to supervise, and I only have confidence in Bess because she's a registered nurse." Which was, on the face of it, pretty neurotic, she knew.

"Ah." Matt dunked the edge of his cookie in his coffee. "New-mom anxiety."

Heat rose in the center of her chest as she waved off her worry. "I know it's silly..."

"But it's the way you feel, darlin'. No shame in that."

Pleased to find him honoring her feelings instead of making fun of them, Sara nodded. "Exactly," she said softly. "Plus, I really don't want to be away from Charley for all the time it's going to take to socialize Champ because then I'd end up feeling I was neglecting him. So it's a real conundrum."

Matt finished off his cookie, understanding again. "How do you formally socialize a puppy, anyway?"

"By introducing him to as many different people and places as possible over the next month. So he'll be comfortable no matter where he is."

"Sounds...interesting."

Sara smiled, suddenly aware how cozy this all felt. With the two of them there, chatting, and the puppy and baby sleeping nearby.

Matt was going to make a wonderful husband and father someday.

Trying not to think about the toe-curling kisses they'd already shared, she admitted, "The outings would be good for Charley, too. He's spent way too much time at home with just me, thus far. But—" Sara took another sip from her mug "—I can't handle both Champ and Charley out in public by myself." Which meant some sort of accommodations would have to be made.

Again, Matt understood. Practical as always, he asked, "So why don't we do it together, then?"

Chapter 4

Sara stared at Matt, as if sure she hadn't heard right.

He understood her confusion. Because he certainly hadn't expected to make such an offer when he'd come over here, either. But something about being around her and Charley made him want to leave his self-imposed isolation behind.

"You want to help me socialize Champ?" she asked, still appearing stunned.

The thought of having to be in contact with the puppy sent a cold chill down his spine. "No. I still don't want to get that close to any dog." Never mind a sweet, adorable puppy who could easily steal his heart if he allowed it. "I want to take charge of Charley while you train Champ."

Sara slanted him a sideways look. "You understand that I would want us all to go out in public together?

You'd have to leave your ranch and come over here, help me load them in my vehicle *every day* for one month, or until Alyssa Barnes is well enough to take over Champ's training and care?"

He figured he could handle that as long as he wasn't in charge of the leash. He nodded, admitting ruefully, "Initially, I figured avoiding dogs entirely was the way to go. But—" he paused to draw another breath "—you've helped me realize that is more apt to provoke questions than avoid them."

Her jade eyes gleamed. "So you're going to take the opposite tact."

He moved forward, hands spread, his voice edgy with tension. "I want to desensitize myself, the way a person would after any trauma."

Sara offered a supportive nod. "Kind of like when you get thrown off a horse. The last thing you want to do is get back on one, but if you don't get back in the saddle as soon as possible, you may not ever be able to ride again."

"Right." The understanding in her eyes encouraged him to dig a little deeper into his feelings. "I'm not planning on falling in love with the pup, or even having much to do with Champ. I just want to be able to be around him and not start thinking about all the things I'd rather not think about."

She looked at him from beneath the fringe of her lashes. "I hear you."

She certainly seemed to. And not just in the way a compassionate woman would, but like someone who had been through her own version of hell.

Matt cleared his throat. Maybe the two of them would be good for each other, after all. "So when and where do you want to start Champ's socialization?" he asked.

She paused. "This evening okay with you?"

"I know what you're thinking," Sara told Charley several hours later. She rushed around her bedroom, trying to get ready.

"I'm getting awfully dressed up for an outing with you and Champ and Matt, but it isn't a date. Even if it is Saturday night. And it sort of feels like it could be one. It's absolutely not."

Charley gurgled from the seat of his battery-operated swing.

"It's just that the Spring Arts and Crafts Fair at the community center is a pretty big deal around here." Sara paused to put on her favorite gold necklace and matching earrings. "Everyone goes, and everyone gets a little bit dressed up. Usually cotton dresses and cardigans for the ladies, and button-up shirts for the gentlemen. And of course—" she mugged affectionately at her son "—adorably cute outfits for the little ones, like yourself."

Her doorbell rang.

Sara glanced at her watch.

"Oh dear." Matt was early. Charley still wasn't dressed, and Champ still had to go out.

Thanking heaven that she at least had gotten in her favorite yellow dress, Sara finished zipping up the back, then eased Charley out of his swing. Doing her best not to get drool on her dress, she carried him to the front door.

Matt stood on the other side of the portal, looking handsome as could be in a tan button-up shirt and jeans. "You okay?"

"Yes." She inhaled a whiff of his sandalwood-and-leather cologne, noting how closely he had shaved. "Why?"

He shrugged. "You're perspiring."

Okay, it really wasn't a date, she thought in wry relief, because if it had been a date, he would have had more sense than to point that out. She waved an airy hand. "I've been rushing around."

"How can I help?"

With a grin, she drawled, "I was hoping you'd ask." She shifted her baby into his strong arms. "Entertain Charley while I gather his stuff."

"Any particular reason why you chose this event for Champ?" Matt asked.

Sara motioned for Matt to follow her up the stairs to the nursery. She stopped by the master bedroom long enough to grab a pair of soft beige ballet flats. One hand on the door frame, she paused to slip them on. "A couple, actually. First, it's indoors, so it'll be well lit and we don't have to worry about the weather. And secondly, there will be a fair amount of noise and excitement and a ton of people there of all ages."

Matt's gaze shifted upward, from her feet to her face. "So there'll be a lot for both Charley and Champ to take in."

A little embarrassed she had inadvertently just given him a glimpse of her bedroom, post wardrobe crisis, she said, "Yes." Trying not to flush, she reached for Charley and put him on the changing table.

She needn't have worried whether Matt would judge her indecisiveness, though. He seemed to have something else a lot more serious on his mind.

"Are you going to have Champ on a leash?"

Was he nervous about being around the pup himself? Afraid that might trigger some sort of PTSD-like reaction on his part? Worried she couldn't handle the puppy in a crowd and might lose track of Champ? Or just not really looking forward to that part of their excursion? She sighed. There was no way to tell, given the inscrutable look on his face. Although he hadn't reacted to the adorable black Lab puppy's presence thus far with anything more than guarded disinterest.

Figuring the best way to engender calm was to exude it, Sara casually let him in on her plans. "Actually, I'm going to carry Champ in my arms tonight. That way, when he starts meeting a lot of different people, he'll still feel safe. And he won't get tangled up around our feet since he's not that great on a leash yet." Although he would get there.

Matt nodded with what appeared to be relief. "What about this little fella?" he asked.

Sara eased off her son's terry-cloth onesie, changed his diaper, then slid on a blue-and-white playsuit. "I'll adjust the BabyBjörn and you can carry him in that, or you can push him in the stroller. He'll probably be happy either way."

Matt considered. "Might be better to put him in the Björn, so he'll be high enough to really see what's going on."

Sara was delighted Matt had no problem being close to her son. She went to get the canvas carrier, and fifteen minutes later, they were on their way. Matt drove his pickup truck. She drove her SUV, with Charley in his infant seat and Champ safely ensconced in his carrier.

From the looks of the crowded parking lot, the festival was already in full swing when they arrived. Sara put her son in the BabyBjörn and then helped Matt ease it over his shoulders. Charley gurgled with excitement and leaned back against Matt's broad chest. The sight of the two cuddled up together so contentedly was enough to make her swoon. As well as wish that Charley had a daddy like Matt in his life, all over again…

Satisfied all was well, Sara smiled contentedly. She snapped a leash on Champ's collar and led him to the grass. She gave him the appropriate command and the little pup promptly relieved himself, while Matt stood a short distance away.

"Good boy, Champ!" she praised him warmly, since one of the things she was teaching him was to go potty on demand. "Good boy!" She scooped him up and together, she and Matt went into the building where the festival was being held. As expected, Charley got his share of affectionate greetings. Sara was mobbed with people wanting to pet Champ, too.

What Sara didn't expect was to run into Matt's sister, Lulu. The dark-haired honeybee rancher was older than Matt by two years, and to twenty-eight-year old Matt's continued aggravation, had been known to be both bossy and protective of all five of her brothers. As well as stubbornly resistant to *their* advice.

"Hey!" Lulu grinned as she came forward to give them all a hug. Hands on her hips, she stood back to look at Matt. "I knew you were donating funds to recruit new volunteers."

Sara had told Lulu and his mom as much, in order to ease the pressure on Matt.

Lulu's McCabe's blue eyes sparkled. "But I didn't

know that she'd talked you into helping out with the puppy raising, too!"

Matt's expression became impatient.

"He's just helping me out with Charley while I socialize Champ," Sara explained.

She realized, too late, she should have added that little tidbit to her email to both women. She hadn't because she had figured it would mean more if they'd heard about that part of the bargain from Matt.

"Even more interesting," Lulu murmured, waggling her brows.

Matt gave his sister a quelling look. "I don't see how," he retorted.

"Well, for months now you've refused to go out with anyone I've tried to fix you up with!"

Lulu had been trying to fix Matt up?

If so, then why didn't she ask me? Sara wondered, a little jealously, given the fact they were both single, the same age and had known each other before. Then she immediately pushed the ridiculous notion away. She was a widow with a new baby who had also made it clear to everyone around her that she didn't want a love life...

Exuding sisterly exasperation, Lulu continued, "Nor would you deign to ask anyone out on your own! And yet here you are...with Sara and her crew...on what certainly *looks* like a social outing..."

Once again, Sara lifted a staying palm and stepped in to clarify. "Only in the sense that the festival is a community event. And we are all members of the Laramie family."

Lulu looked at Matt, wordlessly beseeching him to verify that was indeed the case.

Instead, to Sara's consternation, the big jerk merely

shrugged and kept a poker face. Mulishly refusing to comment either way.

Determined to set the record straight, Sara continued firmly, "If we want Champ to get used to all sorts of crowds and venues, we have to bring him to all sorts of gatherings. Some big, like this. Some medium-sized. Some small and intimate."

"Uh-huh," Lulu said.

Sara flushed. "I know what you're getting at, Lulu, but this is not a date!"

Lulu grinned. Looked from Sara to Matt and back again. "Methinks the lady doth protest too much."

Heat continued flooding Sara's face as she recalled, without wanting to, the kisses she and Matt had shared on his ranch. "We're just friends," she repeated.

"Mmm-hmm." Lulu beamed with excitement. She patted both their arms before she moved off. "Let's see if you two stay that way..."

"You know, you could have helped me out with your sister tonight," Sara said later, when they got back to her ranch and put an exhausted Champ and Charley to bed.

Matt folded his arms across his chest. "You seemed to be doing okay."

"She thinks we're dating!"

The corners of his eyes crinkled. "So?"

"So, we're not!" Sara shot back heatedly.

Mischief glimmered in his gaze. "Okay."

In deference to the sleeping little ones, she kept her voice low and tranquil. "What do you mean, 'okay'?"

He looked her in the eye. "Okay," he replied genially, giving in, "we're not dating."

"But...?" she prodded, sensing there was a lot more

going on in that handsome head of his. Emotions she needed to know.

He looked down at her patiently. "It occurred to me that if I help you with Charley every day for the next month or so while you socialize Champ, people are going to see us together. A lot."

As always, his ultramasculine presence made her feel intensely aware of him. Her pulse raced. "Which is why we should make it clear to everyone we're just friends."

Something flickered in his expression, then disappeared. "We can do that."

"But..."

Matt rubbed his hand over his jaw. "People are going to think what they want to think anyway. So why not stay mum and let them jump to whatever conclusion they're going to jump to anyway."

She shivered under his continued scrutiny. "I don't want to pretend that I have feelings for you that I don't have."

He moved toward her, throwing her off her guard once again. "You have to have feelings for someone to go out on a date with him?"

"At least a basic attraction."

The wicked gleam in his eyes said if he thought she would allow it, he would kiss her again.

The trouble was, she knew she would.

"I think we already established we have that," he deadpanned.

She tingled all over, recalling his embrace. Lower still, she felt a melting sensation. Sara swallowed and moved toward the kitchen, picking up a few burping cloths and bibs that needed washing. Her back to him, she took them into the utility room and dropped them into the hamper that held Charley's baby laundry. She turned around to face him again. "I told you those kisses weren't going to happen again."

He moved to let her exit. "I'm not going to lay odds one way or another."

Being alone with him always seemed like a dangerous proposition to her way-too-vulnerable heart. Never more so than now.

Feeling a little overheated, Sara removed her cardigan and draped it over the back of a breakfast room chair. "But you think I am going to kiss you. Eventually."

His smile widened. "Definitely a possibility."

She lounged against the counter and searched for a way to keep them in the just-friends zone. "Look, Matt, I'm not going to lead you or anyone else on. I *don't* want to get married again."

He shrugged and ambled closer, his eyes never leaving hers. "Great, 'cause I don't want to get married, either."

There was no doubt about it. Matt McCabe had to be the most infuriating man ever! Ignoring the skittering of her heart, she tipped her head up, refusing to get sucked in by the blatant sexiness of his gaze. Feeling parched, she went to the fridge and took out a big bottle of sparkling water. "Then what do you want?" she asked.

He watched as she filled two glasses with ice and quartered a lime, already seeming to be mentally making love to her.

"Besides a warm, willing woman to make love with…who doesn't expect any more from me than I want to give?"

Her knees suddenly weakened treacherously, for no

reason she could figure. Trying not to fantasize what that would be like, she cleared her throat and prodded, "Besides that."

"Well, then, it'd have to be, for my mother and my sister to stop haranguing me."

Glad to have something else to focus on, Sara worked in the lime wedges and filled their glasses with sparkling water. "Are they badgering you about something else besides the therapy-puppy program?"

Matt nodded tersely. "My mother wants me to participate in the West Texas Warriors Association programs for ex-soldiers returning to civilian life."

So I'm not the only one who senses you're struggling, Sara thought, feeling simultaneously comforted and worried. She handed him a glass and, together, they went into her living room to sit down.

Always ready and willing to lend an empathetic ear, Sara took the sofa. "Why does she want that?"

Matt sat in a big upholstered chair, kitty-corner from her. A faraway look came into his gray-blue eyes as he took a long, thirsty drink. Then let out a ragged breath. "She thinks the only people who will ever be able to truly understand what I saw and experienced while overseas are other military personnel."

As much as Sara tried, she couldn't begin to imagine what he'd been through. Or more important, how he felt now. "Your mom might have a point."

He rested his glass on one muscular thigh. "Did Anthony go to WTWA?"

"No," Sara admitted with heartfelt emotion. "And I wish he had."

"Why?"

Regret tightened her throat. "Because there were

times when he was just so remote from me. Kind of shut down and moody, and I didn't know how to deal with that."

Matt's eyes darkened. He took another sip. "You could have just let him be."

Sara nodded. "That's what I ultimately did do."

Matt studied her. "And now you regret it."

"Yes." Sara's voice caught, and the sorrow inside her welled. "Because now he's gone," she confessed, as her vision blurred with tears, "and I'll never know what he was going through, or not going through." Unable to sit still a second longer, she set her glass aside and rose. Moving to the desk, she took a tissue from the box and dabbed her eyes. "Or what I might have done differently to help him reconnect with me."

Suddenly, Matt was behind her. Hands cupping her shoulders gently, he turned her to face him. Threading a hand through her hair, he cupped her cheek and lifted her face to his. "That was his choice, Sara," he said gruffly.

Was it? she wondered, even as she sank into Matt's warm, comforting touch.

The next thing she knew, Matt's other arm was around her waist, bringing her closer still. "I think letting him have his space was a good thing," he said.

As she met Matt's gaze, she could see he really felt she had nothing to regret. Relief flowed through her. Followed by a surprising willingness to let him comfort her.

Maybe she hadn't really done anything wrong.

Or been remiss…

Maybe her late husband's death was part of a larger destiny…one neither she nor Anthony had any control over. As she looked up into Matt's face, she noted *he* seemed to think so.

Aware maybe it was time for her to move on, just a little, she let herself drift toward him a little more.

His other hand slid up, into her hair, and cupped her face as he tenderly murmured her name. Desire sifted through her. And then all was lost as his head lowered, her eyes shut and he fit his lips over hers.

If the first time he had kissed her had brought her back to life…the second time opened up her heart. Simultaneously erasing her need to grieve and heal in private…and keep any future romance from her life.

His kiss was slow. Exploratory. As ever so tenderly, he brought her all the way out of the past, and into the present.

And still he kissed her, inundating her with the heat of him, his masculine strength and tenderness. His tongue tangled with hers, giving as well as taking, persuading, seducing. Slowly, purposely demanding everything she had to give.

Until she kissed him back, hotly, ardently. Her arms were wreathed about his neck, her breasts pressed against his chest and there was nothing but need and more need.

And still the clinch continued, his caresses filling her with everything she had ever wanted and required. Lower still, she felt the depth of his passion. Shivers swept through her. She melted against him, her insides fluttering even as she struggled to keep her feelings in check. He was so hard and strong. The feel of his body pressed up against her sent a maelstrom of ardor pulsing through her, and an even stronger wish to connect with him, heart and soul, woman to man.

But it was too soon for them to search out such intimacy.

They both knew that.

With a sigh of regret, she tore her lips from his.

"We're just supposed to be friends, remember?" she reminded shakily.

"I know." He rested his forehead against hers and released a ragged sigh, revealing himself to be every bit as ripe for a reckless red-hot love affair as she was. He straightened reluctantly. "I'm not going to apologize." Mischief gleamed in his eyes. "But I know what our bargain was…"

It simply wasn't going to deter him in the least.

Which was a problem, Sara thought, as another wave of longing sifted through her. Given how much angst they both still had to grapple with in their personal lives.

With effort, Sara gathered her defenses and looked deep into Matt's eyes. She couldn't help her late husband, true. But she might still be able to help Matt reach out, the way Anthony hadn't. Even if he resented her interference…

Still in the circle of his arms, her hands lightly splayed across his chest, she drew a bolstering breath and firmly and calmly steered the conversation back to what they had been discussing before their embrace. "Is that why you don't want to be involved with the WTWA? Because you're afraid if you do participate in any of their programs, they won't give you your space?"

Expression gruff and forbidding, he let her go, stepped back a pace and told her, "I'm not afraid, darlin'. I just don't have time to join anything until I get the Silver Creek pastures fenced and ready for grazing, since Cullen wants to be able to use them by next fall at the very latest."

Sara knew a fake excuse when she heard one. Matt could call on his four brothers, and his father and sister, and endless McCabe cousins, and get all that done in no time. "You're making the time to help me," she pointed out, refusing to back down with him, the way she had with Anthony.

"Yep." His eyes glittered with something akin to anger. "And look what that's reaped. Endless questions from you. Matchmaking from Lulu."

She knew he was signaling her to back off, but her heart was telling her to behave differently.

Defiantly, she closed the distance between them. Took his big hand in hers. "I just want you to be happy, Matt." She squeezed his fingers firmly. "After all you've given to our country," she told him, "you deserve it. All our returning warriors do."

He looked down at their joined hands for a long moment, his expression inscrutable. "You mean that?"

His hand felt so warm and strong beneath hers. She looked into his eyes. "Yes," she said huskily, "I do."

His gaze roved her face, lingered on her lips, then returned to her eyes.

"You know what will make me happy?" he finally said.

Another kiss, she thought hopefully, suddenly having second thoughts about the deal they'd made. And becoming aware of the fact that she wouldn't mind someone warm and willing to make love with, too, someone who wouldn't ask her for things she couldn't give, not ever again.

And that would be Matt.

"What?" she returned softly, thinking this was it, the moment he would make his move on her, again. And this time, foolish or not, she would not stop him.

"What do you want from me, Matt?" she asked softly, aware she would do whatever she could to help him come back to life, in the same way she now was.

His mouth took on a harsh, formidable line.

"No more questions."

Chapter 5

Sara realized they needed to take a step back from each other so, for the next week, she arranged to meet Matt at their destinations. It was a little harder, getting both the puppy and her son in the car simultaneously without his help, but it made Champ's training a lot less intimate.

There was little time for them to say much at all to each other as they took the little puppy for thirty-minute visits to the preschool, the pet store, the local farmer's market, an office building that had elevators, and the ladies' auxiliary group at the community chapel.

Matt just strapped on the BabyBjörn and amused Charley while Sara took charge of Champ and his leash.

When they were done, she thanked him, he nodded his acknowledgment, and they went their separate ways.

It was so to the point, in fact, that she was sure they'd be able to get through the rest of the month without getting any closer when, of course, all hell broke loose, and she had one of the worst nights ever as a new mom and temporary puppy trainer.

So, an hour before they were to meet, she called Matt and left a message on his voice mail, telling him that evening's training was off.

Thirty minutes later, her doorbell rang.

Matt was on the other side.

He looked as if he had been in the shower when she called. His hair was still wet and smelled of shampoo, his clothes clean and rumpled. His handsome face etched with concern, he asked, "What's wrong?"

And for once, she had no idea at all how to answer that.

Silence stretched between them. Matt caught the fleeting glimpse of unhappiness in Sara's eyes.

"Nothing," she finally said.

Wary of adding to her distress by saying or doing the wrong thing, he looked down at her. He had never seen her looking so bedraggled. Or fatigued. She had spit-up and drool and what appeared to be baby food smeared over her loose white blouse. Her fair skin was unusually pale, her jade eyes were red and puffy—as if she'd been crying a lot—and her golden-blond hair was escaping from the knot at the nape of her neck, going every which way.

All of which combined to make him wonder what in heaven's name had been going on over here, since he had seen her the previous day.

She'd been completely pulled together, as usual, then.

His heart going out to her, he walked all the way inside and shut the door behind him. Closing the distance between them, he put a comforting arm around her shoulders. "Didn't sound like nothing, darlin'," he pointed out gruffly. In fact, in the recorded message, her voice had been clearly distraught.

She extricated herself deftly and eased away. Spying a soiled disposable diaper on the coffee table, next to the impromptu changing area on the sofa, she picked it up and carried it to the trash. "I didn't get any sleep at all last night."

He could see that, too. If he looked past the puffy redness, he could see the circles beneath her eyes.

Clearly, she'd been through hell.

A second later, he began to realize why when Champ let out a happy bark, did a little leap and then scrambled up and over the three-foot wooden side of the whelping box. Free, and deliriously happy to be so, the puppy came skidding toward the two of them at full blast.

Simultaneously, Charley—who'd been sitting in his high chair—let out a wail.

Sara scooped up Champ before he could head for the foyer staircase. She started to hand Champ off to Matt. Then appeared to abruptly remember their deal. She took care of Champ, he wrangled her baby.

A furiously wiggling Champ in hand, she sent a distressed look back to the now wailing baby. Tears gathering in the corners of her eyes, she sighed and said to Matt, "Would you mind?"

No wonder she was exhausted. And appeared at her wit's end. He would be, too.

"I'm on it." He went over to pick up the still-sobbing Charley. Who stared at him through tear-blurred eyes.

The six-month-old baby looked every bit as tired and stressed out as his mommy.

Only Champ was full of energy. Sara carried the writhing puppy outside and set him down on the grass.

Matt followed, baby in his arms. "Charley teething again?"

Sara made an empathetic face. "No teeth have come through his gums yet, but I think he still is." Her shoulders slumped. "That's not the problem."

Matt moved close enough to inhale the faint scent of lilac clinging to her skin. "Then what is?" he asked, tamping down the urge to take her in his arms and hold her close as she needed to be held right now.

She retorted, "Champ finally figured out how to get out of his pen!" Aware the puppy had finished, she snapped a leash on him and guided him back inside the house.

So he had just witnessed.

Unsure whether it was frustration or fatigue causing her to respond so emotionally, he pointed to the large wire dog cage in the corner of the living room that, so far as he could discern, anyway, had gone unused. "You've got a crate right there," he said, while Charley curled up against him, peering over his shoulder.

"Yes." Sara perched on the back of the sofa, leash still in hand. She looked down at the adorable puppy now resting at her feet, like the perfect little angel he apparently had not been. "And every time I put Champ in that crate, he goes crazy, barking and trying to get out. Which in turn makes Charley start to cry. The more Charley cries, the more Champ barks."

Matt was beginning to see why she appeared so completely wrung out. "And this went on all night?"

She drew a deep bolstering breath, the action lifting the swell of her breasts in a way that reminded him of all the things he was forbidden to do, as per the terms of their bargain. “Yes.”

Matt pushed away the yearning to make love to her. One day things could change—in fact, he hoped they would—but right now they had immediate problems to solve. He shifted Charley to his other shoulder. “What are you supposed to do to stop that?” Charley nestled his head in the crook of Matt’s neck.

Sara smiled at the way her son was cuddling up to Matt. She came closer, looking a little more tranquil now. “Get Champ used to the crate.”

Matt noticed how soft and kissable her bare lips were. Remembering how sweet she tasted, he said, “And you haven’t been able to do that so far.”

She flexed her shoulders. Linked her hands behind her neck, stretched in a way that made her physical fatigue all the more apparent. “No.”

Resolved to help her, Matt mulled all this over. “He’s okay when you put him in his little crate in the car.”

“I know.” She pointed to the airline-style plastic crate she used for travel that was next to the door to the garage. “And I tried putting Champ in that last night and it didn’t work, either.”

“Why not?”

She huffed out a breath. “Do you think I would be this exhausted if I had figured that out?”

He flashed her a crooked grin. “Sorry. Didn’t meant to imply—”

“I’m ineffective?” Sara frowned as more hair fell out of the schoolmarm bun at the nape of her neck. She removed the elastic that had been holding it. Her hair spilled to her shoulders in a golden cloud, and she combed her fingers through it, still voicing her frustration with unchecked emotion. "Well, apparently I am, at least when it comes to training a puppy."

Champ seemed to know he was in trouble. He sighed loudly, and put his chin on his outstretched paws.

Aware this would be a lot easier if there were two adults and one puppy and one baby, Matt continued walking an increasingly drowsy Charley back and forth. "You've never done this before?"

"No." Sara sighed and stared down at the leash in her hands. "My parents didn't allow pets when I was growing up. I didn't have time for an animal when I was in vet school. And when I got married, my husband informed me he didn't really want a pet. So, I never got one."

A fact, Matt noted, that seemed to frustrate and disappoint her.

Sara's soft lips twisted in a self-effacing moue. "I've delivered puppies and kittens and taken care of them in a veterinary medicine setting, but the rest of it is all new to me."

It wasn't like her to just give up on searching for a solution. Unless she was as privately depressed as she seemed to assume he was. "Did you ask the people in charge of the puppy-raising program?"

She looked down her nose at him. "Yes. Of course I asked. They said that I need to leave Champ in the crate until he stops barking and then take him out. Praise him for good behavior. Give him a chance to run around and relieve himself and get some water. And then put him back in. If he barks or otherwise misbehaves, ignore him. When he's quiet, take him out."

Made sense. "Has that worked?"

Sara threw up her hands. "Not so far. He never stops

barking, and Charley won't stop crying." Without warning, the tears she'd been holding back streamed down her face.

"Hey," Matt said, wrapping his free arm around her shoulders and pulling her in close, the way a good friend—not a lover—would. "I'm here now. It's going to be okay."

Sara sniffed and buried her face in his shoulder. "I don't see how," she muttered against his shirt.

Deciding the hell with the rules of their baby bargain, Matt ran a hand down her spine, soothing her as best he could with one hand. "I'll supervise Champ, get him to calm down and maybe even sleep for a while, too," he promised, as Charley, alert to the sound of crying, leaned over to look at his mother, perplexed.

"How?" Sara cried, even more distraught.

Matt had always been good at problem solving. "You leave that to me," he told her firmly, then seeing that Charley was about to burst into empathetic tears, said, "Why don't you take Charley upstairs? So both of you can get some rest."

Sara straightened. "It's too late in the day for a nap."

Clearly, Matt didn't think so.

"Dinner will be in another hour…"

"I'll wake you whenever you want." He handed her the baby and took the leash. "Go."

She paused, clearly tempted, yet worried, too. She looked deep into his eyes. "Are you sure you want to take care of Champ?"

"Yes," he said, and found to his amazement, it was true.

There were larger issues at stake right now than what had once been the stuff of his nightmares.

Seeing her doubt, he pointed out, "I've been around Champ all week. And it hasn't been a problem. In fact, it's gotten easier for me every time I've seen him." He squared his shoulders. "This will be another way of getting back in the saddle, so to speak." It didn't mean he had to fall in love with the little pup, or even get emotionally attached.

Sara glanced down at Champ, who was now settled next to Matt's feet, gazing upward adoringly.

She started to relax.

Ready to do what was needed for all concerned, Matt cupped a hand on her shoulder. "Everything down here will be fine," he reassured her gently. "Now go. Sleep. I'll take care of Champ."

Sara woke several hours later to the smell of something delicious—and no barking. Beside her on the king-size bed, a pillow framing either side of him, Charley yawned and stretched. Sara sat up and saw it was seven thirty.

As she'd feared, they were way off schedule. Which wasn't such a problem for her, but it might be for Charley. And Champ…

They would just all have to make-do. Hopefully, with Matt's continued help.

She ran a brush through her hair and put on a clean shirt, then carried Charley to the nursery for a diaper change. When he was changed, they went downstairs to find Matt in the kitchen, the leash attached from the pup's collar to his belt. Champ was lying on the floor beside him, watching Matt intently, the scene so calm and cozy it brought sentimental tears to Sara's eyes. Surreptitiously, she wiped them away. She must still be way overtired, although she admitted, the nap had done her good.

Matt turned to greet her with a smile. She did her best to smile back. Gesturing at the slow cooker on her counter, she asked, "What's this?"

His gaze radiated casual affection. "Beef stew. I put it on this morning." He came closer, inundating her with the fragrance of his soap and cologne. "Champ and I took a ride over to the Silver Creek to pick it up while you all were napping. Brought it back and plugged it in here to continue cooking."

Sara put aside the notion of what it might be like to have him here with her like this every evening. As much as she might need and want the help, it wasn't part of their bargain. Hence, it wasn't going to happen.

Ignoring the new skittering of her pulse, she lifted the lid. Saw chunks of beef, potatoes and carrots simmering in a rich, thick gravy. She shook her head in admiration. "Well, it looks and smells amazing."

He grinned proudly. He took a spoon out and scooped up a bite. Blew it softly to cool it, then offered it to her. "It's my mom's recipe."

Sara tasted the delicious entrée. Grinning, she gave him the thumbs-up. "You really cooked this yourself?" she asked. As they stood there, side by side, it was all she could do not to think about kissing him again.

"I did. I like to have something good waiting for me at the end of a long day in the field."

As she met his eyes, a new spiral of warmth slid through her.

"I also brought over half a pecan pie and makings for salad. I figured since I was inviting myself for dinner, I should contribute."

Charley reached out and grabbed the sleeve of Matt's shirt in his small fist. Ignoring the tender look he threw her son, Sara swallowed through the dryness of her throat, and said, "I'll owe you a home-cooked meal, then."

His eyes locked on hers. He responded with lazy pleasure. "I'll take you up on that."

Deciding she had been ensnared in Matt's keen gray-blue gaze for too long, she said, "Mind holding Charley for a minute while I get his dinner ready?"

"My pleasure." Matt shifted the little boy into his arms, grinning as Charley gurgled and patted Matt's broad chest with the flats of both hands.

Sara warmed the chicken and vegetable baby food in the microwave, spooned it into a trisectioned baby dish, and added a little applesauce, too. She nodded at Champ, who was still resting at Matt's feet. "How did you get him to be so quiet and calm?" Since the pup had discovered his ability to be a little escape artist, he'd been brimming with adrenaline and the need for adventure.

Matt shrugged. "Simple. He's really tired. We did some leash training around the yard when we got back."

Sara turned her attention away from the compelling sight of her son snuggling up to Matt. So this man was not just strong and protective, he was amazingly tender, too. So what? That didn't change anything between them. And if she allowed herself to think it would, they'd both be in big, big trouble.

She went to find a bib for Charley. "Thank you. I know this wasn't exactly the bargain we made."

Matt's eyes tracked her every step as she moved

around the kitchen. "Deals change. Especially in emergencies."

"As much as I loathe to admit it, this was definitely an emergency."

He soothed her with a look that was sexy and self-assured. "Nothing a little sleep for everyone wouldn't cure."

Sara frowned. "The problem is, how am I going to get Champ to be quiet tonight?"

Matt shrugged. "If you want, I can manage his crate training, too."

Sara paused in the act of filling a sippy cup with milk. "You know how to do that?"

Matt nodded. "None of the strays we'd ever brought in had ever been in a crate, so yeah. I could do it. Take him home with me, if you want."

Sara was tempted. Really tempted to just back out of the commitment she'd made. "Everyone signs a contract when they agree to help raise a puppy. To have Champ anywhere else overnight, I'd have to request formal permission."

Matt's eyes darkened. "Which you'd rather not do."

Sara sighed and admitted ruefully, "This is already embarrassing enough. I'm a veterinarian. I should be able to handle a puppy."

Empathy colored his low tone. "You're also a new mother. Taking care of an unhousebroken puppy and a baby simultaneously is a lot."

Oh no. "Did Champ…?"

"Yep. I found the cleaning supplies. Although," he said, lifting one strong hand, "it's really my fault. I know what happens when they start to sniff and circle. I just wasn't fast enough."

Was there no end to this man's generosity? Now that he had started to rejoin the community, anyway. "Well, thank you," she said softly, realizing that she may have misjudged him completely.

His gaze warmed. "No problem."

Sara measured Champ's food into his dish. She petted his head gently, smiling when he wagged his tail, then set it down in front of him. Straightening, she went over to wash her hands, then took Charley from Matt and settled him in the high chair. *As long as things are suddenly so cozy between us...* "Can I ask you something?"

"Sure." He winked, teasing. "Not sure I'll answer..."

Oh, cowboy, Sara thought as his low husky murmur sent another wave of desire rippling through her. She settled in front of her son and began to feed him. Then turned back to Matt, her demeanor as calm as it was curious.

Once again, their eyes locked. Held.

"Why did you come over here in such a hurry this afternoon?"

Chapter 6

Why did I rush over here this afternoon? Matt asked himself as he got the makings for the salad out of the fridge.

So many reasons…

Darkness had fallen outside, but the kitchen lights cast a warm and cozy glow that made the room feel close and intimate, and Sara look all the prettier.

He let his gaze sift over her, taking in the honey-gold hair falling over her slender shoulders, the subtle rise and fall of her breasts beneath her loose apricot tunic. Refusing to let his gaze go any lower, he said, "You sounded really distraught on the phone when you left the message canceling our plans."

She tilted her head. "So you thought something was wrong."

His gaze lingered briefly on her lush, kissable lips.

Returned to her eyes, thinking how relaxed she was now compared to how she had been when he'd arrived. Chuckling, he rolled up his sleeves and walked over to the sink to wash his hands. "Wasn't it?"

She wrinkled her nose and gave him a teasing once-over. "Thank you for coming to our rescue."

He tried not to think about her touching him every place her eyes had been. "That's what we McCabes do." With effort, he tamped down his growing feelings. Flashed her the kind of easy smile he gave all his friends. "Help our neighbors."

"Your family should know about this." He admired how her skinny jeans molded her feminine curves. Damn, but she was sexy. "Why?"

"They wouldn't be so worried about you if they did."

He divided the small package of field greens between two salad bowls. Added a package of slivered almonds and a smattering of fresh raspberries and blackberries. Realizing he'd forgotten to bring anything to dress it with, he paused, hands on his hips. "I love my family, but they need to mind their own damn business."

She lifted a skeptical blond brow. Seeming to read his mind, she got up to get vinaigrette and poppy seed salad dressings out of the fridge. She brushed up against him lightly as she set the bottles down on the counter in front of him. "So they can't be worried about you the way you were worried about me?"

She had a point. Except… "I haven't called them crying."

She blushed. "I wasn't crying."

He gazed down at her, aware it was taking everything he had not to haul her into his arms and kiss her again. And this time he wouldn't be just consoling her. "You definitely sounded like you had been."

She averted her gaze and inhaled a deep breath. Her lower lip quivered slightly, as if she might burst into tears yet again. "How about I take Champ outside while you sit with Charley, and then we can eat?" she asked huskily.

Able to see she needed a moment to collect herself, he nodded. "Sounds good."

Her brief respite outdoors gave him a chance to kick himself in the rear for inadvertently saying the wrong thing to her again. When she and Champ came back in, Charley was still in his high chair. He had finished his applesauce. So Sara gave him a smattering of Cheerios to push around the tray while Sara and Matt enjoyed the dinner he'd prepared.

Keeping the conversation businesslike, he asked, "So what do you want to do about the training opportunity we missed this afternoon?"

"I phoned the Laramie Gardens senior living center before I called you and rescheduled for tomorrow afternoon at four p.m." Sara added butter to a piece of the crusty bread she'd added to the feast. "Do you think you'll be able to do it?"

He nodded.

She took a sip of mint iced tea. "I'd understand if you want the weekend off."

Was she trying to put distance between them, or simply being considerate? Her expression gave no clue. "Are *you* taking the weekend off?" he asked, just as quietly.

"No." A contented smile lit the pretty features of her face. She looked over at her son, then down at Champ, who was snuggled up against her feet. "I want them both out and about every day."

Matt shrugged, beginning to relax again, too. "Then I'll help you every day."

She finished her salad and started on her stew. "Is it getting any easier for you to be around dogs now?"

Yes and no, Matt thought. He still did not want to get emotionally attached to Champ, but he savored the time he spent with Sara and Charley and Champ. Maybe because, in their own way, they'd become a little team.

But there were also still times when he'd be out and he would see an older dog that would remind him of Mutt. And that always led to the mixture of grief and crippling guilt that left him unable to sleep.

Aware Sara was waiting for his answer, but knowing she didn't need to be burdened with his problems when she already had so much on her agenda, he shrugged and said with an accepting smile, "Hey, this is America. Land of the free and the brave—and the pets we love. So if I ever want to be able to go anywhere—" and he did, especially with Sara and crew "—I just have to suck it up and deal. You know?"

"I do." They were both finished eating. Sara looked down at the floor where Champ was curled up, sound asleep. She disengaged the leash from her belt, and rose.

Champ slept on.

Soundlessly, she moved away from him and carried her dishes to the sink. Matt followed, just as stealthily. "It used to bother me to be around married couples," she confessed, her soft lips twisting ruefully. "Or people in love. Or women who were expecting who had their husbands at their sides." She bent over to put their dishes in the dishwasher, inadvertently giving him a nice view of her slender ankles, taut calves and sleek thighs.

She shook her head. "It just made me so acutely aware of everything I'd lost and what I'd been through with Anthony's death."

Matt joined her at the sink. Sensing he wasn't the only one who needed to talk about the most difficult moments of his life, he asked, "Did they ever figure out what happened to cause Anthony's car accident?"

"They definitely know he was going too fast when he came to that bend in the road, and that he missed the turn. But there was no drugs or alcohol involved. He didn't have his phone with him, so he wasn't texting or on a call."

"So it was just a freak accident or a moment of inattention."

Regret flickering in her eyes, Sara dipped her head, admitting, "I asked him to run into town and go to the grocery store for me. So maybe he had his mind on that."

Matt knew the path she was traveling. It wasn't good. He cupped her shoulders. "It wasn't your fault, darlin'. Accidents happen."

She nodded, whether in agreement or to end the conversation he did not know. She cleared her throat. "Dinner was delicious, by the way."

He got the hint. Subject change. Now. He smiled, still wishing he could kiss her, and not have her take it the wrong way. "I'll tell my mom you liked her recipe."

She held up a hand. "Whoa there, cowboy. If you do that, you'll also be telling her the two of us had a dinner together that you cooked."

Matt ran a hand across his jaw. "Hmm. How about that."

She narrowed her gaze. "Still using me to get your family to back off?"

At this point, it would be more accurate to say he was using his family as an excuse to spend time with her...and Charley...and Champ.

But sensing she might not want to ponder that right now, given the convoluted way their renewed friendship had all come about, he merely shrugged. Ready to let things stand as they were, for the moment, anyway. He regarded her curiously. "Is that a problem?"

She shrugged. "Only...possibly...for you."

As much as Sara had enjoyed the pleasure of Matt's company, she knew they still hadn't solved the problem of how to get Champ to stay in his crate. "So how is this going to work again?" she asked Matt as bedtime for the little ones approached.

He took the towels he'd brought in from his truck. They were worn but clean. "We're going to rub these towels over our skin and get our smells on it," he demonstrated as he talked, "and then put them in Champ's wire crate, and then he is going to go in, too."

Sara followed suit, moving the terry cloth across her throat, her hands and forearms.

Champ looked surprised when Matt picked him up, cuddled him briefly, then put him in the wire cage, next to the comfort towels. When the door clicked, he began to bark. Unperturbed, Matt stretched out in front of the crate and slid his fingers through the metal grate.

To Sara's surprise, Champ stopped barking. He lay next to Matt's hand, sniffed, and then with a loud sigh, settled, too. As she watched the two of them interact, Sara couldn't help but drink Matt in, head to toe, in all his masculine glory. His hair had dried in rumpled waves that were both sexy and invitingly touchable, his face closely shaven. Clad in a washed-'til-it-was-soft ivory chamois shirt that stretched across his broad shoulders and muscular chest, and faded jeans that did equally nice things for his hips and legs, he was every inch the indomitable Texan. Ex-soldier. Rancher. Daddy and husband-to be…?

With a sigh, Sara forced herself to stop thinking about what an eligible man Matt was, and how attracted she was to him. Then she asked, "Now what?"

Matt smiled up at her, oblivious to the unexpectedly sensual nature of her thoughts. "We sleep."

Sara blinked. "On the floor?" Yes, there was an area rug, but beneath that it was solid oak. Which would definitely not be comfortable!

Matt's smiled widened. He looked like a cowpoke on a campout. He winked. "Well, not you and Charley, naturally."

Sara went over to give Charley's swing another turn. As her son began to sway again contentedly, she walked back to Matt. Guilt assailed her. "But that won't be comfortable for you!"

He folded his hands behind his head. "I wouldn't say no to a pillow."

She hunkered down next to him, aware there were limits as to what she would ask of him. "Matt…" she cautioned softly, wary of upsetting Champ, who would then upset Charley again.

Matt caught her hand in his and squeezed her fingers tenderly. "Do you trust me, Sara?"

She looked into his gray-blue eyes. The answer to that was easy. "Yes."

He gripped her hand again and continued looking deep into her eyes. "Then trust that I can handle this."

With the situation under control, Sara thanked Matt again, and then took Charley upstairs. She bathed her son and got him ready for bed. Gave him the last bottle for the evening, read him a story, rocked and sang to him, then put him in his crib.

Short minutes later, Charley was sound asleep.

She turned on the baby monitor and eased from the nursery.

As she walked back into the master bedroom, the outside lights clicked on. After slipping the portable monitor into her pocket, she grabbed the items Matt would likely be needing if he were staying the night, and walked back downstairs to investigate.

Matt was standing in the moonlight, watching Champ romp in the grass. He stood, legs braced slightly apart, hands shoved in the pockets of his jeans. Aware the spring night was beginning to get a little chilly, she walked over to join him. Once again, she felt as if she and Matt were leaders of the same team. A family team.

Barely able to comprehend just how comfortable that felt, Sara turned her attention back to the black Lab rollicking in the grass.

Amazed at how easily Matt had taken control of what had seemed to her to be a completely untenable situation, she inclined her head at Champ. "He didn't make a sound, not that I heard."

Matt turned to her, his handsome features bathed in the glow of the lamps above. The corners of his mouth lifted into an amused smile. "Yeah well—" he shrugged his wide shoulders "—he didn't go to sleep, either, but that will come."

Sara bet it would. "I noticed you moved the crate closer to the sofa." Where she had also deposited a pillow, blanket, washcloth and towel, toothbrush and toothpaste.

"As long as he's right next to me, I think he'll be fine."

She studied his profile, deciding he was way too sexy, whatever the time of day or night. Way too capable and masculine and kind as well.

Aware she could fall all too hard for the handsome rancher if she weren't careful, Sara folded her arms in front of herself. "I get that this approach might work tonight..." Who wouldn't feel safe with Matt stretched out beside them?

He turned. Seeming to zero in on her nervousness, he leaned in close, his smile slow and sure. "But...?"

Inhaling the intoxicatingly familiar scent of him, she edged back. "What about tomorrow?" She couldn't help but ask. "Are you doing this so you'll have to spend the night every night?"

"Hmm." He looked over to see her shivering in the night air. "Hadn't thought of that." He wrapped an arm about her shoulders and brought her in close to his side. His eyes gleamed devilishly. "But ah...now that you mention it..." he teased her softly, bending down to whisper in her ear "...the idea does have a certain appeal."

He favored her with a flirtatious smile that did funny things to her insides. And the chase was on.

Sara tried not to think how much she enjoyed having

him around, or how easy it would be to start depending on him. Even though their deal was set to go on for only three more weeks. She cleared her throat. "Seriously…"

Matt tightened his arm around her shoulders, in a friendly squeeze, then let her go. All Texas gentleman once again. "Seriously," he said drily, "he will get used to the crate in the next twenty-four hours or so and soon it will feel as cozy and safe to him as your arms."

Relief mixed with the desire starting up inside her. As their glances meshed and held, all Sara could think about was kissing him again. Not that she had any business doing that, either, when he was clearly a man who needed a wife and children, even if he hadn't realized it yet, and her heart was locked up tight. "I don't know how to thank you enough for all your help. I was at my wit's end."

He knit his brows together and teased in a soft, low voice that sent thrills coursing over her body. "Well, there might be a way."

Her heart skittering in her chest, Sara lifted her chin. "And what is that?" she asked, almost ashamed to admit what favors she could think of, off the top of her head.

Smiling, he stepped a little closer to her. "My family is having a potluck at my parents' ranch on Sunday afternoon. Lulu's bringing her Honeybee Ranch food truck which is going to make its debut in downtown Laramie next week. She's going to be testing a couple entrées. Everyone else is bringing sides."

Giving herself a second to recoup, Sara checked on Champ, who was still running circles in the grass. Finally, she turned and hazarded him a glance. "Sounds fun."

"Glad you think so," Matt said, and flashed his most persuasive smile, "because I'd like you to go with me."

"As a friend."

He made a seesawing motion with his hand. "Like I said, we don't have to label it."

Was he trying to confuse her? She stepped closer, too. "But your family will assume it's a date."

His hands settled on his waist. "Possibly."

Talk about infuriating. She lifted a censuring brow. "Or probably?"

"Does it matter?" He studied her for a long moment, and then his shoulders flexed in an offhand shrug. "You and I will know what it is."

Except, Sara thought, working hard to conceal her traitorous emotions, she really didn't.

She knew what she foolishly wanted it to be…a start to something more…that could lead to either a really close lifelong friendship, the kind where they could lean on and be there for each other, no matter what… Or… they could reach for something even more romantic and fulfilling, that would rid her of her grief and guilt, and ease the physical loneliness she felt. Even if it weren't dating, per se.

Unfortunately, she realized, taking in his casual expression, it did not seem as if she and Matt were on the same page.

He continued, matter-of-factly, "A favor from one friend to another."

As it turned out, Matt was correct. Champ did sleep through the night, and he did not bark again in his crate, so long as Matt was next to him. It was a little odd having the big, strong rancher there in the morning when she and Charley woke up, but as the morning progressed, she got used to the sight of him in rumpled clothing with dark tousled hair and a day's growth of beard. And she knew she could really get used to him making blueberry pancakes for them all and then accompanying her while she took Champ and Charley outside to enjoy the beautiful spring morning.

By the time Matt left to go back to his ranch, to shave and shower and tend to things there, Champ was so tuckered out he went willingly into his crate, curled up next to the old towels that smelled like her and Matt, and fell sound asleep.

The trip to Laramie Gardens went well, too.

"I can stay," Matt said, when they got back.

Wary of getting too dependent on the handsome cowboy, Sara shook her head. "No, I've got it," she said.

And to her satisfaction, she did.

Still, it was nice to see him again the next day when he arrived a little after two in the afternoon to pick them up for the potluck.

She had missed having him around.

And unless she was mistaken, he seemed to have missed being with the three of them, too.

It would have been nice, however, to clarify exactly what this was to him. A date? A return favor for a friend? A simple social occasion between platonic friends?

There was simply no clue on his ruggedly masculine face. Other than the fact that, to her increasing frustration, he absolutely did not want to put a label on whatever this was.

When they arrived at the McCabes' Bar M Ranch for the family dinner, cars and pickup trucks lined the drive. Lulu's Honeybee Ranch food truck was at the end and delicious smells were wafting through the truck's open service windows. They'd barely parked when members of his family started coming up to greet them.

Cullen and his wife, Bridgett, came over to introduce their fifteen-month-old son, Robby, to Charley, and their beagle-mix, Riot, to Champ.

The second oldest of the McCabe brothers—the widowed surgeon, Jack—had his daughters, aged three, four and six in tow. "They want to meet your two fellas," he told Sara drily.

"I told you the baby would be cute!" Lindsay, the oldest, said.

"I think I like the puppy better," Nicole, the middle daughter, exclaimed.

"I like 'em both," Chloe, the youngest, declared.

Sheriff's deputy Dan McCabe and his wife, Shelley, brought over their four-year-old triplets, who promptly knelt to pet both dogs.

"Are you two going to get married?" one asked.

"No!" Sara and Matt said swiftly, while the adults laughed.

"Never say never," Chase McCabe said, as he and his wife, Mitzy, pushed the stroller that held their quadruplets. The two had been sworn enemies, until a business calamity the previous Christmas had brought them together. He wrapped an arm around his wife's shoulders. "We're living proof that miracles can still happen, even in this day and age!"

"I wouldn't mind receiving one," an aproned Lulu said, coming up to join the group.

"Your time will come," Matt's dad, Frank McCabe, predicted warmly. He walked over to welcome Matt and

Sara, too. "Don't let them tease you too much," the tall, silver-haired rancher quipped.

Sara smiled back. "I can handle it. What I do need to know is where I should put the strawberry shortcake we brought for the potluck."

Frank directed, "Rachel is setting up a buffet on the screened-in back porch."

Relieved to be away from any of the questions she had a feeling were going to be coming up from the siblings, Sara headed for the rear of the house while Matt and his dad took charge of Charley and Champ.

Matt's mom, Rachel, was indeed on the back porch, setting out a lovely spread of homemade dishes. During the week, in town, the petite dynamo put her silvery blond hair up and wore suits and heels befitting her job as a tax attorney. On weekends, she left her hair down and dressed like a rancher's wife in jeans, boots and feminine cotton blouses. "Where would you like these?" Sara asked, showing Matt's mom what she had.

Rachel smiled. "Over here."

Sara stepped back. "Anything else I can do?"

"If you want to help me finish setting the table I won't say no." Rachel handed over a basket of silverware. "So how have you been?"

"Good," Sara was surprised to admit, even more so since Matt had come into her life.

Rachel went down the row, placing napkins. "How's Matt?"

Sara tensed. "Isn't that a question for him?"

"It would be—if he would ever tell me anything." Rachel paused. "Really, how does he seem to you?"

Torn, Sara hedged, "I'm not sure I can describe…"

"Try."

Finished with the silverware, Sara started putting out the glasses. "He's been very kind and helpful with Charley and Champ…"

Rachel added plates. "The word around town is that you've been seeing each other almost every day."

Sara nodded. "That's true."

Rachel straightened. "Are the two of you dating?"

Heat spread from the center of Sara's chest, into her face. "Matt—and I," Sara added uncomfortably, "would prefer not to put a label on it."

"So, in other words, yes."

Gosh, Rachel was persistent! But then so were most of the McCabes. And most moms, when it came to protecting their offspring.

"So, in other words," Sara corrected, taking an equally persistent and matter-of-fact tact, "Matt and I are reestablishing a friendship we both thought was long over. We're finding we had more in common than we knew." She flashed a friendly smile. "So, it's all good."

Except for one thing…

Figuring as long as they were talking candidly, she could ask a question or two also, Sara moved a little closer and continued, "What I don't get is why you and the rest of the family are so worried about him. I mean, he's as stubborn as he always was, but he seems fine to me." More than fine, actually, given what had happened to him and Mutt.

Rachel sighed. "I guess it's because, until very recently, he had seemed to be spending too much time alone. Not dating anyone. Which in turn made me wonder if he's really over the other military widow he was involved with."

Other military widow? Sara blinked, feeling gob-smacked. "What are you talking about?"

Rachel paused. "You don't know about Janelle?"

Feeling like she'd just taken a blow to the chest, Sara shook her head. "No," she said, just as Matt walked up to the porch, Charley in his arms.

The silence, already really awkward and rife with emotion, turned even more so. A fact Matt was quick to pick up on.

"Really, Mom," he drawled, "meddling already?"

The older woman straightened. "We were just talking."

Matt gave his mother a chastising look. "Well, now you can stop because Lulu is about ready to start serving the entrées."

Matt turned to Sara with a smile that did not quite reach his eyes. "Lulu is dying to have you try her honey chipotle chicken wings and honey barbecued ribs…so if you're game…"

"I am."

Luckily, there were no more questions about her and Matt's "romance" or lack thereof from anyone else in the McCabe family during the rest of the party.

When they went home, Matt took Champ out for a last outdoor break and some water, while Sara put an equally tuckered out Charley to bed.

When she came down, Champ was snoozing away in his crate, and Matt was standing in the kitchen, waiting to speak with her. "Sorry about my mom. She can't seem to help herself."

A mother herself now, Sara understood the fierce need to protect, so she waved off his concern. "It was fine." Sara began to put some of the leftovers that had been sent home with her in the fridge.

Apparently for Matt, it hadn't been. "What did she say?"

The real question was, what did Matt *not want* Rachel to reveal? Deciding this was an opportunity to satisfy her own curiosity, Sara shot him a commiserating look and said, "Your mom mentioned a military widow named Janelle."

Matt's stoic reaction did not change.

Swallowing, Sara continued, "She seemed to think there was some parallel between your relationship with Janelle, and your renewed friendship with me."

"There isn't."

Silence fell and he offered nothing more.

Not willing to even consider being in a relationship where she was repeatedly shut out emotionally, Sara decided to let it—and consequently, him—go.

"Okay."

Her heart aching, she pivoted away.

He put a hand on her shoulder. Waited until she made a half turn. "That's it?" he demanded curtly. "Just… okay? No more questions?"

Sara drew a deep breath, unwilling to take all the blame for the new tension between them. "You don't like questions," she reminded him, reining in her emotions, too. Even as her skin heated at his gentle touch. "And I don't like having to ask, so…" Deciding it was best they curtail this conversation, she started to show him the door.

He caught her hand. His gray-blue gaze was sober, intent.

"What do you want to know?"

Chapter 7

Sara turned around. She'd had all evening to think about this, and she knew that if she and Matt were ever to get really close—as close as she wanted them to be—he was going to have to let down his guard a little. "Were you in love with her?"

He released a short, impatient breath. "I thought I was."

She walked into the kitchen and took two cold sports drinks from the fridge. As she handed him one, their fingers brushed and a thrill swept through her. "Are you in love with her now?"

Twisting off the cap, he shook his head.

Surprised how much this meant to her, Sara tensed. "Are you sure?"

He took a long drink, then studied her over the rim of the bottle. The corners of his sensual lips curved up.

"You're not going to rest until you hear the whole sad story, are you?"

Why lie? She didn't know why it mattered so much to her, she just knew that it did. Shrugging, she took a drink, too. "Probably not."

He took her by the hand and led her into the living room, settling on the middle of the sofa. Happy he was about to confide in her, she took the place beside him.

He squeezed her hand, letting their clasped palms rest on his thigh. "A year into my last deployment, one of my buddies was killed while out on a mission. I accompanied his body back to Virginia, where his wife and his family resided."

Sara could only imagine how difficult that had been for him.

As Matt continued, his face became etched with grief. "I was a pallbearer. Everyone was as distraught as you might imagine, and after the service, at the gathering back at the house, his widow, Janelle, and I talked a lot. She wanted to know a lot about her husband's last days. If I thought Dirk had been happy and I told her—honestly—that she had meant the world to him."

Matt swallowed and his voice grew hoarse. "When I got back to my unit, I got all the guys to make a video, recounting some of their best memories of Dirk, and I sent it to her and his family.

"They were really happy to have it. Janelle wrote and thanked us. One email led to another." He shrugged. "And pretty soon we were talking regularly. Six months later, when I had a few weeks leave, she met up with me in Italy." He cleared his throat as an indecipherable emotion crossed his face. "And we went from being friends to something more."

"You were serious about her," Sara guessed. They were sitting so close she could feel the heat emanating from his powerful body.

"Very." Matt's expression turned brooding. "Anyway, one thing led to another, and before we knew it, we were talking about being together when I left the service.

"At first," he admitted, a mixture of regret and self-admonition filling his tone, "the plan was that I would move to Arlington, get a job there when my tour ended. So we could really date." He exhaled. "Then, she decided that even though we'd only been in a relationship a few months, it was silly to pretend we *weren't* going to end up together."

Talk about jumping ahead! Sara thought in surprise. "And you were good with that," she surmised.

"Initially, yeah." Matt nodded curtly, remembering, clearly as caught off guard then as she was now. He shifted toward her, a soul-deep weariness in his eyes. Compassionately, he related, "Janelle was big on advance planning. And I gave her that because I know sometimes when you're dealing with a loss, you just need something in the future to hold on to, in order to keep going."

"Something to give you hope," Sara said softly. That you can actually control.

Matt squeezed her hand, as if glad she understood. "Right. Anyway, Janelle wanted us to share a home together when I did get out of the service, *but* not the one that she had lived in with Dirk, so she put her house on the market, and sold it, and started looking at high-rise condominiums."

"While you were still on active duty overseas?"

"Yes."

Maybe it was Matt's rugged physicality, but Sara couldn't picture him residing happily in the city, any more than she could see him ever sitting at a desk all day. He wasn't really a suit and tie kind of guy. Casually, she asked, "Were you interested in living in a skyscraper?"

"No. And, in fact, I didn't want her to buy *anything* in Virginia with me in mind because I had already purchased the Silver Creek here, and knew that ultimately I wanted to live in Laramie County. She didn't even want to visit Texas. So we started arguing."

"Over email," Sara guessed.

"And via Skype."

"That doesn't sound fun."

"It wasn't." Matt sighed. "Anyway, I tried to put myself in her place."

That sounded like the gallant man she knew.

"I attributed her need to be near her own family and sort of control everything about our future relationship to the sudden, unexpected way she had lost Dirk. So I finally relented and said we'd live wherever she chose, at least for the first few years. Work obligations would likely dictate it after that. I'd keep my ranch—as an investment and a retreat."

"Sounds fair." Sort of…

"And in return, she agreed not to actually purchase anything until we could look at properties together."

"Sounds practical."

He nodded. "When I got out, I went straight to Virginia, instead of Texas, to see her. I just intended to stay a couple weeks. Then I figured we'd travel to Texas to see my family. I wanted her to meet everyone…"

Also reasonable, Sara thought.

"…and at least see the Silver Creek before returning to Virginia to look for work, but that wasn't in her plans. She said there was no time for us to go to Texas to see my family. She'd already set up properties for us to look at, and appointments for me with job recruiters who specialized in placing ex-military in the Washington, DC, area."

That, Sara thought, was incredibly, ridiculously presumptuous. She tried to put together everything she already knew about him. "And this was after your base was attacked and Mutt died." And he had probably needed his family more than ever, even if he hadn't told them what had happened.

"Not too long after, yes."

"And Janelle knew that?" *Knew you were still reeling?*

Again, a terse nod. "We didn't talk a lot about the attack on the compound because of what she'd already been through, losing Dirk and all, but yeah, she had all the details my family didn't."

Which meant they'd been close. "And she still didn't cut you any slack?"

"I didn't expect her to," Matt said gruffly.

But his ex should have been understanding and sympathetic, Sara thought resentfully. She should have wanted Matt to spend time with the rest of the McCabes. She should have wanted to meet them, too. "So what happened next?"

He stood and walked over to the fireplace. "We did what we always did when a conflict arose—we argued. More bitterly than ever. I told her there was no way I was going to work in an office, or be security somewhere. I wasn't sure what I wanted to do at that point, but I did know that I wanted to be outdoors, and that I was perfectly capable of finding my own employment without her help."

Sara joined him at the mantel. "I'm guessing that did not go over well?"

He turned to face her. "Janelle was furious. She said if I wanted to be with her, I was going to have to honor all her demands." Matt shook his head in irritation. "I'd had enough of all the conditions. So we broke up and I came back to Texas."

Sara took his hand and squeezed it. "I'm sorry." It sounded like he had been through hell.

"I'm not." His gaze narrowed. "All that made me realize that an emotional connection and physical chemistry aren't sufficient for any couple."

She breathed in the masculine fragrance of his skin and gazed up at him. "What do you need to be happy?"

He flashed her a roguish grin. "The kind of easy, satisfying relationship all my siblings seem to be getting, the kind my parents have."

Finding his low, husky voice a little too enticing for comfort, she returned, "That's a tall order, cowboy." But an oh-so-delectable one.

He wrapped an arm about her waist and reeled her in to his side, his mouth hovering over hers. "Maybe," he told her huskily, "not as tall as you think."

Sara had been telling herself she'd been exaggerating the impact of their previous kisses.

The practical side of her only wished that was the case!

The moment his lips were on hers, drawing her in, she was as lost in him as ever before.

Sara knew they should slow things down. Get to know each other again a whole lot better before attempting any kind of physical intimacy.

And while that made sense on a purely intellectual level, emotionally she needed him to put the moves on her. Make her feel all woman to his man. Sexy, vibrant and alive.

For months and months now, she had been living in a dark lonely place, her only joys her infant son and the animals she cared for.

Matt made her feel as if she could have more.

Maybe not forever.

Maybe not in any truly meaningful or long lasting way.

But she could have pleasure, she discovered, as his hands slipped beneath the hem of her shirt, caressing her back and better molding her against his hard, muscular planes.

She went up on tiptoe, wreathing her arms about his shoulders, even as he clasped her closer. And still he kissed her, deeply, irrevocably, his lips seducing hers apart and his tongue tangling with hers. She felt the pounding of his heart, the depth of his desire. She tasted the essence that was him.

And still she wanted him.

Wanted *this*.

Matt hadn't intended to let them get any closer than they already were. Hadn't planned to take her in his arms and kiss her again, because it would add a whole host of complications to an already tenuous situation.

She was vulnerable.

So was he.

In different ways, to be sure, but the bottom line

was he was not what she needed. And, despite the passion flowing between them, he did not want to take advantage.

But remaining emotionally aloof around her was proving to be a futile task when she melted against him, kissing him back, again and again and again. The blood thundered through him and he reveled in the soft surrender of her body pressed against his.

With a groan, he tore his mouth from hers. Breathing raggedly, he closed his eyes. "If I don't leave now..."

"I know." She kissed his throat.

With another groan, he looked down at her. "Sara..."

She unbuttoned his shirt. "I want you to stay, Matt." Her gaze zeroed on his. She lifted her chin, challenging him to dare to try and chastise her for choosing to live her life anyway she chose. She pressed another kiss on his collarbone, shoulder, jaw. "I want to make love."

He emitted another lust-filled sigh.

Then seeing the raw need, and the fierce determination in her eyes, decided, why fight it?

She was an adult. They both were. And if this was what they needed...

"Upstairs?"

She nodded and took his hand.

There was plenty of time as they made their way to her bedroom to change their minds.

They didn't.

Instead, she drew him over to her bed, then lifted her arms to encircle his shoulders and kissed him with a wildness beyond his most erotic dreams. With her breasts pressed intimately against him, her hands sliding up and down his spine, she rocked against him in a way that had all his gentlemanly instincts fading.

Drunk with pleasure, he undressed her and filled his hands with her lush, delectable curves. She was incredibly beautiful, soft and silky all over, damp with desire.

She stripped off his shirt, dropped her hands to his fly. His jeans came off, then his shorts.

He let her call the shots, let her be in control, until they were almost there. Then he laid her back on the bed and slid between her thighs.

She gasped as his hand found his way to the feminine heart of her. Shuddered as he helped her find the release she sought. He found a condom. Slid upward. Lifting her to him, easing in, then diving deep. She closed around him like a tight, hot sheath, and together, they soared toward a passionate completion more stunning and fulfilling than anything he had ever felt.

Afterward, they clung together in silence, still shuddering, breathing hard. But as normality returned, so did Sara's usual reserve. To his disappointment, Matt felt the barriers around her heart going right back up.

When she turned on her side, away from him, he bent over to kiss her bare shoulder. "Hey…" he said softly, wanting her to know this was not casual. Not… meaningless.

She waited, not moving.

But how to approach it? In a way that wouldn't insult. "Maybe we should forget about not using labels."

This caught her attention.

She turned back to him, caution in her pretty green eyes. "And do what?" she asked in surprise.

"Date."

Chapter 8

"Oh, Matt," Sara said wistfully.

She draped the blanket around herself and moved elegantly to her feet.

Regret flowing through him like the tide, he sat up, too, and reached for his boxer-briefs. Damn it all. He had known it was too soon to make love to her. Given what had just happened between them, though, it shouldn't be too soon to ask her out. In fact, that should have happened first. Probably two weeks ago, after the first time they kissed.

"If you're worried about this making things too complicated between us, you needn't be," he said gently, determined to ease her worries and lighten her mood. He sent her a look filled with mischief. "Complicated is just fine with me."

With a low laugh, she shook her head. "Oh, Matt,"

she said again. The picture of sated elegance, she gathered her bra and panties off the floor. Managed to don her panties with the blanket still around her.

With a faint shake of her head and a soft exhalation of breath, she let the blanket fall all the way to the floor. Giving him a fine view of her curvaceous backside in the process. And though he could no longer see what lay beneath her floral print cotton panties, he remembered the petal softness well.

He felt himself grow hard again.

"Tell me what's on your mind," he encouraged.

Keeping her back to him, she slipped on her bra and fastened it in front. "You don't have to be gallant." She looked at him with weary embarrassment as she pulled her arms through the sleeves of her blouse and shimmied into her denim skirt. "I get what this was." Barefoot, she disappeared into the adjacent bathroom and came out with a brush.

Aware it was just as arousing to watch her dress as it had been to undress her, he shifted on his jeans. Reached for his shirt, too.

"For both of us," she added, suddenly looking a whole lot more practical and a lot less emotional than the situation warranted.

"Hmm." Matt stroked his jaw in a parody of thoughtfulness. "A long time coming, maybe?" he teased.

She nixed his guess. "Rebound sex."

To Matt, that was both good news and bad. Bad in the sense that she put it in the category of something not necessarily to be repeated again. Good in that… He studied the flush in her cheeks and the shimmer of feminine embarrassment in her jade eyes. "You haven't…?"

Her tongue snaked out to wet her lower lip. “Not since Anthony,” she confirmed softly. Then demonstrated the kind of mutual interest he hoped she would. Swallowing, she looked him in the eye. “And you?”

He was pleased to report, “Not since Janelle.”

He’d thought the fact he didn’t bed women recklessly would be of comfort to her.

Instead, it only seemed to confirm what erroneous conclusions she had already made. “See?” She leaned against her dresser, arms folded in front of her, satisfied her point had been made.

Their lovemaking had been rebound sex. Nothing more. Nothing less.

Matt finished getting dressed. Hands spread in a gesture of supplication, he walked toward her. “I hear what you’re saying, darlin’, but I don’t agree.”

Her chin lifting, she gave him a challenging look that made him want to ravish her all over again.

“If I just wanted to…um—” he tried to think of a respectful way to put it, and failed “—I could have. As could you.”

She uttered a smothered half laugh, then sent her glance heavenward, sighed. “What’s your point, cowboy?”

He looked down at her arms, which were still crossed militantly in front of her, and knew he had his work cut out for him.

That did not make him any less intent on persuading her to give him…them…a chance, however.

He took another step closer, and looked deep into her eyes, reiterating gently, “It means, Sara—” he took her resisting body all the way into his arms "—that maybe the fact we chose here and now means something."

As Sara gazed up into Matt's ruggedly handsome face, she wanted to believe that. *So much.*

Especially since she'd had a secret crush on Matt for years that had only faded when she got married. After she lost her husband, and Matt returned to Laramie County, that desire had come roaring back. Hence why it wasn't a surprise to her that they had ended up in bed.

She also knew the night had been an emotional one. For them both. He yearned for the kind of satisfying romantic relationship most of the members of his family had. She did, too. But she also knew that kind of romantic love did not happen on a whim. And what they'd enjoyed just now—satisfying and wonderful as it was—had been wildly, recklessly impulsive. Which was something she had never been.

Sara sighed. She wished he didn't look so damn hot, even in his disheveled state, because it was *not* helping matters. "Look, Matt, I'm not the same person you remember."

She focused on the disbelief in his eyes.

"Why do you think that?" He continued to study her as if trying to figure something out.

Heat gathered in her chest and spread through her throat to her face. She knew she had to be completely honest with him, or even a friendship between them would never work. She knotted her hands in front of her. "Because the last decade has changed me."

He pulled her against him for a sweet and thorough kiss that quickly had her tingling from head to toe. He lifted his head, then swept his hand through her hair. "We're both definitely older and more mature."

She splayed a hand across the center of his chest. "And guarded in ways that the people closest to us don't want to see or accept." Beneath her fingers, she could feel the strong and steady beat of his heart.

"It's like there's this wall," Matt said.

She wet her lips. "Around our hearts."

A contemplative silence fell.

She remained in the circle of his arms. "The thing is, I like having that wall around me," Sara said, appreciating how protected and cared for she felt when she was with him, even though she knew her heart was very much at risk. She lifted her head to look into his eyes. "I feel like it keeps Charley and me safe."

And while such emotional independence was good for her, it might not be good for him.

And because she cared about Matt, she wanted what was best for him. Always.

The corners of his lips lifted ruefully. "You may have noticed I like to keep my distance from people, too, darlin'." He paused, as if sensing that in this one area they were really in sync. His gaze darkened. "The quiet and solitude…the lack of demands…can bring a lot of peace."

She took his hand and led him through the bedroom doorway, back down the stairs. As they landed on the first floor, well away from the temptations of her bed, she drew a deep breath, confessing, "The thing is, my friends and family keep urging me to open up my heart again, and go back to being my 'old hopelessly romantic self.' But I can't do it. I don't want to be that vulnerable or emotionally dependent on anyone again."

So he needed to know this was as close as they were ever likely to get. She wasn't even sure this was sustainable, given how conflicted she was feeling right now.

"Never mind anyone's wife," he deadpanned.

Were they really talking marriage now? "Or significant other." She didn't want that kind of pressure, to make everything turn out all right.

By the same token, she wasn't promiscuous. So she couldn't just have random one-night stands and feel good about it, because that wasn't the real her, either.

Sara's brows knit together. "Why are you smiling?"

He shrugged and flashed her an indulgent smile. "I just find it ironic..."

"Because?" She went into the kitchen to get something to drink.

He followed beside her. "Weddings were all you ever talked about when we were teenagers."

How well she remembered. Her favorite magazines when she was in high school had been centered on being a bride.

She poured him a tall glass of lemonade and handed it to him. "That's because I thought marriage to the love of your life was the key to living happily ever after." How that dream had crashed. "Now I know it isn't."

He regarded her over the rim of his glass. "Because Anthony died."

She sipped the tart, icy liquid. Waited while it soothed her dry, taut throat. "There's that."

He sat down at the breakfast table. As she started to

walk by, he hooked an arm about her waist and drew her down onto his lap. "And what else?"

Sara set her glass on the table beside her. She figured as long as she was baring her soul, she might as well tell Matt about this insufficiency, too. "I don't know if it was me." She let her fingertips dance across the broad plane of his shoulder.

"Or Anthony. Or the fact that we had such a whirlwind romance, and then rushed into marriage before he left for the Middle East. But…" She bit her lip in chagrin.

Matt studied her, as always seeing so much more than she would have preferred. "You weren't happy together?"

Finding it impossible to talk about this when she was so physically close to Matt, Sara stood and paced a distance away. Taking a deep, bolstering breath, she forced herself to continue, as frankly as possible, so he would understand what a very bad bet she was as a life partner. For Anthony, and now for Matt…

"Our reunions while he was in the army were always wildly passionate and then so horribly bittersweet and sad when he had to leave."

She could see Matt understood; he had been through the deployment miseries himself.

Doing her best to suppress the remembered hurt, she swallowed. "Then, when he finally did come back for good, he was just… Our relationship was just…so different. He didn't talk to me anymore." She'd felt like she barely knew him, and vice versa.

"PTSD?"

She stuffed down another wave of pain. “Like you, he said not.”

Matt’s gaze narrowed. “You think otherwise.”

“I don’t know.” Without warning, Sara found herself blinking back tears. “There were a lot of days he seemed completely fine, happy even.” When she had a ray of hope. Enough to want to start a family with him. She shook her head, still struggling to contain the raw emotion welling within her. “Others, where he was drinking too much. Flying off the handle. Taking reckless chances.” To the point she had been worried and on edge.

Matt leaned toward her, his forearms on the breakfast table between them. “So when your husband’s car went off the road one afternoon, in that freak accident, leaving you alone and pregnant…”

And sad and guilty and so much more.

Matter-of-factly, he surmised, “You decided that was it, as far as ever getting married again went. At least to an ex-soldier.”

“Yes.” Yet life went on. And she had Charley, and for a while anyway, little Champ. And now, temporarily anyway, Matt…?

She swallowed hard, confessing honestly, “I miss my husband every day and I deeply regret that Charley will never know his father, but—” She paused to corral her emotions and draw an enervating breath. “Being a single mom isn’t so bad.” Doing her best to look on the bright side, she lifted her arm expansively. “I get a whole king-size bed to myself. Never have to negotiate what’s for dinner. Or share the remote.”

“I can see the pluses of that,” he rasped.

As their eyes met, his filled with heat.

"But you still want to do whatever-this-was-tonight again," Sara guessed.

He stood, all Texas gentleman. All honorable McCabe. "When you're ready." Which he seemed to fully expect her to be one day. "Yeah," he said softly, coming over to kiss her one last, completely thrilling time. "I do."

Matt was out in the field, taking down more fence the next morning when his oldest brother, Cullen, drove across the semi-open field and stopped just short of him.

Matt put down his tools and walked over to greet him. "Hey. What's up?"

Cullen emerged from his pick-up truck. "Thought I'd come out to see how things were going out here." He gazed around Matt's ranch, surveying the progress that had been made. "Pretty slow, from the looks of it."

Sensing a talk he didn't much want to hear coming on, Matt pretended not to understand where this all was headed. "You accusing me of being lazy?"

"Nope. Just impractical and stubborn to a fault is all."

"Thanks, bro."

"You're welcome."

They exchanged grins. "As you know," Cullen continued, serious now, "I've got a lot of calves about to be born and I need a safe place to put them and their mamas until they're weaned. I was hoping to lease pasture here, on the Silver Creek, by next month."

The thought of having cattle trucks in and out, and hired hands disrupting his solitude set Matt on edge. With a sigh, he walked back to pick up some of the debris. He carried it over to the bed of his pick-up truck.

With as much patience as he could muster, he reminded, "I told you it would probably be another year. Maybe two before I'd be ready for that."

Cullen nodded. "And I offered to bring some of my men over to speed things up. So you could start making money instead of just spending it."

Matt gathered another half-dozen rusty metal posts. "Thanks. I've got it covered."

Cullen stepped in to help. "You sure?"

Matt considered. He was getting better, thanks to Sara, and Charley, and Champ. He still had a ways to go. "Yep. So maybe you better start looking elsewhere for pasture to lease."

Together, they carried the trash over to the bed of the truck, dumped it on top of the rest.

The awkward silence stretched.

"You know, I may only be half McCabe," Cullen finally said.

That again? Aware he wasn't the only family member who'd had issues, Matt held up a staying hand. "You know you're as much a part of the Rachel and Frank McCabe clan as the rest of us."

"Now, yes," Cullen admitted candidly. "Thanks to some recent revelations, brought about by my lovely wife. But there was a time, when I was sixteen and I first came to live with you-all, when I was just like you are now, little brother."

Matt preened. "Incredibly handsome and charming?"

Cullen guffawed—as Matt meant him to do.

Eventually, the twinkle in Cullen's eyes faded. He got serious again. "I had walls around me a mile high. The way you do now."

Matt didn't need reminding that the war had changed him, and not for the better. He scowled impatiently. "What's your point?"

Cullen shrugged. "Just that it's a lonely way to live." His voice grew rusty. "If it weren't for Bridgett and Robby and Riot, and the unexpected way they came into my life..." He paused to shake his head, his affection for his wife, baby and puppy as clear as the blue Texas sky overhead. "Well, let's just say I would not be anywhere near as gloriously happy as I am now."

Matt knew that. He met Cullen's eyes. "I'm glad you all have each other," he said. And he meant it.

Cullen clapped a brotherly hand on Matt's shoulder. "I want you to have a wife who loves you... *and* a family of your own...complete with kids and a dog, too."

Funny, Matt was feeling the same.

That did not mean it was going to happen.

Not with his limitations and Sara feeling the way she did.

Still, the time they were spending together...their passionate lovemaking...had showed him they could have something incredible.

Something enduring.

And Sara was right.

Their relationship didn't have to necessarily be formal or traditional. With time, they could—and would—fashion an arrangement that worked well for them.

And for now, that was enough, Matt told himself firmly. It was going to have to be.

"How's it going?" Matt asked when Sara let him in later that same day. One thing was certain: the mommy in charge looked extraordinarily beautiful in navy leggings and a long-sleeved blue-and-red-striped shirt. Her hair was swept into a loose sexy knot, and her skin was glowing luminously. It appeared whatever misgivings she'd had about their reckless lovemaking had been put to rest by their long talk and amazing good-night kiss the evening before.

He knew he felt good about it. Then and now.

As if it were the beginning of something magnificent…

"Oh, Matt, you have to see this!" Sara announced happily. She made a sweeping gesture toward the center of the living area. "Charley is attempting to crawl."

Matt followed her out of the foyer and hunkered down beside Sara's son. The infant was lying on his tummy on a play quilt spread across the floor. Soft, cloth infant toys were scattered around him. Some within reach, others purposefully not.

"Go for it, Charley," Sara cheered.

Charley gurgled merrily in response, seeming to understand perfectly what his mommy wanted from him.

Impressed, Matt watched Charley lift his head and all four limbs in the air with astounding athleticism, while his tummy remained flat against the blanket.

"It looks like he's pretending to fly," he said, as Charley "pretend-soared" a little more, making enthusiastic noises all the while, then abruptly ran out of steam and let his limbs collapse around him.

Matt eased the toy Charley was reaching for a little closer. With a grunt and a smile, the baby turned over onto his back and rolled the rest of the way toward it.

When his fingers closed on it, he gurgled happily and lifted it to his mouth.

"Way to go, little man," Matt praised, gently touching his baby-soft cheek.

Charley gurgled happily and kicked some more.

Matt looked over at the whelping pen—which was empty— and the crate. Also empty.

Sara knelt on the other side of the blanket. Her son between them. Noting how quiet it was, Matt looked around some more. "Where's Champ?"

"At the WTWA facility in town, working with one of the trainers. I'm supposed to meet up with them in about an hour."

"Is that why you texted me that I didn't need to set aside time to help you-all out today?" Or was it because they'd made love the night before, and she wanted her space, to further reconsider their plunge into physical intimacy?

Although she was clearly happy to see him, there was no clue on her pretty features as to what else she might currently want from him. At least in the romance department.

Sara looked at him from beneath her lashes. "I don't really need you to go with me to pick Champ up, since there will be plenty of people who can help me get Champ and Charley in the SUV simultaneously. But—" she watched as her son rolled back onto his tummy again and set his sights on another toy "—if you want to tag along, it *might* be fun."

He picked up on her cautious tone. "Might be?"

Abruptly, Sara looked torn. She rose lithely and walked over to the kitchen, where she'd been removing the stems of fresh strawberries. "Alyssa Barnes, the wounded infantry soldier who is going to train Champ, was just transferred to a rehab unit in Laramie, for the rest of her three-week recovery." Sara's voice took on an unexpectedly emotional note. "Her parents are bringing her over to WTWA, and she's going to meet Champ for the first time."

So much for her having her affection for the puppy under lock and key.

Noticing her eyes had taken on a suspiciously moist sheen, Matt gave Charley an affectionate pat, then rose and moved to her side. All the while giving her the chance she needed to compose herself.

Out of the corner of his eye, he watched her pull herself together. Their fingers touched as she handed him a luscious red berry, then took one for herself, too. "They're expecting the meet and greet to really boost Alyssa's morale."

At her invitation, Matt helped himself to another berry. "She's having a hard time?"

Sara nodded, her expression grim. "Numerous surgeries, infection, a lot of setbacks." She handed him another couple of strawberries before putting the bowl back in the fridge. "And she has another grueling three weeks or so of PT to go before she'll be well enough to work with Champ completely on her own. But her sister and parents have all pledged to help with that while she's on the mend. So there's no doubt she'll get there."

"When will you be turning Champ over to her?"

"We've set the date for the reunion picnic."

So Sara still had time to come to terms with the goodbye to little Champ.

As did he…

Deciding they needed something else to focus on, Matt observed, "The strawberries are great, by the way."

Sara laid a hand over her heart. "The first real bounty

of spring, at least in my view!" She sighed, happy color coming into her cheeks. "I love it when they're sweet. And tart, too."

Unable to resist, he teased, "Kind of like you?"

"Whoa there, cowboy." She splayed her hands across the center of his chest, blushing for a completely different reason now. "Laying on the charm a little thick today, don't you think?"

He smirked in response.

If that was her not-so-subtle way of telling him to stop flirting, he wasn't making any promises. Paternal instincts kicking in, he turned to check on Charley. The little boy was lying on his back, contentedly inspecting a stuffed toy in his hands.

Satisfied they had time to banter, he turned back to Sara. Let his gaze drift over her lazily. "What else do you like in the spring?"

"In terms of fresh produce?" she asked, deliberately misunderstanding what he was asking. "Pretty much everything…"

"So," he drawled back, "the way to your heart is definitely via your taste buds."

He could handle that. He eased his hand through the wisps of hair at the nape of her neck.

She gasped as he rained a few kisses over the soft, feminine slope of her throat. "Very funny."

Not enough? "A few hot, sexy kisses, then." He gathered her close.

Sara groaned. "Matt…" She used her splayed hands to put pressure on his chest.

Much more of this playing around and he'd be wanting to make love to her, here and now. "Okay." He let her go reluctantly. "But just for the record," he said with a wink, "I'm available whenever…and wherever, darlin'."

His mischievous attitude had replaced the heavy drama of the night before, just as he had hoped. Sara looked happy again. Turned on. Almost carefree…

"Oh, I think you've made that pretty clear, cowboy." Sara responded with a candor he hadn't dared expect.

He noticed she wasn't saying yes, exactly. Nor was she saying no. But they were definitely in "maybe, when the time is right again" territory.

He could definitely deal with that.

She drew a bolstering breath. "In the meantime, it's time for us to go. We've got a schedule to keep."

"OMG! This little guy is so cute!" Alyssa Barnes said as she sat and cuddled Champ in her arms.

Champ, never one to turn away any adoration, licked the red-haired former army sergeant under the chin.

Alyssa looked at Sara, her freckled face alight with joy. "Thank you for stepping in temporarily so I'll still be able to join the program as planned and help train this little guy."

"No problem." Sara smiled. "You should thank Matt, too. He's also lent a hand."

Alyssa looked at Charley, who was cuddled up as snugly in Matt's arms as Champ was in hers. "Is this your little boy?" she asked the two of them.

Sara wasn't surprised she'd made that assumption. Matt cared for her little boy with all the love and tenderness of a Super Dad. "Charley is my son," Sara clarified.

"Oh." Alyssa looked taken aback, and no wonder, given the affection flowing between the two. It wasn't just Matt who was completely besotted. Charley snuggled up to Matt with total adoration, too. "I thought…" she stammered.

Sara cut her off with a relaxed lift of her hand. "We're just friends." *Although, part of me would like to be so much more...*

"Right." Alyssa paused. Her brow furrowed. She looked down at the black Lab in her arms. "Is it okay if I spend a little more time with Champ?"

Sara looked at Alyssa and her sister, who was there to assist since the former soldier was still in a knee brace, moving stiffly. "Take your time." She and Matt left them in the group meeting room and shut the door behind them.

"Sara? Matt?" Hope Winslow-Lockhart, the director of WTWA public relations, strode toward them. Elegantly dressed as always, the tall blonde executive asked, "Could I have a word with the two of you?"

"Sure," Sara and Matt said in unison.

They walked down the hall and moved into Hope's office.

She gestured for them both to take a seat. "I wanted to update Matt about the progress we are making with the volunteer recruitment initiative, so he'll know how his very generous donation is being spent."

She logged on to her computer and showed them both the new social media page that had been set up.

"We want to add videos of all the people who help teach each service, therapy or companion dog. We're going to use Star—Champ's mother—and compile the video we already have of her during her pregnancy and the birth of her litter, to the very first eight weeks of her nine puppies' lives, while they were all still at Sara's ranch. And then get film of every person working with every puppy after they left the litter. We want to show how the aptitude of each dog is evaluated and let everyone know that in this case it really does take a village to train a dog.

"So, if we could get someone—say Matt—to film Sara on his phone, as she works with Champ, it would be really great."

"I can do that," Matt said.

If he did, it would mean they would be spending even more time together, Sara thought with surprising happiness.

"And of course we'll get film of Alyssa Barnes as she bonds with Champ, too."

"What do we do with the videos?" Matt asked.

Hope handed over a paper. "Just email it to the editor's address. She'll take it from there." The PR director reached for another page. "I also wanted to let you both know that we've got a couple new support groups starting next week."

Her expression sobered slightly. "One for widows and widowers of military personnel."

Sara leaned forward slightly, not sure she'd heard right.

Hope continued, "The other group is for ex-soldiers who are transitioning back to civilian life."

Matt looked about as happy as she felt. "Tell me my family didn't put you up to this," he said brusquely.

Expression tranquil, Hope shook her head. "I was just hoping you both might choose to participate."

"I'm doing okay," Sara said, still feeling a little rattled at having been singled out this way.

Hope smiled. "I know that," she said with her trademark gentleness. "It's why I thought you might be a good role model for the new widows."

Sara drew a breath. Was it stuffy in here or what? All she knew was she suddenly felt slightly claustrophobic. Needing fresh air, she rose. "I don't feel like I'm quite there yet."

Hope stood, too. "Then you could show the others what it's like to be midway point in your recovery," she suggested candidly.

Sara caught a glimpse of Matt's stone face, and forced a smile. "Thanks for the invitation," she said, flashing a polite but firm smile, "but I am too busy with Champ and Charley right now to even consider taking on anything else."

Hope managed not to look disappointed. "Maybe later?"

"I'll definitely think about it," Sara fibbed. Even though she knew she wouldn't.

Hope turned to look at Matt.

Not surprisingly, he merely stood and said, "Sorry. Not my thing."

An hour later, Matt drove Sara, Charley and Champ home. They woke Charley getting him out of his car seat, which he was not happy about. And when Sara sat down to feed her son his dinner, he was even crankier.

"Think it's his teeth?" Matt asked, when Charley refused both his baby food and bottle.

Aware she had just been wondering the same thing, Sara looked in his mouth. The lower gum was pink, and a little more swollen than it had been earlier. "Maybe."

She got out the numbing cream. And a teething ring

from the freezer. Charley accepted the first, and batted the second away.

Meanwhile, little Champ—who hadn't seemed to miss Sara and Matt at all while visiting with Alyssa and her sister—chowed down on his puppy food with enthusiasm.

Deciding her son wasn't liable to eat or drink anything until he was in a better frame of mind, Sara took him out of his high chair and, humming softly, danced him around the kitchen.

The movement was enough to make him stop crying.

Matt watched, smiling. "You're really good with him."

High praise from a noted source. Sara smiled back, glad she had opted to invite him to stay on for a while longer. Which he had oh-so-willingly accepted. The fact was, she needed Matt near her tonight. "So are you."

He cleared his throat. "Sorry Alyssa Barnes thought..."

Sara waved his unnecessary words away. "I'm not. It was an easy mistake to make."

Eyes darkening with indecipherable emotion, Matt continued, "I'd be incredibly happy if Charley were my son."

So would I, Sara thought.

She waited.

The disloyalty she expected never came. Wondering if she *should* feel guilty, she frowned.

Matt studied her.

"Does Hope ask you to join a support group a lot?" he asked.

Ah. She'd been wondering if he would bring that up. Though, like her, he didn't really want to seem to talk about it. "This was the first time."

He sauntered closer, his expression curious. "Did it upset you?"

Good question. Initially, she'd felt shocked, almost insulted. Then scared of what taking a step like that would bring.

Aware Matt was waiting for her answer, and that this was a very raw subject for him, too, she chose her words carefully. "I don't want to start moving backward. I worry that dwelling on my loss in a support group, week after week, would lead me to do just that. And that would be bad for me and for Charley, and really, anyone close to me." It seemed to her that Anthony's death had hurt enough already.

Matt nodded. He took her hand in his, gave it a heartfelt squeeze. "Now you know how I feel," he said.

"About joining a group where you're forced to share your feelings with everyone?"

He nodded. "It's not that I mind talking about what's going on with me, privately, from time to time, when it seems appropriate. Or when I just need to vent."

He drew her slightly closer, and Sara tightened her fingers in his, loving the solid masculine warmth of him.

"But making 'true confessions' isn't something I can do on demand," he finished gruffly.

Sara sighed and rested her head on his shoulder. "Me, either."

Another silence fell, more companionable this time. With a soft sigh, she lifted her head. Their eyes locked, and as she gazed into his eyes, she couldn't help but think how right it felt, being with him. Whenever, wherever…

She smiled as her next idea hit. "Maybe we can be each other's support-person," she said.

Matt bent his head and kissed her tenderly, once and then again. "I'd like that," he said.

As he gathered her close, Sara knew she would, too. Even though she still wasn't certain when—or even if—they would make love again. Or be anything more than increasingly good friends.

Chapter 9

Sara glanced at the clock for what seemed like the hundredth time in the past half hour. Charley cooed from his seat in the windup swing while Champ watched patiently from inside his crate.

"It's weird, isn't it?" she said, checking her cell phone to make sure the battery was fully charged. It was. "Matt is usually so punctual. Early even." He was never late for Champ's training sessions. And he hadn't said anything about missing this one before he'd left last night.

Although, she admitted to herself, it was possible he'd been distracted by the intimate conversation and the kisses they'd shared…and had simply forgotten to tell her about an impending scheduling conflict.

"But there are innumerable reasons why he could have been held up, too," she told her young audience, as she twisted her hair into a knot on the back of her head and secured it there with a couple of pins.

This was definitely not the same situation as the day Anthony never came back from the store. Although, she admitted to herself anxiously, it sure felt like it. Worse, she'd put some dinner on, in hopes that Matt might stay after they were done. A sign she was beginning to care too much?

Luckily, she had no more time to ruminate on it.

The sound of a pickup truck in her driveway signaled she had company. She moved to the front door and heaved a sigh of relief when she saw Matt climbing out from behind the wheel. With a friendly lift of his hand, he strode toward her.

As he neared her, she saw the shadows beneath his gray-blue eyes. His hair was wet, his handsome jaw clean-shaven except for one strip of beard along his jaw where he had missed. "Sorry," he said gruffly, as he moved in close to give her a friendly hug hello, inundating her with the brisk, masculine scent of him. "Time got away from me."

Sara smiled with a mixture of happiness and relief as she nestled against the hard, unyielding muscles of his chest. "Take a breath, cowboy," she teased, still tingling all over when he let her go. "It's all good. Although, I have to ask… Are you okay?"

His brow crinkled in surprise. "Yeah, why?"

Might as well be honest. Blushing beneath the appreciation in his gaze, she ushered him across the entry and into the main living area of her home. "You look like you haven't slept in a couple of days."

He tilted his head in acknowledgment, looking as if

he wanted nothing more than to make love to her again, then shrugged. "A lovesick cow kept me up all night."

She squinted back at him, not sure whether he was joking or not. "Seriously?"

He cast fond looks at their two young charges, then turned his attention back to her, tipping the brim of an imaginary hat. Obviously enjoying how flustered she'd become, he gave her a cocky grin. "Yes, ma'am. Had a three-year-old Brahma stumble onto my property in the middle of night, bellowing at the top of her lungs." His lazy grin widened. "I had to catch her and put her in the barn, then look at the brand and the ear tag and figure out who she belonged to."

Although cattle did occasionally get loose, the timing of the escape could have been a whole lot better, Sara thought. Even as the large-animal veterinarian in her wanted to know, "Was the cow okay?"

"Physically, she was fine," Matt reported soberly. "I'm not sure her heart was all that great." He strolled closer, recalling with a smile. "She was in heat. In search of a bull down the road."

Now it was beginning to make sense. "At Chance Lockhart's ranch, Bullhaven, where there are dozens of prime bulls," Sara guessed, trying not to think how right it felt, having Matt here with her this way.

"Yep," he related. "But my unexpected visitor was not a cow meant to breed rodeo stock, so she was out of luck." He shook his head, chuckling. "Not that this deterred her, given the raging state of her hormones. Anyway, she never let up her bellowing all night." Mischief lit his sexy smile as he locked eyes with Sara. He took her hand and pressed it comically over the left side of his chest. "The heart wants what the heart wants, I guess."

Sara's sure did. Fingers tingling at the brief contact, she stepped back and propped her hands on her hips, surveying him. "If you didn't look so tired, McCabe, this would be funny."

"Actually," he said and shoved a hand through his hair, setting the damp strands to right, chuckling all the more, "it's still kind of funny. Anyway, I talked to her owner around dawn and he came to get his lovesick cow around eight this morning."

Sara could imagine what a relief that had been. "Were you able to go back to bed?" she asked before she could stop herself.

His sleep habits were really none of her business.

And she *really* didn't need to imagine him naked between the sheets of his bed. Or wonder what it would be like to be there with him…

Oblivious to the unprecedentedly ardent direction of her thoughts, Matt gave another negative shake of the head. "I had to deliver a big load of mesquite to a barbecue restaurant chain in San Antonio. Just got back a little while ago from that. Went to shower, and here I am. A little late…"

Which explained his wet, shampoo-smelling hair and soap-scented skin.

"…but ready to go." He pulled out his phone. "So want to get started on teaching Champ the sit-stay command?"

Figuring the more on task they were, the better, Sara smiled. "Let's do it."

Luckily, Charley had nodded off in the battery-operated swing while they were talking. Hence, Matt's only responsibility was manning the video camera on his cell phone while Sara put Champ through his paces.

"Okay, Champ, sit," Sara commanded.

The puppy settled on his haunches, while looking up at her.

"Good sit!" Sara praised warmly, giving him a treat.

She lifted her hand in a halting manner. "Now stay."

Understanding, Champ remained where he was.

"Good boy!" Sara crooned, while Matt looked on proudly, too. "Good stay!" She treated the pup again as he looked up at her intently. And on they went. Practicing walking on a leash, by Sara's side, without pulling ahead or to the side. Sitting and staying longer. Sitting and staying with lots of warm praise and no treats.

Champ aced it all. And like the magnificent helper he was, Matt captured it all on video on his cell phone. When they'd finished, he promptly emailed it in to the puppy-training group at WTWA.

Aware how much she was going to miss these evenings together when their bargain inevitably ended, Sara asked, "Would you mind sending me one, too? I'd really like to have it."

"No problem," Matt said with a genial smile, doing that, too.

Sara gave Champ food and water and put him back in his crate to rest. Charley was waking up from his little nap, so she lifted him out of his swing, handed him to Matt, and then began preparing her son's dinner of baby food, too.

A supremely contented look on his face, Matt held Charley in his arms while lounging against the kitchen counter. Watching them, Sara couldn't help but think what a great daddy he was going to make some day.

Probably husband, too. He was such a natural on the domestic front.

It was too bad she wasn't interested in getting married again.

Unaware of the romantic nature of her thoughts, Matt surveyed her thoughtfully. "Is it going to bother you to have to give Champ up at the end of the month?"

Tingling everywhere his glance had touched, and especially everywhere it hadn't, Sara shook her head. With effort, she drew on a skill she had learned in vet school. "I know this is only temporary so I'm making sure I keep my professional distance and don't get too attached."

Although he looked skeptical, as if wondering if that could actually be done with a puppy as cute as little Champ, Matt reached over to grab a tissue and dabbed some drool from Charley's chin. "That's good."

Matt shot Champ, who was now snuggled up against the grate drowsily watching everything that was going on, a gentle look. "What about Champ?" Without warning, he sounded a little worried. "Is the pup going to have a hard time leaving you?"

Wasn't that just the five-million-dollar question.

Sara exhaled. She lifted her gaze to his, answering carefully. "If it were just Champ and me and Charley all the time for a month, and this home was all he knew, he likely would, at least for a short while."

She held up a hand before Matt could interrupt.

"That's why we're getting him used to all sorts of different situations and places and people. To help prepare him for the extensive training and varied experience he's going to have over the next two years."

Matt nodded approvingly, although he still looked

a little apprehensive. "He is a pretty calm and outgoing little fella."

Smiling, Sara reflected, "He's definitely got the heart of a service animal. Plus, he seems to automatically sense where he is needed...as was demonstrated when he met Alyssa Barnes and some of the other soldiers at WTWA." She released a breath. "So, as long as there is a soul in need of comforting, or a wounded vet in need of assistance, I think he's going to rise to the challenge and be just fine. And I know he will be loved, wherever he goes, by whomever he is with."

Matt seemed to trust her assessment. "Good to hear," he said gruffly.

Wondering if Matt were beginning to get a little too attached to the pup-in-training, despite his previous aversion to all dogs, Sara reached for Charley and settled him in his high chair.

Turning back to Matt, she asked casually, as if she hadn't been hoping this would be the case all along, "Would you like to stay for dinner?"

There were a lot of reasons why he should decline, Matt thought. The first being the reason he had been unable to sleep the night before, even before the lovesick cow showed up.

His first visit to the West Texas Warriors Association facility had been as difficult as he'd expected. Seeing the veterans who'd been getting rehab in the glass-walled physical therapy center stop what they were doing long enough to greet Champ warmly had brought up a lot of memories. Good and bad. And though he hadn't had any more nightmares since he had started helping out Sara, Charley and Champ, he had feared he might be thrust right back into the darkness if he did go to sleep. Which in turn had made him wonder if he was doing the right thing in spending so much time with them, given Sara's ever-present need to move on to a happier, trauma-free life. So, aside from the few kisses they'd shared the night before, at the evening's end, he was putting the brakes on the sexual part of their relationship, too.

At least for now.

Until he was sure he could be what she wanted and needed…even in an untraditional, non-married, sense.

"I mean I do owe you a meal, and then some," Sara continued, an uncertain smile curving her soft lips.

Damn. The last thing he wanted to do was hurt her feelings. And given how delicious whatever she was cooking smelled…he'd be a fool to turn it down. Pushing the troublesome thoughts away, Matt straightened. "Love to, darlin'," he said. Maybe this was just what he needed. Maybe *Sara* was just what he needed. "What can I do to help?"

Relief showed in her slender frame and a smile lit up her face. "Finish feeding Charley for me?"

Their hands brushed as she handed him the dish of baby applesauce and some sort of meat and vegetable entrée. Aware all over again how silky her skin felt, it sparked in him a fierce longing to rediscover every glorious inch of her soft, womanly curves. Matt released a rough breath as he pulled up a chair in front of the infant. "I think we can handle that."

Charley watched him raptly, seemingly as happy to have Matt there for dinner as Matt was to be with them. He could so get used to this. In fact, he had a suspicion they all could. “So how has your day been?” he asked Sara, over his shoulder.

As she moved about the kitchen gracefully, he admired how pretty she looked in her yellow button-up blouse, knee-length denim skirt and brown leather moccasins. “Very busy. Since plans are underway for the WTWA service-dog reunion.”

“Oh, that’s right.” Matt shifted his chair so he could see her, and Charley, too. “You’re having it at the Blue Vista?”

“Yes. We’re having it here at my ranch.” Pleasure teased the corners of her lips. “I’ve got plenty of room. Anyway, I volunteered to help send out the invitations and gather the RSVPs this year, so whenever Charlie and Champ were down for a nap I was busy doing that.”

Matt watched Sara put together roast chicken sandwiches on fresh-baked wheat bread, with slices of tomato, red onion, and colby-jack cheese. She added chipotle mayo, then slid them onto the panini press. “Am I on the invite list?”

She looked up, her expression inscrutable. “Did you want to be?”

Two weeks ago he would have said hell no. Two days ago, after making love to Sara, he would have said hell yes. Now…after visiting the WTWA with her…he was on the fence.

To go and be around all his fellow soldiers and the dogs they loved could mean triggering a new slate of hellacious memories. However, to not go would be signaling to Sara that she—and the dog she was training—weren’t important to him.

Assuming his answer was no, Sara turned away from him and kept her poker face. She removed the sandwiches from the panini press and slid them onto a plate. "I'd like to have you here," she said gently, "but it's not required. Not by a long shot."

Actually, Matt thought, it was. Especially if he didn't want some other ex-soldier making a move on her. Because whether Sara realized it or not, something was happening with her, too. Her heart was opening up again to new people, new experiences. Same as his.

"I'll not only attend," he promised, reaching over to briefly touch her hand as she put the plates on the table, then returned to the stove to get the rest of the meal. "I'll help out in any way I can."

Sara couldn't say she was surprised that Matt had volunteered once again. The McCabes were gallant to the core.

There had been a moment there, however, before he had accepted her invitation, when she'd sensed something troubling him again.

That worried her.

It was moments like that, when she didn't know what was going on with him emotionally, that had destroyed her marriage to Anthony. She didn't want a similar exclusion wrecking her rekindled friendship with Matt.

Thankfully, he looked okay—albeit still a little tired—now. And maybe that's all his hesitation had been, she thought. The fact he was feeling tired and overwhelmed after a very long day.

Bolstered by the positive turn in her thoughts, she ladled chicken tortilla soup into bowls, set them on a tray, along with the condiments, and carried it to the table.

As she sat down opposite him, he regarded her with interest. "So how is this event usually set up?" he asked, adding shredded cheese, sour cream, pico de gallo and guacamole to his fragrant soup.

"It's very casual. We set up on the lawn. All the attendees bring food and outdoor folding chairs. A couple of people usually man the grills. Mostly, people sit around and share stories, and meet each other's service animals, and at the end of the reunion, we take some pictures."

"How many people attend?"

Sara stirred condiments into her soup. "Last year it was around two hundred. I think we're on track to do about fifty more than that this year. And, of course," she said, tilting her head, "we have invited all the people who have expressed an interest in volunteering in our puppy training program, too. So it could be about 275 total, I think." She smiled at Matt, glad he was going to be joining them. "We probably won't know for sure until the day of, since not everyone RSVPs."

"Can you handle that many people here?"

Matt looked out the window. Dusk was falling, but they could still see the rolling green lawn that surrounded her ranch house.

Sara nodded. "As long as the weather is nice, we can absolutely accommodate everyone. If it's not," she frowned, relating, "then we have to move it to the WTWA building, which can hold that many people and their dogs at one time. Although it won't be as cozy, since they'll be scattered over three floors and a covered outdoor area."

Matt paused, taking it all in. "Let's hope for nice weather, then..."

They talked a little more.

Sara noticed that Charley was chewing on his hand,

as if his gums were bothering him again, so she brought out a teething ring from the freezer and handed it to him.

Matt laughed as Charley promptly stuck it in his mouth and rubbed it back and forth across his gum. “Got to hand it to the little guy,” Matt claimed, as proud as any father. “He figured out what makes him feel better right away.”

Sara nodded.

Like Matt, her son preferred being self-sufficient. As did she, actually. Until now…

Now it was nice having Matt around to help, keep her company and make her feel like a whole lot more might be possible in life again.

She looked at his empty sandwich plate and soup bowl. “What about you, cowboy?” she asked. “Can I get you anything else?”

He shook his head.

“No, but it was delicious.”

“Thank you.”

Silence fell.

As the awkward pause drew out, Sara looked from Matt to Charley and back again. It was hard to tell who was losing steam faster now that they’d eaten. She smiled at Matt. “I was going to ask you if you wanted to hang around while I made an apple crumble for dessert…but I’m thinking I should offer you a mug of really strong coffee, then send you home instead.”

“Both sound really good, don’t they, Charley?”

Her son kicked his legs in response and then leaned over and reached for Matt, batting his forearm persistently.

Matt turned to slant Sara a questioning look.

"I think he wants you to hold him," she explained. The really funny thing was, Sara wanted Matt to hold her, too…

By the time Sara had the dessert in the oven, Charley's head was drooping over Matt's shoulder. Sara glanced at the clock, belatedly realizing, "Oh, honey, it's past your bedtime."

Charley offered her a drowsy smile.

"Anything I can do?" Matt asked, still looking a little ragged around the edges himself.

Sara glanced at the puppy still sound asleep in his crate and shook her head. She gestured expansively toward the sofa. "Just have a seat and keep an ear out for the timer on the oven."

Matt offered her a mock salute. "Will do."

Charley's bedtime routine of bath, storybook and bottle took about twenty minutes. When she'd finished, she eased her sleepy son into his crib and kissed him good-night.

Wondering how Matt was faring, she went back downstairs. Found him with his eyes closed and his head resting on the back of the sofa cushion, his breathing deep and even. Long jean-clad legs sprawled out in front of him, brawny arms folded across his chest, he looked incredibly solid and masculine.

Not sure what to do—leave him be and let him spend the night—or wake him and send him on his way, she edged closer still.

And that was when he stirred, his eyes opening to look up into hers.

Matt blinked. Scrubbed a hand over his face. Groaned. "I nodded off, didn't I?"

"It's fine."

"No. It's not." His voice was a low sexy rumble in his broad chest. Appearing upset with himself, he shifted, moving his weight forward on the sofa cushion.

Her heart going out to him, she moved closer still. And that was when she saw the ugly red wound on the inside of his palm. "Oh my God, Matt," she gasped. "What is that?"

Chapter 10

Matt got up from the sofa. "It's just a splinter," he said, folding his arms against the hard muscles of his chest and shrugging off her attempt to look at it.

Sara moved in and took his hand anyway, turned it over so she could see. Damn, that was an angry-looking wound. "Did you do this today?"

He shrugged nonchalantly, then lifted his eyes to meet hers. Their gazes clashed as surely as their wills. His scowl deepening, he admitted, "This morning. I was in a hurry. Didn't bother to put on my work gloves."

A wave of concern rushed through her. Followed by a surge of emotion that was even harder to rein in. Still holding his gaze with effort, she fought back a sigh. "You know when the skin around it starts to get red like this, that it's getting infected?"

"I'm going to take care of it."

She dropped her hand. "Really?" Beginning to realize why he hadn't already done so, she challenged softly, "How? Given the fact the splinter is in your right palm and you're right-handed."

He cocked his head. Unable to argue with her assertion, finally said, "My brother Jack's a surgeon."

She nodded, amenable. "You could definitely drive into town and let him take care of it. Or—" she paused to let the sheer practicality of her offer sink in "—you could let me remove it."

His eyes flashed, and another jolt of awareness swept through Sara. Reminding her just how very much she still desired him.

"Or I could just let it be until it's convenient."

Sara thought about the complications that could ensue. Like sepsis.

Determined to help him, whether he wanted her to or not, she stepped closer and curved her hand over the flexed muscles of his bicep. "Not a good idea," she persisted.

He exhaled wearily.

Suddenly she was lumped in with all the other meddling, overprotective members of his family. And though she wasn't eager to become a nuisance to him, she also couldn't knowingly let him walk out of there without caring for him, with the same kindness and concern he'd been bestowing on her.

The oven timer went off.

Glad for the respite from their stare-down, Sara pulled the apple crumble out of the oven and set it on the stove top to cool. Giving Matt no chance to argue further, she went into the adjacent room, came back with a black bag in one hand, a first-aid kit in the other.

A surgeon was a surgeon, after all.

And if she could help…

When she breezed back in, she could see he had made up his mind to cooperate with her. Whether because it was easier than arguing with her, or the splinter hurt as much as she imagined and he really did want it removed, macho attitude aside.

Not that it mattered to her, since she wouldn't have been able to bid him adieu without the gnawing guilt that she hadn't been as neighborly to him as she should have been.

He watched as she inched on a pair of sterile gloves. Then leaned toward her and joked, "I thought you only worked on large animals."

Refusing to let him ruffle her, she narrowed her gaze. "Exactly."

He couldn't help it; he laughed. "Yeah, well, just so you know," he returned, as sexual chemistry arced between them, hotter than ever, "I'm only letting you do this because I still want some of that dessert."

The practical side of her believed that. The apple crumble did smell good.

Almost as good as he did.

"Mmm-hmm." With practiced efficiency and a poker face, she tore open a packet of antiseptic and cleaned the surface of his wound.

Although no sissy, he grimaced and hissed when she touched the skin.

She could see why. The thick jagged splinter was really in deep. Sympathy reigned. What was it about men that made them feel they had to conceal anything that might be conceived as a weakness? "Has this been hurting this bad all day?"

His expression remained impassive.

Sara retrieved a packet of sterile stainless-steel instruments from her bag. "Why didn't you tell me when you got here?"

"I was already late." He shrugged his broad shoulders. "And it wasn't anything you or anyone else needed to worry about."

She glanced sideways at him, then returned her attention to the foreign object needing to be removed. "Stubborn and self-sufficient!"

He chuckled again. "Hey..." He looked her up and down with lazy male confidence. "Look who's talking!"

She flushed despite herself. "I'm a mom." She focused on making a narrow incision in the top layer of skin. "I have to be competent in all areas of my life."

He watched her use the tweezers to deftly remove the wood. "Well, so do ex-soldiers and ranch owners."

"Touché." Smiling, she coated the area with an antibiotic cream from her home first aid kit. "There. All better." She put on a bandage. Started to move away.

He caught her by the elbow.

A shiver moved through her.

"Thank you," he said sincerely.

As their eyes met, emotion shimmered between them.

"You have to take care of yourself," she said, suddenly afraid he wasn't.

He threaded a hand through her hair, his expression gentling all the more. "What I really want to do," he confessed, his mouth lowering to hers, "is take care of you."

Sara wanted that, too.

So very much...

The next thing she knew, she was all the way in his arms. They were kissing and touching in one long sensual line. Her body responded with a lightning bolt of desire, and now that he was deepening the kiss, another more powerful wave had started to surge. Followed by a riptide of longing and suppressed need, an aching awareness of just how alone she had been.

He tasted so incredibly good, she realized. Felt so strong and so right. She groaned as his hands cupped her breasts, his thumbs rubbing across the crests. She curled against him. She had never wanted someone so completely. Or felt so wanted in return.

Matt lifted his head. "You better tell me to leave," he warned gruffly, "if you don't want me to make love to you again."

She laughed shakily. Determined to keep this light and easy and sexy. "Actually, I do. And you should..."

Matt laughed wickedly, as Sara hoped he would. He lifted her in his strong arms and settled her on the island. His gaze still holding hers, he caught her around the middle, guiding her legs snugly around his waist. He reached inside her shirt, undoing the clasp of her bra. She shuddered in anticipation. Smiling, he molded her soft curves with the palms of his hands, then bent his head and kissed her again, deeply, evocatively, until her heart was racing and she was tingling all over.

And still their mouths mated.

She shifted her hips, encountering rock solid hardness, heat. His hands moved to the bare skin of her thighs, and her skirt hiked up, nearly to her waist.

"You feel so good," he whispered, leaving a trail of fevered kisses across her jaw, down her neck. She quivered as his caressing palms went even higher. Then lower. Easing beneath elastic. Finding the feminine heart of her with butterfly caresses. Slow. Deliberate. Determined to help her find release.

She shuddered again, so close to heaven. "Oh, Matt," she whispered, arching with need, "you feel so good, too."

His gray-blue eyes darkened with pleasure.

She shuddered and he coaxed her to respond even more, to let all her inhibitions float away. Until her body pulsed and she tightened her legs around his waist and melted against him.

She had time to draw a breath, and then his mouth was on hers again, hot and hard, and they were kissing as if the world were going to end. She lost her panties. He lost his jeans.

Her nipples budded. The skin between her thighs grew slick once more. She opened herself up to him, longing for the ultimate closeness. He found a condom; she sheathed him. He gripped her bottom and stroked her where their bodies met. And still they kissed. Taking their time. Building their pleasure, pacing their movements, propelling each other to the very depths. Until there was no more holding back. They were racing to the very edge, soaring, climaxing, then ever so slowly coming back down.

Sara didn't want the moment to end.

And neither did Matt.

Holding each other. Touching…loving…kissing… They moved upstairs to her bedroom and started all over again. The second time they made love to each other that night was even more thrilling. Sara let her head rest on his chest and she fell asleep, wrapped in Matt's arms.

And woke alone, at midnight. To the sound of Champ whining impatiently.

Sara threw on a robe and went down to let Champ out. To her aching disappointment, Matt was gone. His coffee and their dessert left untouched.

Sara spent the rest of the night and the morning wondering and worrying. She didn't know why Matt had left without a word to her. Not even a note. She only knew that on some level it really bothered her because it was just too reminiscent of the way her marriage to Anthony had deteriorated before his death.

For so many reasons, she had done nothing about her husband's mysteriously distant behavior.

But she could do something about this.

Even if it was to only find out for certain what was going on with Matt, and by extension, them. So she gathered her courage, called her friend Bess Monroe, and asked the rehab nurse if she could come out and sit for Champ and Charley for a few hours while she went out.

Bess, who was still single and had a raging case of baby fever, was delighted to help out.

Her friend looked over the instructions Sara had written out. "When will you be back?"

"Not sure. An hour, maybe two." How long did it take to get answers and then recover and restore her pride? "But I'll have my cell phone with me."

"No worries." Bess paused, then lifted a thoughtful brow. "Are you okay?"

Well, no, actually... Sara flushed and turned away from her friend's probing gaze. "Why?"

"You look like you haven't slept."

A malady that seems to be going around. Sara collected her phone and keys, and slid them into her bag. "Charley is teething," she said, although that was not what had kept her awake.

"Ah," Bess sympathized. "Well, have fun."

Sara smiled. *Will I? Or will this be something else I'll come to regret?* "You, too."

It only took ten minutes to drive to Matt's ranch. As she drove through the gates of the Silver Creek, she couldn't help but notice the progress he was making these days, clearing the land and taking down aging fence. He had mowed some of the pastureland, too, which gave it a neater, more manicured appearance.

Maybe there was a method to his solitary endeavors, she thought. Certainly, no one could argue with the effort he was making to turn his land into a thriving enterprise.

She found him about a mile or so back from the road. He was working on fence today. Wearing jeans and a tight black T-shirt that showed off how fit and taut his tall body was.

Surprised to see her, he lifted a hand in greeting and strode toward her, wary concern on his handsome face. The brim of his hat shaded his eyes. "Everything okay?"

She ambled close enough to see the darker rim of his gray-blue eyes. "I'm not sure." She rocked back on the heels of her Western work boots and drawled, "Did I do or say something wrong last night?"

His eyes widened in consternation. He surveyed her slowly, head to toe, as if he found her completely irresistible. "What do you mean?"

Trying not to think how attracted she was to him,

too, Sara wrinkled her nose. “The way you left. Without a word.” *Or a kiss goodbye.*

He flashed a too casual smile. “You were so sound asleep. I didn’t want to wake you.”

I wouldn’t have minded. “Is that all it was?”

Something akin to guilt and regret moved across his face. He paused. Like he wanted to say something but didn’t know how. The moment passed without revelation.

“What else could it be?” he finally said in return.

“That’s just it.” Sara shrugged in escalating frustration. She knew he’d been hurt, and was wary of making another mistake of the heart, too. “I’m not sure.”

Abruptly, Matt looked as impatient as she felt. Their eyes locked for a breath-stealing moment. “I thought I was doing the right thing, quietly letting myself out. Avoiding doing anything that would have seemed… presumptuous.”

Given the fact they had just rekindled their friendship, and were keeping things casual, he had a point.

He folded his arms across his chest. “I’m not sure what your rules are, or would be, even if we were dating.”

“Which we aren’t,” she added tartly. Which was another problem.

“So…” He continued to study her, rocking forward. “I’m not sure why you’re so unhappy.”

Because I feel shut out and abandoned. Even though technically I have no right to feel that way.

Her humiliation and embarrassment increasing by leaps and bounds, she forced herself to behave like the mature adult she was. “You’re right,” she acknowledged with a heartfelt sigh. “There was absolutely nothing wrong with what you did last night." *Even though I really wish our evening together ended differently.*

She swallowed around the dryness in her throat.

"I'm not sure why I'm so upset," she blurted out reluctantly, aware their passionate coupling had left her feeling way too hormonal. When he continued watching her, as if perplexed, she threw up a hand, adding, "It's not like we're in love or anything."

His brow lifted in surprise and his hands fell to his sides. "Do you want to be?"

To her shock, Sara realized the answer to that was yes.

But not with just anyone. With Matt. And honestly, how crazy, how unforgivably reckless, was that?

Deciding to exit before she made an even bigger idiot of herself, she lifted her hand. "I've got to go."

"Sara..."

She spun around and began hurriedly walking away. "I just came over to tell you there's no need to come to my ranch this evening," she said over her shoulder. "Bess Monroe is going to help me with Champ's training."

He caught up with her in six long strides. "Wait!" He put a gentle hand on her shoulder, staying her forward progress, then moved around so she had no choice but to look at him. "Are you sure?"

That was the hell of it, Sara thought, looking into his mesmerizing gray-blue eyes. She wasn't sure at all. Not of what had happened between them. Of what she wanted. Or especially what he felt.

All she knew was that there were times when she felt incredibly close to Matt. And others when there was an emotional wall between them higher than any she had ever felt with her late husband.

And that wasn't good.

Not at all.

"Yes," she said, forcing one last completely fake smile. For both their sakes, she had to be a heck of a lot more cautious. "I am."

Chapter 11

Matt didn't come over that evening, nor did he call.

Or respond to the text message she sent him the following day telling him that he wouldn't be needed to help her with Charley and Champ that night, either.

And while she expected that he appreciated the break from the daily baby and puppy duties, she also sort of expected that he—like her—would be missing the time they usually spent together.

Apparently, he didn't.

And Sara was still trying to figure out what to make of that at six o'clock that evening when her doorbell rang.

Matt was on her doorstep, with Lulu and their mutual friend Bess Monroe flanking either side of him. He looked incredibly handsome in a charcoal suede blazer, starched blue dress shirt and dark jeans. His dress boots were shined to perfection, and since he was holding his stone-colored hat against the center of his chest, she could see that he had gotten a haircut. He'd also done a very nice job shaving. A sandalwood and leather fragrance clung to his jaw, stirring her senses all the more.

Sara blinked. "What's going on?" she asked.

Grinning, Lulu breezed in. "My baby brother has finally come to his senses, that's what! He's taking you on a date!"

Bess waltzed in after her. "To help make that happen, he enlisted our help. We're baby and puppy sitting for you!"

Sara's jaw dropped. Talk about presumptuous! After leaving her hanging, wondering about whatever he was thinking and feeling after their falling out, for nearly two whole days!

Temper rising, she jammed her hands on her hips. Tilting her chin, she formed an officious smile. "I hate to break it to you, cowboy, but it's customary to *call* and ask a woman if she would *like* to go out with you, before you make these kinds of arrangements."

He flashed a sexy grin. "Thought about it." His eyes sparkled the way they always did when he got under her skin. He ambled a little closer, purposefully invading her space. "Figured you'd say no…so I decided to take matters into my own hands."

Sensing fireworks, Bess and Lulu eased away. Sara scowled, even as her heart panged in her chest, trying to think about what it would be like to kiss him again.

Which, after the way he'd left her two nights before, was definitely *not* going to happen. Not ever again!

She glowered at him, letting him know that it was going to take more than a simple dinner out to make things right between them. "You know," she snapped, "you are not the only one around here who does not like to be told what to do!"

His laughter was throaty and implacable. "Figured. Did not dissuade me in the least."

Sara shut her eyes briefly and rubbed at the tension in her temples. She thought she'd felt ridiculously off-kilter before he arrived. Now with him here standing next to her, his big imposing body taking up all the space, she didn't know whether to ignore her hurt pride and forgive him, or do what she'd decided to do earlier, and keep her heart safe and him at bay.

It was pretty clear, however, as he gave her a slow, thorough once-over, what he wanted to do. End their tiff—and all the rules and non-rules they'd set up thus far—by kissing her senseless.

"Don't argue with the man," Lulu admonished.

Ever the romantic, who never seemed to have a boyfriend of her own, Bess chimed in, "I'll help you get ready!" Giving her no chance to argue, she steered Sara up the stairs.

Figuring she could use a temporary respite from Matt's seductive presence, Sara went along docilely. But her mute cooperation ended the moment they entered her bedroom and shut the door behind them. "Listen." She whirled on her longtime friend. "I appreciate you and Lulu trying to help, but I don't view Matt like you two seem to think."

Not since he sneaked out in the middle of the night, and then defended his actions in a way she'd been unable to argue with, at least on a practical level.

Lulu paused. "Not boyfriend material?"

Given how easily he could break my heart? "Definitely not," Sara said.

Bess shrugged. "So kick him out. The three of us will have a gals' night."

While that would have been a wonderful idea two weeks ago, now Sara hesitated.

Bess grinned. "Just what I thought." She wagged a teasing finger. "You can deny it all you want, girlfriend, but you're crushing on Matt every bit as much as he's crushing on you."

Oh heck, why deny it? Especially when he was there, looking so fine. It wasn't like either Bess or Lulu would believe it anyway.

Bess gave Sara an encouraging hug. "Give him a chance." She shook her head in exasperation. "Do you know what I'd give to have a man look at me the way he just looked at you?"

Probably the same thing I'd give, Sara thought. *Everything.*

She sighed, conceding, "Okay, but we're not staying out late." For both their sakes, she was going to insist they be more cautious than they had been. *What was it they said? Slow and steady wins the race?*

Bess waved an airy hand. "Whatever." She disappeared into Sara's closet. "Although if you're home by midnight," she called over her shoulder, "I'm going to be really surprised."

Sara took half an hour getting dressed, and the wait was well worth it, Matt noted happily. The red sheath molded to her slender curves, while the knee-length hem and sleek alligator heels worked together to draw attention to her showgirl-perfect legs. She'd put her hair up in a loose twist at the back of her head. Tendrils escaped, slanting provocatively across her forehead and the nape of her neck.

Resisting the urge to haul her close and press a string of kisses up the slope of her throat, he said thickly, "Wow."

She shook her head at him, but not before he tracked the softness of her lips and the flush in her cheeks.

Lulu and Bess elbowed each other, mugging. "She does clean up pretty good," Bess teased.

Sara gave her friends The Look. "Okay, you two."

She turned to give them instructions on Charley's and Champ's care for the evening. Then, giving Matt a cautious glance, said, "Ready?"

He held the door for her. "Absolutely."

"So where are we going?" she asked, her expression inscrutable.

Lamenting the fact he had almost blown the only real chance he'd ever had with her, he took her by the arm and led her outside to his pickup truck.

"The Laramie River Inn outside of San Angelo." It was the best place for a gourmet dinner in a one hundred mile radius. He'd had to do some mighty fine persuading to get a reservation on such short notice, even if it was a weeknight.

She lifted a delicate brow. "You must really be trying to impress me."

He opened the passenger door. "Or make up with you," he ventured.

She pivoted and challenged him with a gaze that was sexy, self-assured and faintly baiting. "That's really not necessary," she said softly.

He figured he'd be the judge of that.

She put her right shoe on the running board of the truck and gripped the handle just above the door. He caught a whiff of her lilac scent, even as his attention drifted lower, to the snug fit of her dress across her delectable hips. Oblivious to his arousal, she slipped into the passenger seat with admirable grace.

He waited until she'd fastened her seat belt, then shut her door and circled around to climb behind the wheel. Figuring the more intimate conversation could wait until he had her full attention, and she had his, he said, "So, what's new on the home front? How were Charley and Champ today?"

While they drove, she filled him in on their antics. He told her about the lovesick cow that had showed up on his property again.

A companionable time later, they arrived at the inn.

A private table near the window, overlooking a field of Texas bluebonnets and Indian paintbrush wildflowers, was waiting for them.

Showtime, he thought. He held the chair for her and she slid into it. The next few minutes passed in silence, as they studied their menus, placed their orders and agreed on a bottle of wine. When their waiter left, she looked wary again and he couldn't blame her. He had been a horse's ass and then some.

Matt reached across the table and took her hand. Regret lashed through him. "I'm sorry," he said quietly, forcing himself to be the gentleman he had been raised to be. "There are no excuses for the way I behaved the other night." He might not have been able to sleep there, but… He swallowed around the tension in his throat, finished soberly, "I should have treated you better."

Her chin lifted indignantly. Clearly, an apology was not what she wanted from him. Then what was?

"We went through this, Matt."

Not well, he thought, because the outcome of their conversation had left her studiously avoiding him.

Determined to set their relationship to rights, he covered her hand with his. "Our friendship is important, Sara," he reminded her, savoring the silky warmth of her skin. "More than that, it's good to have you in my life again after all these years apart."

Finally, a chink in her emotional armor.

She released a slow breath, his honesty engendering hers. With a reluctant smile, she admitted, "It's been good to have you in mine." She paused to survey him with slowly building mischief. "I remember you as a kid. It's been nice to get to know you as a grown-up."

He nodded, thinking of all the ways they had both changed, and still likely would. "You, too," he said gruffly.

They fell silent as their first course was delivered.

When the waiter left, he leaned toward her. "Look, I know you don't want to get married again. You made that clear." He forced himself to be honest in a way he hadn't been with anyone else. "The truth is, I'm probably not husband material, either."

For a moment, Sara didn't move. Then something like disappointment flickered in the jade depths of her eyes. "I don't know how you can say that," she returned finally.

He watched her drag her fork idly through her salad. "Because it's true. My time overseas changed me."

She discounted his declaration with a shrug.

"Things…like Anthony's death…have changed me, too."

He knew that. He figured it was why she was so scared, so ready to run at even the slightest disagreement or disappointment.

They could still work this out.

They *would* work this out.

"Then we're on the same page," he told her seriously. "Because I want to stay close with you. Not lose track with each other the way we did before we each left for college. So whatever you want. If you prefer us to be just friends," he vowed, even as his body ached to make love to her again. "Or friends with benefits." His voice dropped a husky notch. "Or something in between, you can have it." He paused to let his words sink in. "All you have to do is tell me what would make you happy."

Sara didn't know what she'd expected when Matt had shown up to take her out on a date.

She definitely hadn't expected him to be so direct, or to chivalrously offer her heart's desire to her, whatever that turned out to be.

He leaned toward her. "Tell me I haven't upset you again."

"No." The truth was he couldn't offend her anew. Because she hadn't stopped being conflicted and confused about their relationship.

One minute she was crushing on him so hard she thought she might actually be falling in love with him. The next she was exasperated beyond belief.

"Do you want to make love again?" he asked, his gaze drifting slowly over her face, before returning to her eyes. "Or go back to simply being friends?"

A shiver of anticipation went through her.

Did she want to make love with him again?

The answer was yes. Definitely yes.

Did she want to wake up alone afterward again?

The answer to that was definitely no.

She did want to spend time with him. Every day. Maybe even every night.

And that could lead to trouble, she knew. Because if she allowed herself to open up her heart again and fall all the way in love with him—and he couldn't love her that way in return—it was going to devastate her.

"Sara?" he prodded softly, reaching across the table to take her hand in his.

He deserved an answer. And an honest one at that.

"I'm not sure what I want my future to hold," she said finally, looking down at their clasped hands. Except she didn't want to be hurt again. Didn't ever want to feel she'd been emotionally shut out and abandoned. Or that she had let someone down by not being what they needed and wanted, either. Because that kind of grief and guilt was not something she could handle again, either.

Matt regarded her patiently. "I get that," he replied gently, understanding—perhaps even sharing—that sentiment.

Sara drew a deep breath. *What was it she'd been telling herself? Slow and steady wins the race? Especially when the most important thing of all was keeping Matt in her life.*

Aware it might be better to ask for too little rather than too much, at least right now, she worked up her courage, looked him right in the eye, and said, "So how about we go back to just being friends?"

* * *

To Sara's relief, Matt took her request in stride. It was almost as if he had expected that the incredible fireworks they'd shared had been too good too last. That the risks they were on the verge of taking were not going to be worthwhile, after all.

He was in agreement with her. Their top priority had to be preserving what they already knew they could have, a deep and lasting man-woman friendship. And though it stung a little to find he shared her ambivalence, she couldn't blame him.

Life had not been particularly kind to either of them in the romance department. To expect that everything would magically work out between the two of them, after reconciling their friendship and impulsively taking it to the next level, was not realistic at all.

And as a single mom now, she absolutely had to be practical.

So, for right now anyway, friendship was definitely the better option.

At least that was what she kept telling herself as the next week passed, without so much as a lingering look, touch or kiss from Matt.

Oh, they still spent plenty of time together when she was training and socializing Champ, and Matt helped out by simultaneously taking care of Charley for her as they all went through their paces, but that was pretty much it.

They didn't share meals.

They didn't exchange confidences.

They didn't do anything that would lead to further intimacy of any kind.

And while it was a relief on one level, it was also incredibly disappointing on another.

She hadn't expected to ever have sex with anyone else after Anthony died. Hadn't even been able to imagine it. So to find out that she could still want someone had been astounding. And to feel wanted in return had been even sweeter.

She also knew if she had to choose between a lifelong platonic friendship with Matt and a fleeting love affair, she would definitely choose the companionship.

So this was definitely the better option.

Especially when she could still share certain elements of the rest of her life with Matt.

"You'll never guess what happened overnight!" she exclaimed, when he met her for Saturday's late-afternoon training session.

He ambled in. The spring day was a little chilly, and he looked as ruggedly handsome as ever in his tan chamois shirt, jeans and boots. "No clue!" he said, stopping just short of her.

Ignoring the way her heart skittered in response whenever she was near him, Sara smiled proudly. "Charley got his first tooth!"

"You're kidding!"

She pointed to her son, who was enjoying some tummy time on his play mat in the middle of the living room floor. "See for yourself."

Matt sauntered over, laconic as ever, and stretched out beside Charley so the two were facing each other. Suddenly looking so very much like father and son it made her heart ache. If only Matt could be Charley's new daddy!

Oblivious to her wish, Matt gently cupped Charley's chin. "Going to let me see, big fella?"

Charley offered a huge grin.

Matt admired the edge of white peeking up out of his lower gum. "Wow."

Charley's grin widened all the more.

Matt peered closer, tilting his head. "Looks like the one next to it is about to push through, too."

Sara joined them on the blanket, kneeling beside them. Beaming, she predicted, "Before we know it, he'll have two teeth!"

Charley gurgled and pounded the floor beneath him with his tiny fists. Rocking forward and back as if that alone would get him somewhere.

"Now, if we could just teach him to crawl instead of roll to where he wants to go," Sara sighed.

Charlie flipped over onto his side, again and again, until he found the toy he wanted and put it in his mouth.

"He'll get there," Matt reassured her, confident as ever. The corners of his eyes crinkled. "In the meantime, we should definitely celebrate his first tooth."

"We should," Sara agreed.

Merriment tugged at Matt's smile. "Think he's too young for ice cream?"

Doing something that fun, even with their tiny chaperones along, always seemed like a dangerous proposition to her way too vulnerable heart. She cleared her throat and lifted her chin. "I imagine he could have a little." It was time they expanded their repertoire of social expeditions again. That did not have to mean they'd end up holding hands or kissing or being tempted to make love again.

Especially if they kept things absolutely casual and platonic.

"You think?" Matt's eyes glittered with anticipation.

Sara nodded, reassuring herself they were doing the right thing. She smiled over at him. "It's such a nice day. The Dairy Barn in town would be a good place to socialize Champ, too."

His gaze traveled over the hollow of her throat, past her lips, to her eyes. He rose and offered her a hand up. "Let's go, then."

Half an hour later, they were pulling into the lot.

As always during their excursions, Matt took charge of Charley, while Sara snapped a leash on Champ and lifted him out of the car.

No sooner had they stepped onto the sidewalk, than a trio of delighted squeals rose from the other side of the decorative fence surrounding the outdoor eating area.

Matt lifted a hand in recognition. "Hey, Jack!" he called to his brother, as Jack's three little girls came running for them, all talking at once.

"It's the puppy, Champ! He's so cute! Can we pet him?"

"Sure." Sara stopped.

"Fancy seeing you two here," Jack said.

Matt shrugged. "We're friends."

A lift of the brow. "Friends? Lulu said you went on a date."

Matt remained impassive. "We did."

"And?" Jack pressed.

Another shrug. "Went right back into the friends zone."

The surgeon clapped a hand on Matt's shoulder, and

spared Sara a genial look. "Mind if I have a word with my little brother?"

"Go right ahead."

Matt walked off, Charley still in his arms, Jack at his side. The three little girls gathered around Champ. Cooing over him and petting him by turn.

"Are you nuts?" Sara heard Jack say. "She's everything you'd ever want in a woman. And she's got a baby you clearly adore."

Mortified, Sara stood frozen in place.

Matt held his brother's assessing gaze with one of his own. "Just helping out."

Was that all it was? Sara wondered, stung by Matt's "this means nothing to me, so stop asking" tone.

The two men continued staring each other down. "Looks like a hell of a lot more than that to me," Jack harrumphed.

Matt scowled, looking trapped.

The three girls went from sitting to standing. Champ continued basking in the adoration.

"Yeah, well, maybe you don't know everything, Jack."

Jack leaned in, his own grief evident. "I know one thing. A woman who hits every wish on your list doesn't come along every day. And when you find her, you have to hold on. 'Cause if you don't…" Jack's voice cracked.

Too late, Sara realized it was coming up on the anniversary of his wife's death. Matt must have realized it, too.

"You're right," Matt said quietly, lifting a palm. "I'm an ass."

"No. I'm sorry." Jack scrubbed a hand over his face. "I shouldn't be pushing you. I just hate to see anyone else give up what they could have, while they still have a chance."

Aware she'd been eavesdropping for far too long, Sara stepped back, looked down. Swiftly became aware the little girls that had been surrounding her were gone…and that she was holding an empty leash.

She gasped.

Then turned in the direction of another trio of excited squeals.

There was Champ, nosing happily along the cement, with the girls accompanying him. And he was almost to the sidewalk that fronted the parking lot! Cars were turning in…backing out.

"Stop!" Sara shouted, fisting the leash and breaking into a run.

Spying what was going on, Jack hopped the waist-high fence.

Her heart pounding, Sara caught up with the puppy and Jack's youngest child. Her arms spread wide, she scooped both of them into the safety of her arms, then for good measure snapped the leash on Champ. Jack lassoed his two older daughters. Matt was suddenly there, too, Charley still cradled safely against his broad chest.

To Sara's immense relief, everyone was all right.

"You girls know better," Jack scolded.

The hell of it was, so did Sara.

Chapter 12

"You can take a breath now," Matt said to Sara, several hours later. They'd brought home takeout for dinner, and he'd stayed to help her for a while after that. Charley was upstairs, in bed, fast asleep for the night, and an exhausted Champ was curled up in the back of his crate, snoozing, too.

"Maybe even try to relax?" He flashed her a sexy half smile, even as worry darkened his eyes.

Sara only wished she could but try as she might she could not seem to let go of the near accident.

She lifted the ice pop mold out of the dishwasher. "I keep seeing it, over and over in my mind," she confessed. She carefully poured diluted fruit juice into each cup of the mold, then slid a pacifier-style holder into each slot.

She slanted a glance over her shoulder at Matt, then

headed for the fridge. He opened the door to the freezer compartment for her.

"It all happened so fast," she lamented softly, setting the tray on a shelf.

She shut the door and turned back to Matt.

Unbidden, an image of Champ headed merrily for the parking lot, Jack's three little girls tagging innocently along beside him, flashed in her mind. And her heart once again filled with terror.

What if she hadn't happened to become aware at that precise instant?

Not looked up and seen…

A huge tragedy could have ensued.

And it would have been all her fault for being momentarily inattentive.

Without warning, her eyes filled and her throat ached. "Oh, Matt," she whispered shakily, putting her hands over her face, as the overwhelming guilt she'd been holding back all afternoon came rushing to the fore.

He moved closer, his understanding, intuitive nature and strong male presence like a port in the storm. He wrapped his arms around her. Moving one hand over her spine, threading the other through her hair, the action as comforting as his presence.

And yet the horrifying images inside her head, the emotion building inside her, did not subside. She gulped around her tears, shaking her head, aware she felt nearly as grief-stricken and guilty now as she had when she'd sent Anthony out on that completely unnecessary errand, only to have him die… "A split second later and…"

He held her closer still, bending down to press his

cheek against the top of her head. "But it didn't happen, darlin'," he pointed out gruffly, wrapping his arms tighter around her.

Sara shuddered, tears still sliding down her face, even as she soaked up his warmth and his strength.

Was this how distressed he'd felt when Mutt was killed? And if so, how had he gotten over it?

All she knew for certain was that in the midst of the calamity he'd stayed really chill, and he was just as calm now. Laudably so. Despite his worry over her.

And while the intellectual part of her admired his unflappable attitude and his ability to simply take the near-catastrophe in stride, her intuitive side worried he might be shutting down emotionally again, the way he had been when they'd first started hanging out.

And that would not be good.

Not at all.

Matt frowned as his cell phone dinged.

Reluctantly, he let go of her and pulled the phone from his pocket. Seeing who it was from, he relaxed and moved to show her, too.

On screen, there was a text message with photo from Jack. Matt clicked over to the attached photo, smiling fondly. "Looks like the girls sent you an apology drawing."

Sara moved in close to see, her shoulder nudging the solid, warm musculature of Matt's chest. The artwork slash note was really cute. With a lot of grass, a puppy on a leash and a stick figure with Sara's name underneath. There were also hearts and flowers, and a big "We R So Soree!" printed across the top.

The message from Jack said, Sara: Chloe understands that although she likes to unhook things a lot, she cannot ever unsnap a puppy's leash from its collar again. (In case you can't figure out the spelling, they are so sorry, and so am I.) Thanks again for helping to save the day. Have a great evening.

Sara sighed. "Well, at least your big brother seems to have forgiven my inattention," she said.

"Now," Matt countered, with a wry smile, "all you have to do is forgive yourself."

Easier said than done, Sara thought.

Although, both men were right. She couldn't keep dwelling on past mistakes. Any more than she could dwell on Anthony's death. All she could do was behave a lot more responsibly in the future.

She went back to the rest of her evening chores: washing Charley's teething rings, putting them back in the freezer to chill, along with the homemade iced fruit pops, and emptying the dishwasher. As she did so, she spied the cartons, too. "You know we never did have that ice cream," she said, bringing out the two striped cartons.

Matt's eyes glinted. "I think I could handle that."

"Butter pecan or coconut almond?"

Matt set his phone aside and lounged against the counter, settling in comfortably and keeping her company, the way he had before they'd decided to put on the brakes. With a warm smile, he teased, "How about a little of both?"

"Sounds good." Sara scooped ice cream into two bowls.

It felt so right, having him with her. She knew she could get used to it. Was that what Matt's family was seeing, too? she wondered, as they sat down at the island, side by side, and began to eat. Why they were matchmaking and pushing her in his direction and vice versa?

Maybe this was something she and Matt did need to frankly discuss if they wanted to avoid awkward encounters in the future. She took a deep breath and turned to face him once again, her bent knees nearly brushing his. "Listen," she said, her spoon idling halfway to her lips, "about what Jack said to you about me..."

Still savoring the bite in his mouth, he grinned. "You *were* eavesdropping, then."

She heaved a sigh of relief at the realization he was amused instead of annoyed by her interest. "Yes," she said, trying not to blush. "I am deeply ashamed to admit that I was."

His brow furrowed. "Just out of curiosity...why were you so interested in what Jack was saying?"

Ignoring the butterflies in her stomach, Sara shrugged. Not about to admit how important it was to her, to be accepted as a suitable friend or companion by Matt's family.

"Because I had initially heard enough to know Jack was talking about me and you."

Needing to know more about what Matt was thinking and feeling, too, she forced herself to go on. "I also knew he was jumping to some pretty outrageous conclusions." Like in some way she and Matt were meant to be, the way Jack and Gayle had been.

An intimate silence fell.

"Yeah, well..." Matt shrugged, not the least bit surprised by his older brother's outburst. "He's still pretty angry about losing his wife in childbirth." Matt's voice dropped a sympathetic notch. "Having to raise Chloe from day one without her mom. And deal with Nicole and Lindsay's grief."

Sara reflected on the unbearable tragedy. "I can't even imagine how hard that has been for him."

With a commiserating nod, Matt finished the rest of his dessert and put his dish aside. Understanding lit his gray-blue eyes. "Sometimes he's okay. He just sort of soldiers on and keeps everything in perspective." Matt exhaled. "At other times, like this afternoon, when he thinks that someone is *not* appreciating what they have, while they have it…" Matt's lips thinned "…he loses it and lets them have it."

Sara understood that kind of irrational jealousy and resentment. She'd suffered flashes of it herself, when in the early throes of her grief over her husband's death.

Matt rubbed at the taut muscles on the back of his neck. "The only problem is, of course," he observed, in a low, matter-of-fact tone, "that not everyone has the kind of love Jack shared with Gayle."

Was Matt talking about himself now? Sara wondered. The fact he had never loved anyone the way Jack had loved his late wife?

Hard to tell.

What she could absolutely discern was that Matt was conflicted about his past, his present and his future, just as she was.

Maybe because whether he wanted to admit it or not, the near miss of an accident with his nieces—and Champ—that day had inadvertently brought up his issues with Mutt, too. Although, no one on the scene at the Dairy Barn, aside from her and Matt, had known about that tragedy.

Deciding it would help them both to relax even further, she stood and beckoned him toward the adjacent living room.

Leaving him to follow at will, she said over her shoulder, "We've talked a lot about me. Not much about you." She sat down, patting the place beside her on the sofa.

As the silence stretched out, the tension between them increased.

"How are you doing?" she prodded.

He came only so far as the edge of the rug in the conversation area. Stood, legs braced slightly apart, thumbs hooked through the loops on either side of his fly.

"What do you mean?" he asked, as if it were no big deal.

Sara waited for him to join her on the sofa.

When he didn't, she pointed out, "You were pretty cheerful when we set out to celebrate Charley's first tooth today. Since Champ was inadvertently let loose… not as cheerful."

His gaze narrowed. "Maybe I just have a lot on my mind."

"Like what…?" she pressed.

"Like, you really *don't* have to rescue me."

The fact she was able to get under his skin so easily, meant he was feeling something. Determined to find out what, she murmured, "I know."

He gave her a deeply irritated look that said, *Do you?*

Feeling a little like she'd just grabbed a lion by the tail, she rose and crossed to his side. As she inhaled the musky scent of him, her heart did a funny little twist in her chest. "You can still lean on me, the way I've been leaning on you the past few weeks."

His expression didn't change in the slightest. Yet he exuded testosterone with every slow, even breath.

"I don't need to lean on you."

And isn't that just the problem. Sara sighed, lamenting the fact this was not the first time she'd found herself in this situation, although she desperately wanted it to be the last.

Heat bloomed in her cheeks. Achingly aware of just how much she was coming to care for him, not just as a friend, but as the most important man in her life, she said softly, "You could if you wanted."

He looked at her for a long moment. "And if I don't...?" he asked.

Sara tamped down the fantasies their previous lovemaking sessions had inspired.

She shrugged, not sure whether to be relieved he was keeping the brakes on the chemistry between them. Or hurt that he wasn't as interested in getting to intimately understand each other as she was.

"Then we don't really have a relationship that is at all equal."

He met her gaze, his eyes dark and heated. "And that's a problem because...?"

"Lopsided friendships never work," she explained, her voice every bit as exasperated as his had been. "At least not long term. And right now," she huffed, wishing she didn't want to kiss him again so very much, "*I* seem to be doing all the taking, while *you're* doing all the giving."

And that was unfair.

He put a hand around her waist and tugged her against him. Then he leaned over and whispered in her ear, "Maybe I like it that way."

The unyielding imprint of his tall, strong body had her nipples tingling and pressing against her shirt. "Yeah, well, cowboy, maybe I don't."

He met her gaze in a way that made all rational thinking cease.

She thought about making love with him.

Holding him through the night.

Waking up together.

And most important, getting closer emotionally.

She had the strong impression he knew what she was beginning to want. And yearned for it, too. But for reasons she couldn't understand, wasn't about to let either of them have it.

He cleared his throat. To her frustration, every barrier that had ever been around his heart, seemed to be firmly back in place. "I probably should be heading home."

Suddenly, that was the last thing Sara wanted. Sensing she wasn't the only one who needed more love and attention in her life, she moved closer still.

This was one of those watershed moments.

"What if I want you to stay, Matt?" she asked, daring to put her own feelings on the line, to admit she wanted to feel incredibly close to him again. The way they felt when they were making love. She paused to look him in the eye. Asked softly, "What, then?"

Matt let his gaze drift over her, taking in every sweet, supple inch. She was so beautiful, so bright and intuitive and incredibly feminine. Had she not been in such a vulnerable state…

But she was.

And, having been raised a gentleman, he could not take advantage of that.

"Probably not a good idea," he said gruffly. Especially when he wanted to make love to her again as much as he did.

The fire of indignation lit her jade eyes. She stepped back, all cordial Texas grace. "Why not?"

He searched for some inner nobility that would give her all she needed—and nothing to later regret. Ignoring the way-too-innocent sparkle in her eyes, he tightened his fingers over hers and leaned in close enough to inhale the fragrance of her skin and hair. Then he let his gaze move wistfully from the playful curve of her lips, back to her eyes. "Because I don't trust myself not to kiss you again," he said, unable to help but admire how pretty and sassy she looked, with her pink cheeks and tousled hair.

Reluctantly, he let her go, stepped back. "And since we agreed to stay in the 'just friends' zone from here on out…"

She reached up to remove the clip from her hair and set it aside. He watched the wavy golden-blond mass fall loose and free to her shoulders once again.

Her lusciously soft lower lip shot out. "What if that, too, was a mistake?"

With Herculean effort, he resisted the urge to pull her right back into his arms. "Look, Sara, I get that you had an incredibly upsetting experience today and you're still shaken up." Just as he was. "You probably still have a lot of adrenaline running through you. But now isn't the time to leap recklessly into something you will later regret."

Sara scowled, her frustration with the situation apparent. "Making love with you is not what I've been regretting, Matt." She looked him straight in the eye. "Pushing you away, trying to put our relationship into some preconceived, predetermined box with boundaries that don't even make any sense, is what I've been regretting."

She was making a powerful argument. And if she hadn't been so susceptible… He swallowed. "You deserve to be married again."

"And I've told *you* that I don't want that!"

Maybe not now. He was pretty sure that would change when she got over the loss of her late husband.

"Charley needs—"

Sara went up on tiptoe. Cut him off with a finger pressed against his lips. "Charley needs people around him who love him and care for him," she asserted in a low, determined tone. "He needs strong, male role models in his life." She encircled her arms about his neck, fitting her soft, supple body against the length of his. "You fill both those needs."

Feeling himself grow instantly hard, it was all Matt could do not to groan. Summoning up every bit of chivalry he had, he unhooked her arms and set her aside. "And I'd like to do so in the future."

She smiled, not the least bit dissuaded. "Great. Charley and I want the same." She reached down to take off her boots.

Mouth dry, he watched her begin to unbutton her blouse. "It's not that simple, Sara."

Passion gleamed in her pretty eyes. She stripped off her shirt. Reached for the zipper on her jeans. "Why isn't it?"

He caught her hand before she could shimmy out of

her jeans. "Because once again you're not addressing what you need."

"Yes, Matt, I am." She moved into his arms, taking the initiative and pressing her lips to his. With a low growl, he found himself succumbing to the desire he had promised himself, for both their sakes, he would never resurrect again. Blood thundered through him, and he reveled in the taste and feel of her. Yet he knew what he had to do.

With a groan of frustration, he sifted his hands through her hair and tore his mouth away. "Sara..."

Her lower lip, so soft and pink and bare, trembled slightly. Yet her feisty resolve remained.

She splayed her hands across his chest. She kissed his jaw, the skin behind his ear. "I want you to stay, Matt." Her nipples protruded from the satin of her bra as she reached for the buttons on his shirt. Twin spots of color brightened her high cheekbones. "I want us to go back to making love, and being there for each other, whenever, however, we each need," she confessed softly, vulnerability shimmering in her pretty green eyes. "While at the same time," she continued persuasively, "not judging each other for any of our flaws. Or resenting each other for what we can't seem to give."

Hands on her shoulders, he forced himself not to think about taking her to bed again. "We need to slow down, darlin'," he warned. "Talk about this."

"Why?" Hurt warred with the frustration in her eyes. "When I feel like you get me and accept me the way no one else does, or ever will! I want to be close to you, Matt. Closer than we've been this last week." Her slender body trembled. "What is so wrong with that?"

Nothing. At least so far as he could figure in his

heart. He could hardly chastise her for wanting to live her life to the fullest in any way she chose, when he was resolved to do the very same thing in his. "You make a compelling argument," he said gruffly.

"Good." She guided him over to the sofa. As soon as he sat down, she slid onto his lap. "Now, where were we?"

Saying to heck with caution, he reached around behind her and unhooked her bra. "In a wagonful of trouble."

She laughed softly. "Trouble can be fun…"

He cupped her breasts, his body hardening as he felt her quiver. "Pretty much everything about you is fun."

She lowered her face to his. "Right back at you, cowboy," she murmured back, then kissed him with a sensuality that further rocked his world. Her soft pliant form surrendering against his, she threaded her hands through his hair, moaning softly. He cupped the silky globes of her breasts with both hands, drawing first one rosy bud, then the other into his mouth. And still she melted against him and held him as if she never wanted to let him go.

Loving her unfettered response, he lifted his head. Exhilarated by the fact she was about to be his…again… he rasped, "Any special requests?"

She laughed softly. "Your choice."

Pure male satisfaction poured through him. "Even better."

He eased his palm past the edge of her panties, finding the damp, soft nest. She moaned as he stroked. Eager to please her, he kept kissing her, while continuing his slow, sensual exploration. He stroked her repeatedly, light butterfly touches that had her shuddering. Kisses and caresses that had her melting.

They switched places and he knelt before her, stripped off her panties and positioned himself between her thighs. Holding her open to him. Loving her. Until she twisted against him, no longer able to hide the totality of her response.

As eager to please him as he had been her, she unbuttoned his belt, undid his fly. Slipping her hands inside, she found the hot, hard length of him.

Their reactions were simultaneous. He groaned. She trembled with pleasure.

Caught up in something too elemental to fight, she bent to love him. Until he, too, could stand it no more. He found a condom. Together, they rolled it on.

With a growl of satisfaction, he stretched out over top of her and brought his whole body into contact with hers. Hands beneath her hips, he spread her thighs and slid inside, penetrating deep. She gasped and kissed him back, to his delight, just as ravenous for him as he was for her. And then they slowed it down. Taking their time. Drawing out the unimaginable pleasure. Until there was no more holding back, no more waiting. She was wrapping her legs around his waist, drawing him deeper, surrendering to his will, even as powerful sensations layered, one over another.

He lay claim to her lips and her body, as he wanted to lay claim to her heart and soul. Until she was kissing him back, more ardently than ever before. And this time, when they came together in shattering pleasure, he knew there was no going back, for either of them.

For long moments they lay locked together, quivering with delicious aftershocks of their passion, catching their breath. Worried he might be too heavy for her, he rolled onto his side.

She moved with him. Emitting a happy sigh, said, "I have to tell you, cowboy, I could sooo get used to this."

He propped his head on his elbow and gazed deep into her eyes. "Same here, darlin'." He stroked his fingers through her tousled hair, pressed a gentle kiss on her temple.

Her gaze grew dreamy. "Want to spend the night?"

More than you'll ever know.

Wary that could ruin everything, however, he clasped her close and pressed another kiss on the top of her head. Wishing things were different, said, "Remember that speech you gave me earlier, about not asking or expecting us to give anything we don't feel able to?"

She nodded.

Rising, he reached for his clothes. "Well, this is one of those things I shouldn't do."

Hurt flickered briefly on her pretty face. "Because we're not married and not going to be?"

That is definitely part of it. But not all. Not nearly. "Because you'll sleep better without me here," he said.

Chapter 13

To Sara's delight, the week that followed was a lot more romantically satisfying than the previous one. Matt showed up to help her every afternoon, then stayed for dinner and the bedtime routines for Charley and Champ. The only thing he wouldn't do…wouldn't even consider doing…was spend the night after they'd made love.

Which in turn made her ruminate. What was really preventing him from actually *sleeping* with her? Was he a bed hog? A restless sleeper? Insomniac? Did he snore? Just really hate to snuggle? Or did this have something to do with the PTSD she'd been suspecting he had? Sara couldn't begin to figure it out, and he didn't want to discuss it, so she was still wondering about his motivation when he arrived at her home late Friday afternoon, just in time for Champ's training session.

"What is he going to work on today?" Matt asked, cuddling Charley, who had just woken up from his nap.

"You'll see." Sara grinned, proud of how much progress the little black Lab was making.

Using a simultaneous combination of hand signal and verbal command, she walked Champ out to the back patio. Said, "Champ, sit!"

He put his rump on the ground, and kept his eyes on her.

"Stay!"

The pup remained perfectly still. She waited a second, then backed up several paces. "Champ, come!"

He rose and trotted to her side.

"Sit!"

He sat obediently.

She patted the ground in front of his paws. "Down."

Champ stretched out, his tummy on the ground, too.

"Good boy, Champ!" Still praising him warmly, Sara hunkered down beside him and petted the top of his head. "Good boy!"

She rose to her feet once again.

"Champ, stand."

He rose with canine grace. Stood looking patiently at her.

"Wow," Matt said. "He's got it all down pat."

Sara smiled proudly. "He does, doesn't he?" She took Champ's leash and led him over to his spot in the grass, where he promptly relieved himself. "I can't wait to show him off at the reunion picnic tomorrow."

"Any final word on where it's going to be yet?" he asked.

Sara nodded, not so happy about the predicted weather, and the necessary change in accommodations.

"The rain is supposed to start around nine this evening and continue until midnight tomorrow. So the event has been moved to the WTWA building in Laramie."

Matt grinned down at Charley, who was now patting Matt's jaw with both of his little hands. He paused to kiss Charley's fingertips, then turned his attention back to Sara. "Will it hold everyone?"

She paused to let Champ get a drink from his outdoor water bowl, then led him back inside. "There are three levels of meeting rooms and a large covered patio out back, so yes, it will." Sara directed Champ to his mat on the floor and handed him a nylon chew bone.

She washed her hands, then took Charley from Matt and settled her son in the high chair next to her. "Although it won't be as accessible an event as usual, due to the fact everyone won't be scattered across one large space."

Looking devastatingly handsome in a blue chambray shirt and jeans, Matt lounged against the counter, arms folded in front of him. His hair was clean and rumpled and he smelled like soap and cologne. The faint hint of evening beard clung to his jaw.

"That's too bad," he said.

As intensely aware of him as ever, Sara shrugged. "It will still be fun." She walked into the pantry and emerged with canisters of flour, regular and confectioner's sugar, and a tin of cocoa.

He didn't look convinced but deftly dropped the subject.

"So. What are you making?" he asked, nodding at the eggs and butter coming to room temperature on the counter.

"Our contribution to the feast. Two large sheet pans of fudge brownies."

He waggled his brows in anticipation. "Can I help?"

She handed him the box of Cheerios for Charley. "Keep me company. And lend a hand if either of our two little ones need something."

Matt scattered dry cereal on Charley's tray. "They look pretty content right now," he observed.

Charley was snacking on Cheerios, watching everything that was going on around him, while Champ was lying on the floor next to Sara, his nylon puppy chew bone clasped between his little paws.

"They do."

Sara slipped a chef's apron over her neck.

Matt stepped behind her to tie it, his hands brushing her spine in the process.

Tingling from even the light contact, Sara smiled her thanks and stepped back to the counter to consult the recipe. "Hard to believe it's his last night here."

Matt watched as she broke eight eggs into a bowl.

"You going to be okay, saying goodbye to Champ tomorrow?" he asked in the gruff-tender voice she loved.

Aware it was her turn to keep her feelings tightly locked away, Sara put the softened butter and sugar into the bowl, and turned the stand mixer on low. "I probably wouldn't be if I hadn't made a point to not get too attached to him." She forced herself to focus on the task at hand. "But I know he's going to be with Alyssa Barnes and her family." And that was, she knew, a very good thing for the returning wounded soldier and Champ.

Matt nodded his approval. "They were really nice when we met them."

Sara measured vanilla into the wet ingredients. "And

she's so excited about working with him, which will in turn help her in own recovery."

Matt stepped back to give her room when she added the flour and cocoa to the mixing bowl. He looked down at Champ, and Sara thought, but couldn't be sure, Matt had a brief gleam of affection in his eyes.

He looked back at Sara, his expression implacable again. "How long will Alyssa Barnes have him?"

"About two years, or however long it takes for him to complete all of his training and be permanently paired with a disabled veteran." Sara spooned the batter into the pans. "At which point, she'll have a chance to start all over again, with another puppy." Finished, she removed the paddle and offered it to him. "Which is what most of the program volunteers do. Helping out like that can be pretty gratifying."

He scooped off a taste with his fingertip and then gave it back to her. "I can see that."

She savored the chocolate mixture, too. And thought about kissing him again. Knowing that if she did, he would not only taste like rich chocolate brownie batter, but also the dark male essence unique to him.

Aware she was running out of time with Champ and Matt, she gathered her courage and said, "By the way, I know our deal was for one month." Which had flown by way too fast. "But I want you to know," she said huskily, "you are welcome here anytime."

Matt wrapped his arms around her waist and brought her close for one long, sweet kiss. Melting into the embrace, she kissed him back, sliding her hands across his solid muscular chest. When he'd finished, he looked down at her tenderly. "You and Charley are welcome at my ranch, too. Anytime." He rubbed his thumb across her lower lip, clearly savoring their time together every bit as much as she. "No invitation required."

Sara and Matt spent the rest of the evening, sharing a quick and easy dinner, and caring for Charley and Champ. When both little ones were down for the night, he helped her cut up the cooled brownies and pack them into foil serving pans.

"Tomorrow's going to be a long day," he said, when they'd finished. "I probably better head on home."

Maybe it was presumptuous of her, but she'd been looking forward to whiling away the rest of the evening with him, now that their little ones were fast asleep.

"Sure?" she said. "There's a new movie on Netflix you might enjoy." She grinned saucily. "I've got popcorn..."

He shook his head. "Thanks, but...some other time, okay?"

He brought her close for a scorching hot good-night kiss, hugged her one last time, then smiled again and slipped out the door.

Flummoxed, Sara stood on the porch waving as he drove away. It wasn't the first time he had exited before ten in the evening, or even the first time he had left without making love with her during the last week.

Since their "misunderstanding," he had been working hard to refrain from any behavior that might seem at all overfamiliar.

To treat her with courtesy and respect and make sure she knew that as much as he appreciated and desired her, that he also respected her space, and her need for privacy.

But tonight his courteous exit felt different somehow. Like some mysterious wall was between them. Like there was something he didn't want her to see.

And late the next morning when he arrived to take her and Charley and Champ into town, he was even more scrupulously polite.

"Is this everything?" he asked, as he stacked Champ's food and water bowls, chew toys, sleep towel and leash in a box on top of his travel and sleeping crate.

"Just about." Sara looked at the water sluicing off the eaves. She slipped on her raincoat and hat. "I just need to take him out to go one last time before we head out."

The only problem was, Champ didn't like the rain or the wet ground. She walked him around and around on his leash, waiting for him to squat and relieve himself. To no avail.

He was having none of it.

Finally, Sara gathered him in her arms and took him inside the house. He was soaked to the skin and shivering. She was equally drenched.

Matt handed her a towel from the stack by the back door. Sara started with Champ's head and ears, and gently blotted the moisture from his silky black fur. As much as she could, anyway. Then she worked her way over his shoulders, down beneath his belly and legs, and paws. He leaned into her, snuggling close, the way he had so many times, and suddenly it hit her. This was the very last time he would be her responsibility. The tears she'd been holding back flooded her eyes.

She blinked them away furiously. Matt turned away. But not before she saw the moisture shimmering in his eyes, too.

Was this what he'd been hiding from her the previous evening? The fact that despite all common sense, he'd gotten attached to little Champ, too?

Several hours later, Garrett Lockhart, the doctor and former army captain who helmed the WTWA and also ran his family's charitable foundation, caught up with Matt near the buffet tables. The one place in the facility where, to Matt's relief, dogs weren't allowed.

"Hey." Garrett grinned at Matt who was there hanging out with Charley. "I just met Champ. You and Sara did a great job bringing the little pup along. He's incredibly relaxed and outgoing."

Except, Matt thought guiltily as Charley kicked his foot against his chest, dislodging his baby moccasin in the process, *he* hadn't done much of anything to help socialize Champ. Yes, he had cared for baby Charley while Sara worked with the cute little puppy. And he'd supervised Champ for a couple of hours while Sara grabbed some much needed sleep. He'd also helped Champ acclimate to his training crate. But he hadn't stopped to personally greet or pet him, or cuddle him the way Sara did, even once.

Not about to publicly admit that, though, Matt smiled, demonstrating the cheerful attitude the event attendees expected to see from him.

"All Sara's doing," he admitted with a shrug, while trying to retie Charley's shoe with one hand. Not easy, given the way Charley was situated in the BabyBjörn hooked over Matt's shoulders. "All I did was watch over Charley here while Sara did all the work."

"Speaking of baby wrangling..." Hope, Garrett's wife, interjected. She smiled when Charley kicked his moccasin all the way off and it went sailing in the air between them. Then bent to pick it up and moved forward to help put it back on. "I have to ask. How *did* Sara talk you into doing that?"

Matt chuckled. This was a little easier to talk about. "Let's just say she's persistent," he teased.

Garrett wrapped his arm around his wife's shoulder, as their five-year-old son, Max, and his little brother, Harry, played peekaboo around their parents' legs. "The mark of a good woman." He bussed his wife's head. "She never gives up."

Hope leaned her head on Garrett's shoulder. "Not when it comes to love, anyway."

The problem was, Sara wasn't in love with him, Matt thought. The only thing she saw him as was a good friend and part-time lover, and although both of them had started out wanting nothing more than that, he was beginning to think they'd been wrong to limit themselves. If they ever wanted to have what Hope and Garrett Lockhart and some of his happily married siblings had, anyway.

And speaking of brothers…

Bess Monroe, Jack and his three little girls came up to join them. "Where's Sara?" they asked in unison.

Matt inclined his head. "Upstairs in one of the meeting rooms on the second floor, convening with all the rest of the dogs in Champ's litter."

Matt looked at Jack and Bess. Was it his imagination or did the two of them have something going on? Besides the decades-long friendship they claimed? His brother had interfered in his love life. Maybe it was time he did the same. "What are you-all doing here together?"

Bess smiled, as Charley's shoe once again went sailing. She knelt to pick it up and handed it to Matt, then nodded at Jack and his daughters. "They're my plus four," she bragged. "Saved me from needing an actual date."

"And—" Jack looked at his daughters fondly "—they wanted to see Champ and make sure he was still all right, after that unfortunate incident at the Dairy Barn."

Matt pointed them in the right direction. And then pretended to need to find a quiet place, to change Charley's diaper and feed him his bottle.

And so it went for the rest of the day.

Charley kept kicking off the one shoe and stayed mostly with Matt, while Sara went back and forth, talking to everyone she'd been working with in the puppy raising program for the last two years, and helping out with the replenishment of the buffet.

Matt stayed on the sidelines as much as possible, glad he had Charley to both distract and run interference for him.

"You didn't get to do as much socializing as I did," Sara lamented much later, when they drove home.

Relieved the event was over, Matt exhaled. "Actually, Charley attracted plenty of people. All of whom wanted to tell me just how cute he was."

Sara grinned with maternal pride. "He is that."

The advantage of carrying around a baby had also prevented him from paying direct attention to any of the service dogs. It had still been hard being at the reunion, though, Matt reflected tensely. Because everywhere he had gone, there had been an active or retired military person and a service dog, reminding him once again of what he really didn't want to remember.

* * *

"Hard to believe Charley is still wide-awake at nine o'clock at night," Matt said.

"Probably has something to do with all that time he spent sleeping on your chest today, at the reunion," Sara mused, bringing in two mugs of coffee for the adults. Hers had cream, no sugar. Matt's was plain, just the way he liked it. Which was no surprise. She did everything just the way he liked it.

She settled next to him on the floor, turning toward him in a drift of lilac perfume. Pretty color highlighted the delicate planes of her cheeks. "You could have put him down, you know, let him sleep in his stroller."

"I know." It had been comforting, having Charley cuddled up against him. While at the same time experiencing what it would feel like if Charley were actually his son.

She looked at him over the rim of her mug, enthusiasm still glittering in her eyes. "What did you think about the event?"

That it had gone on way, way too long. For him, anyway. For everyone else it had concluded far too soon.

He took a sip of his coffee, and found it as perfectly brewed as always. "It's a good organization."

Her soft, bare lips formed a sexy smile. "Thinking of joining it?"

Given the way he was feeling right now? No. He also knew what Sara hoped to hear. And for reasons he couldn't begin to decipher, he did not want to disappoint her. "Maybe later," he hedged. That was, if his plan to keep desensitizing himself to dogs worked as he hoped.

Determined to steer the conversation away from the

stuff that still haunted him, he returned his full attention to Charley, who was still stretched out on the play rug between them. Head up, his tummy flat on the floor, he was trying to pull himself forward by moving his arms. Unfortunately, he did not have the strength for his weight.

Matt smiled tenderly. He shifted the toy Charley had his eye on a little closer. Charley reacted by bouncing up and down, the movement just enough to allow him to capture the stuffed ducky.

He chuckled. "Got to hand it to the little fella. He's still trying to figure things out."

Sara sighed with maternal frustration.

Matt knew she wanted to solve all her son's problems for him. Rather than let him work this out for himself.

"I've been trying to show him how to crawl," Sara said.

"Oh yeah?" Matt waggled his brows, attempting to tease her into relaxing about her son's lack of progress on the physical agility front. He nudged her bent knee playfully with his. "Want to try teaching me?"

She returned his look with mock indignation. "No."

He chuckled, playing along with her stern reproach.

Sara watched her son roll right back over on his tummy and begin the search for a way to crawl again.

She took a deep breath, continued bringing him up to date. "I've stretched out right beside him and got up on all fours, and rocked back and forth, just as he is now, and then demonstrated it to him by moving one arm and leg forward slowly, and then the other."

Interesting.

And something he really would not have thought of doing himself.

But then, he'd been brought up to be a McCabe man and McCabe men solved their own problems.

"And what does he do?" Matt asked.

Listening to the adult conversation, Charley lifted his belly up off the floor, and began rocking back and forth in earnest.

Sara ran her hands through the silky strands of her hair. "Usually he just plops down and looks at me as if to say, *What in the world are you doing, Mom?* And then he rolls around to get whatever he wants."

Matt shrugged. "Well, as long as he's mobile."

Sara's lower lip shot out in frustration. "It's important he achieves this milestone."

"Even if he's not quite ready?" Matt said, as Charley planted both hands and feet on the floor, and then lifted his tummy and bottom as high as he possibly could, a move that put his body into an inverted U. As usual, he got stuck in that position, and let out a frustrated scream.

Sara reached over to help her son get unstuck and fall gently back into a seated position. "I honestly think he'd be happier if he could get around." She handed Charley a small stuffed blue bunny.

He lifted it to his mouth, and chewed on a corner earnestly.

Matt looked around. With all the dog paraphernalia gone, the living area seemed oddly barren. He soothed Sara as best he could. "Well, it won't be as hard for you to work on this with Charley, now that Champ isn't here."

Sara immediately teared up. She looked like she had lost her best friend.

"Sorry," Matt said hastily.

Shaking her head in abject misery, she rose, ducked into the nearby powder room and shut the door behind her.

Matt looked at Charley. Glad he was too young to understand that Sara was crying. He leaned forward conspiratorially. "I know your mommy *says* it's too much but we may have to get her a puppy of her very own—to keep."

Sara came back out of the bathroom, her spine stiff with indignation. She glared at Matt. "Don't you dare."

He was about to ask why not, when she lifted a silencing palm.

"I have to get over the loss first," she explained firmly. "And then, and only then, will I consider what else might be in our future."

Sara used the time upstairs, getting Charley ready for bed and tucked in, to further compose herself. When she came back down, to her surprise, Matt had put their coffee mugs in the dishwasher. His hat, rain jacket and cell phone were nearby.

"You're getting ready to leave?" she asked in surprise, aware she had been acting a little hormonal.

Or maybe just grief-stricken.

She really had gotten used to having the little puppy around. Even though she had known all along she would not be able to keep him.

He shrugged, his emotions as tightly wrapped up as hers had been vividly on display. "I figured it's been a really long day."

She caught his arm before he could move past her, her fingers closing over the swell of his bicep. She knew she'd been crabby. She also knew he'd been sort of withdrawn and brooding all day.

She'd thought maybe it was because there were so many dogs and military people at the reunion picnic. That it had been hard for him to be around that. Now she wondered if more was bothering him.

"I still have energy," she said. When it looked like he was going to protest, she lifted her palm in the age-old sign of peace. "You look like you do, too." She paused to look him in the eye, figuring if she couldn't help her son learn to crawl, she could at least encourage Matt to open up to her about what was bothering him. "So what's really going on here, Matt?"

He held her eyes with his mesmerizing gaze, making her feel all hot and bothered. "You want me to be blunt?"

She checked her need to throw herself into his arms and kiss him until all her excess emotions fled. His body language and curt tone made it clear he was not in the mood for romance.

"Of course."

He stuck his thumbs through the loops on either side of his fly and rocked back on his heels. "The reason I've been here almost every day the last month is now residing elsewhere with Alyssa Barnes."

She studied him in consternation. "Meaning what? I'd have to get another puppy for me to take care of in order to keep you dropping by on a regular basis?"

Frustration tautened the handsome planes of his face. Abruptly, he looked like he didn't know what to make of the new phase of their relationship, either.

With a sigh, he resumed his usual easygoing manner. "I love Charley. You know that." His gaze gentled. "I love hanging out with you, too."

"Love hanging out with" was not the same as *love*. At least not the kind she wanted, deep down. But maybe he was right. Maybe, like Charley's crawling, their relationship would continue to develop in its own way, its own time. *If* she didn't push. She jerked in a bolstering breath. "Then why not just build on that?" she asked softly.

A contemplative silence fell. Leaving her feeling like there was still so much she didn't know about him. Might never know, if it were up to him.

His gaze drifted over her, lingering on her lips before returning to her eyes. "You want to keep seeing each other as much as we have been?"

Sara nodded. "I want to keep making love with you, too."

He groaned, then, looking more conflicted than ever, said, "Sara… I know we said we'd just keep things casual and figure out what to do one day at a time…without making demands on each other. But maybe, given how upset you are at having to give up Champ, even though you knew all along this was coming…"

His words sounded perilously like a breakup speech.

Distraught to find herself close to losing even more in the space of one day, and all because he couldn't handle the loss they'd both been braced for any more than she could, she said, "I know you tried to keep your distance from Champ, and in a way, you did, but your heart aches, too, Matt. Don't deny it."

He scrubbed a hand over his face, abruptly looking as miserable and distraught as she felt. "Not trying to," he said gruffly.

She held out her hands imploringly. "Then what are you trying to do?" she asked, tears blurring her vision.

His expression immediately contrite, he moved farther away from her. "What I've been trying to do for weeks now. Look out for you and your needs," he said, his voice turning even raspier.

She knew he thought disappearing to deal with his grief would somehow spare her, the way he'd tried to spare his family after the attack on the compound. But it wouldn't. Not now, when the only two people in the world who knew exactly what they were feeling was themselves.

She studied him, her heart racing. "You want to be gallant? You want to care for me?"

Frustration warred with the exasperation on his face. "You know I do."

In a panic, fearing she would lose him, too, Sara moved in and wrapped her arms around his neck. "Then kiss me, Matt," she whispered, lifting her lips to his. "Just kiss me."

And so he did.

Matt had never imagined he would be in a position to use the chemistry he had with Sara to gain entry to her heart. But their situation was so complicated he had no choice but to use whatever advantage he had to get close to her. To let her know he wanted her in his life, not as some occasional lover and casual friend, but as a real viable part of his everyday existence.

He wanted her to be able to come to him, as easily as he had been coming to see her the past month. He wanted to share her worries and her triumphs regarding Charley. Be there every evening for dinner, and be able to go home after to his place and know she not only understood, but was okay with it.

So when she took his hand and led him upstairs to her bed, he went. Kissing her the entire way.

And when she started to disrobe, he helped her. Just as she helped him.

Naked, he pulled her to the edge of the bed, knelt on the floor in front of her and nudged her thighs apart. She gasped and caught his head as he found her. Satisfaction roaring through him, he breathed in her sweet, musky scent and explored the silky heat, the taut pearly bud.

And still he ravished her, again and again, until she was calling his name and coming apart in his hands. Loving the no-holds-barred way she surrendered herself to him, he moved up again. Kissed her fiercely, deeply. Taking her the way she demanded to be taken, completely, irrevocably. Until there was no doubt she knew how much he wanted her. There was no stopping the building sensation. And she was clamped around him, urging him on to a soul-shattering climax, and then slowly, sweetly back down again.

For long moments after, they clung to each other. He savored the feel of her wrapped up in this arms, cognizant of just how fragile the moment was. Because he knew he was going to have to get up, get dressed and go home, if he didn't want to fall asleep.

And he would leave.

Eventually.

Once they'd both had their fill.

Right now, he needed and wanted to hold her, just a while longer.

Chapter 14

Sara woke to the sound of a loud gasp and guttural moan, followed by a piercing "No" and the most primal scream of terror and agony she'd ever heard. She bolted upright at the same time as Matt, who was wild-eyed and sweating, swung both arms up to shield his face and reeled backward.

Swearing, he lunged forward, at least so far as the covers tangled around them would allow. Then let out another chilling shout of anguish. "Mutt! Oh my God!" His voice broke as tears streamed down his face. "Mutt!"

Before she knew it, Sara was crying, too.

Desperate to end his nightmare, she grabbed Matt's arms, attempting to wake him. At the same time, Charley started to cry in the nursery down the hall.

"Matt!" She shook his shoulders, harder now.

Still in the midst of his night terror, he threw her off.

Torn between her need to minister to Matt and comfort her son, Sara bolted from the bed. She grabbed her robe and raced down the hall, shrugging it on as she moved, listening to the heartbreaking sounds of her son's sobs, and the diminishing cries of Matt.

Her heart pounding, she switched on the nursery light and moved to her distraught son's side. "It's all right, baby, I'm here," she soothed, as she picked up her wailing infant and held him to her. She swept her hand reassuringly down his back. "Hush now, baby, Mommy's here. It was just a bad dream."

Charley burrowed his wet face into her shoulder. She sat down with him in the glider, and still crooning gently, began to rock back and forth .

Charley drew a shaky breath and snuggled even nearer, not crying now, but clinging to her as if his life depended on it.

She sang his favorite lullaby, felt him relax even more, as Matt's chaotic voice faded and the upstairs fell completely silent once again.

Eventually, Sara realized Charley was once again sound asleep.

Carefully, she eased him back into his crib. Stood there a moment, her hand resting lightly on his chest. She felt his breathing, deep and even. Relieved his own upset had been so short-lived, she turned and crept out of the nursery, walked down the hall into the master suite.

The king-size bed was empty.

Matt was dressing quietly in the moonlight. Head bowed, broad shoulders hunched forward in defeat, he looked as completely destroyed inside as she suddenly felt.

Not sure how to comfort him, she walked in. Her emotions in turmoil, she took a stabilizing breath. "You're awake."

He offered a terse nod in response, then boots in hand, headed past her without a word down the stairs.

Barely able to contain her hurt and confusion, Sara followed. She'd expected him to accept her comfort as readily as Charley had. Instead, he seemed to wish they were a thousand miles apart.

She understood he was embarrassed.

He had no reason to be.

Determined to make him understand and accept that, she intercepted him at the door. "You don't have to leave, Matt," she told him quietly. "In fact, I'd prefer you didn't. Not until we've at least had a chance to talk."

He shoved a hand through his hair and let out a long breath. Looking frustrated that she needed him to spell it out for her. Even though that was apparently the last thing he wanted to do.

More determined than ever not to part like this again, with both of them locked in their own private version of hell, she moved into the doorway, further blocking his exit. Ignoring the tight lines around his mouth and the shadows in his eyes, she asked, "Is this why you've never wanted to stay the night with me? Have you been having nightmares all along?"

Matt wasn't sure how to answer that, because first, he didn't want her to know how long and how often this had been going on. He didn't want anyone to know. And second, he wasn't exactly sure what had happened tonight.

Only that their lovemaking had been more incredible

than ever. He hadn't intended to fall asleep and tempt fate. But she'd wanted him to stay a little longer and he'd been too damn weak and greedy to say no. So he'd cuddled her close, savoring the delicious feel of her soft body pressed up against his. The next thing he knew, he was waking up, sweating and alone, to the sounds of Sara running down the hall, baby Charley crying his heart out. The state of the bedcovers, his own pounding pulse, echoing shouts and aching throat had him surmising the rest…

He'd been dreaming about the compound again.

The suicide bombers.

The explosions…

And the sheer hell and heartbreak that had followed.

"Was your bad dream about Mutt?" she persisted, her soft hand curling around the taut muscles of his bicep.

Why deny it? Suddenly too weary to stand, he sat down on the stairs to pull on his boots. He had to get out of here, if he wanted even a prayer of shaking off the residual terror and grief. He also knew, after what she'd just witnessed, she wasn't going to let it go. So it was either talk it out now, or face it later.

"Have you been having nightmares?" she asked again, sitting next to him on the tread.

He grimaced. "Sometimes." But they had faded when he had started spending time with her and Charley and Champ. Not gone away entirely. But lessened, just the same.

Until tonight, anyway.

Tonight it had been as bad as it had ever been.

He blew out a breath.

She wound her hand through his. "Why didn't you tell me?"

He looked down at their entwined fingers, wishing they could forget all this and just go back to making love. "I did."

She studied him a long, heartrending moment. Compressed her soft lips together, but still left her hand in his. "Ah no, cowboy, you did not…"

Okay, so I didn't exactly confess to chronic night terrors. Tightly, he reminded her, "When I said you'd sleep better without me here…that I wasn't marriage material…that's what I meant."

She swiveled to face him, her bent knee bumping into his thigh. She looked incredibly vulnerable, even as naïve hope shone on her pretty face. "You can get help for this at the WTWA. They have support groups…"

He laughed harshly at even the suggestion of such a miracle. If miracles existed, Mutt would not be dead. Restless, he let go of her, stood. "Like you said, dwelling on the grief of what happened would only set me back. I want to move forward."

She rose with elegant grace. Her lower lip trembling, she pointed out, "Except you're not okay, Matt."

Wasn't that a little like the pot calling the kettle black? He lifted a censuring brow. "Projecting a little, are you?"

Sara flushed, indignant. "I'm trying to move on," she said, mimicking his coolly deliberate tone. "Build a new life for myself and Charley."

He tamped down his anger and resentment with effort. Shrugged. "Well, so am I."

His words hit their target.

Her face turned a blotchy pink. "I can't go back to living the way I did when Anthony was alive."

"I'm not asking you to."

She slammed her hands on her waist, and tilted her head up to his. "Aren't you?"

"First of all, I don't inflict my bad moods on you, which is why I'm trying to leave here tonight. Second, I'm not reckless."

"But," she interrupted, eyes glittering emotionally, "you are clearly suffering from post-traumatic stress."

He scoffed and leaned back against her front door, arms folded in front of him. "What makes you think that?"

She went utterly still for one long moment. "Besides the nightmares? The fact that you're not taking care of yourself as well as you should...a fact that was demonstrated when you let that splinter in your hand go untreated, even though it was clearly painful and you knew you were risking infection."

"I told you I would have gotten around to that. I delayed because I wanted to be with you."

Sara looked like the last thing she wanted was to be anyone's excuse.

Valiantly, she forged on, "You also avoid anything that reminds you of your loss. Like dogs."

"Hey," he said, smiling thinly, not about to criticized for that, "I managed to be around Champ."

She paced the foyer like a prosecuting district attorney before the jury. "But you weren't exactly comfortable at the WTWA reunion picnic, were you? All those servicemen and women. The dogs they loved..."

The memory caused his gut to twist.

He grimaced. "What's your point?" he demanded gruffly.

She stepped toward him, hands outstretched, like the relentless do-gooder she'd been when they'd met. "The point is I care about you, Matt, so much. Charley loves you. Champ adored you, despite the fact you avoided him as much as possible. And you cared about him. I saw it before we left for the picnic, when I realized—" her voice caught on a half sob, and it was a moment before she could go on "—we were going to have to say goodbye to him today." Eyes brimming with tears, she continued, "I know you, Matt. Not just on the surface, but deep down. You're meant to have a dog and a family of your own."

Matt only wished that were the case. He regarded her bleakly, his misery increasing by leaps and bounds. "Charley would probably tell you differently, given how I terrified him tonight."

She nodded then murmured softly, "Which is why I'm *suggesting* you get the help you need."

Except it wasn't really a choice. Not in her view, anyway. And the last thing Matt wanted was a repeat of his previous failed relationship. Or a new onslaught of the kind of badgering he'd received from his family. "Suggesting," he queried lightly in return. "Or commanding?"

Her shoulders stiffened in defiance. "I am not trying to order you around."

"Sure sounds like it," he scoffed.

Another tense silence fell. "I want to know you're taking care of yourself the way you should, Matt. I want you to be able to stay the night with me, to sleep here."

Matt wanted that, too. More than she knew. He also knew it wasn't going to happen. Because as hard as he tried, he couldn't just erase that part of his life. Couldn't will the nightmares away.

And he damn well wouldn't risk hurting or frightening her—or, God forbid, Charley—again.

Desperately trying to hang on to what they'd had, he countered just as persuasively, letting her know his own requirements for happiness. "And I want what we've had up to now, Sara. To live each day to the fullest and hang out together and help each other…and when we're both feeling it, make love with each other."

Her lips quivered as much as the rest of her. "I want that, too, Matt." Her eyes glistened with worry and hurt. "I also want to know that you're not going to go off the rails, the way my husband did."

Was she talking about the accident that had cost Anthony his life? "I don't drive recklessly, or go into a curve traveling way too fast."

Sara swallowed, looking uncomfortable again. "I'm not talking about car wrecks, per se."

He studied her in confusion, sensing something new about to be revealed. "Then what are you talking about?"

Her breath caught. "Suicide."

Matt stared at Sara. "Anthony's death was ruled an accident. I know, because my brother Dan was the first deputy on the scene and I talked to him about it at the time."

Sara paused.

"You yourself told me tests showed there were no drugs or alcohol involved. He didn't have his cell phone with him, so he wasn't texting or looking at that. He was simply going too fast for the turn, and drove off the road. And that explanation makes sense. Given Anthony's post-war inclination toward reckless driving."

Looking terrified and distraught, and uncertain, she lamented, "But what if it was more than that?"

He shook his head at her. "Now you're the one going over the edge..."

She held up a hand, wordlessly asking him to hold on a minute. Then went to the computer set up on the desk in the living room. He'd never really seen her use it, he realized belatedly, as she turned it on and sat down in front of it. When the screen lit up, she motioned him over.

There were two different log-in icons on the desktop computer. She pointed to Anthony's, then typed in the password. His home screen came up. She clicked on the icon that held the Word documents and pulled up a list of files. They were arranged by date.

She clicked on one that was titled Pros and Cons.

When it came up, she sat back and motioned for him to read it over her shoulder. He moved in.

Under pros, it said:

1) Life insurance
2) Military benefits for surviving spouse
3) No more fights
4) No more regrets
5) No more worrying about not being the kind of dad our kid will need

Under cons, it said:

1) Will never know if it's a girl or a boy
2) Sara might never forgive me

Matt turned back to Sara in shock. This was damning, but not entirely conclusive. Unless she knew something else. "You think Anthony was struggling with whether or not to commit suicide?"

She got out of that document and opened up another file.

It appeared to be a personal letter, written six months before his accident.

Sara,

I'm so sorry. So very sorry…

Matt looked at her. "Did the two of you have a fight when he wrote that, an argument of some sort?"

She threaded her hands through her hair, pushing the heavy length of it off her face. "I don't know what happened on that date. I've also gone back in my work calendar and so far as I can tell, that day was like any other."

"But something is nagging at you," Matt guessed, seeing her continued distress.

Sara nodded. "It was around that time that he told me he wasn't sure if we should keep trying to get pregnant. Maybe it wasn't a good idea for me to have a baby."

She shook her head, her sorrow clear. Tears of regret misted her eyes. Knotting her hands in front of her, she continued explaining softly, "That's all I'd been holding on to while he was overseas and I disagreed. He backed off and we kept trying but he became even moodier and more shut off, and… I don't know. As I mentioned before, our relationship wasn't good when he died. We'd become strangers, sharing the same house, sleeping in the same bed."

"Yes, I remember. I'm so sorry, Sara."

"So that letter he started and never finished, it could have been about whether or not we should have a baby..."

Or, Matt knew, it could have been the beginning of a suicide note that was also never written.

Sara reached for a tissue and blotted the dampness from beneath her eyes. "I don't think Anthony ever had nightmares. Not that I knew, anyway. But maybe it would have been better if he had, instead of stuffing all his conflict down, deep inside."

"So he came back from his tour in the Middle East with issues about what he saw and experienced there."

Sara gave a stiff, jerky nod.

"Did you ever tell anyone about this?"

"No. Just you."

"Why not?" he asked.

"Because he didn't want me to and I didn't have any proof of anything anyway, except he was closed off, moody, reckless. And none of that proved anything!"

She gestured impotently at the computer. "Don't you think if I thought there was even a chance he would do something crazy like take his own life that I would have found some way to intervene?"

Matt knew she would have.

"But I didn't think whatever was going on with him was anything that couldn't be fixed by opening up a new chapter in our lives."

"And starting a family," Matt guessed.

Wearily, she began to cry. "And I didn't come across these two files until about four and a half months after he died, and by then I was nearly six months pregnant. I didn't see any reason to speculate about what he had been thinking and feeling that day. I already felt guilty enough for sending him on the errand that led to the accident that caused his death." She shook her head in quiet misery. "I didn't want to burden anyone else with the question of what we will never know for sure."

Except, Matt thought, he was pretty sure Sara still had her suspicions. And those doubts were clearly tearing her apart. "I can see why you'd want to protect Charley," he said carefully.

She shoved her chair back, rose and gazed at him in a way that made his chest go tight. "Then you can also see why if you're going to be around us, as much as you have been, Matt, you have to get help dealing with your grief and guilt over Mutt's death."

A support group wasn't going to fix that.

Dwelling on it wasn't going to help.

He knew that. And somewhere, deep down, so did she.

Calmly and patiently he pointed out, "I can see why you're worried, but again, Sara, I'm *not* your late husband."

Her lips formed the stubborn line he knew so well. "I know that." She stepped toward him beseechingly. "But I also know that I can't take a chance that anything will ever happen to you." Tears streamed down her face. "I didn't do anything when it came to Anthony. I sensed he was in trouble. That he was shutting down. The same way your family and I have intuited you are privately struggling."

She shook her head, the mounting despair and fear emanating off her as she choked out, "I don't want to look back on this night and wonder what might have happened if only I'd been able to convince you to do what Anthony never would."

So this was it, then? he wondered furiously.

She told him how it was going to be and he was just supposed to forget what he wanted and needed—which was solitude and the time and space to heal on his own—and instead mindlessly cede to her demands?

"Look, Sara, I'm sorry for all you've been through. If I could undo it for you…and for Charley," he said, his voice catching, "I would."

She studied him, tears glistening in her eyes. Evidently sensing what he already knew—that they were at a crossroads. "But…?" she prodded shakily.

Knowing he had to be honest, even if it hurt, he looked her in the eye and went on implacably, "I won't be in a relationship where I'm told how, and where, to live my life. I did that and it didn't work. I was never more miserable." He shook his head, recalling, aware a line had been drawn, and she had drawn it. "I'm not doing it again," he said flatly.

Sara regarded him as if she could not believe he was countering her wishes. Even when she had given no notice to his. "So what are you saying, Matt?" she asked in shock, her eyes filling with tears.

The truth, Matt thought.

The sad, awful, heartbreaking truth.

That, as much as they both might have once wished it, the two of them were never meant to be.

And, given the fact they were oceans apart in what they each required to be happy, probably wouldn't be able to go back to friends with benefits, or mere friends, either.

Which left them with only one option.

He exhaled roughly and shook his head. “That it’s over, Sara. You’ve made it clear. It has to be.”

Bitterness and regret sweeping through him, he turned on his heel and left.

Chapter 15

"Hey, stranger." Bess Monroe grinned as Sara walked into the WTWA facility. "Did you plan to attend tonight's support group for military widows?"

Was that tonight? she thought uncomfortably. Apparently so.

"Ah, no." Although Sara had been wondering...hoping, actually, that Matt might have decided to partake in the support group for returning veterans, which she definitely knew was being held this evening.

"I just came by to see if one of Charley's moccasin-style booties is here. He didn't have it on when we got home from the reunion picnic Saturday evening, and it wasn't in the car, so I thought someone might have found it here."

Bess gestured at one of the elevators. "Let's go to the Lost and Found and see."

Bess led her upstairs to the administrative offices. “So how’ve you been?” she asked, chatting amiably.

Horrible. “Good,” Sara fibbed. She caught the rehab nurse assessing her with clinical expertise. “Why?”

Bess touched her arm gently. “You look tired.”

Because I haven’t been sleeping at all since Matt and I broke up. Not that we were actually a couple. Still, sometimes it felt as if we were.

Bess opened the storage room door. “I thought Charley might be getting another tooth.”

Sara smiled wanly. “He is. But now that I’ve learned all the ways to ease his discomfort, he’s okay most of the time.”

“Good to hear.” She pulled out a large plastic tub marked Lost & Found. “See it anywhere in here?”

Sara sorted through the collection of jackets and T-shirts, socks and shoes.

Bess perched on the edge of the desk with her arms folded in front of her. “So what is bothering you? I can tell it’s something.”

Finally, Sara thought, something they could talk freely about. She lifted her head. “I’m worried about Matt.”

Bess was not surprised. “A lot of us are,” she replied kindly. “Although he has seemed to be doing a lot better since he started hanging out with you and Charley.”

Sara nodded. That was true, too.

Bess continued to study her. “Is Matt going to continue helping you and Charley out, now that Champ is with Alyssa Barnes?”

Sorrow pinched Sara’s gut. “Probably not.”

“Really?” The other woman blinked in surprise.

"The two of them looked so cute together on Saturday. Almost like father and son!"

And what a good daddy Matt would be, Sara thought wistfully, if only things had worked out between the two of them. "I know." She bent her head and went back to looking through the bin.

Predictably, her friend, sensing trouble, did not give up her questioning. "So…what's going on?"

Should she say something or say nothing? Sara wondered. In the end, she couldn't risk doing nothing. Again. Even if doing nothing was meant to protect the ex-soldier in her life.

She swallowed around the ache in her throat and looked at Bess again. If anyone would know how to help, her friend the rehab nurse would. To her relief, Sara found that her affection for Matt gave her the courage she needed. "I found out Matt's been having nightmares related to his time in the Middle East."

"Does he talk about them?"

"Not really—" *not the way I'd like* "—and he doesn't want me to mention it, either." Which left a great big emotional wall between them. The kind so insurmountable it had torn them apart.

Bess nodded in understanding. "I'm guessing you suggested he talk to someone here."

"I did. And that did not go over well. He pretty much ended our, um—" *love affair* "—friendship," she said finally. Without warning, Sara spied what she had been searching for. She plucked the lost baby moccasin out of the box. "Here it is." Although she had gotten what she needed now, she continued sitting for a moment, suddenly too weary to move.

The last few days had taken a lot out of her.

In fact, she felt as depressed, deeply saddened and empty inside as she could ever remember feeling.

Bess moved next to Sara. She put an arm around her shoulders. "One of the things I've learned in my years as a rehabilitation nurse is that whenever trauma or tragedy occurs in a family, it hits *everyone* close to them, too." She paused to let her words sink in. "Even when the wounds aren't visible."

Sara blinked back tears and looked over at her friend. Bess took her hand, and they went to sit on the sofa along the wall.

Kindly, Bess explained. "Take Matt's brother, Jack, for instance. Jack's a civilian, but when his wife, Gayle, died during the birth of their third child, he was completely thrown by the loss, as were his kids."

Sara wiped her tears away. "But they've recovered."

Bess hesitated. "His situation is definitely a work in progress."

Which meant he had hope about reaching reconciliation.

Whereas she…

"The point is, Sara, Jack knows he needs help after what happened. And he isn't afraid to ask for it."

Matt was in the pasture, tearing down old barbed wire fence with a vengeance, when he saw his mother's SUV driving across the field, toward him.

Knowing she'd likely heard through the Laramie grapevine that his "friendship" with Sara was kaput, he swore. Sensing a lecture of some sort was likely coming, he set his tools down, yanked off his leather gloves and strode toward her.

Rachel propped her hands on her hips. "And here I thought you were getting better."

He bypassed her and went straight for the big insulated water jug sitting on the bed of his pickup truck. "Thanks for the observation, Mom."

She watched him mop his face with his sleeve. "You're not returning messages again."

Matt tipped the jug and opened the spout, then drank deeply of the cold water. "Probably a reason for that."

"You don't want us to know you and Sara broke up."

Heart aching, he drank again. This time, to quell the sudden tightening of his throat. Feeling suddenly, unbearably, weary, he leaned against the side of his truck. "We were never a thing."

His mom scoffed, "Come on, now." Her expression as impatient as her voice. "Your family isn't that clueless. You were definitely a couple, even if you never identified it as such."

He didn't care what "evidence" his lawyer mother had uncovered. With a shrug, he turned his glance away. "It doesn't matter."

She narrowed her eyes at his terse words. "Why not?"

Matt sighed. Knowing the maternal inquisition would not end until he gave his mother something concrete to go on, he explained, "Because Sara found out I've had a few nightmares, and has demanded that I go to this support group at WTWA, and I'm not going to do it. I'm also not going to fight about it with her, so she and I are…not going to be friends or anything else anymore." It hurt, just saying the words.

Rachel nodded. "I see." A mixture of pity and disappointment gleamed in her eyes.

Matt knew Rachel didn't mean to judge him, but she was. Everyone was. He tensed all the more. "Look, Mom, I know you and Dad want me to be married and have a family," he began.

And part of me wants that, too. Or did. With Sara.

"And…?" Rachel prodded.

Matt spread his hands wide. Digging deep, he forced himself to be completely candid. "I want what you and Dad have. A relationship that's easy. That just works. And if I can't have that, then hell… I'm not going to have anything," he finished honestly.

His mother stared at him as if he'd grown two heads. "A relationship that's easy…that just works," she repeated in shock. She stepped nearer, her brows knit in confusion. "Is that what you think your father and I have?" she demanded.

Matt didn't know why she was so surprised. Sensing another critique coming on, he returned, "I know it is."

She matched his low, fierce tone. "Then you're wrong. Marriage only *looks* easy on the outside. When you're in it, it's anything but. A successful union takes work and effort and putting your partner's needs ahead of your own, and having them make the same sort of sacrifices for you. Because if you're both *giving* ninety-five percent, and *taking* five percent, a relationship will always work."

He understood selfless teamwork. It was what made military units thrive. "And that's what you and Dad do?"

"Yes," Rachel said softly. "We always put each other first. And we always will."

That made sense now that he thought about it. His parents were always helping each other out, caring for each other, loving each other, finding ways to make even the most contentious situation work out in a way that ultimately satisfied everyone. It was that kind of loving unity that had made their family thrive. Matt gulped. "I'm not sure Sara and I can do that, Mom. We're so different."

His mother offered a wry smile and shook her head. "Maybe not as much as you think. Given how stubbornly you're both behaving." She touched his shoulder with maternal affection. "Sara wants you to live life fully. She wants you to be able to sleep at night, to not be so shut off. Now tell me, Matt. What exactly is so wrong with that?"

"I know this was tough for you," the counselor said, as the group disbanded. She rose and intercepted Matt before he could get out the door. "But I'm happy you were here tonight, and happier still that you've also agreed to see one of our counselors, one-on-one."

"I appreciate the opportunity."

"It'll get better."

Will it? he wondered, thinking how he had initially let Sara down.

"Just give it time."

"I will," Matt promised. Because time was the one thing he suddenly had plenty of.

He ran into Bess Monroe as he headed down the stairs. She grinned at him, offering the encouragement, "Getting started is always the hard part!"

Bess was right. Taking advantage of all the WTWA had to offer hadn't been difficult, Matt thought. The really tough part was what was coming up next. Because he was on his way to the Blue Vista to see Sara.

Except…she wasn't at the ranch she'd shared with

her late husband. She was here. In the flesh. Coming out of one of the *other* support group rooms. He blinked. “Sara?” he said hoarsely.

Surprise lit her pretty features. “Matt!” she said, coming to a halt right in front of him. Not looking nearly as unhappy to see him as he would have expected her to be, given the way they had parted several weeks ago. For a moment, her gaze devoured him, head to toe, as if checking for any further injury. She lightly clasped his arm. “I’ve been wanting to talk to you.”

“Same here,” he countered gruffly.

Bess passed them again and said, “My office is empty. Third floor.”

Sara looked at Matt, an inscrutable question in her eyes. “Sounds good to me,” he murmured. Whatever afforded them privacy.

They climbed the stairs, neither speaking until they got inside Bess’s office and closed the door behind him.

Sara turned to face him, looking more gorgeous than ever in a pretty pink dress and white cardigan. “As you can probably see,” she said, her intent gaze giving him courage, “I had my first group session.”

“So did I,” he forced himself to reveal with unflinching honesty.

Her breasts rose as she inhaled a shaky breath. “Wow.”

“Yeah, wow.” It had been a rough road, getting him to the recovery process, but now that he was here, he was not giving up. Not on healing. Not on her. Not on the two of them and the future he knew in his heart they were destined to have together.

“I guess great minds do think alike.” Her eyes were kind. Hopeful…

He wrapped his arms around her waist and tugged her against him. "I'm sorry," he said hoarsely.

"I'm sorry, too. Really, really sorry. I was way too hard on you."

"You gave me the kick in the pants I needed."

She splayed her soft, delicate hands across his chest. Her palm settled over his rapidly beating heart. "The thing is, Matt, we both need help. I realize that now." Her lower lip trembled with emotion and her eyes sparkled with tears as she gazed up at him.

Shaking her head in silent regret, she confessed, "I accused you of not wanting to deal with what happened when Mutt passed. Well, I haven't dealt with what happened when Anthony passed." Her low voice caught. "And I know that I have to do that before I have even a chance of moving on."

The heartache of loss was something they both shared. "I need to do that, too," he told her. The difference now was that grief was bringing them together, instead of driving them apart.

And together, he knew, they could do anything.

They continued staring at each other, breathing raggedly. Filled with hope.

"So…we're both getting counseling," Sara said, mulling that over with a mixture of satisfaction and relief.

"We are," he told her tenderly, taking her face in his hands and rubbing his thumbs over her cheeks. His throat felt tight and his easy speech deserted him. "But I don't want to just work on myself," he murmured softly. "I want to work on us, as a couple, too."

Sara blinked in amazement. "You do?"

"Yes, darlin'." He bent to kiss her, softly and sweetly, with all the tenderness she deserved. He paused, shook his head in remorse, admitting, "I've missed you more than words can say."

"Oh, Matt," Sara trembled in his arms. "I've missed you, too! So much!"

He gathered her close, and they kissed again, even more poignantly this time. With heartfelt regret, he admitted, "I never should have walked out the way I did, but," he paused to draw a breath, "our time apart reinforced something that deep down I think I've known all along."

"Which is…?" Sara asked, going completely still.

Matt sifted his hands through the silk of her hair, tilting her face up to his. "That you and I are made for each other. We might have our struggles and imperfections, but together we make sense."

Sara beamed with unmistakable happiness. "I couldn't agree more, Matt."

He nodded in relief. Knowing there was still more to work out, he forged on gruffly, "I want to do the things that will make our relationship selfless enough and strong enough to last a lifetime," he confessed raggedly, telling her all that he'd hidden, all that was in his heart. "Because I love you, Sara. With all my heart and soul."

"Oh, Matt," she whispered back joyously. "I love you, too!"

She lifted her head to his, and their lips met in a searing kiss that sealed the deal, and then another that was deeper and more long lasting, more passionate.

Finally, Matt drew back slightly. Grinning, he cleared his throat and drawled, "So now…for the *really* important part…"

She listened, ecstatic.

He took both her hands in his and clasped them tightly. "I want us to have a future together. You, me, Charley and whatever canine companions we bring into our lives."

Sara's smile brimmed, mirroring the happiness he felt. "Sounds perfect to me!"

He dropped down on one knee, ready and able to give her everything she ever wanted and needed. Solemnly, he asked, "Good enough to marry me when the time is right?"

"Oh, Matt," Sara whispered. She knelt and tugged him close. Their lips met in another sweet and enduring kiss. "There's nothing I want more!"

Epilogue

April, three years later...

"Mommy, when is my baby sister finally going to crawl?" Charley asked, his cute little face scrunched up impatiently.

"I don't know if Kristen will crawl," Sara told her son honestly as she set her six-month-old daughter on the play mat spread out over the living room floor.

Grinning, Matt picked up Charley and held him in his arms. The two handsome fellas went nose to nose. "You never did."

Charley blinked in amazement. "I didn't?"

Matt shook his head, then relayed proudly, "You went straight to walking."

"Wow," Charley breathed, and he and Matt settled on the floor next to Sara and the baby.

"Wow is right." Matt leaned over and bussed their son's head. "Your mommy and I were really amazed when we saw you pull yourself up on the side of your crib and start walking along the rail."

Charley climbed onto Matt's lap and rested his hands on Matt's broad shoulders. Never at a loss for questions, asked, "How old was I, Daddy?"

Matt ran a hand lovingly over his back. "Eight months and two days."

Tilting his head, Charley considered. "Is that good?"

"Very good," Matt praised.

"I think Kristen will do very good, too," Charley pronounced solemnly. He got down to play with his baby sister. He showed her toys, and pretend-read to her from one of the cloth-covered infant storybooks.

Nearby, their adopted eight-year-old retired service dog, Mollie, watched happily from her cushion next to the fireplace, her big blond head nestled on her paws.

Looking every bit as contented as Sara felt, Matt settled closer to her, wrapped his arms around her waist, nuzzled her hair. "So what do you think, wife?" he murmured in her ear as their kids continued to play. "You want to grill out tonight, since the weather is so nice? Or go into town and eat?"

Aware it didn't matter what they did, because they were always incredibly happy when they were together as a family, Sara turned toward him and smiled. "Either option works for me, cowboy."

Soaking up his strong, masculine warmth, she wreathed her arms about his neck, kissed him on the cheek, then gazed adoringly into his gray-blue eyes.

It was amazing how much the support they had both received from the West Texas Warriors Association had not only helped them both resolve their own grief but helped others suffering from similar calamities heal as well.

She'd gone back to work part-time as a large-animal vet, and still shepherded a new litter of future service puppies into the world every year.

Matt had finished revitalizing his ranch and now ran a little cattle, alongside his brother's herd, too.

When they'd married, a year into their official courtship, she'd sold the Blue Vista and moved into his ranch house at the Silver Creek.

It hadn't taken long to convert the big empty space into their home, or for them to decide to expand their family. And now Charley and their dog, Mollie, and their new baby girl, Kristen, loved it there as much as she and Matt did.

To the point that life just didn't get any more perfect.

She smiled. "I think I'd like to stay here. Tomorrow is the service dog reunion. We still have a lot to do to get ready to host it, once the kids are in bed."

Matt grinned in easy agreement then winked. "And after that, I can think of another thing or two to do."

She laughed at the sexy mischief in his low tone. The soul-deep tenderness and affection in his smile. And felt an answering love filling her heart. "I can, too, cowboy," she whispered back playfully, kissing him again, slowly and sweetly. "I can, too..."

* * * * *

SPECIAL EXCERPT FROM

HARLEQUIN

SPECIAL EDITION

Before he testifies in an important case, businessman Michael "Mikey" Fiore hides out in Jacobsville, Texas, and crosses paths with softly beautiful Bernadette, who seems burdened with her own secrets. Their bond grows into passion...until shocking truths surface.

Read on for a sneak peek at
Texas Proud,
the latest book in
#1 New York Times *bestselling author Diana Palmer's Long, Tall Texans series!*

Mikey's fingers contracted. "Suppose I told you that the hotel I own is actually a casino," he said slowly, "and it's in Las Vegas?"

Bernie's eyes widened. "You own a casino in Las Vegas?" she exclaimed. "Wow!"

He laughed, surprised at her easy acceptance. "I run it legit, too," he added. "No fixes, no hidden switches, no cheating. Drives the feds nuts, because they can't find anything to pin on me there."

"The feds?" she asked.

He drew in a breath. "I told you, I'm a bad man." He felt guilty about it, dirty. His fingers caressed hers as they neared Graylings, the huge mansion where his cousin lived with the heir to the Grayling racehorse stables.

Her fingers curled trustingly around his. "And I told you that the past doesn't matter," she said stubbornly. Her heart was running wild. "Not at all. I don't care how bad you've been."

His own heart stopped and then ran away. His teeth clenched. "I don't even think you're real, Bernie," he whispered. "I think I dreamed you."

She flushed and smiled. "Thanks."

He glanced in the rearview mirror. "What I'd give for just five minutes alone with you right now," he said tautly. "Fat chance," he added as he noticed the sedan tailing casually behind them.

She felt all aglow inside. She wanted that, too. Maybe they could find a quiet place to be alone, even for just a few minutes. She wanted to kiss him until her mouth hurt.

Don't miss
Texas Proud *by Diana Palmer,*
available October 2020 wherever
Harlequin Special Edition books and ebooks are sold.

Harlequin.com

SPECIAL EXCERPT FROM

LOVE INSPIRED SUSPENSE

INSPIRATIONAL ROMANCE

A K-9 officer and a forensics specialist must work together to solve a murder and stay alive.

Read on for a sneak preview of
Scene of the Crime *by Sharon Dunn,*
the next book in the True Blue K-9 Unit: Brooklyn series available September 2020 from Love Inspired Suspense.

Brooklyn K-9 Unit Officer Jackson Davison caught movement out of the corner of his eye: a face in the trees fading out of view. His heart beat a little faster. Was someone watching him? The hairs on the back of Jackson's neck stood at attention as a light breeze brushed his face. Even as he studied the foliage, he felt the weight of a gaze on him. The sound of Smokey's barking brought his mission back into focus.

When he caught up with his partner, the dog was sitting. The signal that he'd found something. "Good boy." Jackson tossed out the toy he carried on his belt for Smokey to play with, his reward for doing his job. The dog whipped the toy back and forth in his mouth.

"Drop," Jackson said. He picked up the toy and patted Smokey on the head. "Sit. Stay."

The body, partially covered by branches, was clothed in neutral colors and would not be easy to spot unless you were looking for it.

LISEXP0820

He keyed his radio. “Officer Davison here. I’ve got a body in Prospect Park. Male Caucasian under the age of forty, about two hundred yards in, just southwest of the Brooklyn Botanic Garden.”

Dispatch responded, “Ten-four. Help is on the way.”

He studied the trees just in time to catch the face again, barely visible, like a fading mist. He was being watched.

“Did you see something?” Jackson shouted. “Did you call this in?”

The person turned and ran, disappearing into the thick brush.

Jackson took off in the direction the runner had gone. As his feet pounded the hard earth, another thought occurred to him. Was this the person who had shot the man in the chest? Sometimes criminals hung around to witness the police response to their handiwork.

His attention was drawn to a garbage can just as an object hit the back of his head with intense force. Pain radiated from the base of his skull. He crumpled to the ground and his world went black.

LISEXP0820